LYRIC OF VULCON

Karin Marchen

Cover design by Kim Dingwall

ISBN 978-0-6481555-3-9

Callistemon Publishing

To my friend and muse. You believed in me.

CHAPTER ONE

Little Prisoner

Today was Lyric's eighteenth birthday. It was supposed to be her day of triumph, the day she fulfilled the hopes and expectations of her family, the day she fulfilled her destiny. She was on the podium in the city plaza, not in triumph but on her hands and knees on the cold, hard, stone. The lovely green dress her mother had made for her, and the intricate braids her mother had woven into her long brown hair were soiled with rotten eggs and fruit. The foul stench filled her nostrils. The crowd chanted, "Eject the Wildling!". Lyric felt the sting of an egg smash on her cheek.

Ahead of her, Lyric could see the man she loved locked in sword combat against his best friend, fighting for his life, and hers. At the other edges of the podium, her father and her uncles were similarly battling against Royal Protectors. She turned her head away from the sting and let the slimy contents of the egg drip down her face onto the stone.

Lyric's eyes fixed on her mother, her face drained and ashen in horror, her gaze soon diverted to the ground in disappointment. Today Lyric disappointed her family and sealed their fate.

This was not the first time the city folk had used Lyric for target practice. Just like the last time, she felt powerless to deal with it. So many rules, so many constraints, so many expectations. Last time she had huddled, waiting to be rescued. This time, no rescue would come.

Grandmother would have known what to do. Grandmother always knew what to do. She always knew what was best. Lyric missed her and needed her guidance, but she was not there.

Lyric felt humiliated and beaten. How had it come to this? Was there something she could have done to avert this? She cast her mind back, picking through the events of her life, trying to find something, anything that could have made a difference. If she had been more obedient from the beginning, would that have made a difference?

When she could eat no more and the grown-ups started talking about important things, it was time to slip away to the fields. Lyric escaped to the nearby pasture after her birthday lunch. Lying on her back in the soft grass near the farmhouse, watching puffy clouds drift across an azure sky, Lyric luxuriated in a perfect day. She wished she could play with her cousins. Lyric knew she had cousins, but they never came to the farm and she was never allowed to leave it. One more year and she would be old enough to start school in the City, old enough to play with other children. For now, she pondered the sky and listened to birdsong and the rip and munch of goats grazing ever closer nearby. Replete from a feast of meats, fruits and cakes, and with the sun gently warming her, Lyric lapsed into an easy sleep.

Something poked her leg gently, rousing Lyric halfway to attention. A second, much firmer poke, finished the job.

"There you are," said a raspy voice, worn by time. "Thought I might find you here."

"Grandmother." Lyric rubbed her eyes and focussed on the frail form. With long, braided grey hair and skin dry, tanned and wrinkled like old leather, Lyric's grandmother looked ancient.

Grandmother Nye leaned casually on the ornate, hand-carved walking stick Lyric's father had made for her when her gait became unsteady. "You're wanted back at the house."

Lyric sat up, nodded acknowledgment, then gazed off into the distance. She watched the white light play around the nearby trees, and the goats in the field. In the distance she could see the great Mount Vulcon, looming tall at the heart of their great island, with its flickering white halo.

Grandmother turned to look in the direction Lyric was gazing. "What are you looking at child?"

Lyric refocussed her gaze back to her Grandmother. The white light around Grandmother was still bright, but it flickered less than it once had. "Grandmother," she said, getting to her feet and trying to dust off the back of her tunic. "Why doesn't anyone talk about the White Fire?"

Grandmother's eyes widened and she stared intently at Lyric before taking a deep breath and calming herself. "Tell me about the White Fire, Lyric."

"You know, Grandmother, the white glow around everything. Around the trees and the flowers and the animals and the people and even around the mountain." Lyric pointed at Mount Vulcon in the distance. "I call it the White Fire because it dances about like fire."

Grandmother looked about, looked at the mountain and turned to walk slowly toward the farmhouse. Lyric skipped and danced around her with far too much energy to walk so slowly. Her bare feet caressed by the cool, soft grass.

"The reason no one talks about the White Fire my child, is because you are the only one who can see it."

"You can't see it, Grandmother?"

"No child."

"What about Mother and Father and Aunt Tyla and Uncle—?"

"No." Grandmother interrupted before the list extended to every person Lyric knew of.

"Oh," Lyric said. Her voice quiet with disappointment and her brow furrowed. "Why not?"

"Dear child," Grandmother said, "only very special people can see the White Fire. No matter what anyone ever says, it is very important that you can see it, and it is very important you keep seeing it. Practise, so you can see it better and better. OK?"

"OK, Grandmother."

"And best not tell anyone else about the White Fire, it will be safer that way."

"Not even Mother and Father?"

"I will tell Mother and Father, and Aunt Tyla too. I will help them understand, but best you not talk to them about it in case someone else overhears you. This is very important. Do you understand child?"

Lyric slowed her skipping and nodded.

Grandmother seemed satisfied and they continued on. As they approached the farmhouse door, Lyric tugged at Grandmother's tunic.

"Grandmother, what if I don't want to be special?"

Grandmother paused at the doorstep, blocking the way. She placed both gnarled hands firmly on her cane and leaned down intently toward Lyric. "I am what I am, child, and you are what you are. All you can do is try and be your best self. To try and do anything else can only end badly."

Lyric didn't fully understand, but it sounded very sensible, "Yes, Grandmother". Grandmother opened the door and led Lyric into the kitchen where the now solemn family were assembled around the long kitchen table.

Lyric was startled by the change in mood. The morning had been filled with cooking and happy chatter. Lyric had helped with kneading bread, stirring cake mixes and cutting fruit. She felt warmth and belonging working with Grandmother, Mother and her aunts to prepare the meal. The lunch was rowdy and joyous with much talk of the harvest and the coming winter. Now the room was suddenly sombre.

Lyric's mother, Adria stood, a picture of self-control, with a soft, welcoming smile. She gestured Lyric to sit on a stool positioned at one end of the solid wooden table. Adria's tanned cheeks were flushed from her labours in the steamy kitchen and the mead the grown-ups shared after the meal. Her soft brown tunic was lightly dusted with flour outlining the shadow of the apron she had worn earlier. Grandmother shuffled off to the side of the hearth, adjusted the cushions and slowly planted her fragile frame in the chair Lyric's father had made for her.

"Is something wrong?" Lyric asked, raising herself onto the sturdy wooden stool. "Did I do something wrong?"

"No, Precious One," Adria said, taking Lyric's hand and giving it a reassuring squeeze before moving away and taking her seat at the table.

"Now that you are in your fifth year, there's something very serious we need to talk to you about." Hann said. Lyric's father was muscular and tanned from working in the fields. His large, capable hands now folded nervously on his knees as he leaned toward Lyric.

Lyric looked back and forth between her parents, confused, looking for clues.

"Keep it simple, Hann," Aunt Tyla said. "Remember she is only a child."

Hann looked back at the gathering with an annoyed frown, but they all nodded agreement. Flustered, he took a deep breath and tried again.

"Precious One, you are very special."

That was amazing. How had Grandmother told them about the White Fire already? They had only just walked into the room and Grandmother had gone directly to her chair without speaking to anyone. How did they all know so quickly? Was Grandmother magic or something? Lyric turned to Grandmother with one eyebrow raised in quizzical surprise. Grandmother just smiled and winked.

"That is why it is very important you are kept safe," Adria said.

"I thought we agreed I was the one to explain this to Lyric."

"You are, my love. I was just—"

"Just what?"

"Helping."

Hann waved his hands in the air in frustration. "I don't need help. I can do this."

"Well, do it then." Adria leaned back and rested one elbow on the table.

"OK. No interruptions."

Adria gestured for Hann to continue. Grandmother chuckled quietly. The aunts and uncles shook their heads in dismay.

"That's why it is so important we keep you safe," Hann said.

Lyric could only manage a feeble nod.

"To be sure you stay safe, you must not start school in your sixth year. You must not do the test."

"But I want to go to school. I want to play with other children."

"I know Precious One, but it is not safe."

"But Father, I'm smart and I'm fast. I can be safe at school."

"No Lyric," Hann said. "You cannot."

"But Father."

"I know this is disappointing Lyric, but on Vulcon, children who are special like you die when they start school."

"Die?"

"Yes, Precious One, die. All able children are tested, and the special ones die."

Lyric's brow furrowed as her five–year–old mind tried to process this. She thought her father may be mistaken but the stern looks on the faces of her family convinced her otherwise.

"To keep you safe, we have decided that the people of Vulcon must believe you are not able. They must believe you are mute."

"What is mute?"

"Mute means not able to speak," Adria said.

Hann cast a stern glare in Adria's direction. Adria put her hand over her lips and looked apologetic.

"I'm not allowed to speak anymore?"

"From today Lyric, you may only speak to the people in this room, and only when there is no one else about. From today, you must stay close to the house and you must never leave the farm. You must never, never go to the City. You must promise to do this Lyric. If you do not do this, you will die, and we will all be so sad that we will die too. Do you promise?"

Horrified at the thought she might die, that her family might die, Lyric nodded.

"Do you promise?" Hann asked again, louder this time.

"I promise."

"Very well then," Hann said, his shoulders slumping in relief. "Would you like some more cake?"

Lyric shook her head. "May I go now?"

"Yes," Hann said, with a sigh

Lyric raced up the wooden stairs to her room. She threw herself onto the bed, the straw in the mattress crunching on impact, and she wept. As her sobbing subsided a little, she could hear the creaking of someone coming up the stairs. Lyric opened one eye to see her mother approach the bed. She rolled over, turning her back on her mother.

Adria crouched slowly beside the bed and placed her hand on Lyric's shoulder. Lyric shrugged it off. "I'm so sorry, Precious One," Adria said. "I know this seems difficult, but there is no other way. When you are older, you will understand. Until then, please try to make the best of it, and know we love you."

Lyric didn't move. She just lay there sobbing quietly. Soon she heard the creaking of her mother descending the stairs and she sobbed herself to sleep. Lyric was still too young to know the word 'prisoner' but she was not too young to know what it felt like.

CHAPTER TWO

Wildling

There is nowhere more mesmerising, more enticing, than the place you are forbidden to go. Lyric's wanderings brought her once again to the South Gate. Her mother told her to stay away from the City, but curiosity brought her here before and she had been safe. She was now in her thirteenth year. Nearly grown up. She could do this. Like last time, she would find somewhere to hide so she could observe. No one would see her. She would be safe.

The South Gate was a gaping archway in the tall stone walls encircling the City. The massive, dark, wooden doors were hewn from cedar trunks and swung inward to allow the passage of people and goods to and from nearby farms. Traffic through the gate was intense in the morning and evening but tapered off during the middle of the day. This was an opportunity to pass without detection. Concealed in a hedge, Lyric could see out along the dusty road and into the City streets beyond the gate. She was practised at concealing herself and just as accomplished at stealth. Lyric waited until all was clear, burst from the hedge and raced through the gate to the shelter of a small alleyway. She crept along the dirt streets, compacted by generations of sandals, wagons and hooves. She moved like a thief, hiding in the corners of mismatched daub house facades until she could be sure the way was clear. Her bare feet were silent on the sun–toasted, dry earth. The sun of early summer was high overhead and there were few shadows other than those cast by roof overhangs and the burgeoning clouds that drifted overhead.

In the distance, the sound of the school yard drew her onward. It was her objective. She mustn't let the children see her, she mustn't talk with them, and it would be far too dangerous to ever play with them. Yet, she could at least watch them, if she could find a safe vantage point. At the end of an alleyway was a small open area with a magnificent tree on the far side. The trunk was thick, and some branches attached fairly close to the ground; an ideal climbing tree. Lyric made for the tree and clambered high into the branches, digging her grimy fingers into the rough bark. Wedged at the fork of a large branch, and concealed by the foliage, she could see down into the nearby school yard.

Lyric watched the children play. The smaller children ducked and weaved among the others in a game of tag. A group of girls with neatly braided hair, spotlessly clean tunics and fine sandals moved small pots around on a wooden slab in a pretend lunch party. One of the taller boys was guiding a wooden hoop around the playground with a short stick while a handful of other boys watched on, waiting their turn. The older boys and girls were clustered in shaded corners at the edge of the playground in small groups, deep in conversation. Periodically one would raise their head and look around, though Lyric could not make out what they were looking out for. She listened to the yells, the shouts, and the squeals of delight. She so longed to join them, but her mother said it wasn't safe. She must stay apart. She must not be seen.

On Lyric's seventh birthday, her mother had declared she was old enough to wander and play on all the fields of the family farm, not just those around the farmhouse. On her twelfth birthday, she was granted permission to explore beyond the farm, but her mother made her promise to be responsible enough to never go near the City. Lyric promised in earnest, keen to taste her new freedom, but over the last year she incrementally widened her territory, and was drawn by curiosity toward the City, keen to see what the lives of other children on the island were like. It would be OK, she told herself, as long as she was careful. As long as she returned home safe each evening. Eventually a bell rang, and the loud, joyful mass of young children tumbled through large doors into the schoolhouse, followed by the older children at a much more considered pace, leaving the playground deserted.

Lyric stayed comfortably wedged in the branches of the tree, her legs dangling through a fork in the branch, the trunk forming a backrest and her arm hooked over a small branch to the side. She was adept at tree climbing. It was a favourite pastime. Lyric could tell just which branches were strong enough to support her weight and being what her father called 'a mere slip of a girl', she could climb to the highest branches possible and see far out over the countryside. She noted how useful those skills were right now. Lyric heard the sound of hooves on dirt and turned to see a donkey, led by a bearded man in drab garb, pulling a cart full of onions. They passed under the tree in the direction of the city centre and the old man didn't look up.

Lyric observed that people rarely looked up, so a high vantage point was usually a safe place to conceal herself. As she strained to watch the cart disappear down the street, some leaves caught in her hair, joining the leaves and twigs already present in the bird–nest of dark, tangled wavy hair. The bright green of the leaves echoed the colour of her eyes and her light olive skin was besmirched by mud and dust, so her face and limbs resembled the bark of the tree in which she was perched, exquisitely camouflaged. Lyric wore a loose, brown tunic, tattered and punctured by the branches and rocks of previous adventures, but it was thick enough to keep her comfortable on the rough bark. She would wait for a while longer to see if the children emerged once again to play.

The school bell sounded again and jolted Lyric to consciousness. She had dozed off in the sultry summer heat and the length of the shadows in the schoolyard told her hours had passed. She writhed and loosened muscles and joints stiffened after so long in a singular position. This time children did not emerge into the yard to play. She thought maybe she could hear them in the distance. It was late, so she must get home quickly, before nightfall, or her parents would worry. When the coast was clear, she scrambled to the ground and bolted for the cover of a nearby alley. Carefully she worked her way along the streets and alleys toward the South Gate until she could see the bushes and fields beyond. She pressed her body close to the daubed mud brick walls and crouched behind barrels and planters to try and conceal herself. She was almost there, almost free of the City. Lyric prepared to make a dash for the safety of the hedge when a group of schoolchildren stepped into the alley exit, blocking her way.

"Look! It's the Wildling!" shouted a boy about Lyric's age, with a neat tunic and brown leather sandals. Bobbing with nervous excitement, he pointed at Lyric, now cowering against a wall at the side of the alleyway.

Lyric turned to flee back the way she had come, but another group of children entered from the other end of the alleyway. She was trapped.

A girl holding a slate in one hand and a leather satchel in the other eyed her curiously. "She's grimy and unkempt like an animal," the girl said, with her head tilted to one side. "My father says she's mute."

Another girl with long black braids responded, "Yeah, my brother says she's mute because she's stupid, just like an animal." Her face crinkled in disdain.

"Get her!" yelled a voice from somewhere in the gathering.

The children dropped their satchels to the ground and began gathering pebbles. Lyric cowered against the earthy wall in terror, shielding her head and face with her arms. She winced as each hurled pebble found its mark, pummelling her arms, legs and body.

Lyric cried feebly, but she must not speak, she could not plead with them to stop. The bombardment continued. Her mother was right. The City was not safe. Children were not safe. Lyric had broken the rules, broken her mother's trust, and now she would die here. Her tears mixed with the dust on her arms and face, forming muddy streaks. Still the pummel of pebbles continued relentlessly and by now some of the boys had found some larger stones to add to the mix.

"Cut it out!" Ordered a boy just arrived on the scene from the street ahead. "Let her go." He stood authoritatively, hands on hips. His deep brown eyes glared furiously at them as his wavy dark brown hair and olive-coloured tunic caught the breeze. The gold of the evening light illuminated him on one side and the White Fire glowed and danced around him. To the cringing Lyric, he looked like a god. The avalanche of pebbles paused.

"But she's the Wildling," a girl with long braids said. "Mama says she's an animal and should have been killed at birth."

"Father says she's too stupid even to attend school. That's why she roams the fields like an animal," an older boy continued.

"What's it to you anyway Benn?" the girl with braids chided. "You her Protector or something?" The gathered children giggled, spurring her on, "Benn Protects the Wildling." she chanted. "Benn Protects the Wildling."

By now another boy, roughly Benn's age, arrived on the scene. Lean and lanky with straight dark hair he surveyed the scene for a moment, "Benn! What are you doing?"

"No one deserves to be treated like this," Benn said. "Not even the Wildling. If we're going to be Protectors someday Rikk, it will be our job to protect the vulnerable. This is about as vulnerable as it gets," he pointed to Lyric cowering against the wall looking terrified. "Besides, as far as we know, she's never actually hurt anyone."

Rikk shook his head as if pondering whether to help his best friend or try and rescue him.

"Benn Protects the Wildling." The children resumed their chant and resumed pelting Lyric with pebbles.

Suddenly there was a deep rumbling and the ground began to shake. Pieces of daub crumbled from walls and fell into the streets, raising clouds of dust. Pots shaken free of window sills smashed on the hard earth below, spilling their contents in all directions. The children squealed and stumbled about as they tried to make their way to open areas, as they were taught to do. Rumblings and shakings of the earth were not unusual on the island of Vulcon.

Benn lurched forward, pushing the children aside until he reached Lyric. He bent over her, shielding her from falling daub and whispered in her ear, "If you can understand me, run. Now!" He pointed in the direction of the South Gate.

Lyric didn't need to be told which direction to go. She leapt up and ran forward with Benn at her side. He held her arm, half dragging her along. After they pierced through the mob of frightened children, Benn stopped, pushing Lyric forward, "Go!"

She fled through the city gate into the hedge on the far side of the road.

Benn walked casually to the hedge and peered through. Unable to see her in the dense mesh of twigs and leaves, Benn turned and walked back toward the gate. He seemed to assume she had made good her escape among the rows of grapevines beyond.

In fact, Lyric was still carefully concealed and motionless in the hedge, her skin poked and prodded by the branches and twigs. She knew it would be safer to head into the fields after the gathering dispersed. She would be far more exposed there than in the hedge, even if she did stay close to the vines.

When the ground was still again, Lyric watched Benn return to the alleyway. He gathered up his satchel and brushed the dirt and dust from it.

"Are you sure protecting the Wildling was a good idea?" Rikk asked, approaching Benn from behind, "I mean, it's not a good look, and probably not a great career move."

Benn swung his satchel onto his shoulder. "Maybe not Rikk," he said and gave him a reassuring slap on the shoulder as he walked past, "but it felt like the right thing to do." Benn turned and waved back at his friend as he walked out through the South Gate. "See you tomorrow Rikk," Benn called before heading out along the road between the fields that led to his home, a small farm far west of the City.

When all was quiet and no-one noticed, Lyric crept from the hedge and wove her way along and between rows of vines in the direction of home. She ran without pausing to catch breath, through hedges, across fields, over the stone bridge and onward until she reached the whitewashed, mud-daubed, stone farmhouse surrounded by fields that she called home. Her skin started to smart from the myriad of scratches inflicted by the hedges. Tomorrow her body would be dotted with bruises from the pebbles and stones, but for now she was safe, she was going home to her family. Now her only dilemma was how to explain all the bruises to her mother.

Lyric skimmed along the hedges as she approached the farmhouse. Such stealth was not usually required on the Nye farm. After all, it was home. This time Lyric was trying not to be seen. Trying to delay the inevitable and postpone the consequences.

She could see her parents and the hired workers out in the fields working on the harvest. The workmen and her father cut the golden, crisp stalks with razor–sharp sickles, dropping them down in a neat row to one side. Hann's powerful movements were rhythmic under his wide–brimmed hat. The large wet patches of sweat that soaked through his linen work–tunic were visible even from a distance. Adria and the other women gathered up the stalks in armfuls, bundled them into sheaves and stood them in neat rows. A horse–drawn wagon plodded along the rows as more workers heaved the sheaves onto the wagon and conveyed them to the great barns near the farmhouse. This process would repeat itself daily until the entire crop was harvested, or until it rained, in which case the remaining crop would be lost. Nothing was ever wasted on the Nye farm though. Should any grain spoil in the field, her father would wait until the seeds sprouted, then turn the goats onto the debris to clean it up. Hann always vowed that sprouted grain made for good cashmere.

Her father and the other cutters swayed to and fro in a singular rhythm in the fading light, singing songs of the harvest, and songs of the bread, beer and straw the barley would provide. Thus, busily engaged in their labours, no one noticed Lyric sneak to the farmhouse and slip through the door.

The kitchen was warm, steamy and filled with the aroma of goat stew. Grandmother stood at the hearth, cane in one hand and using the other to stir the pot over the fire with a long wooden spoon. Grandmother still wanted to help with the harvest in the fields but now even more frail and resembling a skeleton with skin loosely drawn over it, she was assigned to preparing the evening meal instead. Her still intense brown eyes followed Lyric as she tried to walk casually across the room.

"So, how was the City?" Grandmother asked.

Lyric froze in her tracks. She should have known she could keep no secrets from Grandmother. "Not so good." Lyric's tensed muscles relaxed, defeated. "I had some trouble with the children there."

Grandmother waved her closer. As Lyric approached, her grandmother poked one of the red marks with her cane.

"Ouch!"

"Pebbles or rocks?"

"Both."

"Hmmm — best go get cleaned up," Grandmother said, returning to stirring the stew. "When you're done, there's some salve on the shelf over there." She pointed with her cane to a shelf in the nook beside the hearth.

"You won't tell Mother or Father, will you?" Lyric asked as she moved toward the washroom.

"No, my child," Grandmother replied. "You will."

To Lyric it felt like a punch in the gut. As she washed, dressed and applied the salve, she rehearsed over and over what she would say.

Returning to the kitchen, Lyric made for the hearth. "Sit down Grandmother. I can do this." Lyric plumped the cushions, then took her Grandmother by the arm and helped her settle into the chair. She hooked the cane on the armrest of the chair and took up the wooden spoon. The stew released clouds of steam as she stirred. Lyric placed another piece of wood on the fire, then placed a second pot, filled with water, over the fire to boil some barley. It was this season's grain, clean and fresh from the harvest.

As the last light faded, and the last of the workers left for their homes, her parents burst through the rear kitchen door, from the farmyard. They were hot, sweaty and grimy from the day's labour. "It's a good harvest this year my love," Hann said as he removed the worn goatskin gloves that protected his hands from the harsh barley stalks.

"Yes dear," Adria said, pinching the gloves from her fingers. "The grains are full and heavy. The crop will sell well." She stowed her gloves on a shelf by the door. Spying Lyric, at the hearth her face beamed, "Hello Precious One." She marched forward to hug her daughter, then she saw them, the red welts, all over Lyric's arms and legs, and she froze. "What happened?"

Lyric fidgeted. "Some children threw stones at me today Mother."

"Oh, my child." Adria approached, wanting to hug her daughter but seeing nowhere to touch that would not be painful, she took Lyric's head gently in her hands. "Which children? Where? Did they come onto the farm?"

"No," Lyric replied. "I was exploring off the farm."

"Where exactly off the farm?" Hann asked. His face was all concern, but his voice was stern.

Lyric took a deep breath. "In the City."

"In the City!" Hann's face was turning red. "By the Goddess! What were you doing in the City? You know it is forbidden."

Lyric nodded feebly as her mother released her hold, "I'm sorry."

"Sorry! You're sorry? You could have been killed." Adria said, her face paling at the thought.

"Did you speak?" Hann asked, still livid.

"No." Lyric shook her head. "That's why the children threw stones at me."

Adria's face softened and saddened. Lyric saw tears welling in her eyes. She could not make out whether they were tears of relief she was alive, or tears of sadness because her daughter was so harshly treated.

Hann's face didn't soften. He took heaving breaths and stomped about the kitchen. "We can't have this. We can't have you risking your life Lyric, there's too much at stake. Grandmother said you needed more freedom, so we gave it to you, but you betrayed our trust. You don't understand Lyric, everything you do has consequences and these consequences reach far beyond you." He finally dropped onto a bench seat beside the table, breathing deeply to calm himself down. "You are confined to the house for the next two cleads and you are confined to the farm indefinitely."

"That's not fair!" Lyric looked to Grandmother for support, but she just gazed into the fire. She looked to her mother, but she just stood motionless, a tear rolling down her cheek. "If you'd just let me help with the harvest, then I would have less idle time to wander."

Hann slammed a fist on the table. "You know that's too risky. The workers, the people of the island have decided that because you are mute, you are also stupid. This is your camouflage, your protection, our protection. If one of the workers were to hear you speak, even just a word. If they knew you were clever enough to follow instructions, to learn how to cut or sheave barley, you – we would all be in great danger."

"I won't do it. You can't keep me prisoner here because I'm supposed to be special. I have to get out and learn things, do things, or I'll end up as stupid and helpless as everyone thinks I am." Lyric clenched her fists by her side in defiance."

Hann was controlled and determined now. "And for that disobedient outburst, there will be no meal tonight." He pointed to the stairs. "Go to your room."

Lyric glared at her father, hissed in frustration and ran up the stairs to her room.

Her bed was usually a comfort but now the linen tick was insufficient to stop the straw filling of her mattress from poking at every welt. She pulled two woollen blankets over the top, but it was still barely enough cushioning. Frustrated and sore, she sobbed herself to sleep.

On the west side of the island, the shadow of the great mount Vulcon was retreating from the ocean shore, past the stubbly coastal vegetation, over the fields and toward the base of the mountain itself. At first light, with the Kreft farm still in shadow, Benn was busily helping his father harvest vegetables and load them onto the cart. Donn Kreft was lean and wiry with shoulder–length greying hair, bound back into a ponytail. Benn felt as though sometimes his father would look at him with sadness, other times with resentment, but Donn was the only parent Benn had, so Benn loved him. Donn resented the hard work of farming vegetables and was grumpy more often than not. Sometimes loving your parent was difficult.

By the time the shadow of the mountain left the Kreft farm, Benn heaved the last melon onto the cart and carefully placed the greens into a separate basket, wedging it toward the front of the load. Donn harnessed the donkey and hitched it to the wagon. Benn waved his father off as he made for the Fiveday market in the City.

"Good luck at the market father," Benn said as the wagon left the farmyard, turning toward the City.

"Catch some good fish for supper," Donn called back.

Fiveday was Benn's favourite day of the clead. With no school and his father off at the markets till dusk, his only chore was to try and catch a fish or two for supper. Lazing by the riverbank suited Benn just fine. Most of his friends lived in or near the City and it was a long way to walk to the Kreft farm, so friends rarely came. Rikk visited once, but Donn was so grumpy towards him that he rarely visited his best friend's home thereafter. Benn would have liked a pet dog for companionship, but his father was adamant there must be no dog on the farm.

Benn gathered his fishing gear into a reed basket. He dug some worm–rich soil from near the donkey pen into an earthen pot and added that to the basket. The Kreft farm was of modest size and wedged between the road alongside the Roredon river and a creek that flowed into the river closer to the coast. The creek was too small to contain any decent–sized fish, so Benn set off for the river, alone.

The mountain's shadow had well and truly passed by the time Benn reached the river. The sky was indigo blue with an occasional wisp of cloud and the air was warming fast in the morning sun. *A great day for fishing*, Benn thought as he selected a grassy embankment under a large elm tree at a point where the river slowed to a lazy flow. He found a long stick and embedded it into the grass, pressed a reluctant worm onto his hook and unwound a length of cord from the wooden spool. Swinging the hook in a circular motion a few times, he tossed it out into the water, fed the hole in the spool down onto the stick, wrapped a loop of cord around his toe and laid back on the cool green grass. Dappling rays of sunlight pierced the foliage and warmed his face and body.

It was only three days since he rescued the Wildling from the mob of children in the City and her frightened face still haunted him. She had looked grubby and unkempt but there was something about her eyes, something about the way she looked at him. Being mute, she couldn't speak, but he wondered if she really was stupid.

Then he heard the cough. A light cough, a human cough. Benn had never heard an animal make such a sound. He sat up abruptly and looked about him. A short distance downstream stood the Wildling, motionless, watching him intently as the dappled sunlight played on her tangled hair, grubby skin and torn clothes. Her bare feet buried in the soft grass. He sprang to his feet and took a step toward her, dragging the fishing cord through the water and nearly tripping. He hopped about, trying to unwind the cord from his toe.

The Wildling smiled, then began to laugh. Her laugh was light and melodic, not at all like an animal. When he finally regained some dignity, he saw her teeth were white and well formed. Not like an animal at all. He looked more closely, if it wasn't for the grime, twigs and leaves, she might well pass for an ordinary girl.

"Hello," Benn said, in the way people addressed a horse in a paddock. Not expecting a reply. He stared at the blue–green marks on her arms and legs. "Good to see you made it away OK. I hope the bruises are healing. Best avoid the City if I were you, not a safe place for you to be."

"That's what my parents say."

Benn was startled. "You can speak! Everyone says you're mute, but you can speak."

"Yes, but please don't tell anyone. It's a huge secret. Please promise you won't tell."

"Why?"

"Father says that if people knew I could speak, I would be in great danger. He says that anyone who knew I could speak would be in great danger too. So please, promise not to tell anyone. I don't want you to get hurt because of me."

Benn doubted her story, but her pleading seemed genuine, as if she truly believed they would both be in peril, so he reluctantly agreed, "OK."

"Promise. You must promise not to tell anyone, not even your parents, not even your sisters and brothers, not even your best friend."

"OK, I promise."

The Wildling seemed relieved.

"Though I don't have any sisters or brothers and my mother died when I was an infant. It's just my father and me on the farm."

The Wildling looked sad for him, "I'm sorry to hear that." She looked over the river toward the golden fields of the Nye farm, "I can't imagine losing either of my parents, though they would be terribly angry if they knew I was here talking to you."

"My father wouldn't be happy about me talking to you either."

The Wildling stood her ground. "Yes, but after my near fatal foray into the City, I'm supposed to be confined to the house. Still, I wanted to thank you for saving my life, so I waited till my parents left to the harvest and my grandmother was asleep and I crept out."

"You're not at all what I expected," Benn said. "I mean, everyone says you're mute because you're stupid, but you can talk, and you're clearly not stupid."

The Wildling looked surprised, then smiled, "Well, thank you, kind sir. I'll take that as a compliment."

Benn smiled.

"Everyone assumes that because I don't speak, I can't speak. Then they assume that because I can't speak, I'm stupid. Still, all those assumptions keep me safe for now, and give me a rather different perspective on people who really can't speak."

Benn found himself having to concentrate to keep up. Not only was she not stupid, the Wildling was clearly clever. "It didn't keep you very safe in the City though, did it?"

"No." the Wildling conceded the point. "You did. That's why I came to say thank you."

"Well, you're welcome."

The Wildling looked directly at Benn. He looked into her intense, green eyes and he felt his stomach flutter. Then she shifted her gaze and seemed to be looking just past him. Suddenly she turned her head toward the Nye farm.

"I must go now," she said. "Grandmother will be waking soon." She moved to walk around him. "Oh, and I think you'll find more fish under the next tree along." She pointed downstream while walking toward some bushes further upstream.

"Wait!" Benn said as she was about to disappear. "Do you have a name?"

"Lyric," she replied, before disappearing into the hedges.

"Bye Lyric," Benn said, not knowing if she heard him. He figured she would cross the river at the stone bridge. After all, it was the only river crossing and if she had swum across, she wouldn't have been as grimy, and her hair and tunic would have been wet.

Benn reset his fishing line and lay back on the bank pondering the encounter. He had promised to keep her secret. He didn't believe she was really in any danger, but it seemed important to her and such a secret would do no harm. Though, it would be difficult not to tell Rikk. Best friends are difficult to keep secrets from.

After an hour without success, Benn gathered up his gear and moved to the next tree downstream. He tried the spot before and never caught a fish. In fact, he lost a couple of hooks and lines, tangled in logs and branches below the water. He set his line where the water looked deep and free of snags. No sooner had he wound the cord around his toe than it tightened firmly and within minutes he landed a good-sized fish, big enough to feed his father and himself.

"And she knows her fishing spots," Benn said to himself as he made his way home with his prize.

The following Fiveday when Benn arrived at the same spot on the river, he looked about for Lyric. He called her name a few times, but there was no reply. He slumped onto the riverbank, disappointed. It would have been nice to have someone to talk to while fishing. The day was still warm but getting cloudier by the minute. No sooner had Benn cast his line than a raindrop hit him on the head. By the time he gathered up his gear it was pouring down rain. Bedraggled and fishless, Benn burst through the door of the Kreft kitchen. He dropped his gear only to observe he was leaving a puddle. "Darn." One more thing he would have to clean up. He didn't look forward to his father arriving home in the evening either. He would be wet and grumpy, even more so when Benn told him it would be vegetable stew for supper.

The next clead, Benn arrived at the river not expecting to see Lyric. Indeed, he concluded she had only ventured out to thank him and he was unlikely to see her again. He settled in his usual spot under the elm tree. A light gust of wind was blowing elm seeds with their papery green sails out onto the river where they floated away.

"Hello."

Benn heard the voice, a girl's voice. It must be Lyric. Who else would come here? He looked about him but could see no one. He heard a giggle from close by. Maybe she was in the bushes. He got up and walked toward them and the giggling grew more intense.

"Why is it," Lyric's voice said, "that people rarely look up?"

Benn looked up into the elm tree. It took a while of searching and squinting until he spied her grimy form, perfectly camouflaged among the branches.

Detected, Lyric scrambled down and landed gently on the grass at the base of the tree making barely a sound.

Benn smiled. It was good to see her. "You seem to have some luck choosing fishing spots, where shall I fish today?"

"Right here should be fine." Lyric settled herself down on the grassy embankment nearby.

Benn proceeded to prepare his line, cast it in and settle on the grass himself. "Don't your parents look after you at all?"

Benn asked, noting her dishevelled appearance. "Maybe even your parents can't catch you to get you into a tub." Benn snickered at his own cleverness.

Lyric looked stung by his words. She looked like she was facing a predator, trying to decide whether to stand still or run.

"I'm sorry," Benn said quickly. "That was stupid and cruel. I'm sorry."

Lyric seemed to relax a little but was still wary. "It's camouflage," she said, picking up an elm seed from the ground and adding it to the nest of items in her tangled hair.

"Well, it's effective. I'll grant you that. You were almost invisible in the tree."

Lyric's satisfied smile gave Benn hope that he had redeemed himself. Suddenly the line went taut. Benn lurched forward to take the cord in hand and Lyric bobbed quietly with excitement. Benn gently drew the line in, then when the marker knot appeared above the water, he gave a mighty tug and the fish landed flopping on the grass between them. In one swift motion, Benn grasped the fish by the tail, grabbed the knife from the basket and thrust it into the fish, through the top of its head. When the fish stopped moving, he looked up at Lyric who was keenly watching the process.

"I don't like them to suffer," Benn explained. "I don't much like the idea of drowning in water, so I figure they would rather not drown slowly in air."

Lyric nodded and observed with fascination as Benn scaled and gutted the fish. He explained each step to Lyric, as if instructing an apprentice. Eventually he looked up, meeting her gaze. He couldn't tell whether he was studying her unique green eyes or mesmerised by them.

"Another?" Lyric asked, breaking the spell.

"If I can. Father was most unhappy I didn't catch a fish last week, so it would be good to make up for it by catching two today." He carefully reset his line and they settled back down on the riverbank on the now flattened grass. Benn was still mulling over what to say next when the line went taut again and another fish was landed. This fish was also dispatched, scaled, gutted and carefully stowed in the basket.

"Now your chores are done, how are you at running and climbing?" Lyric asked with a wicked smirk.

"Very good at running, the fastest in my school."

"Good." Lyric took off toward an oak tree downstream.

"Wait up! By the Goddess you run fast." Benn followed behind, the basket tightly in hand.

Lyric let out a squeal of delight as she reached the tree and launched herself onto the lowest branch. Benn watched as she dug her fingers and toes into the rough bark. He dropped the basket at the base of the mighty tree trunk and propelled himself up after her.

Benn talked as they climbed, "Do you know you have green eyes Lyric?" He paused momentarily for a response but didn't expect one. "Everyone on the island has brown eyes, but your eyes are green like leaves and forest. Maybe you're part plant. Could be that's why you're so darn good at climbing trees." They climbed high into the branches finally wedging themselves in some sturdy tree forks. Benn gazed about. Afternoon light flickered through the green canopy. The air was still, and the rich smell of earth and oak and summer filled the air. Cicadas pausing at their approach resumed their song, and a startled squirrel darted away along nearby branches. They watched its panicked flight and giggled. It was terrified of the big creatures invading its territory albeit with no intention of doing it harm.

It was a formidable climbing tree. Within the protective halo of its foliage, they wouldn't be easily seen. At Lyric's prompting, Benn talked about school, the children, the games they played, and about Rikk. Lyric seemed to hang on every word. He could only imagine how lonely it must be to not be allowed to go to school or play with other children.

They stayed there for a while, until the gold light of the late afternoon sun punctured through the foil of leaves. When daylight all but faded, Benn announced, "I have to go home now, or Father will come searching for me." They clambered down.

"Will I see you next week?" Benn asked.

"Maybe. I'll try, but I can't always make it."

Benn looked toward the farmland on the other side of the river. "Father says the Nye farm is one of the biggest farms on the island. He says it goes all the way from the river Roredon to the Haunted Forest and from the seashore to halfway up the mountain. I guess there would be plenty for you to do there to keep you busy." Benn began to gather up his fishing basket and head off in the direction of his home. "OK then, I'll see you next time you can get away."

Before passing between two bushes, Benn looked back, but Lyric was already gone. "By the Goddess she is fast," he muttered to himself.

As he neared the farm, he could see the wagon approaching. Without cargo to weigh it down, it bounced about on the dirt road. Despite the rough ride, Donn was smiling, and he waved when he saw Benn. Benn held up the basket and waved back. All the signs pointed to a very good day at the market and Donn was in a pleasant mood. Benn thought it one of the most pleasant and satisfying days he had ever spent. He was already looking forward to the next time he saw Lyric.

So it was thereafter. On the Fiveday, when the weather was fine, and she could get away, Lyric would head for the river and if Donn had headed off to the markets as scheduled, Benn would be there. She would show him where to catch a good fish and then they would wander and climb. In the autumn, they danced and rolled in the fallen leaves. They ate plump grapes, juicy apples and crisp pears from their families' gardens. In winter, it was too cold to catch many fish, but they would lay on dark grey slabs of rock in the sun to warm themselves, gazing at the mountain peak that was, on occasion, lightly dusted with snow. It was never cold enough on Vulcon for snow on the plains. Lyric, always barefoot, grimy and in tattered tunics, seemed immune to the cold. In spring they ran along the riverbank and inhaled the perfume of myriad flowers. They caught fish and rabbits for Benn to take home to his father, so he would think Benn was spending his time productively. They roamed widely, to the foot of the great Mount Vulcon, at the centre of the island, and westward to the ocean shore. Benn would talk of school and Lyric would talk about the goings on of the farm and help Benn to notice the trees, flowers, animals and the intricacies of nature around them. The Goddess had provided them with a bountiful land indeed.

The grain harvest was in and the orchard trees on Vulcon were laden with ripe fruit. It was a good season and there would be ample food for winter. It was morning on the last day of the last clead of the summer school holidays.

Lyric made her way to the riverbank, just over the ridge from the Kreft farm. She climbed high into the elm tree, their elm tree, and settled herself on a sturdy branch, leaning back against the tree trunk, to wait for Benn. It was a bountiful year for the elm tree too. The tips of the branches were clustered with the last of the green, papery seeds and with each gust of wind, some would dislodge and flutter slowly to the ground, or be carried off in the wind. Lyric sat there taking in the rich smell of the bark, listening to birdsong and watching the cascade of elm seeds when it happened.

Lyric was watching the bright dancing white light around each seed. Sometimes it seemed as though she couldn't just see it, but she could also feel it. She selected a seed wafting slowly down from high in the tree and reached out with the part of her thoughts which seemed to feel the White Fire and imagined she was holding the seed in the air. The seed stopped, hovering in the air as all its fellows continued to waft gently downward. Lyric was so startled she broke concentration and the seed resumed its dancing descent. She closed her eyes, breathed slowly, calmed herself and prepared to experiment on another seed.

"Hello Lyric."

Benn's voice shattered her concentration. It took Lyric a moment to regain composure. "Hello Benn," she said, gracefully climbing down and alighting on the soft grass beside him.

"See, you've taught me to look up," Benn said with a wink and a grin.

Benn had been exuberant and joyful at the beginning of the summer school break with the promise of fun times ahead. Lyric observed, however, as the summer cleads passed by, he became progressively more distant. He talked less, brooded more, and started to make comments like, "You know, it won't always be like this." Lyric dared not question further. She thought her life perfect and didn't want anything to change.

Lyric had wondered whether Benn would even come today, and what kind of dark mood he would be in if he did. His chirpy greeting buoyed her spirits, but his mood soon became solemn, pensive even. Lyric waited patiently for him to speak. He had grown taller and more angular in the year since they first met, but then so had she and her tattered tunic failed to conceal the curves of a young woman.

Lyric observed that, like herself, Benn brought a satchel full of food provisions for the day. She was pleased he at least intended they should spend the whole day together. Lyric became impatient and gestured toward the mountain, "Shall we walk to the mountain today?"

Benn shook his head, "No, not the mountain today." he gestured downstream, "I'd rather walk down to the beach. I don't know when I'll get the chance to swim at the beach again."

Lyric looked puzzled, but happily set off downstream. As they walked, Benn chatted about the farm and the harvest. He lamented at the low prices his father was receiving for the fruit and vegetables in town. He talked about how difficult his father found the farm work when he was at school. With ample hired help and a bountiful harvest, the Nyes were experiencing no such difficulty, so Lyric was happy to let him speak and she listened as empathically as she could. As they made their way, the river became progressively wider, the shrubs lining the riverbank gave way to ancient willows waving in the breeze. The water seemed to move slower, eventually seeming to stop altogether and the willows gave way to windswept, sparse grey bushes with harsh scratchy twigs and the fields yielded to rocky outcrops and arcs of small beaches with grey gravelly sand.

The pair scrambled onto a large flat rock, shaded by a small tree, its branches contorted by the relentless ocean winds. They gently placed their satchels, before racing off to the smaller waves on the sheltered end of the beach. They swam, splashed each other with the cold water, chased each other about and swam again. When they were exhausted and hungry, they returned to the rock.

Benn emptied out his satchel displaying apples, pears, plums, boiled eggs and a gourd of fresh water. "What have you got?"

Lyric brought out bread her mother had baked the previous evening, goat's cheese, almonds and figs, and a small pot of quince paste, sweetened with honey and sealed with wax. It was a feast worthy of the last day of the summer break.

"I really love figs." Benn reached over to grab the figs. Lyric quickly snatched a couple of figs to herself and smiled, "You're not the only one." She half bit and half sucked the smooth sweet flesh into her mouth, savouring the flavour and texture. Next she broke off a piece of bread, applied some goat's cheese and quince paste with a small wooden spatula, and took a bite. She closed her eyes as she chewed it slowly.

"Is that as good as it looks?"

Lyric nodded and smiled, so Benn set about compiling a similar creation. He savoured the first mouthful.

"This is so good Lyric," he said, his voice muffled by the mouthful of food. Benn gazed out to sea. "I wish every day could be like this. I wish things didn't have to change."

"Things don't have to change," Lyric responded. "We can keep things just as they are."

Benn's expression became grim again.

As soon as they had consumed all they could eat, Lyric jumped up and pointed to the beach, "Let's swim again?" Not waiting for an answer, she raced down to the sand.

By the time Benn stowed the remnants of lunch back into their satchels, carefully tied the tops closed with leather thong and made his way to the water's edge, Lyric found a patch of coarse wet sand and sculpted a giant scallop shell into its surface.

Benn dropped to his knees in the damp sand beside her. "That's really great, Lyric," he observed, "It looks just like a shell."

Lyric smiled, because he liked her sculpture, and because it felt good when he said her name.

"Listen, Lyric," Benn became serious and began to rub his lower lip with a finger from his left hand while supporting his chin with his thumb, the way he did when he was nervous and uncomfortable, "There's something I have to discuss with you."

"OK," Lyric said, and commenced another shell sculpture in the wet sand. She sensed he was going to say something important.

"As you know, last year was my last year at school," Benn pushed on, "I don't know how much you know about what happens after school. Life gets more serious. We have to grow up. I'm in my sixteenth year now and I guess you're in about your fifteenth."

"Soon, my birthday is in Autumn."

Benn continued, "we can't stay as children forever, even if we want to." Benn paused to consider that further, "Well, maybe you can. Maybe that's the hidden blessing in being wild, and exiled."

Lyric considered reacting, but it was important to hear Benn out, so she just kept sculpting sand while listening carefully.

"Because none of the girls in my year were found to be Seers in the test at the start of school, they will all be going to apprenticeships to become Homemakers, and some of them will also learn trades. Some will serve their apprenticeships at home, some with family and some in the community. Some will even be chosen to be apprenticed at the Palace and learn to serve the royal family." Benn pondered for a moment, then mused, "Funny how none of the girls seem to be Seers anymore. The kids at school said it used to be common, and it's supposed to be passed down from the mother to the daughters. Somehow the gift of the Sight now only resides with the women of the royal family. I guess if I'm going to be bonded to a Seer, like my father wishes, it'll have to be the Princess."

The section of sculpture Lyric was working on suddenly became mush under her hands. She nervously tried to re-craft it, hoping Benn wouldn't notice.

Benn was gazing out to sea. "The boys will all go and do two years at the Protector Academy," he continued. "Then most of them will do apprenticeships and learn a trade. Some will be selected to continue at the Academy for a further year to learn to become Protectors for the island of Vulcon, for the City, and maybe even for the Palace and the royal family. Though, you do have to be bonded to the Queen to be the highest Protector in the land, the Royal Consort. I'm hoping to do something like that. I can't think of any trade I want to learn. I'm smart and fast and strong, I think I'd make a great Royal Protector."

Lyric turned away on the pretence of scooping up more sand, but mostly to hide her grin. Sometimes Benn was so full of himself. But she had to admit, he was smart and fast and strong and not ugly. He was going to make a great Protector for someone. She felt a great sadness that it would never be her. She was the Wildling, a freak, and definitely not a member of the royal family. He deserved better. He deserved a more normal existence. She would have to be content with being his friend.

"Anyway," Benn started drawing with his finger in the sand. "The Protector Academy is a boarding school. I have to live there for five cleads of each moon and I only get to come home to help on the farm for the sixth clead of each moon. Also, father found out I've been spending some time with you. I think he left the farm to look for me the other day and saw us. He's furious. He says that if I associate with you, my chances of becoming a Royal Protector are zero. He says I have to become at least a Palace Protector, or he'll be doomed to poverty for the rest of his years. He only let me come out today if I promised to break it off."

Lyric bit her lip to avoid showing emotion but she could no longer bring herself to move sand about. The current work seemed more of a pile now than a sculpture.

"You see Lyric, I can't see you anymore. We can't play anymore. Do you understand?"

"You said you would be home for the sixth clead of each moon. We could spend time together then." She could feel tears welling in her eyes.

"No Lyric, my father will be watching me like a hawk when I am home. To make sure I don't disrupt his plans for my career, he'll make sure he is with me all day every day. There just won't be a chance."

Benn looked as forlorn as Lyric felt. He moved to wipe away a tear running down her cheek. Lyric felt a tingle in her gut at his warm, gentle touch.

"I'm really going to miss you Lyric. I've enjoyed our adventures and conversations," Benn said as he began to clear his throat and snuffle the way men do when they don't want to be seen to cry. He turned away to wipe his eyes with his palms.

"Benn, no," was all Lyric could say, determined not to sob in front of him.

A gust of cool wind chilled them through their wet clothes.

"We should go now, Lyric. It's a long walk home and our clothes won't dry well after dark." He put the satchels on one shoulder then reached down to help Lyric to her feet.

Standing, she was less than a cubit away from him. Even with wet clothes and a cool breeze, she felt a rising heat inside. Their eyes met. Her eyes searched his for hope and his eyes searched hers, but she didn't know what they were searching for. Benn leaned slightly forward for an instant, then pulled away and turned toward home.

"You clean up well after a swim," Benn said as he marched off. Lyric, confused and heartbroken, walked behind. "If it wasn't for the mess of hair and the tattered tunic, you would look presentable."

Lyric blushed. The swim uncovered her skin from its shield of grime. It was tanned and smooth.

They walked mostly in silence and arrived back at the elm tree by the river just after dark. The light of the full moon lit their way for the last part of the journey home.

"Well, time for me to go then," Benn stood and looked at her one last time.

His face was serious, his brows furrowed in a frown and his eyes showed a penetrating intensity she had not seen before. She couldn't fathom his emotions. For reasons she couldn't explain, he rushed forward and swept her up in a gentle hug. Startled, Lyric just froze, feeling oddly flushed yet soothed in his arms. She breathed in the scent of him. He smelled like spices.

She struggled to decide on the best course of action and tried
hard to contain her emotions. Eventually she wrapped her arms
around him, held him, and tried to make this embrace last
forever. She was still struggling to be an edifice of self–control
when he finally released her and began to march up the
riverbank toward his home.

After Benn disappeared from view, Lyric dropped to the soft
earth and sobbed. She wept for hours, rolling about in grief, in
the moonlight, under their tree. She wept until there were no
tears left in her, until she was once again covered in grime, once
again looking every inch the Wildling.

Lyric's mother taught her that feelings held back could twist
and distort a person from the inside. She let them out, all of
them. Now she must be strong again. She picked herself up and
began the long walk home. Benn was right, she was growing up
too, changing. She must speak with Grandmother, but it was late.
It would have to wait until morning. Maybe she would be
thinking more clearly then.

Lyric kept her friendship with Benn a secret from her
parents, and her mother was too emotionally close to Lyric to
detect it. Grandmother knew though. She had known from the
beginning and Lyric told her everything. One summer day, Aunt
Tyla had burst into the kitchen soon after Lyric's parents left for
the fields. She flapped about the room like a captured bird until
Grandmother called her over to the hearth. Lyric went out to the
garden to let them speak privately. Sometime later Aunt Tyla
emerged, calling out "I promise," as she closed the door behind
her. Calmer now, she walked over to Lyric and gave her a huge
hug. She said, "Take care Precious One," and turned to walk
home. Aunt Tyla then made a point of visiting Grandmother
every moon, spending some time alone with her while Lyric's
parents worked out in the fields.

Still feeling a great wound inside from the day before, Lyric sat to breakfast with her family. This was a busy time of year and there was much to do on the farm.

"Don't worry about cleaning up breakfast Mother, I'll do it."

"Why, thank you Lyric," Adria responded. She eyed Lyric with curiosity, "Are you OK, Precious One? You look like you've been crying."

"I'm fine Mother."

Hann leaned over for a closer look at the hint that something might be wrong. "Are you sure Lyric, you look pink around the eyes? Are you feeling well?"

"Really, I'm fine." Endless days of her parents working hard and paying her little attention, and today of all days, they decided to have an 'intensely caring parent' episode. Lyric fought off the frustration and suppressed the urge to start sobbing all over again. She began to clear dishes from the table. "Go. There is much work to be done. I'll be fine here with Grandmother."

"Alright, Precious One." Adria gave her a hug and pushed away her hair to kiss her forehead. "You know you can talk to me if anything is troubling you?"

Lyric wanted to sob and tell her mother everything, but her parents had a consistent history of confining her at the slightest hint of trouble, so she suppressed the sob welling up inside and just nodded before pulling herself away and proceeded to clear the remaining dishes.

Her parents gathered up their hats and work gloves and headed for the farmyard.

"At last!" Grandmother said in her raspy voice. "I thought they'd never leave."

Lyric plumped and placed the cushions on Grandmother's chair by the hearth then helped her from the bench by the kitchen table. Grandmother wore layers of cashmere and wool these days; a thick tunic and multiple wraps and blankets. She found it difficult to keep warm, even in the summer with a fire in the hearth. Lyric could tell why. As she aided her Grandmother, she could feel only bones under parchment–thin skin. There was almost nothing left of her but her indomitable spirit. Lyric gently helped her onto the cushions and arranged blankets over her lap, then moved toward the dirty dishes.

"They can wait," Grandmother called after her. "First, tell me about yesterday my child."

Lyric pulled the small stool she kept for the purpose, from beside the hearth and sat beside her grandmother's knee. She told of the day at the beach, of Benn going to the Academy and how he would not be able to spend time with her anymore. The grief welled again, and Lyric began to sob. She could be herself around Grandmother.

"Now, now, child." Grandmother lifted Lyric's chin with her bony fingers, wiping away tears with a soft linen kerchief. "Your heart is broken. You have my permission to weep today as much as you want, but tomorrow you must put the weeping aside and decide what to do."

"What is there to do?" Lyric said with the stilted voice of one still sobbing inside. "When Benn is home, his father will be watching him all day, every day. There will be no chance to spend time with him."

"Remember child, friendship is a powerful and vital thing, not to be surrendered easily. You say Donn will be supervising Benn all day?"

Lyric nodded, Grandmother's fingers still under her chin.

"Ah, but what about at night?"

Lyric's eyes widened.

"If I remember correctly, the sixth clead of each moon is the clead of the full moon." Grandmother folded her hands on her lap and gazed at the fire with a smug smile. "I remember Donn Kreft. A much happier soul when his wife Myra was alive. When she was killed it was a double tragedy. He's not been the same since. Fixated on the poor boy's career."

Lyric barely heard this. Her spirit was buoyed. There was hope. She began to hatch a plan. She stood to return to her chores, then sat back down.

"Is there something else child?"

Lyric paused a moment to gather the words, "The White Fire."

"Ah yes, have you been practising. Do you still see it?"

"Yes Grandmother, I see it very clearly now, even more than before."

Grandmother seemed satisfied, but when Lyric did not move from the stool she asked, "Is there more?"

"I was watching the White Fire around a falling elm seed and I started to play with it." Lyric watched for a reaction, but Grandmother just looked at her, listening intently. "I made it stop falling down."

"Really?"

"Yes, it just hung there, suspended, until I was distracted then it fell down like all the others."

"This I did not see my child, but elm seeds are small and not easily seen from awhen." Grandmother turned and gazed into the fire. "You know what you must do, don't you child?"

Lyric frowned as she pondered. "Practise?"

"Yes, my child," she turned to Lyric and smiled. There was a glint in her eye that Lyric had not seen for some moons. "Yes, you must practise. Practise where you will not be seen."

"Thank you, Grandmother." Lyric jumped up and kissed Grandmother on the forehead. "I love you Grandmother."

"I love you too, dear child," Grandmother said and cosied herself for the first of many naps that day.

Lyric had hope and things to do. There was much to plan. She cleaned the kitchen in record time and set off for a small copse of trees in the centre of one of the larger fields. Most of the fields had a copse of trees at their centre to provide shelter for the goats during harsh weather. This copse was large enough to shelter Lyric from view.

Deep in the heart of the copse she plucked a leaf and placed it on the ground. She sat cross-legged on the ground beside it. The White Fire danced around the leaf and Lyric focussed on it, willing the leaf to rise. She focussed, she willed, she held her breath, but all that happened was she broke wind. The leaf didn't budge. She lay back in frustration then breathed slowly to calm herself. Closing her eyes, she tried to remember exactly how she made the elm seed hover: what she was thinking, how she was feeling. She opened her eyes to see the upside-down face of a goat kid looking at her. The goat bleated on seeing movement and Lyric laughed, pushing the goat aside as she sat up. "Off with you, I'm busy." The kid ran back to the comfort of its mother.

The leaf was gone. Probably eaten by said goat. Lyric plucked another and resumed her position. Again, she focussed, she could see the white light around the leaf. She breathed deeply and let herself feel the flickering White Fire, then she gently imagined the White Fire carrying the leaf upward. The leaf gently lifted from the earth to hover level with Lyric's eyes. Lyric gently lowered it to the ground, then sprang to her feet with excitement. The goat kid returned, and Lyric moved to hug it for joy, but it ran away.

Lyric found a good–sized stick and placed it on the earth in front of her. The White Fire was weaker around it than around a living leaf, nevertheless Lyric watched it, felt it and imagined it moving upward. The stick rose to just above Lyric's head, and with a small twist of imagination, Lyric made it spin, like sticks do when they are caught in a river eddy. She reached out and plucked the stick from the air. The moment she touched it she could feel it gain weight in her hand.

Excited now, she spied a large log. Lyric looked carefully around to ensure there was no one about and she focussed on the log. Presently it was hovering a cubit above the ground, dripping earth and sending the creatures inhabiting it scurrying in all directions. She gently lowered the log back down. "Sorry to upset your home," she whispered to the creatures. Clearly the White Fire did not concern itself with the weight of an object.

"I wonder," Lyric whispered, even though there was no one to hear but the goats grazing in the field nearby. Lyric looked at the White Fire around her hands, then closed her eyes and felt the White Fire flowing around and through her. She focussed, imagined, and felt her feet leave the soft earth. She opened her eyes when she felt her head tap on a tree branch. She was hovering about two cubits above the ground. After taking in the perspective, she moved herself sideways and upward until she was sitting on a sturdy branch. For a while she sat there, pondering, trying to understand her discovery, what she could do. Eventually she focussed again and lowered herself gently to the ground.

Lyric arrived home in time to help Adria prepare lunch and tried to act as though nothing had happened.

"You look like you're feeling better now," Adria said, touching Lyric's cheek.

"Yes Mother, I feel much better now." She looked toward Grandmother who was observing her with a wry grin. She felt like an emotional stew; grief, hope, wonder and excitement all jumbling around inside her, coalescing into purpose, gelling into plans. Secret plans.

This was a carefully planned day. Lyric had practised in the copse of trees almost daily since she discovered her ability. She was older now, better prepared. She could do this. On the first day of the school year all the new students were tested. For years her parents told her that children who were special did not survive the test. Her parents kept her on the farm, isolated, telling her only what they thought she needed to know. Now she would see for herself. She knew from her conversations with Benn, where and when the testing would occur.

Her best chance of getting into the City quietly and unseen was after dark. The moon was nearly full, and the sky was clear. She would find her way. Lyric went to bed fully clothed and ready to go. She waited until her parents were asleep, then crept quietly down the stairs and across the kitchen toward the door.

"Going somewhere?" A raspy voice whispered from the corner. Grandmother was now far too frail to climb the stairs to her bedroom, so her bed had been moved down to the kitchen, along a wall near the hearth. Lyric could just make out her hollow face in the light from the embers.

"Don't worry Grandmother, I'll be fine," Lyric whispered.

"Yes, my child, you will." Grandmother smiled and snuggled under her covers.

Lyric quietly raised the bar of wood that secured the door at night, and slipped out. She turned and focussed, closed the door quietly and replaced the wooden bar on the inside. Pushing her woollen cloak back, she dashed toward the City.

By the time she arrived at the city wall, the moon was high in the sky. The city gates were closed at night, so Lyric made for a section of the wall where bushes extended to the very base of the structure. The smooth stones fit neatly together with no chance of a foothold. She wondered why Vulcon City had such high walls and secure gates when there were only Vulcon citizens on the island and the visiting Phoenecian traders came only by ship. Grandmother said it was to protect against the evil spirits of the Haunted Forest, lest they come and attack the citizens by night. Father said it was nothing more than a superstitious ritual superseded when the current Queen's mother decided the city gates were a useful way of controlling the flow of goods into the City so the farmers could be taxed. The Nye family, like other farmers, felt the sting of the taxes following every harvest.

Once she was certain there was no one about, Lyric focussed, felt the surge of the White Fire and elevated herself over the wall and down into the darkened city streets below. Alert and watchful, she crept along the shadows to the heart of the City, emerging between a row of shops at the City Square. On the far side lay the walls of the Palace, in front of which was the podium. On the right of the Square stood the grand buildings of the Protector Academy, cold and grey in the moonlight. On the left of the square was the once grand and fortified Seer Academy. As no Seers had been identified for generations outside the royal family, the building fell into disrepair. Paint and render eventually fell away giving the building a tattered appearance. The rightmost building of the Seer Academy was a large hall running alongside the road to the Port. This was Lyric's target. Keeping close to the buildings, she made her way around toward it.

A small, brown dog leapt out from one of the shops barking loudly at her. Lyric's heart skipped a beat as she darted for the shadow of the alley beside the shop.

The shopkeeper, a rotund, balding man, came out. "What is it boy?" He looked around then focussed on where the dog was barking. "Is there someone there?" The dog led him to the alleyway, where it stopped, still barking loudly. The man squinted to see in the shadows. "It's OK boy, there's no–one there." He picked up the still barking dog and carried it inside. "Must have been a rat," he announced to the family inside and securely closed the door.

Lyric worked hard to maintain focus as she hovered high in the alleyway, pressed motionless against the dark wall of the building. "Luckily people rarely look up," she whispered, lowering herself gently and silently to the ground. When she arrived at the hall, she circled it, noting there was only one entrance consisting of two massive wooden doors, blocked by a wooden bar that would take a very strong man (or two lesser ones) to lift it. Checking again no–one was about, Lyric focussed, raising one end of the bar enough so that one of the two great doors could be pushed open. She slid through the gap, closed the door and lowered the bar on the outside behind her. She was in darkness.

Lyric felt for the small leather bag on the girdle at her waist and carefully pulled out a candle, a small piece of parchment and a flint, taking great care not drop any of the items, as they would be difficult to find again in the darkness of the hall. There was a small, barred window high on the wall to the right, but it let in very little moonlight. Lyric sat on the floor, cradling the precious items in her tunic. She laid the parchment on the earthen floor and chipped the flint over it to create a flame. Lyric coaxed the tiny flame until it was strong enough and lit the candle before extinguishing the parchment. The tiny flame swelled, and the hall illuminated.

A large, square, stone depression lay in the centre of the room with a small canal to a barred opening under the wall on the left side. Inside the depression were a series of painted, flat, flagstones sitting atop other rocks. Partway up the wall on each side of the entrance door were two wooden parapets. Each edged by 'fence' of woven sticks. There was an opening at the side for a ladder, but any ladders were long since removed. Lyric focussed and elevated herself to one of the parapets. She could get a good view of the hall from between the sticks but felt exposed by the entranceway. Then she saw that the other parapet contained some old baskets. Focussing, she floated across to the other parapet. She positioned a large basket near the entrance, wrapped her cloak around her, settled herself as comfortably as she could, and blew out the candle.

The groaning of hinges as the large wooden doors opened, roused Lyric from a deep sleep. Light from the high window began to illuminate the room. The air was now chilly. Lyric wrapped her cloak tight for warmth. Peering between the woven sticks, she could see the depression in the floor was now filled with water until only the flat surface of the flagstones remained visible. Water from the City's canal reticulation system had been shunted into the building until the desired water level was reached. The floor looked remarkably clean for a rarely used, thatched hall. She figured it was probably cleaned and swept the previous day. Royal Protectors brought in a small wooden table and set it in the far–left corner while others set up two cushioned divans and a wooden chair a little in front of the parapets. She wondered why the furniture was set so far forward, then she took in the neglected state of her parapet. The floor, sticks and baskets were covered in a thick layer of dust, that now infested much of her cloak. Most of the baskets were upright, but one which was fallen on its side was full of webs and spiders. Each corner of the parapet was arched in dusty spider web. It would not do to have dust and spiders sprinkling down on the royal family's divans.

Lyric resolved to remain as still as possible, lest she stir up dust. A trickle of dust from the parapet, or worse still, a sneeze, would surely give her away. Moving ever so slowly and carefully, Lyric adjusted her position to see through the largest gap in the sticks. She heard the royal family before she saw them.

"But why do I have to stay ALL day Mother?" a loud voice whined.

"Because you need to learn how to conduct the testing properly," an authoritative female voice replied. "There must be no errors. If any child is a Seer, they must be identified now."

Lyric could only see them from the top as they entered the room. The heads of the mother and daughter were draped with fine purple scarves, sitting unevenly over ornately braided hair. The scarves were encircled and held in place by fine gold crowns, of which the Queen's was the larger, with a prominent ruby embedded centre front. The Royal Consort moved forward around them to the left wearing the red tunic of the Royal Protectors with a shining, panelled, copper overshirt, the front of which formed a breastplate. He bore a wooden platter on which sat a glazed pottery cloche. He placed the platter carefully on the table in the far corner of the room. Other Protectors draped grey towels over the wooden chair, before retreating from the hall, closing the doors behind them and leaving the royal family alone.

"Mother, why can't I just stay for part of the day? This is a boring, peasant kind of place." The Princess moved to brush imaginary dust from her divan before settling onto it, displaying a long, yellow tunic, split at the sides and embroidered with an intricate blue design around the edges.

"Hush Brata," the Queen said. "You must learn to do this well and develop the stamina to attend to the task all day if you are to keep your throne. Fail at this and you will find yourself in a 'peasant kind of place' all day, every day for the rest of your life. Besides, it's not like you have something more important to attend to." The Queen perched expectantly at the centre of her divan, displaying a similarly cut tunic, in purple with yellow embroidery around the edges.

"I was going to select my dress for the opening of the Protector Academy school year. That's important."

Lyric saw the Queen's head turn toward the Princess, but no word was spoken. Lyric imagined that the Queen was glaring at her daughter as the Princess promptly fell silent and looked away.

The Royal Consort, walked to the chair and sequentially removed his sword, belt, breastplate overshirt, metal wristbands, and sandals, laying them carefully on the floor beside the chair. "Ready my Queen."

Lyric could see that Royal Consort Dunn was a tall, muscular man, his dark hair, with wisps of grey at the sides, was tied back in a short, tight ponytail at the nape of his neck. He went and rapped on the door. It opened just far enough to admit the first terrified child. The Royal Consort turned and walked toward the pool of water, sighing in resignation as the Queen stood and moved slowly toward the child.

"Welcome child," the Queen said in a soft, reassuring tone, "Do not be afraid, you are among friends."

The young girl bowed to her Queen and moved furtively forward to where the Queen gestured. Spying the Princess reclining on her divan as she passed, she bowed to the Princess too. Princess Brata nodded and forced a condescending smile.

"What is your name child?"

"Leesa of Wright, your highness."

"Well Leesa of Wright, you get to play a fun game today child." The Queen gestured toward the pool of water and her Royal Consort, who was also feigning a welcoming smile. "You see these stones across the pool?"

The child surveyed the scene and nodded.

"The stones are painted different colours. You get to tell my Royal Consort here which stone to step on next. If he makes it to the other side without falling into the water, you get to eat a piece of delicious cake from under that cloche in the corner, and then you go home." The Queen pointed in the direction of the table. "If he falls in, the test is complete and you may go home, but there will be no cake. Do you understand?"

The child nodded again and studied the rocks.

Satisfied, the Queen returned to her divan and sat down to watch.

"Where shall I step first little one?" Consort Dunn asked, trying to look friendly and enthusiastic.

"The yellow one."

Consort Dunn stepped onto the yellow rock and it was sound. He smiled in relief.

"The black one." The child pointed at the selected stone.

Consort Dunn obediently stepped onto the black rock, and it was sound.

"The brown one," the child announced, more confident now.

Consort Dunn stepped onto the brown rock. It wobbled and tipped, toppling him into the water. The splash from his hulking body wetting all the rocks in the pool and much of the floor around.

The child looked shocked. Consort Dunn sat up and gave a large, fake smile. The sight of him was so peculiar that the child burst out laughing. As Consort Dunn stood and moved to the edge of the pool, water dripping from his thick tunic, the Queen rose and moved toward the child.

"You have done well child," she said. "Now go knock on the door and you will be allowed to go home."

As the bedraggled Consort Dunn drained himself at the edge of the pool, the child did as she was told. The door opened and she exited with a smile. The next child was pushed in through the opening.

Lyric watched on in silence, not daring to move, as the test was repeated, over and over. She smiled each time Consort Dunn dragged himself from the water. She wondered if this was the worst day of the Consort's year. At midday the test was paused when a meal arrived for the Royal Family. Consort Dunn dried himself with a towel and sat on the wooden chair. No cushions for someone so sodden, Lyric thought.

One by one, the royal family left the hall to attend to their toilet as the remnants of lunch were removed. Lyric was thankful she had brought neither food nor water. She did not need the distraction of having to toilet.

In the afternoon the process continued. This time the Princess Brata took on the role performed in the morning by the Queen. After each child, the Queen would critique the Princess's performance.

"You must be more friendly and welcoming, Brata," the Queen said, often. "If the child is too frightened, you won't get an accurate result. Remember, the child must think this is a game."

"I don't see why we bother Mother," Princess Brata whispered after her third admonishment. "No Seers have been detected for years. They're surely extinct by now."

"We must be certain," the Queen said, half whispering, half hissing.

Princess Brata rolled her eyes and proceeded to welcome the next child.

Eventually the light from the window began to fade. The Queen halted proceedings to order torches be brought in and lit.

"How many more?" Princess Brata asked the last Protector, as he made for the door.

"Four, your highness."

The Princess heaved a sigh of exasperation. "I'm sure I have mastered the process, Mother. Can I go now?"

"No! But you may take a seat, and I will finish. I can't have your poor attitude affecting the final tests."

Princess Brata plopped herself on the divan and reclined with a satisfied smile as she watched her parents process the last of the children. Lyric was glad it would soon be over. She was stiff and sore from sitting confined in a singular position for a long time and she was feeling the need to pee.

The final child was a young girl, Tegan of Felder. When she made her way to the edge of the pool, she looked up at Consort Dunn, wearily faking a friendly smile, his hair and clothes still dripping.

"You are very wet," the child said with an expression of concern. "I will try not to get you any wetter."

Consort Dunn smiled as the child studied the pool. The last child of the day was also the most caring. "Where shall I step first, little one?" Consort Dunn asked for the final time.

"The yellow one."

Consort Dunn stepped onto the yellow rock and it was sound. By now he knew it was.

"The black one."

Consort Dunn obediently stepped onto the black rock. It was still sound.

"The black one to the side," the child pointed.

Consort Dunn stepped onto the stone and it too was sound.

Before each selection, Tegan would stare at the far wall of the hall for a moment, as if there was something there, but the wall was blank. Lyric sensed what was happening and felt a surge of excitement. Tegan of Felder, who would have thought? The Felders farmed the extensive vineyards and orchards northwest of the City.

The child continued to indicate stones, and each proved sound. When Consort Dunn stepped onto the far edge of the pool, he wore an expression of feigned pleasure. "Well done child. Thank you for keeping me dry." He then looked toward the Queen who was already making her way to Tegan.

Even the Princess Brata sprung to her feet. "Yes, yes, well done child!"

The Queen placed her hand on Tegan's shoulder. "You have done very well indeed Tegan of Felder." She steered the happy Tegan around the pool and toward the table at the corner of the room.

Consort Dunn met them at the table and lifted the cloche to reveal three, rectangular, golden pieces of cake.

"Choose whichever piece you like, child." The Queen gestured the excited child toward the cake.

After pausing to consider the offering, Tegan selected the middle piece. "Thank you, your Highness," Tegan said as she turned to walk toward the door.

"You must—" Consort Dunn said before the Queen could raise her hand to interrupt him.

"Where are you going child?" The Queen asked.

"The cake looks delicious. I want to share it with my best friend."

"No, no, no," the Queen said, stepping in front of Tegan and blocking her path. She crouched down to the girl's height. "This cake is only for you child. After all, you are the one who earned it. Please eat it now so we can watch you enjoy your reward."

Obediently Tegan took a bite of the cake. "Hmm, honey cake. I love honey cake." Tegan munched another mouthful. "This is the yummiest honey cake I've ever eaten," Tegan said as she was about to pop the final portion in her mouth. "It makes my mouth tingle."

"Secret royal ingredient," Princess Brata said, smiling as Tegan devoured the last mouthful.

"Excellent," the Queen said. "You'd best be getting home now. It's late and your parents will worry."

Princess Brata walked Tegan to the door, knocked for the Protectors to open it and gently ushered her through.

When the door closed behind Tegan, the royal family stared at each other in silence for what seemed to Lyric a very long time.

"So, Seers are extinct by now?" The Queen glared at the Princess.

Princess Brata stood there, looking decidedly ashen, eventually shifting her gaze to her father.

"It is done," Consort Dunn said, gathering up a towel and drying himself off.

"Indeed," the Queen said.

As Consort Dunn put on his sandals and the fixings of his Protector uniform, the Queen and the Princess walked to the far table. The Princess lifted the cloche and the Queen tipped the remaining pieces of cake onto the floor, stepping on them to squish them onto the rough stone surface. "For the rats."

The party made its way to the door and the Queen turned toward Consort Dunn. "Have the family watched. You know what to do."

"Yes, my Queen." Consort Dunn knocked for the door to open.

"I want this room sealed for one clead," the Queen said to the Protector at the door. "Then have it cleaned."

The Protector bowed and the mighty door was closed.

Nice of them to leave the torches on, Lyric thought. She waited until she could hear the Protectors walking away, then focussed and floated her way down to the floor, preceded by streams of dust. It was difficult to focus, her tummy hurt. Rather desperate, she ran over to the canal and peed in it until she felt relieved. Hungry, she went over to the table. She found the cake thoroughly pressed into the dust and dirt. Why have dirty, gritty cake here when there is good food at home?

When the City was silent and the torches began to dim, Lyric went to the door and focussed, slowly raising the bar on the outside until she could open a door just far enough to slip through. She pulled the door quietly closed behind her and allowed the bar to slip back into place. She wrapped her cloak tight around her and made for the shadows. By the time the moon was high in the sky, she was home. She floated up to her window, entered quietly and put herself to bed. She was so tired that even worrying about her parents' reaction the next day couldn't keep her awake for long.

CHAPTER THREE

Places of Learning

The morning sun was already high in the sky and blasting through her window onto her face when Lyric finally roused from sleep. This was excellent, her parents would be out working the fields and she wouldn't have to face them till at least midday. She could hardly wait to tell Grandmother what she had seen. Lyric felt a tightening in her chest when she came down the stairs to find her parents and Aunt Tyla sitting at the table looking at her expectantly.

"Where were you yesterday?" Hann asked, tense with self-restraint, before she reached the bottom step.

Lyric looked to Grandmother for support, but she just sat in her chair, gazing at the fire in the hearth, wearing a smug, knowing smile. "I was in the City."

Hann heaved a sigh and slammed a fist on the table in frustration. "We've told you, repeatedly, it is not safe in the City for you. You know we have forbidden you to go there."

A year or so ago, Lyric would have cringed and apologised, but she had been to the City and back, safely, without aid. She was more capable now and this fuelled her confidence. "You told me many things Father. Now it's time for me to see for myself."

Lyric saw the colour rising in her father's face and his fists tense. Adria placed her hand on his arm, and it stilled him for a moment.

"What were you doing in the City?" Aunt Tyla asked. She seemed the calmest of the trio and she kept glancing toward Grandmother.

"I went to see the testing of the children for myself."

"You what?" Hann jumped to his feet. "Do you have any idea how dangerous that was? You could have been killed!"

"It's alright Hann," Aunt Tyla said. "She has clearly survived." She turned back to Lyric, "Were you seen?"

Lyric shook her head and leaned against the pole at the foot of the stairs. She didn't fancy approaching the table just yet.

"What did you see?"

"You told me that if children were found to be special when they were tested, they would be killed. Well, one little girl, Tegan of Felder, was clearly a Seer, and she wasn't killed. She was given cake and sent home to her family."

Hann slumped back down and the adults, even Grandmother, exchanged looks of sadness and concern.

"This is very important Lyric," Aunt Tyla said. "Did you eat any of the cake?"

Lyric shook her head. "No, the Queen trod the remaining pieces into the floor. It was too nasty to eat when I got to it."

They heaved a collective sigh of relief.

"What?" Lyric asked, looking at them in turn. "What's going on?"

"Have you heard of the Fading Ill, Precious One?" Adria asked.

Lyric nodded. "How is that relevant?"

"The Royal Physician tells everyone that Fading Ill is a terrible sickness, inflicted upon families by the Goddess." Adria said.

"But the Goddess doesn't work that way," Grandmother interjected, pointing her lumpy, bony finger toward them.

"Indeed," Adria continued. "We have seen that the Fading Ill is a slow death from poison."

Lyric felt the pit of her stomach sink. "You mean, the cake?"

They all gave a long, slow nod.

Lyric's knees started to feel weak at the thought of how close she had come to eating the cake. She sank down and sat on the stairs.

"That's why we make the rules we do, Precious One," Adria said. "To keep you safe."

Lyric felt a surge of frustration. "I'm not a little child any more Mother. I don't need rules to keep me safe, I need information. Don't you see, making countless rules and keeping secrets is what put me in danger?"

Aunt Tyla and Grandmother exchanged a knowing look and nod. Adria looked confused and Hann leapt to his feet.

"The rules have kept you safe!" Hann stomped toward the farmyard door and firmly put the large wooden bar in place across it. "You are forbidden to leave the house for the rest of the clead." He then marched over and dropped the bar across the door to the front yard. "You are forbidden to leave the farm, permanently!" He stood by the door, feet apart, arms folded, frowning at Lyric.

Lyric felt hot with anger and frustration, but she also felt a sense of how much damage unleashing those feelings, in light of her new capabilities, could do. She breathed deeply a few times to calm herself and focussed. The bar on each door lifted simultaneously and fell uselessly to the floor with loud, clattering thuds. Lyric got to her feet and glared her astonished father in the eye. "No," she said, calm and cool now. "I'll not be a prisoner here anymore."

Her mother, father and aunt stared at her, their faces pale in disbelief. Lyric thought she even saw a hint of fear in their eyes.

"Told you," Grandmother said, smirking in her chair. "The child needs somewhere to practise."

Aunt Tyla was the first to collect her wits. "The farm is too small," she said. "Too many workers, she would be seen."

Grandmother nodded agreement and turned to Hann. "You need to find somewhere safe. Somewhere far from here. Somewhere people never go." She pointed her bony finger at him. "And, she's going to need a horse."

Under Grandmother's glare, Hann was unable to protest. His arms slumped in defeat.

"And, she's going to need breakfast," Aunt Tyla said, gesturing to the bench seat.

"Of course." Adria sprang to her feet with new purpose. "You must be famished, Precious One."

"Yes, Mother." Lyric was stunned by the change in mood, sensing that not just her position in the family had changed. The carefree child who had roamed freely over the farm was gone.

Two days passed. Lyric and Adria were just finished preparing the evening meal. Lyric took a plate and sat on a stool beside her grandmother and helped her eat. As Grandmother was now almost devoid of teeth, Lyric cut and crushed the food into very fine portions and loaded the spoon. Grandmother still had enough strength to bring the spoon to her mouth, but Lyric wondered how long it would be before her beloved Grandmother would be too weak to do even this.

The door to the farmyard burst open, and Hann entered. He pushed the door closed behind him and leaned upon it in sad silence.

"Is everything OK?" Adria asked, hastening to his side. "How was the market?"

"The market was fine. We sold everything." Hann placed a mighty hand around Adria's shoulder and rested his head on hers, seeking comfort.

"What's wrong then?"

"I ran into Mikk Felder on the way out of the City. His daughter Tegan has fallen ill. He was grateful to the Queen for graciously sending her Royal Physician to tend the child, but the physician pronounced that the child had Fading Ill, and all hope has been lost."

The family were frozen in silence for what seemed like an eternity. Grandmother placed a reassuring hand on Lyric's arm and searched Lyric's eyes for a reaction. Adria wrapped her arms around Hann and they just held each other. Lyric saw tears welling in her Grandmother's eyes that matched her own. She put down the plate and hugged her Grandmother, gently so as not to break her. When she looked up, her father was wiping his eyes with his sleeve and her mother wiped hers with her apron.

"Such a sadness," Grandmother said. A tear rolling down her cheek.

"What can we do?" Lyric asked, looking at each of them in turn.

"There is nothing we can do my child," Grandmother replied. "The two will be lost."

"Two? What do you mean two?" Lyric sprang to her feet. "What aren't you telling me? I'm so sick of secrets."

"Come sit, Precious One." Adria gestured toward the table and Lyric slowly took a seat at the end of one of the wooden benches. "We've seen this happen before. When the child is identified as a Seer, the child is poisoned by the Queen. This you know."

Lyric nodded.

"It is known that the gift of Sight is passed down the female line. So, if a child is found to be a Seer—"

"Then the mother carries the gift of Sight?"

"Exactly. To prevent further Seers being born—"

"The Queen kills the mother too?"

"And makes it look like an accident."

"That explains it."

"Explains what?" Hann asked.

"After the testing, the Queen instructed the Royal Protectors to have the Felder family watched." Lyric looked at each member of her family in turn, but they had nothing further to say. "How soon?"

"The accident usually occurs around a moon after the child dies." Grandmother said.

"So, I have time to stop it?"

"No!" Hann stepped forward and Adria raised a hand to stop him.

Grandmother continued, "If the mother dies, the Queen will stop at that. If she discovers you can speak, or worse still, if she discovers your gifts, then the mother dies and the Queen will come after you."

"And us," Hann added.

"And Aunt Tyla and her family," Adria added. "And all will be lost."

"What can I do?" Lyric asked. "I must do something."

"The most powerful thing you can do, my child," Grandmother replied. "Is practise. If you do that, then these murders can be the last."

"Very well." Lyric could see the wisdom in this, but she still felt sad and helpless.

"On that note," Hann said. "While I was in the City today, I bought a couple of suitable horses."

"What? Where are they?" Lyric glanced at Grandmother who smiled and waved her to go. It was a bittersweet moment, sadness, helplessness and frustration, now overlaid with excitement. Grandmother was right, she needed to look forward, to find a way to prevent further murders.

Hann opened the door to the farmyard and the three tumbled out to see two horses tied up at the edge of the yard. Both were mares, one was chestnut and the other a dappled grey. "These were wild caught, so they're rugged and sure-footed. They were trained by my friend Jonn so they are docile and well-behaved."

Lyric could barely believe she would have a horse. The grey turned and took a step toward Lyric before reaching the end of its tether. That was all the hint Lyric needed. She walked slowly up to her and ran her hand over the warm, grey neck. The horse turned its head and nudged Lyric in the chest so hard she almost fell over.

"Perhaps you should have the other horse, Precious One," Hann said, walking toward them. "She seems quieter."

"No, Father," Lyric said standing close to the horse's shoulder where she was out of range of its head. "I want this one, and I'm going to call her 'Nudge'."

"I guess I'll have to think about what to call the other one then." Hann ran his hand down the Chestnut horse's mane. "How about 'Poppy'?"

They all agreed 'Poppy' suited her well.

"She's red like a poppy flower," Adria said, beaming from a short distance away.

Hann leaned over Poppy's neck toward Lyric, "For the next two days we'll bring your riding skills up to speed and on the Twoday we'll set out to find you somewhere to practise. A sanctuary where you can practise in safety."

Lyric nodded, smiled and wrapped her arms around Nudge's neck. Now she had two friends.

Lyric and Hann were gone for over three cleads. They returned late one evening, tired and hungry, to a toasty hearth and a lavish meal. Adria hugged them within an inch of their breath as they each dismounted and ushered them inside. Lyric thought Grandmother had grown even weaker while she was away. She sat on the stool and spooned food into Grandmother's mouth before going and eating her own. Grandmother kept smiling and holding Lyric's arm.

"We found a safe place," Hann said as he sat down to the table and proceeded to describe the journey in great detail. Adria savoured the story as much as the food and asked many questions. Lyric barely got a word in edgeways. After helping her mother clear away the dishes and tucking Grandmother into her bed by the hearth, she went upstairs and sat on the edge of her own bed. Thoughts of her adventure were still twirling in her head when she flopped down sideways, still fully dressed and fast asleep.

When Lyric finally came downstairs the next day, the house was almost deserted.

"They thought you needed more sleep after your journey," Grandmother said quietly as Lyric approached her chair. Grandmother coughed and spluttered, her breathing louder and harsher than Lyric remembered.

Lyric tended to the blankets and throws. She moved to ensure the thickest blanket was wrapped around Grandmother's feet. "Grandmother. Your feet are so swollen. What's wrong?" Lyric wrapped them as snug as she could.

Grandmother waved a dismissive hand in response to Lyric's question. "Come, sit child," she said between heavy breaths, and gestured for Lyric to sit on the stool beside her. "My time is nearly done, dear child."

"No, Grandmother."

"Hush, child. It has been a good life, and you have brought much joy to my last years. Thank you."

Lyric gently took her Grandmother's cool and frail hand, tears rolling down her cheeks. "Please don't go, I need you."

"Yes, yes. I have been speaking at length with Tyla. She sees as clearly as I do, if not better, as she has greater distance. She understands. You must seek her for counsel in my stead."

Lyric nodded.

"And you must practise. Promise me you will practise."

"I promise."

Grandmother tightened her grip on Lyric's hand. "Now remember this; be brave when you should, firm when you must and kind when you can."

"Yes Grandmother."

"It is important, Lyric. Say it." Grandmother grasped Lyric's wrist with her other hand and held it tight, insistent. "Say it."

"Be brave when I should, firm when I must and kind when I can."

"Excellent." Grandmother seemed satisfied and relaxed her grip. "Know you are special, the Gift of the Goddess, and know I love you."

Lyric sniffled and wiped tears from her face. "I love you too, Grandmother."

"Enough," Grandmother said, releasing Lyric's hand and waving her away. "You have breakfast to eat and an adventure to have." She winked at Lyric. "And I need my morning nap."

Lyric should have known that her plan for the day could not be kept secret from Grandmother.

Lyric scuttled along behind the hedges of a dirt road in the Western farmlands, north of the Nye farm until she reached an intersection. On the other side of the hedge were three cloaked, hooded figures on horseback, standing quietly, waiting. A small wagon approached, pulled by a single donkey. It was late morning and most of the farmers had already carted their produce to the market and the roads were deserted. This wagon was late.

Lyric peered through the twiggy hedge. As the wagon approached the crossroad, it creaked under the weight of its cargo. The riders moved onto the road, blocking its path.

"Jillen Felder?" a male voice asked.

"Yes?" the lone woman driving the wagon replied.

"Step down from the wagon," a female voice commanded.

"Why? Who are you?"

"Do you dare refuse an order from your Queen?" The cloaked figure pulled back her hood to reveal ornately braided hair, a simple gold tiara, and a stern expression.

"Sorry your majesty." Jillen looped the reins onto a wooden peg and jumped down from the cart. "I didn't recognise you." She curtsied low.

The third figure walked their horse to the rear of the wagon. The rider dismounted and a young woman's arms adorned with bracelets reached out from the cloak to untie and pull open one of the sacks on the wagon and remove a piece of fruit. "Look Mother, pomegranates. I do like pomegranates."

"The last of the season." Jillen began to fidget. "They are sweet. Do help yourself."

The Queen nodded toward the tallest cloaked rider. He dismounted, walked around Jillen to the wagon and drew his sword. He sliced through the rope binding another of the bags, then suddenly thrust back striking Jillen hard in the back of the head with the hilt of his sword. Jillen dropped to the ground like a rag doll and lay there motionless.

"Is she dead?" the Princess asked, biting into her pomegranate to access the sweet arils. The red juice staining her hands and lips.

The Protector Consort pushed back his hood and nudged Jillen's head roughly with his foot. "Yeah, she's dead."

"You know what to do."

"Yes, My Queen." He strode to the other side of the wagon and with a mighty heave he tipped the entire wagon and its contents onto the body. The donkey fell sideways with it, struggling and hawing in fright. "Shall I kill it too?"

"No. If the wagon tipped accidentally, the donkey would have fallen with it and remained there until found."

The Protector Consort came back around toward his horse.

"Are we done now, Mother?" the Princess pulled back her hood, showing her face stained with deep red pomegranate juice. She looked as if she had sucked blood. "I have some new dresses to try on today."

Lyric grunted in incredulity. How could these people show such little regard for the lives of the citizens?

The Protector Consort immediately threw himself onto the hedge where he heard the noise and grasped. His hand found the back of Lyric's tunic and she was hauled, kicking and writhing, over the hedge and held facing the Queen. "Shall I kill her? We can't have any witnesses." He raised his drawn sword toward Lyric's neck.

"Wait!" The Queen eyed Lyric with disdain. "Let me think. If we leave another body and blood here, it won't look like an accident, will it?"

Lyric saw the sword lower. The Queen wasn't the only one thinking hard. Lyric needed a plan, fast.

"So, this is the Wildling?" The Princess approached, peering at Lyric as if she was a weird, exotic creature. "She's very dirty." The Princess sneered. "Strange green eyes." She turned toward her mother. "Maybe I could keep her as a pet?"

The Queen shook her head. "Don't be silly Brata. This creature is mute, stupid and cannot be trained as a pet. Last thing I need in the Palace is another creature that can't be trusted." The Queen's gaze bored at Lyric. "I know. We'll take her to the copse of trees we passed on a farm near here and kill her there. Then it won't be connected with the accident and there will be no witnesses."

"Excellent idea," Princess Brata said, launching herself back onto her horse. She arranged her cloak and pulled her hood back over her head. She took the reins of the third horse as the Protector Consort began to march Lyric down the road, holding firmly to the back neckline of her tunic.

The Queen replaced her hood, fell in beside Brata, and they walked their horses behind the captor and his captive.

Lyric must make an escape, preferably without breaking camouflage. She focussed on the fabric at the back of her old, worn tunic, then pulled away hard. The fabric tore around the Protector Consort's grip and before he could grasp again, she dived through the hedge and fled along it. By the time the party could look over the hedge, Lyric had concealed herself in it, some distance away.

"Well that was incompetent," the Queen said with disdain.

"Shall I go hunt her?" The Protector Consort looked nervous and apologetic.

The Queen pondered a moment, "No, don't bother. She's mute, remember? It's not like she is going to tell anyone what she saw."

They laughed together as the Protector Consort stowed his sword in his belt, mounted his horse and drew his hood. The party turned toward the City.

"Did you see how fast she was Mother?" Princess Brata said. "Just like a rabbit. She was my height and around my age too. We could have been sisters."

"Don't talk nonsense Brata," The Queen shook her head. "You could not have been sisters."

Damn right we couldn't, Lyric thought to herself as she waited for them to move out of sight. Lyric returned to the wagon to see the twitching, grey–blue limbs of Jillian Felder poking out from beneath the toppled wagon, the site strewn with pomegranates and the donkey still struggling on its side in the harness.

"I'm sorry I couldn't help you today," Lyric said to the body under the wagon. "I'll try to stop this from happening to any other family on Vulcon ever again." She turned to the tiring donkey, "I can still help you." She released the donkey from its harness. It struggled to its feet, brayed, then trotted off toward home.

Lyric opened the door to the Nye kitchen to find her parents and Aunt Tyla seated at the table benches, ashen and silent. Grandmother's chair beside the hearth was empty. On Grandmother's bed, her blanket rippled over the frail form completely concealed underneath. Lyric felt like she was hit in the head and the gut simultaneously. She ran over to the bed, dropped to her knees and sobbed into the soft folds of the blanket. They buried Grandmother near the copse of trees where Lyric first practised, and Lyric missed her.

Benn went off to Protector Academy, and Lyric missed him too. On the last clead of each moon, Lyric would venture near the Kreft farm and discreetly observe from carefully chosen hides in nearby trees and bushes. Suspicious that Benn was still spending time with the Wildling, Donn, became intensely protective. During the clead when Benn was at home each moon, Donn didn't let Benn out of his sight from dawn till dusk. But the nights were well lit by moonlight, at least when the sky was clear. That gave Lyric an idea.

It was a long and tiring day. There was much to be harvested from the orchards and stored in late autumn. With his father watching Benn every waking moment he was home, there was no opportunity to sneak away. Donn even accompanied him when he went fishing at the river. The days of roaming the countryside with Lyric were clearly gone and Benn would have to get over it. Still, he missed her. He closed the shutters against the moonlight that penetrated his room and threatened to interfere with his slumber. He flopped onto his bed and was soon asleep.

In the middle of a curious dream in which he was battling against the Royal Protectors, he was roused to consciousness by a persistent tapping. He groaned and sat up, his mind confused as to why he would be fighting against the very Protectors he was training to become, and annoyed by the 'tap, tap, tap' on the shutter. Perhaps it was windy, and the shutter was loose? He dragged himself to the window and opened the shutters.

The sight of a girl, standing in her twig–adorned, grimy finery in the moonlight snapped him awake. She looked like an elfin ghost, but he recognised her. "What are you doing here, Lyric?" Benn whispered, surprised to see her.

"Hello Benn" Lyric said in a soft voice, quiet enough to avoid waking Donn. "Let's play," she said with a wicked, welcoming grin as she gestured toward the river.

"Are you mad? My father would lock me up and throw away the key if he found out I was spending time with you." Benn was trying to be emphatic quietly, so as not to wake his father. "Oh, now I remember, you are mad."

Lyric stood there in silence, looking hopeful.

This was a bad idea. If he were caught, his father would never trust him again. Then again, his father didn't trust him now, so what did he have to lose? "Wait a minute," Benn whispered, closing the shutters for privacy. He threw on some thick clothes against the cool night. Eventually he clambered out of the window into the moonlit garden and together they ran off over the ridge and down to the river. The river shone like mercury in the moonlight and the trees loomed like grey ghosts around them.

"Do you remember how to climb?" Lyric began scrambling into the branches of their tree.

She was still so fast, Benn felt like he was struggling to keep up as he climbed behind her, finally he perched on a high, solid branch beside her, their feet dangling.

"Actually, it's really good to see you. I've missed our chats." Benn said, gazing absently at the ground below. "What have you been doing?"

"You know, the usual." Lyric absently toyed with a yellow leaf. "Roaming the countryside, observing things, trying to stay out of trouble and out of sight. You?"

"The usual. Studying at the Academy, helping out on the farm."

Lyric plucked a twig and poked him playfully. "Tell me about the Academy."

Benn told Lyric about the adjustment to boarding school, and about how having his friend Rikk there helped a lot. He talked about the classes, the professors and the antics the students got up to. He told her how the earth tremor last clead disrupted classes as students and professors fled headlong outdoors.

Lyric listened intently, asking questions about the details. Benn figured he was the only one with anything interesting to talk about, and the longer he talked, the more time he could spend away from his confined and regulated life.

"I can't really talk to Father about what happens at the Academy as it always ends in a lecture about how I should be doing more to get selected for the final year of training. Rikk just wants to talk about training and girls, especially the girls in the Royal Court. But you Lyric, you're undeniably a good listener. I feel I can talk to you about anything."

"Thanks."

Sometimes he envied Lyric's freedom to roam the fields as she pleased, but lately, as he thought about what the future would hold, he felt a bit sorry for her. She was to inherit the family farm and it would provide a good living for her. Still, if she didn't reveal her ability to speak, she would never find a partner and have children, so the farm would be run by an administrator or distant family member and be lost from the family at the end of her lonely life. If she did reveal she could speak, at best the community would be angry at having been deceived and disrespected and at worst, if she was right, she would be killed. He knew from watching his father toil that a farmer's life was a difficult one. Perhaps there was some sense in his father wanting him to be a Royal Protector at Court. The prospects certainly seemed more promising.

"Do you know anything about the testing of the children this year?" Lyric asked.

Benn looked at Lyric with a quizzical raised eyebrow. This wasn't the type of question she normally asked. "Sure. What about it?"

"Well, what happens?"

"One by one the children go into the Great Hall of the old Seers Academy and the royal family test them to see if they are Seers. There hasn't been a Seer detected for many years now. The Queen and the Princess are the only Seers remaining on the island."

"I see," Lyric mused. "What if the Princess wasn't a Seer?"

Benn squirmed. "According to our Civics professor, she would then have no right to the throne. Only a Seer can rule Vulcon." Benn paused to consider. "I know you don't know any better Lyric, but you mustn't ask such questions. That's treason-talk."

"Sorry," Lyric said, looking away from Benn and staring at the ground.

"Besides, if the royal line were not Seers, then there would be no Seers on Vulcon to fulfil the prophecy and all could be lost."

"What prophecy?" Lyric suddenly seemed animated again.

Benn couldn't understand why this should pique her interest. "The High Priestess gave us a religion class a few weeks ago and told us about the prophecy. It was made by a powerful Seer of Vulcon many generations ago. I think I remember it:

In the time of rule by deception, a Great Seer will arise from the people of Vulcon.

A gift from the Goddess.

The Great Seer will halt the murders of children of Vulcon, save the people from the Horrific Catastrophe, and usher in a period of peace and prosperity to last for twenty generations."

Lyric froze.

"What's the matter?" Benn asked.

Lyric looked about her as if trying to gather her thoughts. "Nothing's the matter. I just thought of a job I was supposed to do on the farm today and forgot."

"OK," Benn said, looking concerned. Sometimes Lyric was difficult to figure out. He could have sworn she was reacting to the prophecy.

"Not very poetic is it?"

"What?"

"The prophecy."

"You're right," Benn said. "After all, it was written by a Seer not a poet."

They giggled together at the thought.

Sometime after midnight, there were episodes when the moonlight was obscured by clouds. Much as he wanted to stay and talk to Lyric for hours more, Benn knew how difficult it would be to see the way home without moonlight and his father would be suspicious if he was too sleepy the next morning.

"I should go now," Benn said, starting to climb down through the branches. "I need to get some sleep. Father has a full day of work planned for me tomorrow."

"OK," Lyric said. She sounded reluctant. Nevertheless, she climbed down, agile as a squirrel, behind him.

They walked slowly back toward the Kreft farm. "There was a rumour circulating about you in the City."

Lyric stopped and looked at him expectantly.

"One of the children at the school said they looked out their window one night and saw you creeping through the city streets. You haven't been in the City, have you?"

Lyric smiled. "What if I have?"

"Be careful Lyric. You know the City is not a safe place for you."

"You're beginning to sound like my father."

They both laughed.

Lyric stopped at the hedge near the house. "See you next moon."

"Bye Lyric," Benn said and headed toward his window. He crept quietly inside and waved once to Lyric before closing the shutters. A few seconds later he opened one shutter just far enough to peak outside. The garden lay empty. Lyric was gone. He felt a sad emptiness inside. He told himself he must not get emotionally attached to her as it would only hurt both of them. They could only ever be just friends. He undressed and climbed back into bed, trying not to look forward to seeing Lyric again soon.

It was Spring and the sky was overcast for most of the last clead of the moon. Lyric didn't visit when there was no moonlight and tomorrow Benn would return to the Academy. He went to bed fully clothed against the chilly night — in a thick tunic and sheepskin coat — just in case and made a half-hearted attempt at falling asleep. Benn thought he heard a rustle in the bushes outside. He jumped out of bed and pulled on his fur-lined boots before opening the shutters to see Lyric crouched there, pebble in hand, ready to tap on the shutter. The yard was suddenly drenched in moonlight. Benn climbed out and they stifled giggles as they ran off toward their favourite climbing tree by the river. The new, light green foliage of the elm tree glowed in the moonlight and they were quick to climb into the concealed safety of its branches.

"Good to see you again Lyric," Benn sighed as they settled on their branch.

"Good to see you too," Lyric grinned, looking at the ground and dangling her feet. "So, what's new at the Academy?"

Benn provided Lyric with a description of student antics and the quirks of the professors, followed by a summary of all they had learned during the last moon, including the finer details of securing a basic dwelling against incursion by thieves.

"My father does that every night," Lyric said. "He trained at the Academy and became a Protector too."

"I didn't know." Benn always assumed there was little to know about Lyric. Sometimes he was reminded otherwise. Benn went on to describe the additional steps of setting up trip lines attached to bells or metal pots to detect any incursion past the defences, and Lyric seemed to find this fascinating.

So it went on, in the last cycle of each moon, if there was a clear night, Lyric would tap on Benn's shutter and they would steal away to roam and play in the moonlight. Benn told Lyric about fencing class, then finding a few long sticks, he gave Lyric an impromptu lesson in fencing techniques. He would describe the hand-to-hand combat classes and show Lyric the moves.

After Benn talked himself out, they would lie on their backs on a rock or a patch of soft grass and just gaze at the stars.

One evening Benn was relating the lessons at the Academy. "Then the High Priestess of the temple came and gave a religion and governance class, but you wouldn't want to hear about that. It's pretty boring."

Lyric jabbed him with her elbow. "Since when do you get to tell me what I do, or don't, find interesting?"

"Really, Lyric. It's nowhere near as interesting as combat or survival classes."

"OK," Lyric said, "When you do a survival class, they teach you about how to read the land around you, so you can use it to survive, right?"

"Right?" Where was she going with this?

"Well, what if the land around you isn't made of rocks and plants and animals? What if it was made of buildings and rules and laws? Wouldn't that make a religion and governance class a survival class in a different type of landscape?"

"You have an interesting way of looking at things, Lyric. I would never have thought of it that way." He settled in for a lengthy explanation. "OK, well the gist of it was that the authority and aid of the Goddess is manifested to us through the gift of the Sight. Then this authority and aid is seated in the royal family with the Queen being the head Seer, chosen by the other Seers to rule our land as the servant of the Goddess. Only that doesn't really apply now as the Queen and the Princess are the only Seers left on Vulcon, so they don't have to be elected anymore."

"Well, that's convenient."

Benn thought the comment too cryptic to attempt a response, so he settled into a more comfortable position on the branch and continued, "Then there's the Cataclysm Prophency I told you about. I guess the Great Seer will have to be a member of the royal family then, since there's no other Seers left. I wonder if it will be in this generation. Who knows, the Queen or the Princess Brata could be the one to save us all."

"But what if the Queen and Princess weren't Seers?"

"Then Vulcon is doomed."

At the end of the second year, Benn was accepted to continue training at the Academy, and he was thrilled to discover his friend Rikk was accepted too. That moon, Benn and Lyric swam in the river in the moonlight on a warm summer night to celebrate.

"You know my father never lets me swim in the river," Benn said as they splashed about. "I have to do it in secret."

"Why?" Lyric asked, grasping hold of a willow branch to hold her still against the current.

"Father won't say. Refuses to talk about it." Benn grabbed a branch too so he could float nearby. "Rikk's parents told him it's because my mother died in the creek. Drowned."

"That's so sad."

"Yeah. I sometimes wonder if her spirit is still here? Maybe that's why I'm drawn to flowing water all the time?"

"And here's me thinking it's my amazing company and conversation," Lyric said and splashed water in Benn's face.

Before Benn could splash back, Lyric released her hold on the branch and floated to grassy bank nearby. Clouds were starting to roll in. It was time to go home.

In the spring of Benn's third and final year at the Academy, the soils were saturated, and the streams and rivers already swollen from days of rain. Benn cooked a breakfast of eggs while his father dressed, then opened the door to the farmyard to see storm clouds looming, ominous and dark. Donn went back inside to find somewhere cosy to wait it out. Benn had just enough time to feed the fowl and move the donkey to a fresh pen before the full fury of the storm unleashed with bolts of lightning, booms of thunder and seemingly endless pelting rain. One bolt of lightning occurred at the same instant as a particularly loud boom of thunder, followed by a hissing noise. For two hours the storm raged and then, with surprising haste, it was gone.

Seeing this as a sign, Benn grabbed his work hat and headed outside. The creek was in full flow, at the top of its banks, with brown, muddy water. By the time Benn reached the other side of the courtyard, the creek was over its banks. Benn felt a pang of panic. He ran toward the enclosure holding the donkey arriving just as the fence, made of woven branches and twigs, was washing away. Donkeys were expensive, they couldn't afford to replace this one, and without a donkey, Father would have to pull the wagon to market himself and Benn knew he was already too old for that.

The donkey was trying to outrun the rising water, braying in distress and pressing itself against the remaining fence. Benn leapt over the gate and tried to place a rope halter onto the struggling animal. "It's OK donkey. Just let me get this halter on and I can rescue you." Benn tried to reassure the distressed creature. If only the donkey would stand still, this wouldn't take so long. By the time the halter was secured, the gate had washed away leaving Benn and the donkey wedged in the top corner of the enclosure with the water still rising.

If he could walk the donkey down into the water and around the remaining gate post, he could lead the donkey to higher ground. He tugged at the rope to try and entice the donkey toward the water, but it dug its hooves into the soft earth, braced its haunches down and refused to budge. "Come on. We have to move!"

The water rose relentlessly. In no time at all it was up to the donkey's knees and even more of the fence was washed away. Benn looked upstream to see a wave of water coming toward them. "May the Goddess save us!" was all he could utter before the wave hit and washed them away. In the turmoil of debris and swirling, rushing, brown water Benn lost hold of the halter rope and they were washed apart.

"Benn!" his father shouted, standing helplessly at the house as the water's edge approached, "Benn!"

Within moments, the creek emptied them into the torrent that was the Roredon river. Out of the corner of his eye, Benn thought he glimpsed Lyric running along the riverbank. The roar of the torrent so loud it drowned out Benn's cries for help. Benn tried to concentrate on staying afloat and avoiding the assortment of debris flowing around him, from leaves and twigs through to barrels and pieces of fence from the farms upstream. There were also some uprooted trees and mighty logs. Benn was a strong swimmer, but he was being buffeted by the current and the debris. Sometimes the current would push him under the raging water, and he would pop up only to be narrowly missed by a branch. He was getting wearier with each dunking. Nearby, the donkey was also struggling desperately to keep its head above the tumultuous surface.

Just as Benn thought he was too exhausted to swim further, a large branch that was making for his head seemed to float around him and hold position nearby. Benn reached out and hauled his arms and chest onto it. It kept his head higher above the water. The donkey also seemed to be swimming higher in the water, its head now safely above the brown, foaming current. Remarkably, all the other debris flowed directly downstream, but the branch with Benn aboard seemed to drift toward the riverbank.

Benn saw Lyric running along the river, racing to the point where the branch was slowing, very near the shore. When the branch lodged against a shrub at the edge of the river, she waded thigh deep into the current, grabbed Benn by the back of his tunic then heaved and dragged his weary body up onto the grassy knoll. Perhaps today was not his day to die after all. Once safely on the embankment, Benn rolled onto his back to see a bedraggled, grimy Lyric looking at his face with deep concern while heaving to catch her breath.

"If you wanted to go for a swim today, you should have said something," Lyric said with a cheeky grin between panting breaths.

Benn looked at her, incredulous. He propped himself up on his elbows. "You were clearly running late, so I went swimming without you." Benn dropped back onto the grass, smiling now at his own wit. Suddenly he sat bolt upright, "The donkey!" He moved to get up.

Lyric touched his arm reassuringly. "The donkey seems to be OK." Lyric pointed to the other side of the creek where the muddy sodden donkey was shaking itself off and starting to graze nonchalantly on the lush pasture of another farmer's field.

"Thank the Goddess." Benn sighed and flopped back down on the grass.

"Benn! Benn!" the breathless voice of a wiry figure who was stumbling toward them from upstream, barely audible above the roar of floodwater.

Benn looked past Lyric and recognised his father approaching as fast as his old, bowed legs would carry him. He sighed in dismay. "I'm OK!" he yelled back, "It's all OK!"

"Get away from him you animal!" Donn waved a clenched fist toward Lyric as he approached, "Get away from my son!"

Lyric's smile of relief turned to a sad frown at this onslaught.

"I'm sorry Lyric," Benn whispered. "You'd better go."

Lyric sighed, then rose to her feet and trotted off over the knoll to the fields of the Nye farm beyond.

Donn eventually arrived at Benn's side. He hugged his son, weeping, "You're alive! By the Goddess, you're alive." They helped each other to their feet and wearily trudged their way home. They would go and retrieve the now contented donkey in a day or two, when the water subsided. The damage to the farm gardens and orchards would take longer to put right.

Lyric's tunic was still damp from the river and the warm breeze felt cool as it penetrated the tattered linen fabric. Safely back on the Nye farm, Lyric approached the path leading to the farmhouse. A figure in a modest dress and fine sandals stood there, watching her. Waiting. The wisps of hair not captured into her long braid were wafting in the breeze.

"Hello Lyric," the figure said as Lyric approached.

Lyric waited until she was close enough to speak softly and yet be heard. "Aunt Tyla." They exchanged a welcoming hug and began to walk together toward the farmhouse.

"Let me guess. You saw that I'm going to have an argument with my parents, and you've come to support me."

"Actually, I've come to support them," Aunt Tyla said with a smirk. "They're going to be blindsided – again." Aunt Tyla gave Lyric a reassuring pat on the back. "You're almost grown up Lyric. You don't need support so much right now as you need someone to cover the blind spots in your Sight."

Lyric sighed. "It's very frustrating sometimes, to not be able to see when the people you care about are in danger. If I hadn't figured out a flood was imminent from all of this rain and headed over to see if the Kreft farm was affected, Benn would probably be dead now."

"I know, Lyric, but the Sight clouds our vision of the events affecting those who are emotionally close to us. The more emotional the connection, the more our Sight is obscured. It is indeed frustrating we can't clearly see the events that will directly affect the people most dear to us. That's why Grandmother charged me with being your mentor after she passed. I'm distant enough to see the events around you more clearly than your parents, and much more clearly than you can." Aunt Tyla stopped to address Lyric before they were too close to the house. "Today secrets will be disclosed, and feelings will be hurt." She took Lyric's grimy hand and pressed it between her own. "Remember Lyric, you and your family need each other, now and into the future. Disagree if you must, but exercise self–restraint, don't damage the bond."

"OK," Lyric wasn't sure what Aunt Tyla meant, but after Grandmother's passing, her Aunt promptly stepped up to provide faithful counsel and Lyric was grateful for the ally.

"Good." Aunt Tyla released Lyric's hand and they kept walking. "And remember, your parents are people too and they were young once. You'd be surprised how much they understand if you give them a chance — and a little time to adjust." Aunt Tyla gave Lyric a reassuring smile as they arrived at the door.

Aunt Tyla entered first to find Adria at the kitchen bench preparing lunch. "Hello sister." They exchanged a welcome hug. Well, Aunt Tyla did all the hugging, Adria managed a half–hug where she tried not to soil the back of Aunt Tyla's tunic with her flour–covered hands.

"Lovely to see you, I hope," Adria winked at her sister as she moved back to roll more flatbread.

"Let me help." Aunt Tyla placed a pan at the hearth and proceeded to fry the flatbreads as Adria rolled them. They hissed and sizzled in the pan and the aroma was homely and enticing.

Hann came in from the fields and parked his hat on a wooden peg by the door. "Oh, hello Tyla. Good to see you." He sauntered over to where his wife was rolling more flatbread and placed his muscular arms around her waist. "Hello, My Love," he said, moving to kiss her cheek.

"Hello Hann," Adria said smiling. Then her face became stern. "No! Go and wash your hands before we have soil in our lunch."

Hann pulled away, still grinning and made for the washroom.

Lyric moved to quietly skirt the scene and make for the stairs, hoping to get to her room and change into a dry tunic before her parents noticed her soggy state. Her father intercepted her on his way to the washroom and gave her an affectionate hug.

"Your tunic's wet, Precious One. Where have you been?"

Lyric cast a glance at Aunt Tyla, who nodded reassurance. "At the river."

"At the river?" Hann said, pulling away from her. "The river is in full flood today. Do have any idea how dangerous it is down there?"

Lyric nodded, hoping the discussion would end there.

"By the look of it, you were in the river," Adria said, studying Lyric more closely now. "What were you doing?"

Lyric took a deep breath. "Rescuing Benn."

Both her parents froze simultaneously and turned toward Lyric.

"You mean Benn Kreft?" Hann asked.

"Most of their farm was washed out, caught as it is between the creek and the river. The water came up so fast that Benn and their donkey were washed downstream into the river."

"So, you took it upon yourself to rescue Benn?" Adria asked.

"And the donkey."

Her parents exchanged worried glances.

"You managed to achieve this without revealing yourself?" Adria was wiping her hands on her apron, devoting her full attention to Lyric.

"Without revealing that I was saving them, at least."

"You didn't speak to Benn, did you?" Adria persisted.

Lyric stood in silence. She kept her friendship with Benn a secret for all these years, knowing her parents wouldn't approve. Only her Grandmother knew, and Lyric guessed that Grandmother had briefed Aunt Tyla. Clearly Aunt Tyla was been discreet. Enough with secrets. "Yes, yes I did."

"What!" Hann almost roared. "Do you realise the risk?"

"Benn and I have been friends for a while. He's very good at keeping secrets."

Hann leaned against the stair post and fell silent. Adria plopped down on the bench seat by the table. Aunt Tyla took the pan off the fire and moved to sit beside her sister.

"How long has this been going on?" Adria asked.

"Since my thirteenth year."

"Does he know of your abilities?"

"No. Only that I am not mute."

"Thank the Goddess for that." Adria looked about the floor as if trying find lost words. "Does his father know?"

"No. He forbade Benn to spend time with me." Lyric sighed. "He thinks I'm some sort of animal."

Aunt Tyla looked at Lyric with a pained expression and placed a reassuring hand on Adria's shoulder.

"Well, I forbid you to see Benn too." Hann said, finally finding his voice. "Are there any more secrets we ought to know about?"

Lyric was fuming inside. "You're one to talk about secrets," she half-shouted. "When were you going to tell me about the Prophecy?"

Hann dropped to sit on the stairs.

Adria's face went ashen. "How did you find out about the Prophecy?"

"Benn told me." Lyric had the upper hand and knew it. "So, I looked forward and saw for myself."

"How long have you known?"

"For over a year." Lyric took a step toward her mother. "When were you going to tell me? When it was too late for me to know what to practise?"

Lyric saw shock on her parents' faces. "With the people of Vulcon keeping me exiled and you causing them to do it with your endless secrets, I've a mind to just let—" Lyric checked herself, remembering Aunt Tyla's warning. "I'm sorry. I'm just so sick of inane secrets. I keep telling you, I need information if I am to keep myself safe. To keep us all safe." Lyric sat down slowly into the chair by the hearth and the room fell silent. The fire crackled in the hearth and a bird warbled in the hedge outside the kitchen window.

Aunt Tyla finally broke the silence, "Adria, what would you have done if your parents had forbidden you to see Hann?"

Adria frowned, then looked up at Hann's bewildered gaze and her expression softened. "I'd probably have crept out and seen him in secret."

"Or run off together." Hann winked at his wife.

"I've seen that Lyric needs Benn. We need Benn," Aunt Tyla said, and winked at Lyric. "Lyric is a capable young woman now. We must learn to trust her."

Lyric took the cue, "I presume you've been laying down plans for some years now?"

The three glanced nervously between each other.

"Well, how about I get into some dry clothes and you can tell me all about them over lunch?"

Adria glanced at Hann who put a reassuring hand on Lyric's shoulder. "That sounds like a good idea, Precious One."

Lyric stood up, and made for the stairs, "Oh, and no more planning without me present, OK?"

"OK," Adria said. Hann and Aunt Tyla nodded agreement.

"When do I get to meet this young man?" Hann asked.

"Not for a while yet," Aunt Tyla replied, rescuing Lyric from the need to respond. "It's complicated. But I'm sure we can trust Lyric to manage it appropriately."

"Thank you," Lyric mouthed silently to her aunt before racing up the stairs.

The following moon, the second last of the final year at the Academy, the night was favourable. Lyric and Benn made for their tree by the river where, concealed deep in the foliage, sitting on their favourite branch, Benn told Lyric of his studies in strategy, politics, negotiation and the laws of the land. He described details of the examinations in each subject. The combat examinations seemed the most challenging, but Benn was very pleased with how he conducted himself. The student Protectors were even posted for a trial clead to the Palace, working with the Royal Protectors. He enthusiastically recounted how, after quickly removing the Princess to the safety of the Palace courtyard during an earth tremor, he was formally introduced to the Princess Brata, the Royal Consort and the Queen herself. Benn gushed details of all the finery of the Palace and its occupants. Lyric loved how Benn told her the minutiae of his life. She would have loved to tell him what she was up to during the cleads when he was away, but her family made a good case that it was still not safe to do so.

Benn was growing taller and more handsome as the years passed, not that Lyric dared really look at him, she just stole glances or spied on him from a distance. Lyric was grateful Benn was her friend. She could expect no more. After all, a handsome, capable young Protector like Benn had many prospects for a good bonding. He valued honesty, and if he ever discovered her secrets, well, Lyric knew he would never consider bonding with a partner who was less than honest, let alone someone who would keep massive secrets from him. She doubted that any man would want to want to bond with someone with her freakish abilities, except for mercenary reasons. So, Lyric resolved it would be best to never bond at all.

The early morning was spent making final preparations. Leather was oiled, tunics were pressed, metal swords, buckles and gauntlets were polished to perfection. Their last night in the dormitories of the Protector Academy was spent and their belongings were packed. The atmosphere was jovial enough, but with a tinge of melancholy. The trainees had become good friends and after the graduation ceremony they would disperse. Each would return to their family home to await the wishes of the Queen. Some would be selected to serve at Court and the remainder would be left to make their way in the world as best they could. As fully trained Protectors, now renowned as capable men of integrity, they had excellent prospects of bonding into prosperous families on the island.

"Nearly done with the leather oil Benn?" Rikk slapped Benn on the back as he approached.

"Yeah Rikk. Here you go." Benn passed the pot and the soiled cloth to his friend.

"I'm going to miss this place," Rikk mused. "We sure had some good times."

"Like the times when you hid all manner of items in my bed? Let me see, there were the rocks."

"And the grasshoppers. That was funny. You nearly jumped clear to the other side of the room." Rikk chuckled at the memory.

"You weren't so amused when I returned the favour." Benn winked at his friend.

"Biscuit crumbs, argh. They tickle and itch and it's almost impossible to get them all out." Rikk frowned and shook his head at the thought.

Now it was Benn's turn to chuckle.

"It's going to be a long moon Benn, waiting for the Queen's pleasure. Not that it will be long for you. I reckon the Princess will be on your case before the clead is out." Rikk nudged Benn's shoulder with his fist.

"I don't know about that. Nothing is settled yet." Benn set about strapping on his sandals. "Who knows, she may even choose you."

"Oh, I hope not." Rikk rolled his eyes and moved in close to whisper. "Not wanting to disrespect your prospective partner my friend, but she is a royal pain." They shared a smirk. "Worst bit is that whoever refuses her does so on pain of death." He paused to consider a moment. "Perhaps I should try to look ugly. I could forego today's shave?" Rikk rubbed the stubble on his chin with his oily fingers.

"What if she likes the rugged, unshaven look?"

Rikk recoiled, "OK, OK, I'll shave." He moved off to get his shaving gear. "May the Goddess help me."

"May the Goddess help us both," Benn whispered behind him.

Benn and the other graduating trainees filed in from the Academy courtyard, through the side door and formed an impressive row in front of the podium. Their hair oiled, combed and bound at the nape with leather thong. The cream tunics were overlaid with a leather breastplate and a wide leather belt that holstered their swords. Their leather gauntlets were overlaid with shiny copper, and oiled leather sandal straps were twined around their ankles. On reaching their designated positions they stood in silence, feet apart and hands clasped in front of them.

On the podium before them were two intricately carved wooden thrones — one larger and more ornate. On either side, a long wooden bench seat. The rear doors opened, and the trainee's proud families flowed through and gathered, jostling for the best position. Some families brought a small wooden stool in case an elderly or frail member needed to sit. Otherwise, all stood for the occasion. Once all were gathered, the rear doors were closed with a defining 'boom' and the mighty wooden bar hoisted into position. Such occasions did not broach interruption.

The procession of dignitaries entered through the side door in order of increasing significance. First came the professors in long, blue, ceremonial dress tunics, followed by the Dean in his blood red ceremonial tunic with gold gauntlets, and the High Priestess of the temple in a flowing white robe adorned with a simple, carved golden girdle. When they were all seated on the benches, the Princess Brata entered, stepping slowly and deliberately, her flowing pastel blue dress inching along the floor behind her. She held her head high and straight as if not wanting to disrupt the ornate braids circling the top of head and held in place with a filigree tiara. She winked at Benn as she walked past the trainees and ascended the steps to the podium. It was a few moments after the Princess was seated when a crier's voice rang out, "Behold, Queen Fakir of Vulcon!"

The gathered crowd craned to get a glimpse as the Queen and the Protector Consort entered. The bodice of her long, purple dress was overlaid with chains of gold and strings of pearls. Her dark braids looped on her head, revealing some strands of silver hair. The loops were topped with a gold crown, at the front of which was an ivory eye with an emerald at its centre. The Protector Consort wore similar garb to the Academy Dean, but with a breastplate of gold. He walked behind the Queen with his sword held up in front of his face — symbolically ready to protect his ruler and spouse. There was much whispering in the crowd as the Queen took her place on the large throne and the Protector Consort took his position, standing beside her holding his sword vertically downward, the tip resting on the floor between his feet.

The Queen nodded to the Dean, who sprang to his feet and walked to the centre of the podium with more energy than his greying hair would suggest, and more than Benn was expecting. He clearly had something to say. After welcoming the royal guests, the families and the remainder of the audience, he paused to take breath, then launched into his speech.

"Thank you for taking time to join us in celebrating the achievements of the fine young Vulcon men graduating as Protectors here today. Each has proved himself worthy by virtue of achievements in combat, strategy, survival, fitness and diplomacy training."

"I'm certain that each of you is familiar with the words of the Cataclysm Prophecy. Although we live in tranquil times, where our children are safe and trade is good, I have no doubt some of the young men graduating today are so skilled and capable, they would be worthy Protectors for the Great Seer herself."

Benn noticed the Queen awkwardly change position in her chair, and the Princess looked pallid and uncomfortable as the words referring to the prophecy were spoken. As it was known and acknowledged that the Queen and her daughter were the last remaining Seers on Vulcon, it was assumed eventually one of them, or their female descendants, would be the Great Seer. From their discomfort, Benn concluded that it was a pressing burden.

The speaker continued, introducing the seated Academy professors in turn, extolling his pride in Vulcon and its achievements, and lavishly praising the Queen, the royal benefactor of the Protector Academy. Finally, he invited each of the graduates to come onto the podium as their name was announced to receive their parchment.

"Eli Attam."

A tall, young man promptly moved forward from the front row of the audience where the graduating class was standing. He proceeded nervously up the steps to the podium toward the Dean. He slapped his closed fist across his chest in salute and bowed low. The Dean returned his bow, uttered words of congratulations, then gestured him toward the Princess who assumed a standing position on the left side of the podium. An attendant handed her a rolled parchment, bound with a tasselled cord. Eli bowed respectfully to the Princess who nodded in acknowledgement, spoke soft words of congratulations and handed him the parchment roll. The process repeated until nineteen young men received their parchments. Benn felt his nervousness increase incrementally as each name was called. He shifted his weight from one foot to another. It would be social suicide to faint at your graduation ceremony.

"We have left the best till last," announced the Dean after what seemed like an interminable pause. "I would like to acknowledge the student who has graduated first in this year's class. He has excelled in all facets of his training. One of the finest young Protectors this Academy has ever produced. Benn Kreft."

Like a released spring, Benn propelled himself forward and onto the podium to the sound of fervent applause. He felt the cold clamminess of his own hand as he clenched it into a fist, beat it to his chest and bowed low to the Dean. "Well done Benn. You have earned this honour. Bear it well," the Dean said as Benn bowed. Benn turned to walk toward the Princess. He rubbed his hand on his tunic. It would not do to shake the Princess's hand with a hand as cold and clammy as a fish. He paused mid–podium to bow to the Queen and to his relief, she seemed most pleased.

The audience applause renewed its intensity as Benn reached the Princess. Benn saw the Princess's face light up as he approached, and it felt like a cold fist slamming him in the gut. He took a deep breath and bowed low.

The Princess smiled, "So good to see you Benn. Congratulations."

"Thank you, your Highness." Benn smiled as warmly as he could. "Such an honour to receive my parchment from you." The words grated as he forced them out.

The Princess blushed and held out the parchment, "I look forward to seeing you again very soon, Benn."

Benn took it graciously. "It would be a pleasure to serve, your Highness." He bowed low, relieved she had not offered to shake his hand. Benn suddenly felt an overwhelming urge to flee. Flee the building. Flee the City. Flee to the river. Sit in the elm tree and hope Lyric would come. He stayed himself.

Princess Brata was still beaming as she resumed her seat.

The Queen nodded to the High Priestess, who stood slowly and glided to the centre of the podium.

"Congratulations young Protectors. You are a credit to the Academy." The High Priestess paused while the audience applauded. "In accepting the parchment, you have become servants of the Goddess, to act on her behalf in the protection of the people of Vulcon. Protect your Queen, the designated Seer of the Goddess. Protect your families and the vulnerable, those who are unable to protect themselves. Be men of integrity and always remember you are first and foremost, servants of the Goddess. May the Goddess bless you and your families."

Applause erupted as the High Priestess turned to take her seat. Benn never had much time for the temple or religion, but something about the words of the High Priestess sent a shiver down his spine. For a fleeting moment, he felt like a man with an important destiny.

The royal procession made its way out through the massive side doorway into the Academy courtyard. Then professors, the graduating students and the audience sequentially filed out through this door and dispersed into the garden.

As Benn emerged, the bright daylight dazzled his eyes. The crowd converged on the centre of the garden to congratulate their students and thank the professors. Benn glanced about to take in his surroundings, it was instinct now to survey any environment for hazards, people behaving strangely, and to note the exits. Against one wall refreshments were being served. Pieces of meat and vegetables, on rosemary skewers, were being cooked on racks over hot coals and served on flatbreads with a selection of sauces in pots. There was an assortment of cakes on pottery platters and sweet treats stacked in pyramids. Large bowls piled high with an assortment of fruits completed the array. Students from the Academy assisted with the serving of wine, water and fermented milk at another nearby table. Benn's keen eyes noted a hooded figure, moving away from the crowd toward a tree in the far corner of the courtyard. It was near the massive wooden doors that opened out onto the plaza. For now, at least, those doors were secured shut by a wooden beam that took at least two Protectors to lift.

"Congratulations son," Donn said, approaching Benn from behind and giving him a hearty slap on the shoulder. "I always knew you could do it."

"Thank you, Father."

"Did you see the way the Princess looked at you, son? I think she likes you." The last sentence half–sung as Donn grinned like a satisfied cat.

"Sure, father," Benn said, wishing the event over before his father did something to embarrass them both, something that unwittingly spoiled his own plans for Benn.

"Look, there's the Dean," Donn gushed. "I must go and introduce myself." Donn scurried off toward the tables dressed in his finest tunic and sandals and with a high–achieving son to discuss.

Relieved, Benn worked his way through the crowd toward the tree, curious about the figure in the cloak. Were they friend or foe to dress and behave so odd? His journey was halted a few times by well–wishers, and just as he arrived at the tree, his progress was interrupted by a firm but friendly slap on the back.

"Hey buddy!"

Benn turned to face his friend. The cloaked figure behind the tree would have to wait. "Well Rikk, we made it, we are now officially Protectors."

"Yeah. Well done taking out the first place Benn. Not that it's a surprise, I've seen it coming for years."

"What's in store for you, Rikk?"

"After congratulating you, I'm going to wander over there, mull around the food tables, mingle, and hope some girl from the Royal Court takes a fancy to me. Failing that, I'm going back to work in the family shop, while I wait for an invitation to be a Protector at the Royal Court."

"I'm sure we'll still get to hang out, after all, we still live in the same City."

"I'm not so sure. How did your presentation to the Queen go?"

"Really well, actually."

"Based on that, and the way the Princess looked at you during the ceremony, I'd say you're going to be betrothed within the week, bonded within a few moons, and as Protector and partner of the Princess, you'll be so caught up in Palace duties, you won't have time to hang out much."

"I'm going to miss you, Rikk."

"Yeah. I'm going to miss you too, Benn."

They exchanged the awkward half–handshake, half–hug thing that men do at times like this and Rikk headed off to mingle. Benn turned back to his task just as the hooded figure stepped out from behind the tree, drawing her hood back slightly so only Benn could see her face. At first Benn took a step back, startled, then as recognition dawned, the colour drained from his face.

"What are you doing here?" he asked. His voice emphatic but muted. "This is so dangerous. Do you know what these people would do to you if they knew who you were?"

Lyric smiled. "Congratulations, Benn."

"You came here to congratulate me? You risked your life to watch me graduate and congratulate me? Oh Lyric, what were you thinking?"

Lyric dropped her gaze to the ground and nodded. Benn looked around, desperately trying to find an escape route for her. The garden was fully walled, the door to the hall was closed and the gates to the plaza were not yet open. Lyric was trapped. To make matters worse, band of Benn's classmates and teachers were making their way from the refreshment tables toward Benn to congratulate him.

"Could it get any worse?" Benn moaned.

The legs at one end of a food table suddenly collapsed sending the delicacies on board sliding gracefully onto the earth below. One of the pots rolled over all the others, smashed onto the edge of a platter, and sprayed sauce over all nearby. A server and some of the ladies nearby squealed. A woman whose tunic was now stained with sauces and juices wailed. All present turned to look at the commotion and rushed to assist, including those who had been marching toward Benn. The Protectors were all trained to be heroes, and there were ladies in distress to be rescued. Even if the rescue consisted of cloths, water, reassurance and setting the table and its contents to rights.

Benn looked toward the large gate to the plaza to see the latch beam lying askew on the ground. He figured that some of the Protectors had probably been in the process of opening the gate when the table collapsed. He saw an opportunity. He reached out and gently pulled Lyric's hood further over her head to ensure she was properly concealed, then took her by the arm. "Come with me," he whispered escorting her toward the gate, "I'll get you out of here." In the gateway Benn paused, turned Lyric toward him and held her by the shoulders. He tried to look her in the eye, but she wouldn't meet his gaze.

"See you in the moonlight?" Lyric mumbled.

"No, Lyric." Benn shook her gently, as if trying to make the words sink in. "We can't wander together anymore. We can't see each other anymore. I'll be moving away, moving to the Palace. I have a new life now." He spun Lyric around, pointing her toward the side of the plaza where the road home began. "Now go, quickly, before you are recognised." Benn gave her a nudge to send her on her way.

"Benn! What are you doing?" A voice called from the edge of the commotion in the garden.

"Nothing Father." Benn replied, still watching Lyric begin to make her way across the plaza.

"Who was that?" Donn reached him and looked past him to see a robed figure walking away.

"It was nobody." Benn sighed, silently begging the Goddess that Lyric was far enough away not to hear those words.

Donn grabbed Benn by the arm and dragged him back toward the garden. Order was being restored and the mood of the gathering was once again becoming festive.

CHAPTER FOUR

Betrothal

Lyric was still close enough to hear the exchange between Benn and his father. Of course, she was nobody. That's how she survived. Still, the sting of the words caused Lyric to hasten her pace across the plaza and through the city streets. Concealed by the cloak, she did not feel compelled to keep to the shadows, she strode with determined haste, dodging the citizens going about their daily lives and nodding to any who acknowledged her as she passed. Lyric was still in shock at the realisation Benn would soon be betrothed to the Princess, that he would be lost to her. By the time she reached the outskirts of the City, the shock gave way to grief and an empty, hollow feeling in her gut. Tears trickled down her cheeks and her panting breaths were interspersed with heaving sobs as she ran along the country roads to her home.

Adria was waiting at the farm gate with an expression of knowing and compassion on her weary face. Lyric ran the final few steps to her mother and Adria hugged her tight. "That's right, Precious One," Adria reassured her, "have a good cry."

Lyric buried her face in her mother's tunic and did just that, leaving a soggy patch of tears on the fine linen fabric. When the sobs started to subside, Adria led her into the kitchen where a pile of fresh fruit buns sat on the table. Beside them two empty plates and two decanters of pomegranate juice.

"For us," Adria gestured toward the table, smiling.

Lyric shed the cloak and sat on one side of the table, placing the cloak on the bench seat beside her. Adria took her seat opposite. They each took a bun. Lyric took a small bite of the warm, sweet deliciousness and washed it down with the juice that tasted like nectar. "Yum."

"I'm glad you like it," Adria said in between mouthfuls. "Now tell me about the problem."

Now, when Lyric was finally at liberty to speak her mind, she was so full of emotion that she could barely find words. "Benn," she started, while Adria sat patiently munching, "betrothal to Princess."

"Yes," responded Adria, "Not an unexpected development. But the betrothal hasn't taken place yet, has it?"

Lyric shook her head and took a swig of juice.

Adria held her decanter between her hands in front of her and gazed at the surface of the remaining liquid. "It won't be long now. A few days at the most. The Princess will take a party of Royal Protectors to the Kreft farm and she will ask Benn to be her bonded Protector, in accordance with the traditions of Vulcon."

Lyric polished off another bun while listening intently to her mother.

"So, Precious One," Adria looked up from the decanter, raised it to her lips and took a sip, "You have a few days to choose."

Lyric raised an eyebrow in surprise.

"Oh yes, Precious One," Adria continued, "You do have a choice. Knowing what you know, you are better placed than anyone to make that choice. Now take a couple more buns, and head outdoors. Cry more if you need to, but when the tears are spent you must find it in you to decide not to weep any more over this. Mull over your choices. You know there is much at stake, not the least of which is the future life and happiness of your dear friend, Benn."

Lyric took the buns as instructed and made for the fields. Her mother was wiser than she expected. Perhaps she had been speaking with Aunt Tyla? Lyric always seemed to think more clearly outdoors. She made for a nearby field and sat in the green swathe of pasture watching the play of afternoon light and shadows on the side of the mountain. So much to consider. So little time.

Graduation was on the Oneday and Lyric spent much of the evening and most of the next day roaming the countryside, restless. There was much she wanted to tell Benn, but Adria insisted that it was still not time. Her mother could give her no other counsel than to do what felt right in her heart. So, she pondered, sulked, pouted, wandered, wept then pondered some more. Finally, sitting in the branches of their tree, listening to the flowing water of the river, the rustle of leaves in the breeze and the light melody of birds, she had a breakthrough.

Lyric reasoned that if Benn knew what she knew about the Princess Brata, he would be unlikely to marry her, unless he really loved her. So, as she was not able to tell Benn about the Princess, she would have to find a way to determine whether he really loved the Princess or whether he was simply bowing to his father's (and everyone else's) expectations. Now that a plan was materialising, Lyric was feeling more confident, more determined and most importantly, more hopeful. With great agility she made her way to the lower branches, leapt softly onto the earth below and headed home to prepare for the evening.

The Twoday evening was clear and the moon was full. Lyric knew this may be the last opportunity she would have to spend time with Benn. She decided that on this, the last evening, she would try to at least look normal. Nice even. She wriggled into a clean, new tunic, combed her long wavy hair, twisted it into a knot and fastened it with a carved wooden pin. She donned her mother's cloak again and set off into the cool night.

Lyric approached the Kreft house warily, taking cover in the bushes near Benn's window. As was her usual custom, she had a few pebbles in her tunic pocket and every few minutes she tapped with one on the window shutters. After what seemed like ages, the shutters opened and a sleepy Benn with hair askew, appeared.

Lyric stood and took a step back, showing herself in the moonlight. "Let's walk."

"Shhh! You shouldn't be here." Benn whispered as loudly as he could muster without waking his father.

"One last walk. Please Benn."

Benn considered for a moment. His face looked pained to see her standing there alone. "OK, one last walk," he said with a sigh, "then that's it. Tomorrow I am to be betrothed and I'll be living at the Palace by tomorrow night. Then there will be no more walks." Benn disappeared to get dressed and run a comb through his hair before scrambling out through the window. The pair swept noiselessly to the roadway, Benn seeking to turn right toward the river and Lyric left toward the City.

"It's not safe to go that way Lyric. You know that. Too many people."

"Not at this hour. Besides, we'll be careful," Lyric whispered, putting her hand behind her ear as if trying to hear something.

Benn paused and listened too. The sound of music wafted faintly from over the next rise. Not the complex, structured music of the Royal Court, but the percussive, melodic music of the working folk. There must be a celebration occurring on a not too distant farm.

"We'll have to be very careful," Benn said, turning left toward the music.

"Yes, very careful."

They set off along the road. Benn told stories of the graduation and the conversations in the garden after she left. "You shouldn't have come to the graduation. It was far too dangerous. What if you were recognised?"

Lyric suppressed a giggle down to an impish smile. "Everyone is so used to seeing me tattered and grubby that they didn't recognise me all cleaned up. As long as I could keep my eyes concealed by my hood, I was safe. Besides, I think you're worth the risk."

"Well, it was wonderful to see you there," Benn said, "I guess it would have been sad to graduate without my dear friend Lyric there to see it."

Dear friend. He called her his dear friend. Lyric wanted to hug and kiss him there and then, but she dared not. She just smiled her well-practiced absent–sweet smile, so he could not really be sure she understood his meaning.

Just before the rise they left the road, creeping along a hedge to the left, which they followed down toward a nearby farmhouse. The barn was well lit, the music, now much louder from this short distance, pouring from the open barn doors.

Lyric could see people inside, some sitting along the walls and some dancing to the music. She moved to go closer.

"Don't Lyric! No closer, we'll be seen."

Lyric ignored him and continued to scurry from hedge to hedge down toward the barn. Benn followed wary and worried behind.

The barn had two parts. One part was a large open area for storing farming equipment with lofts above for storing onions and hay. The cleared open area was now hosting the party. The other part housed the stables. Lyric made a beeline for the door to the stables. She quietly lifted the shaft, opened the door and slipped inside. Benn followed silently and pulled the door closed behind them.

Gaps in the wall let in slits of light, illuminating the golden straw piled in the corner and the beasts secure in their stalls. The barn smelled of animals and hay overlaid with the aromas of food and wine wafting in from the next room. There was a muscular grey working pony, a donkey and three brown cows. Lyric and Benn crept up to the gaps in the wall and peered through.

"There's been a bonding ceremony," Benn whispered, "See, over there, the happy couple near the table with the food on it."

Lyric saw them. The bride was wearing the most beautiful gown Lyric had ever seen. It was cream linen with a diagonal of coloured fabric flowers and leaves sewn onto it. The bride's hair was shiny, combed and tied in an upsweep adorned with tiny field flowers. The groom looked dashing in a cream tunic with an embossed leather overshirt and ceremonial sword. "Lovely," was all she managed to whisper.

"The ceremony is finished, and this is the after–party," Benn said.

Still spying through a gap in the wall, Lyric could see the musicians off to the side, well most of them anyway. There were a couple of young men seated on stools beating on wooden drums wedged securely between their knees. The drums were painted in bright motifs and topped in taut, white goat hide. Three others were standing, swaying to and fro to the beat while blowing into pan flutes. There was also the strumming of stringed instruments, but those players were off to the side and Lyric couldn't make them out from her tiny peephole.

Lyric started tapping her foot to the music, "Let's dance."

"You don't even know how to dance," Benn said.

Lyric looked wounded.

"OK then. I'll teach you." Benn turned toward her and the expression on his face changed. He was looking at her very intently, the lamplight filtered through the wall and danced on her face. This time she didn't look grubby. She figured he finally noticed she was washed and clean. He took both her hands gently in his, looking at them as if they were something amazing.

"You really are beautiful when you clean up, Lyric," he pulled her gently into the open space in front of the stalls. "Now, follow my lead." He moved from side to side, and Lyric matched his movements. As he expanded the dance steps in time with the drumbeats, her feet effortlessly followed.

"That's great, Lyric," he said, and smiled encouragement. "It's almost like you've done this before."

Lyric hoped he wouldn't see her blush in the dim light. Benn had called her beautiful and she felt as light as a cloud. Elated, she just wanted to dance, and dance, and dance.

They danced and twirled until they were exhausted, then they collapsed onto the pile of soft straw to rest a bit.

A beam of bright sunlight through the stable door hit Lyric's closed eyes and pulled her to consciousness. Dazzled when she opened her eyes, she shielded her face with her arm. She looked beside her and there was Benn, still sleeping soundly. She could feel the heat of his body beside her. Her movement woke him, and he leapt to his feet.

"Oh no!" Benn almost shouted, "We fell asleep!" He dashed to the door, opened it slightly and peered out. Satisfied the coast was clear, he looked back at Lyric, sleepily rising from the hay. "I have to go." Benn came back and helped steady Lyric as she stood up. "You should go home now. Quickly, before you are seen."

He moved back to the door and paused to look back, "I wish I could see you again, but I can't. Not ever. Goodbye dear Lyric." Benn slipped through the door, and he was gone.

Lyric stood still, first confused by the haste, then feeling suddenly empty and alone in the barn which seemed much less magical, and much more smelly by daylight. She pulled stray strands of straw from her hair and brushed others from her tunic. She scooped up the cloak and put it on. Thankfully, after a night of celebration, the farmer was too weary to tend his animals at first light, so Benn had escaped the stable unseen. But the animals were hungry, calling out for their breakfast, and all the smelly manure produced during the night would need to be attended to. By the time Lyric peered through the door to check if the coast was clear, the farmer was already walking across the farmyard toward the stable door. Lyric looked around frantically, but there were no other exits, not even a loft in which she could hide. Just as she was considering the option of diving deep into the pile of straw, the earth began to shake.

Lyric saw the look of terror on the farmer's face as he stumbled to the middle of the farmyard, away from anything overhanging, then lost his footing, falling face down onto the earth. Lyric, sure–footed from years of running and climbing, left the panicked animals behind and dashed to the shelter of a nearby hedge. By the time the shaking of the earth subsided, Lyric was scuttling along the hedges and fences, and nearly at the road. She paused a moment to mumble thanks to the Goddess for such timely intervention.

At the roadway, Lyric paused. In the distance to her right, she could see Benn arriving home. The sun was still low in the sky and the shadow of the mountain still covered the fields of both her family's farm and the distant forests in front of her. Benn would be able to creep in through his window before his father tried to rouse him. To her left was the distant City and a small royal procession was making its way out through the South Gate. It centred around a horse–drawn chariot, so gilt with gold that the reflection of the morning sunlight upon it could be seen like a beacon even from this distance.

Lyric had not yet made a final decision. She needed more information, and she knew the direction she chose now would narrow her range of choices. As inviting and safe as home looked in the distance ahead of her and as appealing as a hot breakfast was to her empty, growling stomach, she did not head in that direction. Instead she draped her hood over her head and face and walked hurriedly toward the Kreft farm.

Benn was breathless from running as he approached the family farm. He too saw the Princess' chariot leave the City and guessed where it was going. He threw himself through the open window and quickly changed into his finest tunic and accessories, his graduation outfit. This was the day Benn and his father had waited for since Benn was an infant. Perhaps Benn's mother would have wanted otherwise for her son, but sadly she had died in an accident and left Benn to be raised by his devastated father. Donn did his best, continuing to work the family farm to keep them fed, clothed and housed. The work was hard and relentless, and Donn soon fixed on the dream of Benn becoming a Protector in the Royal Court and keeping him in the manner to which he would like to become accustomed, at least during his final days. Now that it seemed so close, Donn had it all planned. He told Benn he would sell the farm if he could, take modest rooms in the City, attend parties, maybe even travel, but always continue to mentor his son in the ways of the world.

By the time the royal procession arrived at the Kreft farm gate, Benn was dressed, groomed and ready. He felt sick to his stomach at the sound of approaching hoofbeats but told himself it was just nerves and excitement.

"Where were you, Benn?" Donn asked, sounding relieved as Benn emerged from his room. "I came to wake you and you weren't there."

"I took one last stroll around the farm Father. I'm going to miss this place."

"I won't," Donn said, attending to his garb for he too was dressed for the occasion.

Benn took position in the centre of their modest living room. He could see out the window to the courtyard. The royal procession arrived and pulled into the narrow Kreft driveway.

Suddenly the humble courtyard seemed tiny and crowded. There were eight Royal Protectors in uniform shuffling along on foot, a shiny sword in each belt. The gilt chariot was radiant in the sunlight, pulled by two white horses in embossed leather harnesses, driven by a Royal Protector and bearing an impatient Princess Brata. Her blue robe wafted in the breeze and her hair was ornately half–braided into a knot, held by shiny gold pins. The procession had an aura of singular purpose as it halted outside the entrance to the Kreft farmhouse.

There was no time for the Protectors to catch their breath. The Princess promptly skipped down from the chariot and hastened to the door accompanied by two Protectors striding to keep up. Benn heard the loud and determined knock of a Protector's sword hilt on the door. The sound reverberated in the pit of his stomach. A tiny voice inside him whispered 'run'. But it was too late. He could not run. He must face his fate. Donn moved forward to open the door.

The Protectors and Donn positioned themselves around the walls. The room was small and that was the only way to clear enough space at the centre. Princess Brata strode toward Benn with a haughty, victorious smile. The perfume of the scented oils with which she was anointed earlier that morning flowed ahead of her. Benn could detect an unpleasant undertone reminiscent of fermented cream. Was this her true scent, the one Benn was to live with every day hence? When the Princess stopped a short distance away, Benn dropped down on one knee and focussed on looking solemn. He didn't have to try very hard. He couldn't help feeling he was being sold into bondage. He turned his head slightly to see his father wearing a look of smug satisfaction that turned to horror as he glanced toward the kitchen.

"Who? What is this?" the Princess said, displeased and pointing. She spied a grimy figure in a dusty tunic move through the kitchen, and grab a fig from a bowl on her way toward the living room.

Benn turned to see Lyric, and the colour drained from his face.

Lyric took a bite from the fig and tried to look confused.

"It's just the Wildling, she roams these parts. We must have left the rear door open," Donn was making excuses for her, trying to maintain the proceedings, "She's of no consequence." There was a distinct tremble in his voice.

Benn winced to hear his father say that, and he could see a hint of pain on Lyric's face.

"Ah yes, the Wildling. I remember you. Go away you, you, creature!" The Princess made a shooing gesture toward Lyric, "A betrothal is taking place. You have no place here."

"Betrothal?" Lyric enquired, trying to look as confused as possible. Benn rose to his feet, looking frustrated.

"It can speak!" the Princess seemed surprised. "Yes, a betrothal, stupid."

Lyric didn't move, she had a quizzical expression.

"That's when I ask Benn here to become my bonded Protector," the Princess continued in a condescending tone.

Benn's father sprang forward, "Sorry Your Highness. I'll get rid of her." He bowed profusely, then rushed toward Lyric, "Get out! Get out! Before you ruin everything." he yelled, frantically pointing back toward the kitchen from which she emerged.

Lyric stood her ground, still looking confused, "Benn already bonded," she said.

"What?" hissed the Princess, "Bonded? Bonded to whom? Bonded when?"

Benn felt forlorn and terrified. He shook his head and silently mouthed "No!" toward Lyric.

"Me," Lyric replied, looking blissfully ignorant of the importance of the situation, "Last night."

The Princess stared at Lyric, her cheeks, then her entire face turned dark red, she scowled, furious, then turned to look at Benn, "Is it true? Were you with this ... this ... thing last night?"

Benn's face dropped. His unfailing honesty had helped him become the top student in his Academy year, but now it was scuttling his plans. "Yes," he conceded, "but it's—" He never got to finish the sentence.

"No!" Benn's father shouted at him, turning his attention from Lyric, "How could you?"

The Princess was fuming, "Indeed. How could you?" she hissed. "I cannot be seen with someone who associates with the likes of that." The Princess pointed a dismissive finger toward Lyric. However, when she realised all in the room were staring at her, she made an effort to regain self-control, then raised an eyebrow and gave a cold, detached smile, as if seeing a solution. She strode up to the nearest Protector, calm, cool and determined. "Kill her," she ordered.

The Protector looked horrified, but he had no choice. If he did not comply, the Princess would just as quickly order his own execution. He steeled himself, pulled his sword and strode toward Lyric with blind determination. He raised the sword high, but as he brought it down a strong hand suddenly clasped his arm.

"No!"

It was Benn.

Everyone in the room was stunned into silence and immobility, except Lyric, who took another nonchalant bite of her fig.

"So, there we have it!" The Princess seethed. "You are her Protector after all." She gathered up her robes and marched for the door, the Protectors moved to follow, shaking their heads in Benn's direction, incredulous. At the door she turned to Benn one more time. "You foolish, foolish boy. The Queen will be displeased. She'll have you executed for this." With that, she and her entourage left the house.

Lyric could hear the Princess in the courtyard, barking orders to her driver and the Protectors, the situation made worse by the limited space offered by the courtyard to turn a chariot and horses full circle. Eventually the footfalls of the party could be heard disappearing into the distance as the procession made its way back toward the City, without its intended cargo.

Donn and Benn remained motionless for a time. Perhaps hoping the Princess would calm down, return to the room and the process could start over. The fading footfalls clearly indicated this was not to be.

"You've ruined everything! Ruined us. Ruined me." Donn yelled at Lyric. "I'll kill you myself!" He drew a knife from his belt and rushed toward her.

Lyric took a step back as Benn stepped forward and easily disarmed the old man, much smaller and more fragile than himself, restraining his thin wrists with his large, strong hands. He guided him, still restrained to a wooden chair in the corner of the room and forced him to sit down.

The old man bent forward, buried his face in his hands and chanted, "We're ruined, we're ruined," over and over while rocking backward and forward on the chair.

Benn stood there, positioned between his father and Lyric, watching his father, vigilant, lest he leap forward again. His career was overturned. His life disassembled and rendered meaningless. All his study, training and striving was for nought. He turned to Lyric with simmering rage.

"Go!" Benn shouted at her. "Get out of here!"

Lyric turned to leave as she had entered, then paused, turned and strode across the room toward the front door. She stopped in the doorway, "Sorry," she said to Benn, then closed the door behind her.

Benn was too angry to realise Lyric had just saved his future, let alone that she was trying to find a way to save his life.

No sooner was the door closed than Donn began to yell. He was shouting so loudly that anyone in the area of the Kreft farm could have heard with ease. However, the Kreft farm was relatively isolated, so Lyric leaving the farmyard, some nearby songbirds, the farm chickens and the Kreft donkey were the only audience.

"I told you, didn't I?" Donn ranted, "I told you, if you kept spending time with that—that—Wildling, she'd be the ruin of you!"

Benn didn't respond, he just stood there, looking toward the door where the Princess and Lyric had exited.

"How could you let it come to this?" Donn was pacing the room, getting progressively more worked up and waving his arms about in exasperation. "What were you thinking, sneaking out last night to spend time with her? That would have to be the dumbest thing you have ever done. Now you've ruined us both. No one will want to work with you, let alone become your partner, once it's known you associate with that— thing."

"She's not a thing, she's a person. Her name is Lyric."

"I don't give a damn what its name is! How am I supposed to show my face in society now? Who will buy my vegetables after this disgrace? You've doomed me to spend the rest of my life in hard labour and social isolation."

By now, Donn was so worked up he was standing directly in front of Benn, who was considerably taller than him. Donn was waving his arms wildly. His face was livid red. "I can't bear to look at you anymore, get out!" He pointed vigorously at the door, "I said, GET OUT!" Donn stomped his foot firmly on the earthen floor to reinforce the command.

"OK. I'll take a walk until you calm down,"

"I don't mean take a walk, I mean get out, and stay out. Don't ever come back."

Benn was shocked. "I'll get my things."

"Your things? Your things? Everything in this house, everything you think you own, I bought from the money earned by my own sweat and toil in those pitiful fields!" Donn waved toward the farm outside.

"You didn't buy the clothes I'm wearing. They, at least, were Academy issue."

"Then leave with the clothes on your back!" Donn was still shouting, "And not a thing more!"

"If you wish."

"Get out! Get out! GET OUT!"

Benn walked toward the door, lifted the latch and turned once more to look at his father and the familiar home of his childhood.

Donn was still in full rage. "Henceforth you are a stranger to me. I no longer have a son. Now get out!"

Benn stunned and pale, closed the door behind him and strode out of the farmyard, across the road, and over the ridge towards the river. As he walked, he picked up a large stick and swiped at the vegetation in his path, out of sheer frustration. It was early Summer, and the green tips of the grasses snapped and bent to Benn's satisfaction at the force of his blows. Unable to think of anywhere else to go, he made his way to their tree by the river. He launched himself up onto a hefty lower branch and sat there, snapping the stick into small pieces and cursing to the winds as he hurtled the fragments toward the river.

As he flung the last piece of the stick, Benn heard a soft voice from near the tree trunk below.

"Sorry."

It was Lyric. Somehow, she had crept up on him and his pent-up rage. Benn looked at his hands as if searching for a fragment of stick to throw in her direction, but all his projectiles were exhausted. "Sorry? Sorry? You've ruined my life and you're sorry?" Now it was his turn to be angry, his turn to yell.

Lyric just stood there, taking the verbal blows.

"Now I have no home, no prospect of a partner. No one but you would want to be associated with me now." Benn mused a moment, "That's it, isn't it? You've been planning this for weeks, maybe even years. Clever plan, keep hanging out with me, ruin my reputation and then you get me all to yourself because I have nowhere else to go. I've always wondered how it is the women in your family seem to win the best Protector graduates from the Academy, bond with them and condemn them to a menial life as farmers and potters. Now I know. I bet it's a plot handed down through the women in your family from generation to generation."

Tears started to stream down Lyric's cheeks.

Benn calmed down a little at the sight of her tears and wounded expression. "I'm sorry," he said. "I'm just, just, so angry with you."

Lyric took a step toward him.

"Don't," Benn warned and held up one hand, "Don't come near me. Not now, not ever again. My only chance now is to stay away from you. To try and find some manual work somewhere and gradually try to rebuild my standing."

Lyric took another step forward.

"I said don't." Benn leapt down from the branch and strode away along the riverbank in the direction of the stone bridge. "Stay away from me!"

Benn strode along the river for a while, then climbed the embankment, finally stopping to sit on top of the ridge where he could look out in all directions. He looked toward the distant City ahead. Below him on his right side was the river and the stone bridge leading to the fields of the Nye farm, somewhere behind and to his left side was the Kreft farm.

Benn eventually noticed Lyric standing nearby. She had once again approached silently from behind.

"Not you again." He was still angry, "I said go away! Stop following me. I don't ever want to see you again."

"It's not safe for you here, Benn." Lyric said.

"You're right, and it's probably not safe to be around me when I'm this angry. So, go away!" Benn waved his arm as if to shoo her away. "You have no idea, do you?" Benn fired the rhetorical question while gazing at the City. "Word of this disgrace would be out all over the City and most of the countryside by now. So, I cannot go to the City, not that any of my friends there would risk the Queen's wrath to try and shelter me. I have no living relative other than my father, who is adamant he is no longer my father, and so I cannot go home. Father kept to himself, so there are no family friends to appeal to, and certainly none who would take the risk of sheltering me. Even my friends from the Academy would be disgraced to be seen with me, so I cannot impose. All I can do is roam from place to place in the countryside and try to stay alive until this all subsides, and I can try to start again. Not so easy on an island, and I have no money to pay for passage on a Phoenician trader ship to leave here either."

Benn was cornered and was coming to realise the extent to which he was trapped. He wiped his face on his arm, determined not to be seen as weakening.

"You would be welcome at our home," Lyric said.

That seemed like a crazy idea. Impose on strangers? Besides, Lyric's family probably had more sense than she and would not offer him refuge, despite her invitation. "How could I possibly expect you to understand? Now stay away from me!" Benn picked himself up and strode off past Lyric, back along the ridge toward their tree.

"My family would keep you safe," Lyric said as he passed by.

Benn shook his head and waved her off, "Go away!"

"We would keep you safe!" Lyric yelled after him as he strode further.

"Go away!" Benn yelled back and started to jog off into the distance. Eventually he stopped and looked back to see Lyric walking slowly in the direction of her home. He sat down again on the green grass. He needed time to think and clear his head, and he was hungry.

CHAPTER FIVE

Taking flight

When Lyric entered the kitchen, forlorn, Adria was kneading dough on the kitchen table. She plied the soft mass with deft, floured hands. Adria quickly wiped her hands in her apron, rushed over and gave Lyric a thorough hug.

"Mother," Lyric began to sob, "I hurt Benn."

"I know, I know, Precious One," Adria crooned, rubbing Lyrics back. "Aunt Tyla said that it must done."

"Was it enough?"

"Yes," Adria held Lyric by the shoulders at arm's length and looked her directly in the eye, "It was enough." Adria smiled and started plucking leaves and twigs from Lyric's hair. "Now, go wash. I'll have lunch ready soon."

Lyric nodded and headed toward the washroom. Her mother had provided some comfort and reassurance, but it was not enough to quell the pain. She had hurt her best friend, ruined his career and prospects, and she could not be totally certain she hadn't done it for selfish reasons. Just the thought of it felt like a great wound tearing itself open in her chest.

"This afternoon you can help me prepare the food for tomorrow's journey," Adria called after her.

Lyric nodded again as she disappeared into the washroom. However questionable her motives, the die was cast. She wiped and rinsed the grime from her skin and hair, trying to wash away the pain and doubt with it. She needed to clear her head and try to fathom a plan to save Benn's life.

Lyric eventually emerged clean, wearing a muted orange tunic Adria had laid out for her. Her long, wet hair was plaited into a single braid, tied at the end with a leather band. She was so distressed on her arrival that she hadn't noticed how steamy the kitchen was. The summer day prevented the heat from the oven escaping the kitchen, even with all the doors and the window shutters open. Lyric saw her mother's face was shiny with sweat, yet Adria worked away with purposeful good cheer.

"Your father is taking some cashmere and other items to your aunt's house in the City, so it's just us for lunch," Adria explained as she ladled out vegetable and chicken soup and slid a plate of steaming, fresh flatbread onto the table. Chickens were a popular recent arrival on Vulcon. The Phoenician traders recently brought a few birds from Egypt where they were the latest 'wonder' livestock. The miracle bird that laid an egg every day. The Nyes were quick to acquire a few birds, rapidly built up a sizeable flock, and sold birds throughout the island. It was soon discovered that chickens were good to eat, so chicken soup was a real treat.

Lyric thought her mother planned this well. Despite the heat, this was comfort food. She let the rich flavours swim in her mouth and felt the heat of the soup as it slid down her throat. It was like a hug from the inside. A salve on the wound.

When the meal was complete and the table cleared and wiped, Adria pulled out four large, leather saddlebags and placed them on the table. During the course of the afternoon, Lyric and Adria filled them. There were bags of flour, biscuits, freshly baked flatbread, two pottery cups, soap and clothes. Slabs of butter, and goat cheese, were each wrapped in waxed parchment. Salt was poured into a tiny pot and sealed with wax. As they worked, they chatted.

"How long?" Lyric asked.

"You'll need to stay at Sanctuary for ten days. Then it will be safe to come home."

"Safe?" Lyric raised one eyebrow and half–smiled.

"Well, safer than now. Safe for a while." Adria playfully tossed a biscuit in Lyric's direction. "Well, you know what I mean."

Lyric caught the biscuit and promptly ate it, mustering a modest smirk.

"Easy now," Adria said. "Save some for the trip."

"But it's so good!" Lyric mumbled with her mouth full of crumbs.

"Then you'll have to remember to come home for more at the end of the ten days."

"Deal." Lyric smiled. She was feeling much better now. Her mother's confidence and good humour were rubbing off on her.

Adria packed the rest of the biscuits into a light wooden box and positioned it in a saddle bag. "You'll have to tell him you know."

"I know." Lyric became serious again. "When?"

"Start when you're well clear of here, when you have reached a place of relative safety in case Benn's initial reactions are … um … not well thought out." Adria paused, looking off into the distance. "Best not tell him everything all at once. Give him time to adjust."

"OK." Lyric had no plan for this. She would have to figure it out as events unfolded.

"When you get to the forest, use what the Protectors fear to make good your escape."

Lyric's initial confusion at this soon gave way to understanding. "Yes, Mother." She was still anxious.

"You're more worried about whether or not he will forgive you, than whether you can keep him safe, aren't you?" Concern evident in her mother's eyes.

"Yes," Lyric said as she wrapped small, firm goat cheeses and passed them to her mother to place carefully in a saddlebag. It helped to know that her mother understood.

"Whether or not Benn forgives you or likes you is beyond your control, Precious One. If you focus on that, you will feel lost, like a down feather on the wind. Focus instead on earning his respect. Right now, you need him to protect you, more than you need him to like you." Adria said. "You can worry about the rest later."

Lyric started to fold and pack clothes. How would she earn his respect? As far as he knew, she ruined his life. As the last items were being stowed in the saddlebags, the door opened, and Lyric's father ambled in with packages in his arms. Lyric flew at him at once and hugged him. He dropped his parcels on the table and hugged her in return.

"Hello Precious One," he said. "Are you OK?"

Lyric nodded, still hugging.

"Is all OK?" he asked, looking up at Adria, with Lyric still suspended around his neck like an orange amulet.

"All OK," Adria said.

"Excellent." Hann freed up one hand to gesture toward one of the parcels on the table. "Brought you back some fish. Since you have the oven fired today, maybe you could make that great roast fish thing you do?"

"Great idea." Adria stepped forward to collect the parcel of fish, tightly wrapped in waxed parchment. "Will you help me Lyric?"

Lyric released her father. He held her by the shoulders and looked directly at her, "You need to get to bed early tonight. You have a big day tomorrow."

Lyric glanced past him toward the doorway.

"Don't worry yourself, Precious One. Your mother and I will take care of it." With that he headed to the washroom to clean up after his journey.

"Indeed," Adria said. "You're not exactly Benn's favourite person right now, so best you are not in the room when he arrives. Early to bed is an excellent idea."

"Getting to bed won't be the problem Mother, getting to sleep will." Lyric helped her mother pack away the contents of the remaining parcels. Hann spent some of the money from the sale of their grain, goat cheese and cashmere on the purchase of spices, and salt. They produced most of what they needed on the farm, but ocean fish and spices were a treat and the salt was always needed, not only for cooking, but also for preparing goat hide for tanning and for preserving meats and vegetables.

Together Lyric and Adria prepared the evening meal. Lyric knew the time would soon be upon them when this would no longer be possible, so she savoured every moment. All the while she worried about Benn. The dinner conversation centred on harvesting as much grain, fruits and vegetables as early as possible and preserving them. The best breeding animals would be marked and most of the rest would be slaughtered before the cool of autumn, their meat and hides preserved for the lean times ahead. Large cellars were discreetly completed at Aunt

Tyla's house in the City, and much preserved produce would be stored there over coming weeks.

By nightfall, Lyric was clean, well fed and cosy warm in her bed as the air temperature fell with the fading light. Her candle was out, and the room was dark. She was supposed to fall promptly to sleep, but she was anxious. Her gut oscillated between pain, flutters and a tight knot. How could one fall asleep with such sensations? She listened out for a sound at the door. It was now well after dark, maybe something was wrong. She couldn't sleep for worry. She just lay there, listening, waiting, hoping.

Finally, a sound at the door. Lyric's whole body shuddered with each knock and her gut wrenched. There would be no falling asleep now. She quietly rolled from her bed, wrapped a blanket around her shoulders and crouched on the floorboards. There was a hole where a knot had fallen out of the timbers and if she positioned herself just right, she could see most of what transpired in the still well–lit rooms below.

Her parents were sitting at the kitchen table, discussing plans for the coming days when the knock came. Adria rose purposefully, smiled victoriously at Hann, then made her way to the door and opened it. "Welcome Benn." Adria stepped aside and ushered Benn into the warm room, illuminated by golden candlelight.

Lyric was simultaneously relieved, excited and nervous. Benn was in her house.

Lyric's father stood and shook Benn's hand, "So, you're Benn then?"

"I am sir."

"I am Hann, and this is Adria. Welcome to our home." Lyric's father gestured toward the seating benches at the table. "Sit down and make yourself comfortable."

Hann took a seat opposite Benn.

"You must be famished," Adria suggested.

"Yes, Ma'am."

"I'll fix you something."

"Thank you, Ma'am."

Adria quickly gathered the plate of food previously stowed in a warmer by the oven and placed it on the table with cutlery and a mug of water.

Benn ate ravenously. "This is delicious," he said between mouthfuls. "Much better than Academy food."

Adria beamed and took a seat beside Hann. Together they watched Benn rapidly clear the entire plate, and down the entire mug of water.

"Where's Lyric?" Benn asked between mouthfuls.

"She was weary and has already gone up to bed," Adria said, leaning toward Hann and wrapping her arm around his.

When Benn downed the last gulp, Hann ventured, "So what brings you here?"

"Well sir," Benn said nervously, swallowing the last of the water, "It's a long story."

"We like long stories," Hann replied. Adria nodded in agreement, then rose to clear the dishes and tidy the kitchen.

"This morning I was to be betrothed to the Princess Brata. By midday I was unbetrothed, homeless and disinherited."

"Why did the Princess not proceed with the betrothal?" Hann asked. "After all, you did graduate at the top of your year at the Academy."

"Because I spent the night with Lyric."

Lyric's father straightened up in outrage. "What?"

"It's alright sir, nothing happened." Benn tried to be reassuring. "We went to a barn where a bonding ceremony was being celebrated."

"That would be the Sansons. Their daughter was bonded yesterday." Adria said.

"I guess so," Benn said. "We danced in the stable, to the music. We sat down to rest on the hay and fell asleep. Next thing I knew it was morning."

"You're sure nothing else happened?" Hann was eyeing Benn with suspicion.

"Sir, I'm not the type of man to take advantage of a vulnerable girl."

"I'm glad to hear it." Hann leaned back and turned toward Adria. "I'm starting to like this young man."

"Please, continue," prompted Adria, returning to her seat beside Hann.

"Well, I raced home and arrived shortly before the Princess. The betrothal ritual had just commenced when Lyric burst into the room and told everyone we spent the night together. The Princess ordered her killed and when I thwarted the Protector, the Princess flew into a rage and left. Then my father flew into a rage, threw me out of the house with nothing but the clothes on my back, and declared I was no longer his son."

"That's a lot of disappointment and trauma for one day," Adria said.

"Yeah! Tell me about it." Benn sighed. "I've spent the whole day roaming the countryside trying to make sense of it all."

"Any luck?" Hann asked.

"Well, I reckon the Princess would have returned to the Palace and related the whole sorry tale to the Queen. The Queen has no sense of humour on a good day, so I expect she'll put out an order to have me killed for humiliating the Princess."

"I reckon you're right." Hann agreed. "There'll be Protectors searching high and low for you by morning."

"Look. I don't want to put you good folk in danger. But Lyric suggested that I may be safe here, that you may be able to protect me." Benn sounded meekly hopeful.

"We can protect you here until morning," Hann said. "Then we will need to move you to a place of sanctuary while we ride out the Queen's wrath."

Adria pointed to a blanket and pillow already laid out on the bed in the corner of the kitchen. "You can sleep there. It will be warm by the hearth."

"Thank you." Benn said, rising from the chair.

"There's a washroom through there," Adria pointed at the small doorway obscured by a curtain, "if you want to clean up before bed."

When Benn emerged from the washroom, Adria was putting away the last of the dishes. Hann stoked the fire and lit two candles. He placed each in a separate candleholder on the table, took one and pushed the other toward Benn. "I'll leave it here in case you need it."

Benn placed his clothes over the back of a chair and proceeded to spread the blanket, as Adria and Hann headed to the stairs. "Goodnight Benn," they said in unison. "Sleep well. You have a big day tomorrow."

At the sound of her parents climbing the stairs, Lyric leapt back into bed, pulled up the covers and closed her eyes.

Adria popped her head through Lyric's doorway, "See, Precious One, all is well. Benn is safe. Now you can sleep."

Lyric smiled. Sleep? She was too excited to sleep. Benn was in her house and tomorrow she would have to find a way to keep him safe. She rolled over, pondering all these things, but the weariness of a long, eventful day soon caught up with her.

Lyric felt a persistent pushing on her arm. It dragged her to consciousness. She forced open her eyes, the room was cool and dark. Even the birds were not yet awake. Adria loomed over her holding a candle which illuminated her face with a flickering, golden glow.

"It's time," Adria half-whispered. "Are you OK to stay awake?"

Lyric nodded and forced herself to sit up. She rubbed her eyes while her mother lit the bedside candle from her own. The candle lights made flickering, ghostly patterns on the walls.

"Be quick now," Adria said as she left the room, drawing the thick linen curtain across the doorway behind her.

Gradually Lyric's wakening mind pieced together the events of the previous day, finally recalling that a sullen, angry Benn was in her house and today was the day she must get him to safety. The pang of realisation and the chill of the night air in her room promptly banished all grogginess and Lyric leapt to her feet so quickly she was dizzy. She found the travel clothes she had set out the night before and dressed quickly. Within minutes she took up her candle and headed downstairs.

Adria soon woke Benn, lit a lantern on the kitchen table and set about cooking a breakfast befitting a long day's journey.

Benn was perched on the edge of the day bed, his face in his hands, slowly dragging himself awake.

"Hello Ben."

Benn's head popped up at the sound of her voice. "Hello Lyric." His tone was sombre, his dark hair all awry.

Lyric felt him gaze at her. He frowned as if struggling to find words. Perhaps he was pleased to see her, perhaps he was still angry she had ruined his life. She couldn't really tell. It felt strange seeing Benn in her kitchen after all these years. Bizarre.

The door to the farmyard opened and Hann appeared carrying a lantern. "Better dress quickly young man. You'll need to be away at first light if you are to stay ahead of the Protectors," he said, on taking in Benn still sitting in his night clothes, with his hair unkempt.

Lyric held out the bundle of travel clothes Adria left on the table for Benn and gestured to the washroom. Benn took them awkwardly and disappeared with a candle into the dark room, drawing the curtain behind him.

Lyric looked out through the open rear door and could see the two horses by lantern light. She ran out to the yard and Hann followed. Nudge's dappled coat glowed in the light of the oil lantern and, true to her name, she gave Lyric a solid, affectionate nudge as soon as she was within range. Poppy's chestnut coat shone like gold in the lantern's light.

"Your horse?" Lyric looked quizzically at her father.

"Yes, Precious One. Benn must take Poppy," Hann said. "She's strong, quiet and reliable, she's done the trip before, so she knows the way, and she's been trained to stick to the trails."

Lyric stroked Poppy's neck. It was warm and soft despite the crisp night air. "But Father?" Lyric knew Poppy was Hann's favourite horse and meant as much to him as her trusty Nudge did to her.

"Hush now." Hann would hear of no argument against his decision. "She'll look after Benn and help keep him safe."

With that, Lyric's protests melted into defeat and she simply gave her father a tight hug. "I'll take good care of Poppy," she assured him.

"I know you will, Precious One," Hann returned the hug and together they made their way back into the cosy kitchen that was luring them with the delicious aromas of a hot breakfast.

By the time Benn reappeared, dressed in a humble travel tunic and overshirt, the breakfast table was laid and the four of them sat down to a hearty meal of scrambled eggs, goat sausages, fried onion and spinach, washed down with honey-sweetened goats' milk.

As they ate, Adria instructed Benn. "The Royal Protectors will leave the Palace at first light and they will go directly to your father's home. Your father is still angry, and he will tell them you have run off after the Wildling. The Protectors will then hasten here."

Benn looked worried. "I'm sorry to put you all in danger."

"We appreciate that Benn," Hann said. "But we must do what is right and prevent loss of life wherever we can."

Lyric said nothing, she just kept eating. It would be a while before they ate this well again.

"To prevent loss of life, we will confess to the Protectors that you and Lyric have run off together. We will point in the direction you have gone but will declare ignorance of your destination."

Benn thumped his fist onto the table. "No! I'll not endanger Lyric. I must go alone. Just tell me where to go."

Lyric stared at Benn in surprise. He was still trying to protect her, even while he was certainly furious with her for ruining his life. Adria's plan may have a chance of working after all.

"That's noble of you, but not possible," Hann said. "You see, Lyric and I are the only ones who know the way, and I will be staying here to protect Adria and the farm."

"I don't understand," said Benn, staring at Lyric who resumed munching, feigning disinterest.

"While you were at the Academy all these years," Hann proceeded to explain, "Lyric has been off in the wilderness creating a Sanctuary. She, and the Sanctuary, have not been found in all this time, so it will serve to keep you both safe now."

Benn stared at Lyric as if she had worked some great wonder. Lyric finished her last mouthful, wiped her mouth on a napkin, rose from the table and placed her plate and cup on the side bench. She smiled sweetly at Benn, took up a candle and disappeared into the washroom. Lyric had impeccable manners for a simple farm girl and she wondered if Benn had noticed

"Hurry and eat up, Benn," Adria said. "It will soon be dawn."

By the time Lyric emerged, Benn had obediently scoffed down two helpings of breakfast. "Thank you, ma'am. That was delicious."

"Clearly," said Adria. She looked pleased that her food was so appreciated by their guest. "Please, call me Adria."

"Thank you, Adria." Benn rose from the table.

Minutes later they were all gathered in the farmyard. The horses were bridled and saddled. The bulging, packed saddlebags were in place, tied to the back of the large rectangular leather saddles and sitting atop the draping cashmere saddle blankets, so they wouldn't rub on the horses. Both horses stood patiently, awaiting their riders. Adria issued both riders with long, cashmere travel cloaks and insisted they wear them. Lyric loved wearing cashmere. It was soft and snug, yet light as air.

"Be safe, Precious One," Lyric's father whispered as he hugged his daughter tight.

"I will."

"She won't be going anywhere unless you let her breathe, my love," Adria said.

"Sorry Addy." Hann loosened his grip and shared a smile with Lyric.

Finally released, Lyric walked over and embraced her mother.

"Remember, be kind. Reveal just a little at a time," Adria whispered in Lyric's ear as she gave Lyric a comforting hug.

"Yes Mother." Lyric rolled her eyes. She wondered why parents felt the need to regularly repeat the same information.

Adria held Lyric's head in her hands, kissed her on the forehead, then released her. Benn stood silently, in awe of a loving family looking out for one another.

Lyric strode toward her father. Hann placed a wooden mounting stool beside Nudge. Lyric took the reins in hand, then in a single leap she threw her leg over the saddle and bags and landed securely in place. Nudge wiggled a little with the sudden weight, then settled, waiting patiently as Lyric positioned her travel cloak over Nudge's back.

Benn approached the other horse with obvious caution.

"Don't worry, Poppy's friendly," Hann said as a gesture of reassurance.

Benn looked only a little less worried.

"You can ride, can't you?" Adria asked.

"Yes of course," Benn replied. "Riding is still compulsory at the Academy. That doesn't mean it was my favourite subject though."

Hann laughed. "Don't worry young man. These horses are much less troublesome than the Academy horses. You may even enjoy the experience."

"Doubt it," Benn mumbled, perched on the mounting stool, with reins now in hand. He too swung his leg over and launched himself into the saddle. It was much less agile and gentle than Lyric's attempt. Still his seat was secure, and true to Hann's word, Poppy just stood there patiently through the whole process.

Lyric smirked at Benn's discomfort. She was raised around horses and was an avid rider for as long as she could remember. It never dawned on her that anyone should have any difficulty in this area. Clearly the Kreft family donkey was not an adequate vehicle for developing horsemanship.

Adria came up and gently stroked Poppy's neck, "Take care to follow exactly in the path of Lyric's horse at all times," she said. "Lyric is the only one who knows the safe path. Follow her instructions exactly if you want to survive. Do you understand?"

Benn looked quizzical, seeming surprised by her sudden gravity.

"Do you understand?" Adria demanded.

"Yes ma'am. I mean, yes Adria."

"Good." Adria relaxed a little. "This is your only chance to be safe, for us all to be safe, don't squander it."

Benn looked confused then gave a sombre nod.

Adria moved over to Lyric's horse. "Ride well and be safe, Precious One. Know that we love you."

Lyric nodded acknowledgment, hoping her mother would stop at this and not say something to embarrass her further in front of Benn.

There was a faint glow in the sky, heralding the impending dawn. Hann extinguished the lanterns. When Lyric's eyes adjusted, she could just make out the farmyard gateway and the farm road beyond. A rooster crowed.

"It is light enough," said Hann. "Go now and be safe!"

Lyric turned to Benn. "Let's ride." She turned Nudge toward the gateway and urged her on.

Benn acknowledged Lyric's parents, then turned his horse to follow Lyric. Poppy happily took position behind Nudge and followed Lyric out the gate. They turned left onto the path that led between fields of pasture and curved gently toward the side of the mountain.

"Remember to use their fear against them!" Adria called out behind them.

Lyric waved a final goodbye to her parents, now standing in the open gateway, and urged Nudge to a trot. Poppy followed briskly behind. Their footfalls rhythmic in the still, morning air. It would be a long day's ride, best to spare the horses and not gallop until absolutely necessary.

The pasture in the Nye's extensive fields was blanketed with dew, rendering them an ethereal, pastel hue in the morning light. The tops of white goats, already busy grazing on the tall pasture that reached halfway up their bodies, were spread out like a splatter of white paint across the scene.

As they trotted the path between the ride fields, Benn was initially quiet. Lyric was convinced the journey would be a tense and silent one, with Benn still angry about her sabotage of his betrothal. He had a right to be. Still, it was uncharacteristic of

Benn to be silent for any great time. She wondered how long it would last.

"Your parents are good people." Benn's voice cut through the morning silence and the sound of hoofbeats.

Lyric smiled, knowing that from behind, her smile would not be seen. It was good he was finally talking again.

"Your mother is a wonderful cook," Benn prattled on. "That breakfast was so delicious. I couldn't stop eating. I hope your mother didn't mind. You probably don't know your father also graduated first in his year at the Protector Academy. I saw his name on the honour tablet in the main hall. He could have been a Royal Protector and had an amazing life at Court. Yet, he seems happy just being a farmer. It must have been love then, because he seems to be quite content, bonded to your mother. Or perhaps it's just all that great food."

Lyric worked hard not to laugh out loud, but she did not reply. She just turned and smiled acknowledgement.

At the edge of the farm, the path petered down to a narrow goat trail that zig–zagged up the low rises at the base of the mountain and then up the mountain itself. Lyric slowed the horses to a brisk walk.

"Why are we slowing down?" Benn asked. "The Protectors' horses are taller and stronger than these horses. At the speed they travel, they'll catch us up in no time. We should be going faster, not slowing down."

Lyric shook her head in disagreement and maintained the same pace. "The horses are heavily laden. We need to make sure they find secure footing and spare them for as long as possible."

Benn cursed in frustration under his breath. After they ascended the first rise, Lyric stopped to look back. The land was bathed in early morning sunlight and the shadow of the mountain was receding toward them. They could see pinpoints of red, seemingly floating on a cloud of dust, rapidly approaching the Kreft farm off in the distance.

"The Protectors are arriving at my father's house," Benn observed. "We need to move faster."

"Not yet." Lyric was calm, keeping Nudge at a steady walk out in front, as they worked their way up the slope. Lyric knew how long it would take them to reach a safe point and there was still a long journey ahead.

"Look, Lyric," Benn said. "They're galloping and we're walking. They'll catch up sooner than you think."

"Not yet," Lyric repeated. Her voice firm and steady. She knew Benn wanted to overtake her and gallop off, but she was the only one who knew the way to Sanctuary. Benn was impatient and frustrated, but he had little choice than to follow behind. Thankfully, Poppy was a calm and steadfast horse and was not acting on the worry and panic of her rider.

Lyric continued to climb the horses methodically up the narrow zig-zag path, and Benn kept looking down the slope, monitoring the progress of the Protectors. They didn't stay long at the Kreft farm before the dusty cloud of red moved back along the road to the bridge and made directly for the Nye farm. Lyric could just make out the billowing of their red cloaks as they galloped along the road.

"We really do need to move faster." Benn sounded even more anxious. "They're nearly at your house!"

"Soon." Lyric was still calm, and still methodically working her horse along the trail, with Benn's horse matching pace directly behind.

"What do you mean soon?" Benn was almost yelling now, "At this rate we're done for. What's wrong with going faster now?"

The horses' ears twitched at the loud voice, but they remained calm.

"Too dangerous," Lyric said. Lyric knew that after yesterday's events, Benn doubted her judgement and it was clear he had little confidence in her ability to keep them safe. It would be a challenge to earn his confidence, before he did something stupid and got himself injured, or worse, killed.

Poppy suddenly stumbled and sent a small rock rolling down the hill. Benn grabbed the pommel of the saddle and held on firmly until the horse found its footing. Benn was so focussed on the Protectors he didn't realise how high they now were, how steep the slope now was, and how narrow and gravelly the trail was.

"Oh, now I get it." Benn seemed a little calmer. "If the Protectors try to gallop up here, they risk losing their footing."

Lyric smiled. "It's a goat track. Powerful horses with long legs are at a disadvantage here." Lyric turned her head to watch the Protectors leaving her parents' farm, galloping along the path the pair had taken earlier in the morning. Lyric and Benn had ascended so far that her house looked like a small toy in the distance. She hoped her parents were OK, then tried to block it out of her mind. She would not be able to think clearly if she thought something had happened to them, and right now she needed to think very clearly indeed. Up ahead, the zig–zag track seemed to disappear at a small ridge running along the side of the mountain. The pair reached the ridge just as the Protectors reached the goat trail. The track split, one track heading north toward the City, the other heading south toward the forest. Lyric turned her horse south and urged it to a trot.

"Not that way!" Benn protested. "It leads to the forest. The forest is haunted. It's dangerous!"

Lyric laughed and walked Nudge onward.

Benn soon caught up. Lyric could see the Protectors had no patience with goat trails, they were trying to cut corners and even gallop straight up the mountainside in parts. The higher they climbed, the more the horses slowed, struggling to find footing on the loose rocky slope. The long, agile legs which made the royal horses fast on flat ground were a liability on steep mountain trails. Lyric kept walking her horse toward the forest, trusting Nudge to stick to the trail, while constantly watching the Protectors. Benn's horse trotted diligently on the trail behind her. She counted eight Protectors in the posse.

In rapid succession two horses lost their footing and tumbled with their riders down the mountainside to the lower slopes. The cries of the riders and horses as they slid away seemed to increase the resolve of the remaining Protectors. Seeing their quarry, they became even more determined.

The Protectors were close enough now that Lyric could see the sweat on the flanks and shoulders of their horses. They were even foaming at the mouth from being ridden too hard for too long. She knew that horses this weary would be even less sure of foot in the rugged terrain. She felt for the horses, they were the innocent victims here. Lyric hoped that none of them would be badly injured, but she was determined to do what was necessary to keep Benn and herself safe.

"Split up!" The leader shouted to his fellows.

The remaining six riders fanned out, some still riding straight up to the ridge, the others fanning out from the track to head directly for them.

Benn was looking more nervous by the minute and Lyric's heart was racing, but she held her nerve and waited until the first Protector reached the ridge where the trail split. "Now!" Lyric shouted to Benn, and egged Nudge to a full gallop toward the forest.

"Yarrh!" Benn yelled, digging in his heels and sending Poppy into a gallop behind Lyric.

Glancing back, Lyric saw four more horses tumble down the mountainside with their riders. They were the ones that had left the trail to make straight for their quarry. Only two Protectors made it to the ridge and were galloping toward them.

The protection of the dense cedar forest was close now and Lyric galloped Nudge into its cool darkness. Benn pulled Poppy up at the forest edge.

"No Lyric. We'll die in there!" Benn yelled. "There's ghosts. There are evil spirits. No–one who has entered the forest has ever come out alive!"

"I have!" Lyric yelled back. "Often!"

Benn was caught between two terrors. Outside the forest the Protectors would be upon him in seconds and he would certainly meet a horrible and humiliating death. Inside the forest lay evil spirits and ghosts and the prospect of a different, but still horrible death.

Lyric was suddenly terrified that Benn would doubt her, that he wouldn't follow her into the forest. How could she reassure him?

"Use their fear against them!" Lyric called out, hoping the echo of her mother's words would be enough.

A brief look of realisation on Benn's face gave way to a look of gritted determination. With the protectors almost upon him, he propelled Poppy into the forest. Lyric led them at a trot a short distance into the darkness, stopping behind some bushes which shielded them from the view of the Protectors. Slowly their eyes adjusted from radiant summer morning sunlight to the dark shadows of the mighty forest. Lyric placed a finger over her lips signalling Benn to be silent as she listened carefully to the Protectors.

"Well, follow them, Swenn."

"You follow them, Natt."

"It's the haunted forest. There are evil spirits in there. And certain death."

"I have a wife and kids to protect and provide for."

Lyric smiled as she felt a sudden, strong gust of wind. It would be helpful. It rustled the bushes, and the trees swayed overhead causing flickers of light on the forest floor. Then came a resounding, unearthly wailing, seemingly from everywhere in the forest. Reminiscent of the muffled sounds of a crowd of people in the throes of an agonising death.

The sound caught Benn by surprise, he let out a shrill scream and shouted, "Ghosts!"

Lyric quickly manoeuvred Nudge close to Poppy, but before she could plant her hand firmly over Benn's mouth, he cried out again.

"We're doomed!"

Lyric's hand silenced him immediately and her apparent lack of fear seemed to subdue him further. Lyric pressed a finger to her lips to signal silence. Benn nodded assent, so she slowly removed her hand from his mouth. She placed a hand behind her ear to signal Benn to listen.

"By the Goddess! It's the ghosts!"

The Protectors backed their horses further into the sunlight.

"Can you hear him? Is he dead?"

The Protectors stood there in silence for a short while, straining to hear. The howls happened again, softer this time. They moved back a little further, clearly terrified.

"Nothing."

"The ghosts have gotten him then."

"Yeah, reckon he's dead."

"Well, there's no point us going in there to find the body. There probably isn't one and if we both die, who will tell the Queen of his horrible death?"

"Reckon you're right, Natt."

"So, we tell the Queen he was killed by ghosts in the haunted forest and the ghosts took the body too."

"Yeah. We as much as saw it with our own eyes."

"Pretty much. At least we heard his dying screams, right?"

"Right."

"Good. Let's go home then, Swenn."

Lyric could hear their footfalls as they trotted their horses back along the ridge. She turned to see Benn with his own hand over his mouth stifling a laugh.

"Gutless wonders," Benn mumbled in between chuckles.

Lyric stifled a laugh herself. She wanted to remind Benn that moments ago he was trapped at the edge of the forest by his own fear, and then screamed like a child at the first noise in the forest. Best not. She simply smiled sweetly at him and turned Nudge to walk deeper into the forest. Benn and Poppy followed.

The forest floor was carpeted in dead leaves, rotting fallen branches and the occasional fallen tree. The cedar and beech tree trunks towered to a dense canopy above, forming a huge, dark, damp cathedral. In places the canopy was broken by gaps and the bushes below took advantage of the penetrating light forming dense clumps like islands in the sunlight.

Lyric walked her horse on into the forest and Benn followed. The trail was barely discernible, but Lyric seemed set on her path. She wove Nudge deftly between the mighty trees and kept a general southerly direction. The sunlight and the mountain peak, the main navigational aids on Vulcon, were obscured so it was difficult for the inexperienced to be sure of direction. It was easy to see how someone could quickly become lost in the forest.

As they neared a clump of bushes, shining green in the shafts of sunlight penetrating the canopy, Benn attempted to make conversation.

"That was a great escape from the Protectors," he said.

He was speaking too softly for Lyric to make out what he said over the rustling of leaves underfoot, so she cupped her hand to her ear to suggest he speak louder.

Instead, Benn worked hard to urge his reluctant horse up beside Lyric. "I said, that was a great escape from the Protectors." Poppy was now brushing up against the bushes.

Lyric pulled up Nudge firmly and froze. "Stop! Don't move!"

Shocked at her reaction, Benn pulled up Poppy and sat very still. "What is it?"

Lyric slid down from the saddle and looped the reins on a nearby tree. "Don't move."

"OK, OK, I'm not moving." Benn sat patiently as Lyric walked quietly and calmly toward his horse.

Lyric took the reins near the bridle and held them firmly. "Slide down this side," she ordered, "Gently and quietly."

Benn obediently leaned backward, swung his right leg over the horse's neck and slid to the ground on Poppy's left side.

"Move away from the bushes."

Benn stepped warily back into the shadow of the forest, "What's wrong?"

Lyric tugged the reins gently to the left and calmly led Poppy to the tree where Nudge was tied. She looped the reins over another branch and walked back to Benn.

"Follow me and stay behind," Lyric said, waving Benn to follow.

Lyric crept up toward the bushes. Crouching slightly, she carefully parted the foliage to peer beyond.

"See," she said, turning to Benn.

Benn peered over her head and gasped. "By the Goddess!"

"You nearly fell into that," Lyric said, moving back and allowing the bushes to close. "On this part of the mountain there are many underground rock tunnels and caves. In places where the roof has collapsed in, it forms a gorge where the trees of the forest floor can't grow. That's why there's a hole in the canopy."

Lyric pointed up at the gap in the canopy above. "But all the light means bushes can grow around the edges of the gorge. Then trees grow up from the floor of the gorge and their canopy just looks like more bushes. It hides the gorge from sight. That's why people die in this forest, they head toward the light, walk through the bushes and fall into the gorges. We have to stick to the forest floor and stay away from the bushes."

Benn nodded. His face was still ashen. Lyric hoped he would trust her more now.

"Come on then. We still have a long way to go before we can stop for lunch."

Lyric took Nudge's reins, walked her to a fallen log she could use as a mounting block, launched herself back into the saddle, and waited patiently for Benn to do the same.

"Now, follow me. Let Poppy stick to the trail and stay away from the bushes."

"Yes Miss!" Benn replied, feigning a salute.

"I know a good spot to stop for lunch, by a creek." As Lyric walked Nudge on into the forest, she could feel Benn's gaze boring into her from behind. He seemed deep in thought, processing what had just happened and the events of the last day. He did not speak again until they stopped. Lyric figured he was pondering which questions to ask, and there would be many.

Eventually, they came upon a creek winding down the mountainside through the forest. Lyric pulled Nudge up and dismounted. She untied the reins, looped one end through a metal ring on the saddle pommel and retied them. This would prevent the reins falling to the ground where Nudge could step on them and become distressed. She led Nudge over to a small, grassy clearing and let her go.

Benn emulated but seemed confused, "Won't they run off?"

Lyric took a package and two pottery mugs from one of Poppy's saddlebags, "They are very hungry and thirsty and there is food and water here. Why would they bother running off?" She made her way to a mossy bank on the creek edge, plonked herself down and gestured for Benn to join her. "Besides, they know the routine. They've done this before."

Benn seemed reassured. He sat down on the mossy bank beside her.

Lyric unwrapped the package. Inside the outer cloth was a layer of waxed parchment containing a few flatbreads rolled around a collection of dried fruits and goat's cheese. Lyric took a flatbread, placed some fruit and cheese in the centre and deftly rolled it into a tube, open at the top and sealed at the bottom. She passed it to Benn and proceeded to make one for herself.

Benn took a bite of the roll. "This is great," he mumbled.

"Didn't your mother ever teach you not to talk while your mouth was full?" Lyric said with a grin.

Benn became quiet and introspective then took another bite.

"Sorry." Realising her carelessness, Lyric became sombre too. "That was thoughtless of me. I didn't mean—"

"It's OK."

"Do you miss her?"

"I never knew her, so I don't really miss her." Benn thought a moment. "But I miss the idea of her, especially when I see other mothers. Watching your mother, who was really good to me, makes me miss having a mother of my own." Benn took another bite, careful to resume speaking only after he fully swallowed it. "And now, thanks to you, I don't have a father anymore either."

"You're still angry with me?"

"Yes. But it seems that right now I need you to survive, so I'm going to try to be nice. At least until I figure all of this out. I think there's something very strange going on."

Lyric smiled and took another bite of her roll. It was a truce then. She could live with a truce, for now.

"So, where are we headed?" Benn asked.

"We're heading to a place I call Sanctuary," Lyric replied. "Like my father said, while you were away at the Academy, I was looking for a safe place to be myself, to practise."

"To practise what?"

"You'll see soon enough."

"Soon enough for you, or soon enough for me?"

Lyric smiled and tried to change the subject. "As everyone is too frightened to enter the forest, it seemed like a good place to start looking for a haven. I eventually found a suitable site, on the far edge of the forest, near the desert. It hasn't been found by anyone in all these years, so I figure it's still a safe place to hide you until the Queen calms down. It helps that everyone thinks you are already dead."

As Lyric completed her explanation, the leaves in the canopy above them began to rustle. A wind was starting to blow. It was quiet at first, a mere whisper, then the roaring, wailing noise grew louder. It seemed to emanate from the forest all around them.

Benn leapt to his feet and went deathly pale. "The evil spirits!" He backed slowly toward Poppy trying to look all around him for the source of the danger.

Lyric stayed calmly on the mossy bank and prepared herself another flatbread roll. "There are no evil spirits," she said before taking a bite.

"What's that noise then?" Benn scanned the forest but started to look awkward as Lyric seemed totally unafraid.

"The tunnels I showed you," Lyric said between mouthfuls. "When the wind blows along the tunnels it makes weird noises. In between the weird wind noises and people falling to their deaths in the gorges, the forest developed a reputation for evil spirits. It keeps everyone away, and has been very effective in keeping me, and my Sanctuary safe."

Benn started to relax.

"Would you like another roll?" Lyric started to prepare it.

Benn returned to the mossy bank and sat back down. He took the roll Lyric offered and ate.

As soon as Lyric finished eating, she grabbed the cups, walked over to the creek and filled them from the cool, clear stream. She held one out to Benn. "Thirsty?"

Benn cleared his current mouthful. "Thanks."

When they had both eaten and drunk their fill, Benn took the cups to the creek and washed them using water and sand, rinsed them and returned them to the saddlebag.

"I've always wondered," Benn said on his way back toward Lyric. "How is it you speak so ... properly? I mean, you speak more like someone at Court than a farmer's daughter. Excellent vowels and all."

Lyric smiled and rose from her comfortable seat on the creek bank. "My parents paid a great deal of attention to my education." She made her way quietly to her horse. "Shall we go?"

"One more question. When I arrived at your house last night, it was like your parents were expecting me. I figured you probably told them to, but this morning your mother was able to tell us the exact course the Royal Protectors would take to try and find us. It was almost as if your mother is a Seer?"

"Yes, Benn. Yes, she is." Lyric moved toward Nudge.

"But I thought there were no Seers on the island except the royal family?"

"That's what you're supposed to think. What we need everyone to think."

"So, there is something strange going on?"

Lyric smiled as she led Nudge to a nearby tree stump.

Benn returned to Poppy and removed the reins from the loop. "It's difficult to tell the time of day from inside the forest. I presume we need to reach this Sanctuary place before dark?"

"It helps," Lyric replied, launching herself back into the saddle from the stump. "Less likely to fall into a gorge that way."

Lyric turned Nudge back to the faint trail and continued plying through the forest and along the mountainside with Benn following quietly behind. Single file didn't really work well for conversation. Lyric was enjoying Benn's company, even though he was still angry with her, but she knew that she must keep her feelings in check. Once he found out how much of a freak she was, she couldn't see how he would to be involved with her and besides, she figured that Benn could never really like someone who had lied to him for most of his life, and then betrayed him.

Lyric continued to weave her horse between the trees at walking pace along a tiny trail around the mountain until flickers of light appeared between the trees ahead.

"Is that the Southern Desert?" Benn called out.

"Yes."

"Excellent. Now we can get out of this gloomy, creepy forest."

Still following the trail, Lyric turned Nudge downhill well before they reached the forest edge. She leaned back in the saddle and allowed Nudge to pick her way carefully downwards between the trees and over their mighty roots. Poppy followed.

Benn let out a cry of dismay. "No! Don't tell me we're not going to the desert."

"Of course we're not going to the desert," Lyric replied. "There are few places to hide in the desert. Especially if you want food and water and not just shelter. Dark, cool and gloomy are incredibly helpful if you are trying to hide."

Benn looked defeated. There was no countering her logic. He continued to look carefully about him as they proceeded. Lyric smiled to herself when she realised that he was trying to memorise the route. Even if he did decide to try and leave, where would he go?

Lyric was keeping a close eye on the daylight. Once the sun set, safe navigation through the forest would be pretty much impossible. Yet the horses could not be hurried at this point lest they trip and fall on the sloping, uneven ground, made even more treacherous by loose rocks and a lacework of tree roots. Lyric observed that a travelling companion, be it her father or Benn, seemed to slow the journey. She was grateful for the long summer days. It would buy them some extra time.

As the light from the desert developed a distinctly golden glow, the ground began to level out. By now Benn was becoming agitated by the fading daylight too.

"Is it much farther?" he called from behind. "I don't fancy trying to follow you through the forest in total darkness."

Lyric smiled. "We're nearly there," she called back. "It won't be total darkness."

Benn seemed reassured and fell back into silence and observation, at least until the light in the forest began to fade. "We're nearly out of daylight," he protested. "The forest all looks the same to me. How do I know you're not leading me into a trap?"

Lyric laughed. "So little faith!" she called back. "What's the matter? Are you having trouble memorising the way with the gloom and repetition of the forest? Is fading light making it even more difficult?"

Having been called out, Benn feigned a look of innocence, but his concern was understandable. As the daylight faded, the shafts of light that had broken through the canopy in places and illuminated the forest were now gone, replaced by a dim, golden glow. Even this was fading, and the forest shadows seemed darker, more ominous, and growing. As visibility reduced, the sounds of the forest became more obvious and the animals of the night began to stir. Owls were hooting and unseen critters could be heard scurrying away in the undergrowth as they passed. Gradually a tattered patchwork of silver began to appear on the forest floor as moonlight penetrated the canopy. The dark tree trunks stood as ghostly sentinels. There was just sufficient moonlight to see by.

Eventually, Lyric pulled Nudge up beside a small clump of bushes. She dismounted and wrapped the reins around the branches of an outermost bush. "We've arrived," she announced.

Benn looked around. There was a small clump of bushes below a tiny break in the canopy, and a larger clump with a distinctly empty centre that glowed eerily silver in the moonlight some distance further into the forest.

"But," Benn said, dismounting and tying Poppy beside Nudge. "There's nothing here."

"Things aren't always as they seem." Lyric smiled and immediately set to removing the saddlebags and saddle from her horse and placed them on the ground near the base of the bush.

"Especially around you," Benn said, and emulated Lyric, removing the saddlebags and saddle from his horse.

Lyric smirked. I suppose it would seem that way to Benn by now. She took two soft rope halters from her saddlebag, each with a metal ring at the base. After applying one to each horse in turn, she removed the bridles and stowed them in the saddlebags. The horses stood patiently, having gone through this routine many times before.

"I hope you know what you're doing?" Benn was watching curiously but was now becoming concerned. "I trust the horses more than I trust you right now."

"And where do you propose to keep them where they won't be seen?"

Benn looked around. There was no sign of an enclosure and a horse stepping into a clump of bushes would meet certain death. Benn shrugged. Lyric hugged each horse around the neck in turn and whispered, "Thank you" before stepping back.

"Go!" she yelled, waving her arms. The horses trotted off toward the desert, weaving between the trees and staying clear of any bushes. Lyric watched them until they disappeared from view. Benn looked to and fro from Lyric to the horses, incredulous.

"So, we'll be walking back to your parents' house then?" Benn was critical of her seeming carelessness.

"We'll get back the same way I always do," Lyric replied. "The same way I have every few weeks for the last few years."

Benn shook his head while Lyric removed the rope attached to her saddle. She headed to a small tree nearby and tied one end of the rope securely around its stubbly trunk. She moved toward Benn with the other end of the rope.

"You first," she said, handing him the rope.

"First where?"

Lyric gestured him to peer between the bushes. A hole about as wide as he was tall, wide enough for a very large person, or a couple of saddles, was gaping there. It descended into darkness.

"Down there?" Benn looked at Lyric in disbelief.

"Yes. Down there. Can you tie this around your waist, or do I have to?"

"Sure. Why go to the trouble of pushing me into a hole when I can just volunteer?"

"You can stay up here if you like. But it gets cold at night, and dark when the moon sets. I think it's going to rain a bit, so it will be wet too. I wouldn't want to try to find my way out of the forest at night either, and I'd rather you didn't fall into a hidden gorge or hole and die, especially after all the effort we've gone to try and keep you alive and safe." Lyric started toward one of the saddles. "Anyway, it's your choice." Lyric again offered the end of the rope to Benn.

Benn walked up, took the rope from her, and tied it around his waist. "I have a bad feeling about this," he mumbled as he edged toward the rim of the hole.

"Now take up the slack in the rope between you and the tree and pass the rope around your waist," she instructed.

"We were taught how to propel down a cliff at the Academy," Benn said. "I've got this. I've got it, but I don't like it." Benn walked to the edge of the hole, tested the tension on the rope and began to propel himself slowly down into the gaping, dark hole. "We were never expected to propel down into complete darkness. A Protector is supposed to be aware of their surroundings at all times."

Lyric heard his mumbling protests grow faint as he disappeared down into the darkness. "When you get to the bottom, untie the rope so I can haul it back up and send down the saddles and bags."

"OK!" Benn's voice projected up from the darkness. "If there is a bottom to this hole and it's not some sort of endless pit."

Presently the protests ceased, and the rope became slack.

"Haul it up!"

Lyric reeled in the rope, tied it around the pommel loop of the first saddle and lowered it down into the hole. The rope wiggled.

"Done."

They repeated the process until both saddles and all the saddlebags were sent into the hole. By now the moon was high and it sent a shaft of white light through the break in the canopy directly down into the hole. No light reflected back and there was nothing but darkness below. Lyric tied the end of the rope around her waist. She passed a segment of the rope around her, took up the tension, and propelled slowly down into the hole. "I'm coming down now," she called to Benn as she went.

"I can tell. You've blocked out most of the remaining light."

Lyric chuckled as she made her way down. Benn received her at the bottom, more by touch than sight, and untied the rope from her waist.

Apart from the dim moonlight coming down from above, there was only darkness around them. Lyric could barely see Benn, but she could feel the heat emanating from him, hear his breathing and smell him. It still reminded her of spices. He was standing very close. She felt her heart racing and struggled to concentrate. Benn was looking around, trying to peer into the blackness, trying to make out his surroundings. By the time he looked back toward Lyric the rope from the top of the hole was slithering down the rock wall and it landed in a pile at Lyric's feet.

Benn was aghast. "I'm assuming there's another way out of here and you haven't just entombed us both."

"Now we won't be found."

"You mean, our bodies will never be found."

Lyric just stood there smiling. She dropped the now useless end of the rope and broke into a laugh.

"You still don't trust me, do you?" Lyric was stating the obvious.

Benn shook his head. "No. I guess I don't."

"I've always made it out before," Lyric said. "Why should I trap myself in here now? It just isn't logical."

She took a flint and tinder from a small rock ledge beside them and pointed to a large pottery bowl, barely visible on the cave floor at their feet. She passed the items to Benn.

"Make yourself useful," Lyric said. "You do know how to light a fire, don't you? They did teach you that at the Academy?"

"Very funny." Benn sneered, struck the flint, and lit the tinder. It provided a tiny fragile light which illuminated a short distance around them. Lyric pointed to a torch beside them on the cave wall and proceeded to coil the rope and stow it on the rock ledge. Benn lit the torch from the tiny flame and placed it back on the wall. The torchlight was caught by a polished silver dish mounted on the wall behind it which radiated the glow in all directions, illuminating the cavern. Benn initially looked with fascination at the ingenuity of the simple device, then slowly gazed around.

"Time to throw some more light on the situation," Lyric said, extracting the flint from Benn's helpless hand lest he drop it. She adjusted the angle of the silver dish then moved forward into the cave.

Benn was rooted to the spot, dumbfounded.

CHAPTER SIX

Sanctuary

To Benn's right, water trickled down from the rock of the cavern wall along the edge of the hole through which they had just descended. Closer to the surface, clusters of small ferns poked out from crevices in wet rock. The flowing water was captured by a carved stone aqueduct which carried it along the wall to a basin at waist height, also carved from the stone wall of the cave. The overflow from the basin trickled into another aqueduct which flowed to a small pool on the cavern floor near the far wall. Benn could not make out where it flowed from there. The water seemed to disappear at the base of the wall. The far wall was solid, roughened, rock.

Along the left side of the cavern, the bases of two beds were carved out of stone, each topped with a simple mattress, stuffed solid with soft straw. Between the beds, carved into the wall was a large hearth capped by a chimney that disappeared up into the stone. Beside each bed, shelves were carved into the rock of the cavern wall, and some were fitted with wooden doors to create cupboards. On the lower open shelves were an array of dishes, cups, pots and pans, and on one of the higher shelves were bundles of rolled parchments. In the centre of the cavern was a stone monolith topped with a mighty wooden slab, complemented by hewn wooden bench seats positioned along each side.

"By the Goddess!" Benn stood motionless, astounded.

"Welcome to Sanctuary." Lyric proceeded to light an oil lamp from the torch, extinguished the torch in a bowl of sand, and watched Benn edge forward and begin to explore.

"There are no doors or windows," Benn said, his mood darkening. "Am I to be held prisoner here then? I don't fancy captivity you know."

"It does seem like there is no way out, doesn't it?" Lyric smirked.

Benn pondered a moment and his mood lightened, "But things are rarely as they seem, right?"

"If you are determined to leave, I'll return you to the surface in the morning. You are here as my friend, not my captive."

"OK, I can live with that for now. I'll reassess the situation in the morning."

Reassured, Benn moved forward and began to run his hand over the carved stone surfaces along the left wall of the cavern, so polished and reflective, with not a chisel mark to be seen, or felt. The minerals in the rock glistened and shimmered in the lamplight.

"The stone is so smooth," Benn said as he explored further. "It looks almost like sand does when it has been struck by lightning. Like it has been melted or something, like some sort of glass."

Lyric smiled to herself, opened a cupboard and removed a linen sheet, a felted wool blanket and a down–filled pillow with a soft linen tick and cover. She dropped the items onto the far bed.

"You can sleep here," Lyric said. "I presume you are able to make your own bed?"

Benn, still looking awestruck, nodded and moved slowly toward the allocated bed. He was still looking around, wide-eyed. Lyric removed a similar set of bed linen from the cupboard and proceeded to make up the other bed.

Eventually Benn formed a question, "Why two?"

"Two what?"

"Beds. Why two beds?" Benn gestured to the beds and smirked. "Were you expecting me?"

"My father would visit sometimes. He made all the wooden things." She finished making up her bed and left Benn to make up his. He seemed a little deflated.

Lyric moved to stow the saddles on a wooden rack near where they lay, and Benn came to help. Together they carried the saddlebags to the centre of the cavern and placed them on the table.

Lyric pointed to some tinder and wood by the hearth and held out the flint, "Would you like to start the fire?"

Benn set to the task and soon the fire was lit.

The fire amply illuminated the entire cavern in a flickering, golden glow, so Lyric extinguished the lamp. There was no need to burn lamp oil if it was not needed. She then proceeded to take a large pot from the shelf and began to prepare a rich vegetable and barley soup from items she and Adria had packed. Benn sat on the bench seat alternately watching Lyric work and gazing into the dancing flames. Feeling restless he moved to examine the parchments on the shelves. They contained the writings of noted authors including poets, politicians, judges, philosophers, mathematicians and geographers of Vulcon, and some from other lands. He saw such parchments in the Academy library but not anywhere else.

"I presume you are able to read." Benn gestured at the parchments.

"Yes, I've studied them all," Lyric said. "I can write too."

"I was thinking," Benn said as he continued to wander about the cave, touching surfaces as if to check they were real. "If you're mother's a Seer and the Sight is passed from mother to daughter, does that mean—"

"Yes."

Benn raised an eyebrow in sceptical surprise, then probed further. "You can read, write, engage in clever conversation and you are a Seer. Why pretend to be mute? Why did you become the Wildling? Why didn't you just do the test as a child and develop your abilities?"

"It's been a long day and I'm sure you're as tired as I am. How about we just eat and sleep and leave that long discussion until morning?"

Benn looked frustrated. Still, as soon as Lyric placed a bowl of soup on the table, he made straight for it.

They ate the soup with bread which Adria had baked for their journey, and some hard-boiled eggs. There were no leftovers.

Replete, Benn leaned back from the table. "This is truly amazing Lyric."

"It's just soup."

"Not just the soup," Benn said, "All of this!" He swept his arm around to indicate the entire cavern. "The craftsmanship is incredible."

"Thank you." Lyric blushed a little.

Benn looked confused, "You mean you created all of this?"

"Well, the cave itself was already here. I just made some modifications."

"The chisel work and polishing must have taken years." Benn looked at Lyric in wonder.

"No chisels."

"What? But how?" Benn's expression a mix of awe and confusion.

"You'll see," Lyric smiled, and moved to change the subject before Benn could voice his objections. "We'll be safe here until the Queen's wrath blows over, and by the end of the ten days, you should have all of the answers you seek. Only, you may not like them."

"I'm not worried about whether I'll like them," Benn said, gazing into the flames. "I'm only hoping I can get my head around them."

Lyric chuckled, gathered up the dishes and took them to the basin. She used soap and a pumice scourer to wash them. Benn found a towel hanging nearby, dried the items and put them away where Lyric directed. The washed items did not seem cold so, out of curiosity, Benn put his hand into the basin water.

"It's warm!" Benn announced in surprise, "How is the water warm?"

"It is heated by the mountain. I'll show you. Put your hand here."

She placed her hand flat on the rock wall behind the basin and Benn did the same.

"Amazing." Benn smiled at Lyric.

"It means the cavern never gets freezing cold," Lyric continued. "Even during the night in the middle of winter, when the puddles have frozen outside."

Lyric looked up, gazed at Benn's face, looked into his eyes and smiled. Benn's expression changed. Suddenly his brows were furrowed, and his dark eyes gazed into hers with a penetrating intensity. The pit of Lyric's stomach plummeted to the floor. Self–conscious and suddenly awkward, Lyric pulled her hand away, stepped back from the basin and gasped as quietly as she could manage. Somehow, she had forgotten to breathe. She turned away, took deep breaths to help regain her composure and walked toward her bed, hoping Benn hadn't noticed.

"I'm tired." Lyric feigned a yawn, removed her sandals and over garments and crawled under the blanket, wearing her tunic as a nightshirt. "We'll talk more in the morning." She pretended to fall rapidly to sleep while keeping at least one eye slightly open so she could watch Benn.

"Looking forward to it." He moved around the cavern and touched the walls at various points, exploring the temperature gradients and marvelling in the smooth stone surfaces, before undressing down to his tunic and going to bed himself. Safe, snug and with a full belly, he was soon asleep.

Lyric lay there awake, with her eyes closed, listening carefully to Benn's every movement and mumble until she could hear him snoring softly. She felt so awake she doubted she would get any sleep at all that night. The events of the day relentlessly swirling around in her head.

Well, at least Benn hadn't screamed and fled, she thought. That was a good sign. But where could he go even if he did? Lyric reasoned he would stay, and make the most of it, even if he didn't want to be there. Then there was the way he looked at her when they stood at the wall. That was intense. She thought it a sign he was still deeply angry with her and the rest of the time he was just being polite. After all, it was usually in one's best interest to be polite to one's prison guard and right now he probably felt like a prisoner here. Especially after she removed the rope which seemed to Benn like their only way out. Lyric couldn't imagine he would ever forgive her for years of lies and sabotaging his betrothal. She would have to try and keep her distance emotionally, so she didn't get hurt. A badly broken heart could jeopardise everything. She must concentrate on sticking to the plan.

With all these discordant thoughts swimming about in her head, and the fire in the hearth slowly dimming, Lyric somehow fell asleep.

Lyric rose early, relit the fire, and prepared a porridge of crushed barley, topped with fresh figs and goats' cheese. She was certain the aroma of breakfast woke Benn from his sound slumber. While Benn got his bearings, Lyric repositioned the silver dishes so that a shaft of sunlight from in front of the recessed wall was bounced around the cavern, illuminating it with bright morning light.

"Good morning," Benn said, dragging himself up to sit on the edge of the bed.

"Good morning." Lyric returned to tending the porridge. "Are you hungry?"

"Very." Benn deeply inhaled the aroma of porridge, "That is a very comfortable bed you have there. I slept like an owl in the day."

Lyric took two pottery bowls and a stone trivet down from the shelf near the hearth and placed them on the table. She then took up two large, thick potholders, and hauled the pot of porridge from the hearth to the trivet. Benn pulled on his sandals, quickly threw his overshirt over his crumpled tunic and perched himself on the bench seat at the table.

Lyric began to ladle porridge into the bowls. When both were full, she applied the toppings and pushed one toward Benn along with a spoon and a silver mug. She poured a white liquid from a large jug at the end of the table into each mug. He looked at Lyric quizzically, she smiled, and he took a sip.

"This is delicious!" Benn said. "Is it what I think it is?"

"Goat milk with honey," Lyric replied, sitting down to her breakfast.

"Where did you find goat milk, and honey, and fresh figs for that matter? I don't recall seeing any in the saddlebags."

"Out there," Lyric pointed toward the far wall of the cavern where a recessed central section was now clearly illuminated. "I'll show you after breakfast."

"Looking forward to it." Benn took a mouthful of porridge. "But not until I've finished off the porridge. This is much better food than we got at the Academy."

"Why thank you, kind sir," Lyric said, trying to look courteous and grand between mouthfuls of porridge. "I suppose at the Academy, sweetening foods with honey was not consistent with their aim of training tough, manly Protectors?"

"Certainly not. Sometimes it felt like a quest to see how much punishment our mouths and stomachs could take. May I?" Benn gestured toward the pot.

"Help yourself," Lyric replied. "I won't need seconds."

Benn didn't need to be told twice. He piled a generous portion of porridge into his bowl, then topped up Lyric's mug before topping up his own.

"So, Benn, now we're both rested, what shall we discuss?" Lyric asked, pausing between mouthfuls.

Benn looked contemplative for a moment, swallowed his current mouthful and said, "I'd like to know why you invaded, no, jeopardised, no, completely and utterly destroyed my betrothal to the Princess Brata."

Lyric popped another spoonful of porridge into her mouth. This was the topic she was expecting, but she sensed he wasn't done yet.

"Because if you hadn't gone out of your way to give the Princess entirely the wrong impression," Benn's voice was raised now, "I wouldn't be fleeing for my life and holed up here. I'd be resident in the Palace. I'd be living in style. I'd be betrothed to a Seer Princess, and I'd still have a father!" Benn shouted the last words while slamming his fist down on the table. His face flushed scarlet.

Lyric swallowed slowly, waiting for Benn's breathing to slow and for his face to return to a more normal colour. Of course, she expected this question, just not the degree of animosity with which it was delivered.

"Tell me Benn," she began slowly and deliberately, "Why do you think the Princess and the Queen did not foresee the disruption of the betrothal?"

"I don't know," Benn replied, frustrated. "What's that got to do with it?"

"Well, they're supposed to be Seers, aren't they? So why didn't they see it? Surely if they had seen it, the Princess wouldn't have reacted as if she was caught unawares. Indeed, she probably wouldn't have bothered to make the trip at all. Why travel all that way to be humiliated?"

"What do you mean, 'supposed' to be a Seer?" Benn was still frustrated, and he looked stymied. He shoved another spoonful of porridge and figs in his mouth. Lyric watched the expression on his face change as he mulled it over while staring at the fire in the hearth. Eventually, he turned toward Lyric.

"You seem to think you know something I don't, so I'll play along. So, why didn't the Princess foresee it?" Benn looked expectantly at Lyric.

"Because if she was a Seer, the issue was too emotionally 'close' to her, so she wouldn't have been able to discern it clearly," Lyric replied. "When Seers try to see the events in their own life, their sight is often clouded by the emotions surrounding the events. The stronger the emotional tie, the less clear the vision. It's a blind spot for Seers."

"There, see!" Benn waved his spoon about. "There's a perfectly logical reason."

"But," Lyric continued "as a Seer, she should have known that."

Benn looked perplexed again.

"So," Lyric mused, "for such an important event, the Princess should have consulted another Seer who could see the situation more clearly."

"The Queen?"

"Exactly. So, why didn't the Queen see it and warn the Princess well in advance? Instead, she let the Princess be humiliated, then retaliated with a vendetta against you as if she was caught totally off guard."

Benn stopped eating and was staring at Lyric now, "Are you trying to tell me that the Queen and the Princess are not Seers?"

"Yes." Lyric scraped the last of her porridge from her bowl and popped it into her mouth. "You've always said you wanted to be bonded to a Seer, and the Princess isn't a Seer. I tried to figure out if you were so in love with the Princess that you would have bonded with her, even if she wasn't a Seer. But at every opportunity when you could have chosen to be true to her, you chose to spend time with me. So, because she wasn't a Seer and you didn't seem to really be in love with her, I meddled. Then, when it came to the crunch, you could have sacrificed me to be with her, but you didn't. You chose to protect me, even if it meant losing the Princess forever. Did I get it wrong? Were you in love with the Princess?"

Benn stared at the fire for a while. "No, you didn't get it wrong."

"You're my friend, Benn. I didn't want to see you bonded in a loveless lie. I'm sorry I hurt you."

Benn looked disarmed by the apology, but he didn't say he forgave her. Maybe he never would. For now, he seemed more focussed on the royal family not being Seers, and the more he seemed to think about it, the more outraged he became.

"You think they've been faking it then, the royal family?" Benn was incredulous. "For all this time?"

"For three generations actually," Lyric said after swallowing the last of her drink. She gathered up her items and headed for the basin, dropping them into the ever-present water. "The Princess isn't a Seer. The Queen isn't a Seer and the Queen's mother was not a Seer."

"But why?" Benn looked curious now.

"Probably because they grew rather fond of the wealth, power and comfort and were disinclined to let it all go when the Sight was lost from their family."

"But how do they keep it a secret?" Benn asked, "Surely their Protectors know?"

"Maybe they do. I don't really know. If they do know and they were forced to choose between the royal lifestyle and disclosing the truth, which would they choose?"

"I rather hope they don't know. Keeping a secret, a lie like that is a great dishonour as a Protector. It could eat up a man's character and spirit from the inside."

Lyric had not thought of that before. She always considered the royal consorts to be either ignorant fools or foul conspirators. Now she just felt sorry for them.

"Do you want the last of this?" Lyric asked, taking up the pot on the table and pointing at the small amount of porridge left.

"Absolutely!" Benn was distracted and waved his spoon. "It's too delicious to waste."

Lyric scraped the remaining porridge into Benn's bowl, then placed the pot in the basin and began scrubbing.

Benn reverted to contemplation. "But if what you say is true," he said, then paused as to make sure he had it straight in his head, "it means, the only Seers left on Vulcon are your mother and yourself."

"And my Aunt Tyla."

Benn's brows furrowed as he considered this further. "So, if the prophesied catastrophe occurs, then the Great Seer would have to come from your family, or we would all be doomed." Disturbed by this information, Benn downed the last of his porridge in silence, proceeded to drink the remaining contents of the jug, and presented the items to Lyric at the basin. As he approached his mood seemed to lighten, as if he was trying to see things, and her, differently. "Well, with a bit of luck the prophecy is false, or the catastrophe won't happen in our lifetime, so there's no need to worry is there?"

"Perhaps not."

"After all, the prophecy didn't specify a date, did it?"

"No, I guess it didn't," Lyric replied. She didn't want to pursue this topic any further just now. There would be plenty of time.

"My turn to scrub," Benn said, playfully nudging Lyric to one side. "There's a towel there. Your turn to dry. Besides, you're the one who knows where all of this goes."

Lyric smiled at his chivalry, dried her hands on the towel and proceeded to dry the items emerging from the basin.

"I wish I had brought along a comb and a razor," Benn said. "I'm probably going to look like a bit of a Wildling myself after a couple of days."

Lyric went to a saddlebag, rummaged deep inside it, and pulled out a tied leather roll. "Father thought you might need this." She put the roll on the table. "I think it contains everything you need to keep yourself looking civilised." Lyric smirked in Benn's direction. "Once we've finished up here, I'll step outside while you get yourself sorted."

"Remind me to thank your father when we get back," Benn said, relieved.

"Would you mind if I asked you a hypothetical question?" Lyric kept drying items, trying to act nonchalant.

"It seems only fair, since I've been asking most of the questions so far."

"As long as I've known you, you've talked about being bonded to a Seer. It is clearly an attractive option when it comes with a Palace lifestyle. But what if it didn't? So, hypothetically, if being bonded to a Seer meant a life of secrecy and seclusion and a Palace lifestyle meant not being bonded to a Seer. Which would you choose?"

Benn paused scrubbing and pondered the question. "Well," he finally said, "I'd choose the third option."

"Third option?"

"Yeah, the third option."

Lyric waited patiently for Benn to continue.

"I'd choose to be bonded to someone I felt compelled to protect and provide for, whether they were a Seer, or at Court, or neither."

"Wow," was all Lyric could manage in response. A new respect for Benn rushed through her like an ocean wave. Away from the influence of his father, Benn was indeed a noble man.

Neither spoke again until the last item was scrubbed, dried and stowed.

"Are we cooped up in this hole for the next ten days?" Benn seemed uncomfortable with confinement.

"Not at all. When you're done in here, I'd like to show you something."

"Where the figs and goat milk and honey came from?" Benn winked at her.

"Where the figs and goat milk and honey came from." Lyric smiled back.

Benn watched Lyric take up two woven baskets from the end of the cavern and step into the archway at the recessed wall where she was immediately illuminated by sunlight. She turned back to smile mischievously toward him.

"Well, come on then." Lyric stepped sideways and disappeared from view.

Benn stepped into the archway to discover the recessed wall was further back than it seemed, with a large opening to sunlight on each side. Outside the left opening, Lyric was standing on a ledge, beckoning him to join her.

As Benn walked cautiously toward Lyric, he saw the ledge was about halfway up a ragged cliff-face which formed one side of a wide, deep gorge. Around the top of the gorge he could see a fringe of bushes, and behind them the tops of the forest trees. Down in the gorge were rocks and ledges and small clearings punctuated with trees, bushes and a range of plants. At the bottom of the gorge was a clear stream which bubbled over rocks and was interrupted by inviting pools. Benn caught sight of some rabbits grazing warily in a small clearing and he thought he saw some chickens beneath some shrubs on the far side. At the mountain end of the gorge, the origin of the stream was hidden by a large fig tree adorned with purple fruit. A snow-white goat with a kid at foot was busy browsing on some bushes nearby. At the ocean-end of the gorge the stream fed into a pool so large it looked like a small lake. The water was rendered dark by the gloom of the massive cavern behind it. Everywhere birds flitted between the trees and there were flowers and butterflies and a fish jumped in one of the pools.

Lyric just stood there a while, watching Benn's face as he took it all in. Eventually he tore his eyes away from the scene before him and looked at Lyric.

"This is— amazing!" Benn said in wonder.

"Glad you like it," Lyric said. "Would you like to explore?"

"Oh, yeah!"

"Follow me then," Lyric said, "and be careful to stick to the path."

Benn couldn't actually see a path, but he was slowly learning to trust Lyric.

Along the ledge, a large bush jutted out over the edge, its branches seemingly suspended in mid–air. Lyric edged between the bush and the cliff wall. Benn followed and discovered the bush hid a jagged path which zig–zagged down the face of the gorge.

Part way down, Lyric paused and pointed, "Figs."

Benn saw she was pointing to the tree at the mountain end of the gorge. "Figs," was all he could manage to say in reply.

When they reached the bottom of the gorge, Lyric handed Benn one of the baskets. "We need to gather some food."

"OK," Benn said. "Where do we start?"

"Let's start with some figs," Lyric said, as they picked their way over rocks and grassy embankments toward the fig tree. As they approached, Benn could see that a dark and mighty cavern loomed behind the tree. The creek seemed to appear from the base of the tree, but Benn figured it probably came from inside the cave.

Lyric acted as a tour guide as they made their way toward the tree, giving a running commentary on the produce to be had. "Up there is an olive tree, and under that bush there are usually some hen eggs. That clump of green at the base of the rock is spinach and over there are some onions."

The more he followed Lyric's commentary the more Benn realised this gorge was not a wild place at all. The natural vegetation was interplanted with fruit and vegetables, herbs and flowers. This was a carefully tended food garden.

"You planted all these?" Benn asked.

"Yes. I was spending so much time here, I figured I ought to plant some provisions." Lyric scrambled over a large flat rock. "Besides, it would also function as a secret reserve of seed material if Vulcon's farms were ever in jeopardy."

Benn couldn't imagine all of Vulcon's farms being in jeopardy to the point where such a reserve would be required, so he just focussed on the skill and diligence with which this garden was created. "Impressive," was all he could muster.

When they arrived at the fig tree, Benn could see it was laden with ripe fruit. Lyric plucked a large, dark one and bit into the soft, sweet flesh, smiling with delight. Benn looked past her into the eerie dark of the cave.

"What's that?" Benn asked, gesturing at the darkness.

Lyric cleared her mouth, "Remember I told you there are large tube–like caves running under the mountainside?"

"Yes."

"Well, this is one of the largest ones. The roof of a large section of the tube has collapsed in, forming this gorge. This cave is the part of the tube which still extends up into the mountain. At the other end of the gorge is the part of the tube which goes down toward the sea."

"What's in there?" Benn edged toward the cave, still curious.

"Bats mostly." Lyric plucked another fig.

Benn reconsidered and moved back toward the tree, "I don't much like bats."

Lyric giggled. "Most people don't."

She now began picking figs in earnest and placing them gently in her basket. "Fancy some figs for lunch?"

"Actually," Benn said, "I really love figs." He began loading figs into his basket too.

"We can get some eggs and spinach on the way back to the cavern."

Having picked all the figs she needed, Lyric headed back toward the cavern and Benn followed, munching on one last fig.

"They taught you a lot about Vulcon's laws at the Academy didn't they?" Lyric asked, strolling along beside the creek.

"They sure did. Hours and hours of lessons on Vulcon's laws."

"So, what can you tell me about the laws pertaining to public use of the city plaza?"

"Why do you want to know that?" Benn was puzzled. This didn't seem to be related to anything he felt was important.

"Just do," Lyric said as if it was no big deal beyond idle curiosity.

"OK. As you know, the city plaza is open to use by all citizens. However, the podium at the centre is restricted for use of the royal family and their delegates only."

"Delegates?" Lyric queried.

"Well, the Queen may delegate someone, like a judge or a Royal Protector to make proclamations from the podium on her behalf." Benn was pleased she was paying attention. He enjoyed instructing Lyric in things she did not seem to already know. "There are always at least two Royal Protectors stationed at the podium to ensure it is not trespassed. Except on market days when the number of Protectors is increased to four."

"Why?" Lyric stepped from one grassy embankment to another as she worked her way downstream.

"Because with the crowds about on market days, it is more likely someone will try to get onto the podium. In the morning it is usually children trying to play, and in the evening, it is often citizens who have consumed too much ale."

"What does the law say happens to those who trespass on the podium?" Lyric jumped up onto a rock and paused there looking at Benn.

"First they are reminded it is illegal to be on the podium and they are instructed to quit it immediately."

"If they still don't go?"

"Then they are forcibly removed by the Royal Protectors and taken before a judge."

"Who guards the podium while the offender is being taken before a judge?"

"On market day, the remaining two Protectors guard the podium until their comrades return. On other days, the podium is left unattended until the offender has been delivered to the judge and the Protectors return to their post."

"What penalty is imposed by the judges?"

"It is considered a moderate offence, so the judge sentences them to a day's hard labour in the Palace kitchen or laundry if they are women. Scrubbing floors, emptying pans and the like. If they are men, it's off to work on the Queen's farms or one of the Queen's construction projects for a couple of days."

"How quickly is the sentence implemented?"

"The judges are very efficient. The offender is usually sentenced and hauled off to commence labour within the hour," Benn said, moving to scramble onto the large rock on which Lyric was perched. "Why the interest? I mean, given our status in the community, it's not like either of us would be foolish enough to trespass the podium if we were ever in the City again?"

"Just curious," Lyric said and leapt down onto the next embankment, leaving Benn alone and confused on the rock.

After exploring, gathering and lunching, Lyric produced two fishing poles and they spent the afternoon fishing in the pools. Once a couple of fish were caught, they headed back to the cavern. The tall walls of the gorge meant evening darkness set in early, and sunrise came late. The night air was crisp, but between the hearth and the heat emanating from the rocks, the cavern was cosy. Benn decided that spending ten days here with Lyric would be no chore at all.

"You know, Lyric," Benn said while gazing into the fire, his belly full after downing the last mouthful of the evening meal, "this place has everything we need. We could stay here forever, just the two of us. We wouldn't have to worry about deceitful Queens and Princesses or Royal Protectors or pushy parents ever again." He gently placed his large, capable, hand over Lyric's smaller one. The warmth of her skin stirred something inside him. He wanted to hold her hand in his. He wanted to hold her in his arms. He wanted to....

Lyric's cheeks flushed and she looked suddenly uncomfortable. She pulled her hand away, swivelled away from Benn and got up to attend to cleaning. "We're due back at my parent's house in nine days."

Benn felt cut to the core. Two weeks ago, he could have had any woman on the island, even the Princess Brata herself and now the one woman he was beginning to see he could spend the rest of his life with clearly wasn't interested in being anything more than just friends. "I see," he said and began to gather up the dishes from the table.

The conversation was strained that evening. When they finally retired for the night, Lyric seemed to fall promptly to sleep. Benn lay there wrestling with his thoughts. Should he compromise his one remaining friendship to try and force something more? He knew he should be concentrating on other important questions, something about Lyric's mother being a Seer, but all he could think about was Lyric and why she rejected his touch.

By the time Lyric awoke, Benn already had a pot of porridge heating over the flames. Lyric dressed quickly and began to prepare fruit to accompany the porridge.

They ate, cleaned up, gathered up the baskets and set out into the gorge on another glorious sunny day. The cavern was cosy, but they were keen to be outdoors. Lyric observed that Benn still hadn't shaved, leaving a distinct dark shadow on his face. This time they explored downstream, toward the cavern at the lower end of the gorge, gathering fruit and vegetables as they went.

After loading some ripe pears into his basket, Benn turned toward Lyric. "I'd like to know why there are no other Seer families left on Vulcon. Why is it that all the children tested at the commencement of school are not Seers anymore?"

"Have you heard of the Fading Ill?"

"Yes. We were taught at the Academy that it was an illness afflicting young children, about school age. They became unwell, progressively worsened, fading away until they died. Apparently, it is much less common now than it once was. Only one or two children every few years are afflicted. I think the last one was a couple of years ago, Tegan someone."

"Tegan Felder."

"But what's that got to do with it?"

"Fading Ill is not a sickness." Lyric looked at Benn with a sad seriousness. "It is a poisoning."

Benn looked deep in thought as he added another couple of pears to his basket, then he froze, the colour drained from his face and he stared at Lyric. "You mean?"

Lyric nodded. "Yes."

"Are you saying the children are being poisoned?" Benn was aghast.

"That's exactly what I'm saying. I saw the poisoning of Tegan Felder myself. If they pass the test, they are given cake with poison in it."

"How could you have seen it yourself? The testing is done in the hall of the Seers Academy and no-one but the royal family and the child being tested are allowed in."

"Yes." Lyric stopped putting fruit in her basket and turned to face Benn. "I crept in after dark and remained concealed there for the day. There are some old parapets in there, I hid among the baskets."

Benn looked like he was trying to fathom how she could possibly have crossed the City, gotten into the hall, accessed the parapets and remained concealed for an entire day.

Lyric continued, relentless. "If children are found to be Seers on testing at the beginning of school, they are given poison. It acts slowly, killing them over a week or so. That's why there are fewer cases each year."

"But that's— that's— murder!" Benn was outraged.

"Yes, and it gets worse."

"How could it get worse?"

"A month or so later, the Queen kills the mother to make sure no more Seers are born in that family and makes it look like an accident. I saw Tegan's mother killed. They hit her on the head, then tipped a cartful of pomegranates onto her."

"But why hasn't anyone done anything about it?" Benn asked.

"A few have discovered the secret and tried to protest or take action. But they are no longer alive. The royal family are very protective, very efficient, and very thorough."

With adequate fruit, Lyric moved on toward the tunnel opening. Benn followed. He took a pear from his basket with the intention of eating it, but he seemed to suddenly lose his appetite and he dropped it back into the basket.

"Those poor children. Those poor families," Benn said as they arrived at the lower end of the gorge. "Why didn't you tell me about this sooner? Why didn't you tell me the truth Lyric? I was your best friend, or at least I thought I was."

"Think about it, Benn," Lyric said. "What would the Queen have done to me if she knew that I knew she was poisoning the Seer children of Vulcon?"

"Executed you, I suppose."

"And what would she have done to you if she thought I had told you the truth?"

"Executed me too, no doubt." Benn looked sombre. "So, you were safe as long as the Queen thought you were a cretin?"

"Yes, and I knew you would be safe as long as you kept the secret of my not being mute and didn't know enough to get you into any further trouble."

"Besides, I'd like to think we were still best friends." Lyric smiled and threw a pear at him. "I'd hate to be telling all this to just anybody."

Benn caught the pear and smiled. "Yeah. I reckon we still are." Then he took a loud crunching bite.

Lyric pointed at the water at the end of the gorge. Benn looked over her shoulder to see a large pool of teal-coloured water partly shaded by a weeping willow tree.

"I fancy a swim," Lyric said, making for the water's edge. She dropped her basket on the embankment and shed her over-clothes down to her tunic, then walked slowly into the water. It felt cool around her feet and ankles. She paused to let her skin adjust to the temperature. "Coming?" Lyric dove down deep beneath the surface, emerging at the opposite end of the pool. Refreshed, Lyric splashed slowly about, shedding the sweat and grime of the last couple of days.

Benn put down his basket, undressed down to his tunic and propelled himself into the water. He swam toward Lyric and hovered in the water nearby. Suddenly, for no reason Lyric could fathom, Benn splashed water at her face. Lyric splashed back, and a splashing duel ensued. It was cathartic. As they splashed, they came closer and closer together until finally they were mere inches apart. Lyric could see Benn's handsome face, glistening with water droplets in the sunlight, gazing at her. Lyric thought his expression strange, as if he were looking at a feast and contemplating where to begin. She looked past the stubble on his chin, took in his aquiline nose and looked deep into his dark brown eyes. They drilled down to her very soul. She felt like a hot ember not being extinguished by the cool water in which she was immersed. Benn was so close she could almost feel his breath on her face. She wanted to move in even closer, but so much depended on her not losing control.

"You're beautiful," Benn whispered. "Did you know?"

Lyric put her hands on his muscular shoulders, smiled sweetly, pushed him under the water and swam away. "You need to shave!" she called behind her when he resurfaced. Lyric made for the shore and Benn followed.

They gathered their baskets and clothes and walked, bedraggled back to the cavern. By the time they reached it, they were nearly dry. Lyric pointed at a snare in a nook of the cavern.

"Do you think you could catch us a rabbit for supper?" Lyric asked as she put her gear down on the table. "I need to bake us some bread, we've run out."

"Sure." Benn dressed himself, took up the snare and headed back out into the sunlight.

After he left, Lyric leaned against the table and breathed deeply. It was often difficult to breathe with Benn so close by. He was all she seemed to think about since the moment he arrived at the Nye farm. It made her stomach churn. This would not do. She pulled herself together. This was not the time to let her emotions get the better of her. Even if Benn forgave her for meddling in his life, he would not want to be intimately associated with a freak. Worse, when Benn knew the truth, he could end up so frightened he may even flee, and she would be too gutted to do what she needed to do. No, this was no time to be entertaining sentiment, or whatever that strange, churning feeling was. Lyric set about getting dressed into dry clothes and making the bread.

By the time Benn returned with a nice big rabbit dangling lifeless from one hand, the bread was ready. Benn set about skinning and preparing the carcass.

"You're very well house trained for a man," Lyric said, setting to work preparing the vegetables.

"Why thank you." Benn smiled back. "On survival camps we were taught to hunt, and cook, and clean our dishes. We even did our own laundry at the Academy. I guess it prepared me well for this situation."

"Indeed, it did."

Benn stopped working on the rabbit for a moment and looked at Lyric. "I have another question," he began. "If the Queen has been killing off all the young Seers, how is it no–one seems to have noticed that only the young Seers were dying?" He watched Lyric while she considered her response.

"According to my Grandmother, when the current Queen's mother was tested as a child, by the Queen of the day and the Head Seer of the Seer Academy, she did not pass the test as a Seer. When that Queen discovered her daughter did not have the Sight, she swore the Head Seer to secrecy and suggested the child should be retested some months later in case she was late in developing her gift. Before the agreed test date, the Head Seer mysteriously died in an accident. The Queen persuaded the new Head Seer that her predecessor had simply delayed announcing the happy news, so they made the announcement together."

"When it became clear the Queen would have no more daughters, there was soon a terrible outbreak of Fading Ill. Most of the victims were Seer children but a few children without the Sight died too, to throw the physicians off the trail. Over the coming years, the Seers of Vulcon started to meet untimely deaths. Accidents, drownings, fevers and many other causes, carefully designed to leave no trail to the Queen. After the last known Seer was dead, a few of the Royal Protectors died mysteriously too."

"So, you're saying the Queen of the day trained some Royal Protectors as clever assassins, used them to kill off Seers, then killed them so there would be no witnesses to the atrocity?" Benn was incredulous. "How did your family survive?"

"Some of the most powerful Seers on Vulcon saw this coming. By the time the deaths began, they had already purchased passage on Phoenician trading vessels and fled to other lands. My great grandmother foresaw this calamity, but the family could not raise the funds for passage off the island. So, my infant grandmother was instructed never to speak, to feign being mute and dumb from her fifth year, just as I was. The Queen saw no point in testing a cretin child who would not be able to complete the test."

"So, your grandmother was never tested?"

"Never tested, and never spoke where she could be seen or heard by other than her immediate family."

"For her entire life?"

Lyric nodded. "The Queen concluded the child was too stupid to bother killing and left the family in peace. Once grown, my grandmother fell in love with a recently graduated Protector of the Academy. The family took him aside and explained the situation. He left the royal household, bonded with my grandmother and became a farmer. They produced two daughters and my great grandmother foresaw that the cretin camouflage would not work the second time. Leaving the farm in the care of a relative, the young family left on a Phoenician trade ship under the pretence of seeking out new crops and livestock. They worked on farms in and around the Phoenician homeland until the eldest daughter, Tyla, came of age. Taking the money that they had saved, they bought cashmere goats from further east and an assortment of grains and seeds and journeyed back to Vulcon to take over the family farm."

"Why didn't the Queen kill the daughters on their return?"

"She got careless I suppose. The old Queen assumed all the Seers on Vulcon were dead, and as grown children of a cretin mother they mustn't have seemed a risk. My mother fell in love with a young man from a noble family who, like my grandfather, graduated first in his year at the Academy. When the situation was explained to him, they bonded and took up residence on the family farm, eventually taking it over when my grandparents became too frail to continue. His father thought the pairing a disgrace and disowned my father. Although my mother was careful to conceal her abilities, the farm grew and grew as my father seemed to have an uncanny knack of knowing when seasons would be good, when rain would fall, and when adjacent land was coming up for sale."

"Your mother's ability gave them an edge?"

"Yes. My grandmother died when I was in my fourteenth year. I still miss her." Lyric paused a moment, wistful. "When I was in my fifth year, the mute cretin camouflage was instigated again. By then the current Queen just assumed the defect ran in the family and I was overlooked for testing."

Seeming satisfied with the explanation for now, Benn skewered the prepared rabbit and positioned it over the fire. Lyric placed a pot of vegetables to simmer at the side.

"OK," Benn said. "There are still some things that bother me about the story."

"Fire away then," Lyric said, planting herself on her bed where she could oversee the food.

Benn took a seat on his bed, opposite her.

"Well, as you know, we were taught about the Great Prophecy at the Academy."

Lyric sensed what was coming. Benn was clever. She knew it wouldn't take him long to start putting the pieces together. She nodded acknowledgement and Benn took it as leave to continue.

"The first part of the prophecy refers to a 'time of rule by deception'. If the royal family pretending to be Seers so they can keep the throne isn't rule by deception, I don't know what is." Benn paused and looked toward Lyric as if to gauge her reaction.

"Agreed," Lyric said, "it certainly qualifies as rule by deception."

Validated, Benn continued. "The prophecy also refers to 'murder of the children of Vulcon'. I'd say poisoning any child who has the Sight qualifies. What do you think?"

"Yes," Lyric replied.

"Even more disturbing than the deception and the murder of the children," Benn said, "is the possibility that the 'Horrific Catastrophe' may therefore occur within our lifetime, and a

'Great Seer' has not emerged. Indeed, it may be possible the Great Seer was poisoned in childhood and will never be here to save the people of Vulcon from catastrophe."

Lyric just nodded slowly and waited. She watched Benn's expression change from a contemplative frown to stunned realisation.

"Hold on. You say the Sight is passed down the female line, right?"

"Right."

"And your mother is a Seer from a long line of Seers?"

"Yes, and my aunt too."

"And you said you were one too."

"Yes, that's right." Lyric just smiled, watching his expression change as he processed the information.

"That means your mother or your aunt could be the Great Seer?"

"Maybe, Benn."

Benn looked incredulous. "I'm sorry, but this is a bit much to process on an empty stomach."

Lyric served the rabbit and vegetables on large platters. They ate in silence, Benn frowning and darting occasional glances at Lyric and Lyric watching Benn closely, waiting for him to pull away, to even attempt to flee.

By the time the rabbit was reduced to a pile of clean bones and his belly was full, Benn looked deadly serious and began to fire more questions.

"So, as a Seer, you came to the graduation ceremony because you could see it would be safe?"

"I came to the graduation ceremony because I really wanted to be there on a day that was so important to you, and because Aunt Tyla saw it would be safe."

"Your aunt?" Benn asked, then realised, "That's right. You were saying a Seer can't see clearly things that are too emotionally close. So, your aunt could see the day clearly, but you were being blinded by feelings?"

"That's right," Lyric confirmed, hoping she wasn't disclosing too much.

Benn's expression became suddenly resolute. "That's a wondrous tale Lyric," he said. "But it is treason. How do I know it isn't just a fiction created by you to win me over?"

"What?" Lyric was exasperated. She took a few deep breaths, giving herself time to think this through. Why shouldn't he be sceptical? After all, at the beginning she wasn't really expecting him to believe any of it. She should be happy he followed the story thus far.

"What proof do you have that any of this is true?" Benn queried. "I mean, all the details and connections and intrigues. They could just be coincidences, cleverly woven into a convincing tale."

"You want proof?" Lyric said as she began to gather up dishes and deposit them in the basin. "Well, then you shall have it. Tomorrow."

"Tomorrow?" Benn almost shouted. "Tomorrow?"

"Yes." Lyric kept calm and self–controlled. "You will have to wait until tomorrow. Then you shall have all the proof you require."

"OK," Benn said, "I shall somehow wait until tomorrow."

"Excellent." Lyric smiled at him. "While you are waiting, would you mind helping with the dishes?"

"Very well." Benn dragged himself to the task. "But if you can't provide proof tomorrow, I'm out of here and you can do you own dishes."

"Agreed." Lyric said. "About tomorrow. There's going to be a lot of rain overnight and the creek may become a bit treacherous. Also, the ground will shake in the morning and the walls of the gorge can be a bit unstable. I would suggest that we remain in the cavern until the shaking has finished."

CHAPTER SEVEN

The Power and the Plan

Benn woke early on the third day, too restless to sleep. So many thoughts swimming in his head. Were the Queen and Princess really not Seers? Were Lyric, her mother and aunt really Seers? Or was this a ruse, perpetrated by Lyric's family every generation to secure the top graduate of the Academy as a bonded partner? After all, Lyric's whole life was a lie. She was neither mute nor stupid, but she and her family kept up the deception for years. Had he been robbed of his rightful place as a Royal Protector and consort by a well-planned deception? In the end, Benn concluded there was no proof to support Lyric's story. No real evidence she or her family were Seers. The predictions made by Adria could just as easily have been arrived at by logic alone, given the circumstances.

Lyric said he would have his proof today. Benn already expected her to postpone till tomorrow, then the next day, and so on until he was too entangled to escape. Escape he must. He dressed quickly and quietly, grabbed a basket from near the cavern entrance and made his way down into the gorge. The earth was damp and there were water droplets on the leaves from rain overnight. Water was dripping from cracks in the walls of the gorge and the air was cool and crisp. Lyric predicted the rain, but it rained often on Vulcon and the creek was just as it was the day before. Benn stepped on protruding rocks to access the far side of the creek, as they did on each of the days before. He gathered some eggs, still warm from the hens, and made for a clump of spinach at the base of the far cliff. He would need a hearty breakfast for he had no idea where or when his next meal would come.

Frustrated, angry and focussed on his task, Benn did not see Lyric emerge from the cavern.

"Benn!"

Benn looked up and forced a smile. "Good morning Lyric," he called back, giving Lyric a casual wave. "I thought we could have spinach omelette for breakfast." He would try to play nice for a little while longer. He needed Lyric's help to exit this trap.

Lyric raced down the path to the floor of the gorge with the speed and surety of a mountain goat.

"It rained overnight, like you said," Benn called out. "But that could have been coincidence, so it hardly constitutes proof. You were wrong about the creek. It's flowing just the same as yesterday. So, after breakfast, if you don't mind, you can show me the way out of here."

Lyric was now standing on a large rock some distance back from the edge of the creek.

"Come over here, fast!" she shouted.

Benn decided her frantic tone and the look of worry on her face were all part of her elaborate ruse. "No Lyric," he called back. "I'm not going to be at your beck and call anymore. The creek is fine, the sky is clearing, and I'm done with being drawn into your elaborate stories."

"The rain that fell on the mountain last night will be coming through the tunnels any time now. Once it arrives, there'll be no way to cross the creek until at least tomorrow."

"Yeah right." Benn sneered then waved her off and resumed harvesting spinach.

It began quietly, the noise. So quietly Benn barely noticed it. It wasn't the wailing of the wind which Benn was now accustomed to, this was a dull roar, getting louder by the minute. Benn stood up and looked about, trying to make out the source of the sound and finally fixed his gaze on the cavern at the mountain end of the gorge. He looked toward Lyric. The fear in his eyes matched the sinking feeling in the pit of his stomach, as a wall of water, taller than a man, gushed forth from the cavern and raced down the creek to the gaping hole at the lower end of the gorge waiting to receive it. All the rocks and bushes that lined the edge of the creek bed, and the rocks he had used as stepping–stones to cross the creek were all submerged under a brown, foaming torrent. Benn stared at Lyric, aghast.

Lyric stood motionless on top of the rock, still well clear of the water's edge. She didn't look afraid, she no longer looked worried, she just gazed past Benn as if looking for something on the cliff wall. Benn saw her say something, but he could not hear over the roar of the torrent. She moved her gaze to Benn and her expression became focussed and calm.

"Move away from the cliff!" she yelled, but the roar of the flooded creek drowned out even a shout.

"What?" Benn called back, cupping his hand to his ear to indicate he could not hear her.

Lyric gestured with her arm that he should come toward her. Benn pointed at the raging creek and shook his head. He thought she mouthed the word 'Damn'. Then the earth began to shake.

All along the gorge, small rocks and soil became dislodged from the walls and tumbled to the earth below. The rock overhang at the top of the cliff above where Benn stood worked its way loose and a huge slab, the size of a farm wagon, plummeted toward him. Benn looked up just in time to see the mighty rock almost upon him. His face terror–stricken, he dropped to his knees and in a futile gesture raised a forearm over his head and closed his eyes tight, bracing for the end.

The end didn't come. When Benn finally opened his eyes, the rock was hovering only a span above his arm. The earth was still shaking, and a multitude of small rocks and gravel were falling from where the rock broke free. The slab of rock, like a mighty black umbrella, was deflecting the debris around Benn. The raging creek roared, the earth still shook and on the other side of the creek Lyric stood calm, motionless, her attention focussed on the rock. Benn stared at her in disbelief and remained frozen there until the shaking of the earth subsided and the debris stopped cascading down. All that remained was the roar of the creek and the rock still hovering unwavering above him.

"By the Goddess!" he said as he started to regain his senses. His hands still shaking, he raised one arm and touched the rock. It felt solid and fixed in place.

Before Benn could calm himself further, or even slide out from beneath it, the massive rock began to move, sideways. It floated through the air toward the creek, just downstream of where Lyric stood, still fixated on it. It reached a point where there were two untidy piles of rocks, one on each side of the creek and both above the level of the flood water. The slab rotated in mid–air, its ends now positioned above the piles and hovered there. A line of bright white light appeared under one end of the rock and disappeared into the mass of stone leaving a small plume of smoke. Moments later a section of rock fell away, bounced on the pile and landed on the embankment nearby. The process repeated at the other end of the rock and a smaller piece fell away, landing at the water's edge. The cavities that remained seemed to fit the boulders at the top of the piles exactly and the huge slab floated gently down into place upon them, forming a rough stone bridge over the raging torrent.

Lyric relaxed her stance and shifted her focus away from the rock. She clambered down from her vantage point and scaled the pile to sit at one end of the new bridge, watching the water pass below. She seemed to be waiting.

Still stunned, Benn eventually pulled himself to his feet and made his way to the bridge, his arms and legs still quivering. He went to the piece of rock fallen at the water's edge and moved to pick it up.

"Careful!"

Closer now, he could hear her above the noise. He pulled his hand away.

"It might still be hot," Lyric said with a cautious smile.

Benn reached down, slower now, held his hand close to the rock and felt the heat it was still giving off. He kicked it gently into the water where it hissed, cracked and split in two. He gathered up one piece and examined it carefully. On one side the surface was rough and broken and on the other, it was smooth, polished and reflective. He dropped the stone and scrambled up to sit at the other end of the stone bridge from Lyric. They were close enough to converse over the flooded creek, but he felt more comfortable keeping a safe distance.

"Is that sufficient proof for you?" Lyric asked with a touch of sarcasm.

"Let me see," Benn said. "Rain overnight — I'd say that's a yes. Flooded creek — another yes. Shaking of the earth — yes again. But you forgot something."

"That I like to play with rocks?" Lyric picked up a loose stone from on top of the slab and casually tossed it into the torrent.

"No, I mean yes." Benn floundered. "I mean yes you clearly like to play with rocks, but you forgot to predict your best friend would be so stupid, foolish and arrogant."

Lyric chuckled. "That's a blind spot for me, remember?"

"Oh yeah. I forgot."

They sat there quietly for a short while, gathering their thoughts and watching the water flow beneath them.

"Really Lyric," Benn finally said, interrupting the silence. "You should seriously consider upgrading to a new best friend. You deserve better."

"I'll stick with this one I think."

"But why?"

"Well," Lyric replied. "He's a good cook, he's good at doing dishes, not a bad hunter, good sense of humour, capable warrior, and he has the endearing habit of repeatedly trying to save my life."

"You forgot tall, strong and handsome," Benn added, managing a smile now.

"I omitted modest on purpose." Lyric laughed and threw a small pebble at him. Benn caught it, smiled and threw it into the creek.

"Seriously though," Benn said after a moment's contemplation. "Thanks for saving my life — twice."

"Three times actually."

"Three? I only count two."

"Well," Lyric elaborated. "Once here today."

"Yes. Thank you."

"Second was getting you away from the Queen to Sanctuary."

"Yes, thank you."

Lyric nodded acknowledgement, "Third was the flood last Spring."

Benn stared at her, quizzical.

"Don't you remember how that tree branch came up just in front of you, and how you and the donkey just happened to float to the shore?" Lyric reminded him.

Benn considered it a moment. "That was you?"

"Yes, that was me," Lyric replied. "It's not easy trying to save someone's life without them knowing you're saving their life. Trying to stop your head from being smashed in by floating debris was no mean feat either. That was powerful floodwater you know."

"I know," Benn said, "I was in it."

"Quite a challenging task actually," Lyric mused, "keeping you above the floodwater and saving the donkey at the same time. I'd never tried focussing on two things at once before. I was impressed the donkey made it."

Benn seemed disturbe. "Then, after you saved my life and the donkey, my father treated you like an animal."

"To be expected when you're the Wildling," Lyric said, trying to keep the mood light.

"Well, I'm ashamed for him," Benn said, "I'd like to apologise on his behalf."

"No need. After all, he's still not sorry."

"Then let me at least say thank you for saving my life." Benn was earnest and looking directly at Lyric.

"You are most welcome." Lyric caught his eye and smiled.

"Well, you did a great job. I would never have known," Benn said. "And thank you again — for all three."

"You're welcome."

"All this time I think I'm protecting you," Benn reflected. "When all along—"

"We're protecting each other," Lyric interjected and flashed him a grin. "Which is why we make such good best friends."

"Indeed, you seem to be making a habit of saving my life. I hope I can do the same for you someday."

"I'm counting on it," Lyric whispered ever so quietly, her voice drowned out by the roaring water.

Benn considered all this and chose his words carefully, "Seers see. That was much more than seeing."

Lyric smiled, "Sight alone won't be enough to save the people. Imagine what would happen if I strolled into the City and announced that the Horrific Catastrophe was imminent, and they must leave Vulcon. I'm just the Wildling remember?"

Benn slid along the rock, a little closer to Lyric.

"Yeah," he said. "At best they'd just laugh and get on with their daily business. At worst the Queen would have you executed."

"Exactly. Both scenarios would result in the death of most of Vulcon's citizens. In order to save them, I have to be able to do more than just see."

Benn understood alright. He stared at her, mouth agape. "It's you!" he said. "You're the Great Seer of the prophecy!"

Lyric just watched the water flowing beneath her and smiled.

"Wow!" was all Benn could say until he took some time to gather his thoughts. "You said you created this place to practise? Is that what you have been doing all these years? Practising to find a way to save the people?"

Lyric smiled again.

"While I was at the Academy learning to be athletic, ambitious and arrogant."

"And self–centred, and condescending and—" Lyric interjected with a wicked smirk.

Benn winced and continued, "You were here, creating this, and practising ways to save the very people who would persecute you on sight?"

"That's about it." Lyric started to smile.

"Well, that sure makes me feel like an under–achiever."

They both laughed at the absurdity of it all.

"So, what do we do now?" Benn eventually asked.

"We gather some food, go back to the cavern and make breakfast. I'm ravenous."

"Sometimes the mundane is very therapeutic." Benn pulled himself to his feet, walked over to Lyric and held out his hand to help Lyric up.

"Sometimes it is." Lyric accepted his help and was gently dragged to her feet.

Benn retrieved his basket, still full of spinach and returned to the bridge.

"If all the facets of the Great Prophecy are in place, the Horrific Catastrophe must be imminent." Benn reasoned, "When is it?"

"I'd rather talk about that later, if you don't mind."

"What is the Horrific Catastrophe? What is going to happen?"

"Later."

"Are you sure you can save everyone?"

"Later. I wouldn't want to spoil your appetite for breakfast."

Benn rolled his eyes in exasperation.

When they reached the embankment beside the bridge, Lyric stopped.

"Would you like some figs with your breakfast?" she asked.

"Not possible today," Benn pointed to the fig tree, "The tree is surrounded by rapids. It's too dangerous to pick them."

Lyric went silent and looked intently at the fig tree. After a few moments, Benn could make out a handful of figs floating through the air towards them.

"That's amazing Lyric!"

As the figs approached, Benn held his basket up and the figs dropped gently inside.

"We should pick some olives while we're here," Lyric said.

Benn held his basket up toward the olive tree.

"It's on this side of the creek," Lyric said. "Don't be lazy. Go and pick them."

Benn looked awkward, then managed a mock salute when he saw Lyric's impish smile.

"Let's pick them together."

After an ample breakfast, Lyric showed Benn her technique for extracting olive oil. She tied the olives in a cloth, hovered the package over a bowl and the mass seemed to squeeze itself in mid–air with the juices trickling into the bowl. When the mass was thoroughly compacted, Lyric took a cup and scooped the oil from the surface of the liquid. They dipped their bread in the oil and Benn pronounced it delicious. Lyric was displaying her abilities freely now and it would take Benn some time to become accustomed to it.

That evening while they were preparing their meal, Benn was pondering. Eventually, while adding pieces of what was earlier that day a fine young, but unnecessary, rooster to a large pot he formulated his question.

"So, you didn't just hang around while I was at the Academy, waiting for me to come home at the end of each clead?"

"No. I could see when the time would be right. When you would be home, when the moon would be full, when the sky would be clear. I would go home then, and head to your farm in the evening. Much of the rest of the time I spent here, fixing the place up, tending the garden, practising."

"And the rocks by the creek," he asked further. "Are they in the positions they fell?"

"Some of them. Each time the earth shakes, rocks fall. Sometimes I just move them to more useful positions. Or just move them out of the way. Besides, father always said I should build a bridge over the creek, for his convenience when he visited."

Benn was trying to take it all in and make sense of the day. "So, that rock cutting thing you do is how you carved out the inside of this cavern?"

"Yes." Lyric started to set the table for dinner. "I like to play with rocks."

They chuckled together and immersed themselves in the mundane.

Still, Benn kept more of a physical distance from Lyric. She was still his best friend, but it was unnerving to think she could probably slice through him at will, just as she did the rocks.

Next morning Lyric woke to find Benn sitting on the edge of his bed, staring at her in a way she had not seen before. She sensed he was keeping his distance and though she could understand why, it still hurt. Things could never be between them the way they were before. Eventually they gathered their baskets and made their way down into the gorge. The waters had subsided somewhat, so more food was accessible. Lyric took Benn to an almond tree he hadn't noticed before and they gathered the drying fruit into their baskets to take back to the cavern. Lyric sensed Benn was full of questions and burning to ask them. She continued gathering and waited patiently.

"Um, Lyric."

"Yes, Benn."

He seemed more nervous around her now. To be expected she thought.

"I'd like to know more about how you move the rocks."

"I use the White Fire."

"White Fire? What's that?"

"To me it literally looks like a white flame. It permeates everything, the rocks, the trees, the plants, the animals, and even people."

"Even me?"

Lyric smiled. "Yes, even you."

"So why can't I see it?"

"I don't know. I'm the only person I know who can see it, most of the time. Not that I know many people." She smiled at Benn. "When the White Fire is really, really concentrated in one place, my parents say they can see it. They say it looks like a bright white light."

"Can you show me?" Benn was curious, a little scared after yesterday's demonstration, but still curious.

"Actually," Lyric said, "I really need to practise a few more times before we return to the farm. Why don't you come along? I usually practise in the afternoons, so we can go after lunch if you like."

"Go? Go where?"

"The desert. It's safer to practise there. No people around and it's more difficult to do any real damage."

"Right." Benn looked uncomfortable about the idea of damage.

They made their way back to the cavern and Lyric raised her basket to capture some apples that were drifting toward them from a distant tree. Benn already seemed to be taking such things in his stride.

"Fortunately, you never needed to use that ability in public. It would have seriously blown your camouflage."

"Almost never," Lyric said.

"What do you mean, almost never?"

"Do you remember the courtyard after your graduation ceremony?"

"I most certainly do. I was so shocked to see you there. It was a huge risk. If my classmates, or teachers, or worse still, my father saw you, the consequences would have been dire. If the table hadn't collapsed and distracted them, I would never have been able to get you out of there alive."

Lyric stared at him, smiling expectantly.

"No?"

Lyric gave a slow nod.

"That was brilliantly done," Benn said. "No one had any idea it was you. Besides, there's nothing quite as distracting to a courtyard full of Protectors than ladies covered in sauce, screaming in distress."

They both laughed, recalling the chaos on the day.

"How did the side gate open?" Lyric asked when she regained her composure. Again, she stared at Benn expectantly. He might as well know the full extent of it.

"Some of the Academy Protectors must have opened it." Benn was thinking aloud. "No, that can't be right, they were all at the table attending to the damsels in distress. But the bar on the gate is massive. It takes at least two big Protectors to lift it."

Lyric was grinning again now. "It weighs less than a big slab of rock," she said, gesturing to the rock forming the new bridge.

"I suppose it does." Benn stared at her in awe.

After the last apples dropped into Lyric's basket, they made their way back to the cavern. Not much was said. Benn had much to ponder and Lyric gave him time and space to process it all.

After lunch, Lyric packed a small satchel of food and water, hung it over Benn's shoulder and took him to the deep end of the cavern, beneath the opening through which they arrived. The rope they used still lay neatly coiled on the ledge nearby. Benn looked confused.

"You were wondering how we were going to get out of here without the rope, right?"

"The thought had crossed my mind."

"Well, this is how I usually come and go. No ropes required."

Lyric moved toward Benn until they were almost touching, she felt hot and the White Fire seemed particularly responsive. "Take my hands," she said, holding her hands toward Benn.

Benn obediently took both her hands and looked searchingly into her eyes. Lyric made an effort to look down from Benn's gaze and focussed her own directly forward, around the level of Benn's chest, "Hold on tight. Don't let go. I wouldn't want to lose you." She felt Benn's grip tighten.

His grip seemed to tighten even further as their feet lost contact with the ground. He was looking around wildly as they drifted upward, eventually emerging through the opening at the top. They moved to one side before gently coming down on a small patch of grass in between two bushes.

"By the Goddess!" Benn said when his feet were once again firmly on the ground.

"You can let go now," Lyric giggled, feeling his firm grip on her hands.

"Oh?" Benn looked down, embarrassed. "Sorry." He released her hands. "Now I see why you don't need a rope."

Lyric shook her hands out, they felt crushed. Benn had a powerful grip. She stepped out from the bushes and they journeyed toward the light of the desert. From the forest edge the desert stretched out, seemingly endless beyond. To their left, the mountain towered in the distance. Far ahead, Lyric could make out a clump of rocks and they set out toward it.

"How are you going to save the people?" Benn asked as they made their way over the hot sand and rocks.

"That's what I'm here to practise. You'll see soon enough."

"Tell me more about the White Fire."

"As a small child, I could see what will be, just as my mother and grandmother could. However, I could also see what looked like a white flame around all things. When I mentioned it to my grandmother, she said it was very important I should continue to practise seeing it, just as I should practise using the Sight.

"Around the time you went to the Academy, Mother taught me a technique she learned from mystics while she was abroad. It was called 'stilling the mind', and I could use it to focus my Sight. One day I experimented while stilling my mind. I asked the White Fire to move a leaf, and it did.

Eventually, my parents agreed I needed a place to practise working with the White Fire, somewhere where I would not be accidentally seen. While you were away at the Academy, my father and I searched until we found somewhere suitable."

"The cavern?"

"Yes." Lyric was happy Benn was paying attention. "The cavern. First, I practised using the White Fire to carve out the cavern. When you first told me about the Great Prophecy, I realised my family had been keeping the secret for many years. That's also when I knew what to practise. I worked on finding a way to use the White Fire to protect people."

"You still haven't told me what the Horrible Catastrophe is."

"I'd prefer to hold that back until our return journey to the farm. It's not the sort of information one would want as a burden for any longer than necessary."

They walked on in silence for a while, Benn processing the new information, and Lyric trying to decide how to ask the pivotal question. To her great relief, Benn broached the subject himself.

"Being able to move rocks and things about," he began, "I bet you're perfectly capable of protecting yourself."

"When that's all I need to focus on, that is indeed the case. But if I am focussed on using the White Fire to protect others, then I cannot use it to protect myself without jeopardising the safety of those I'm trying to protect. Up until now, the only way I have protected myself is by camouflage. As the Wildling I am an annoyance to people, a target of derision even, but I am not seen as a threat. This has been my protection. I've limited experience trying to protect myself when I'm being myself. I do not want to get into a situation where I have to use the White Fire to harm people to protect myself."

Benn stopped walking, frowned, then looked deeply concerned. "Really?"

Lyric also stopped and nodded.

"Your father should be able to protect you in such situations, shouldn't he?"

Lyric shook her head. "I need someone who is highly trained and very familiar with the City and the Royal Protectors. Someone who is not otherwise engaged for the next year and ideally someone who has graduated top of their year at the Academy." She walked on, looking at the ground, hoping for the response she desperately needed to hear.

Benn's face went ashen, his eyes widened, and his mouth gaped. He shouted, "What? The Horrific Catastrophe will occur within the next year?"

Lyric nodded feebly. Had she revealed too much too soon? Shouting was not usually a good indicator of coping.

Benn marched onward. "You need a better Protector than me. You need someone stronger and more experienced. Someone like the Academy combat professor or a Royal Protector."

"And what do you think would happen if I marched up to any of those people and asked them to protect me while I try to save the people of Vulcon?" Lyric was trotting to keep up with Benn's now powerful strides.

"At best they would send you on your way," he eventually conceded. "At worst they would report you to the Queen and you would be executed or assassinated."

"Exactly."

Benn's stride slowed as he started to calm down and he noticed Lyric's difficulty keeping up. "Can I have some time to think about it?"

"Yes." Lyric and Benn walked on in silence. She always expected the question to be daunting but she had not expected it would be such a conversation killer.

A short while later they were circling around the rocks. A rock, apart from the clump, embedded in the desert sand, was carved in the shape of a chair. The surfaces were too smooth for chisels and it wouldn't take Benn long to guess how it was formed.

"I'm going to try and get a solid practice session in before we head back to the cavern," Lyric announced, stopping a short distance from the front of the stone chair. She took the satchel from Benn's shoulder and dropped it gently to the ground. "Best if you remain here."

Benn obediently stood beside the satchel as Lyric took her seat in the chair. Lyric wiggled until she was comfortably positioned, closed her eyes and breathed deeply. She drew the White Fire up from the earth, through her feet and into her body where she allowed it to build up until she felt she would burst with it, then she released it, allowing it to flow through her. Once the flow was established, she opened her eyes slightly. Benn's face was pallid and washed out in the bright light. His expression frozen somewhere between astonishment and fear. His knees gave way and he dropped to the sand, staring in disbelief, speechless. Fortunately, she would be able to practise a few times before they returned to the farm. Benn was going to need some time to adjust.

Lyric continued until the colour returned to Benn's face and he was sufficiently bored to rummage about in the satchel, searching for a snack. She drew the White Fire back down into herself and let it flow back into the earth. When she finally arose from the chair and walked toward Benn, he was crunching a big bite out of a pink and yellow apple.

"Wow!" Was initially the only word he could muster between mouthfuls. When he regained presence of mind, he held out another apple and a goatskin of water, "Would you like something to eat and drink?"

Lyric took the apple and gulped down some water.

Benn loaded their items back into the satchel and Lyric led the way back toward the forest. They had not gone far when Benn quietly uttered, "Yes."

Lyric stopped in her tracks and stared at him. "Yes?"

"Yes, I will try and protect you while you try and protect the people of Vulcon." He stopped walking. "After all, it is the craziest, most illogical, bravest, noblest thing I have ever been asked to do." Benn laughed.

"So, you'll help me then?"

"Of course, I'll help you," Benn said. "After all, you've always been able to talk me into anything."

Lyric's face lit up and she was bobbing up and down with excitement. "Thank you, Benn." She leapt forward and hugged him. Benn just stood there rigid and reserved and Lyric quickly pulled away. She knew he was doing this out of a sense of duty, and she sensed their close bond was disrupted, probably forever. But at least he said yes, and now she had the best Protector on Vulcon to help her.

Benn resumed walking and whined, "I guess there's no chance of just leaving the island on a trading vessel until it's all over then? That is the logical thing to do you know?"

Lyric ignored his protests and almost danced toward the forest, as if a burden was lifted from her shoulders. Benn plodded slowly and deliberately behind her, as if carrying a great load.

That evening, Benn finally shaved.

Benn seemed more cheerful. He happily prepared breakfast and was waiting, basket in hand, by the cavern entrance when it was time to go and gather the food. The level of the creek subsided the following day, exposing the stepping-stones they previously used to cross, but the surfaces of the rocks were still wet and shiny and most likely slippery, so they continued to use the new bridge. As the morning drew on, Benn developed a troubled frown, which Lyric attributed to the burden of responsibility he had agreed to take on. It wasn't until their baskets were filled and they began the walk back to the cavern that the true reason for the frown was divulged.

"I presume you'll be practising again this afternoon?"

"I'd like to practise on each of our remaining afternoons if possible. Is there a problem?"

"Well, you get to spend a few days practising to protect the people," Benn said. "But instead of practising to protect you, it would seem I get to spend a few days sitting in the sand snacking on fruit. I feel as though I should be practising too. It's frustrating."

"What would you like to be practising?"

"I haven't done any sword training or strength training for weeks now," Benn continued. "At this rate I'll be a mountain of mush by the time I'm really needed. We didn't bring a sword and there are none in the cavern, so I guess I'll just have to wait."

Lyric's face lit up, "I have an idea. Come with me."

She placed her basket on the grass and skipped off toward a slab of rock at the edge of the creek. Benn placed his basket and followed. Soon they were standing together beside the rock.

"I don't have any bronze, but I can fashion a sword from stone. It will be shaped like a sword but much heavier," she explained. "Though, it will be brittle like stone, so you won't be able to use it to hit anything hard. Will that help?"

"Actually, I think it would be perfect. I could train through the positions and movements and the extra weight will serve as weight training."

Lyric smiled, then focussed on the slab of rock. It lifted into the air and rotated around its long axis until the flat sides were vertical. A point of bright light appeared at one end and bored into the stone leaving a wisp of smoke. Smoke began appearing from cracks that formed along the top and bottom and crept along the full length of the rock. Suddenly the rock on either side fell away revealing a perfectly formed polished stone sword hovering in mid-air above a pile of rock fragments. Benn immediately stepped forward to take the sword.

"Stop! It's hot remember."

Benn took a step back, "I forgot. I'll wait till you cool it in the water."

"Rock isn't like metal," Lyric explained. "When you cool it suddenly in water, it tends to crack. Remember the rock fragments when I made the bridge?"

Benn nodded, recalling how the piece of hot stone split in two when Lyric moved it into the water to cool. "What do we do then?"

"We'll let it cool slowly and come back for it after lunch."

"You're just going to leave it hovering there?"

"Exactly." Lyric walked back to her basket.

Benn looked at the hovering sword for a moment, shaking his head. Eventually he turned away and collected his basket too.

After lunch they came down from the cavern to find the sword still hovering where they left it.

"It should be cool enough to touch now, right?" Benn asked.

"I think so. Touch it and see."

Lyric smiled as Benn cautiously approached the sword and gingerly stretched out a finger to touch the hilt. The sword was now cool, and Benn placed his hand around the hilt to claim it, but it wouldn't budge. It remained hovering in the same spot. He turned and looked quizzically at Lyric.

"It's going to be heavier than you expect," Lyric cautioned. "May I suggest you place a hand under the blade, the other under the hilt and brace for some weight before I release it."

Benn did as Lyric instructed. As soon as he braced, he could feel the weight of the sword slowly sink onto his hands. It was about three times as heavy as the combat practice swords he used at the Academy. He gently lowered the sword onto the grass below. Now that he knew the weight of it, he took it by the hilt and heaved it into the air.

"Is it OK?" Lyric asked, after he waved it about a few times.

"It's great. Excellent shape, excellent balance, and very heavy." He heaved out the last word as he swung the sword high and the glassy surface glinted in the sunlight. "It will do very nicely."

Benn placed the sword in his belt and the pair returned to the cavern, gathered their provisions and made for the practice site in the desert.

For the next few days they kept to a routine. Gathering provisions from the gorge in the morning and making their way to the desert in the afternoons. Lyric would practise channelling the White Fire until the shadows were long on the ground. Benn would train nearby with his sword. Lyric thought he looked stronger and more confident with each passing day and it made her happy to see him happy. Still, he treated her with a distant deference now. He avoided standing or sitting too close, avoided touching her unless necessary and was very polite and reserved in his conversation. This tugged at her heart and she missed the carefree days when they roamed together along the river.

After supper on the ninth day, Lyric reminded Benn they would have to leave early the next morning. She packed a satchel of provisions for the journey home, set aside some breakfast, and discarded any remaining food into the gorge. Benn helped her clean and get the cavern in order before they retired for the night.

Before Benn blew out his lantern, he rolled over in his bed toward Lyric who was cosy under her covers and was intent on getting to sleep.

"In case I forget to tell you tomorrow, Lyric," he whispered, "this has been the most amazing ten days of my life. Thank you." Then he blew out the light.

"You're welcome," Lyric whispered in the darkness, and promptly fell asleep.

In the morning they were awake early. They dressed, ate and cleaned up in record time. At Lyric's request, Benn piled their saddles and equipment under the cavern opening. Lyric sat with her eyes closed on the end of her mattress, now devoid of the bed linen, which was carefully stashed away.

"What are you doing?" Benn asked, heaving the second saddle onto the heap.

"Bringing back the horses."

"Oh," Benn said in a whisper, "That's important. I'll leave you to it then." He added the bridles to the top of the pile then went and sat at the table until Lyric was done.

"They're here," Lyric said, opening her eyes. "Are you ready to go?"

"I am." Benn sprang to his feet and met Lyric near the pile of riding gear. "I didn't know you could move animals about too."

"I don't know if I can," Lyric said, "But I can move their halters, especially if they have a metal ring in them."

"Ah, so that's why you left the halters on them," Benn smiled, taking Lyric's hands ready for the ascent as if it were a perfectly ordinary thing to do. "Clever."

They elevated upwards and out through the opening of the cavern. The horses were waiting, just outside the bushes. Lyric focussed again and the bridles rose out of the opening. Benn took them and they went limp in his hands. He seemed accustomed to such things now, so without further ado, he proceeded to bridle and tie up both the horses.

By the time he was done, the saddles appeared, followed by the saddlebags, and Benn set about securing these on the horses in turn.

Lyric excused herself, "There's something I have to do. I won't be long." And she darted back into the bushes.

Benn busied himself with checking the girths one more time.

Lyric soon emerged and approached Benn, "I've just had an idea."

"What?"

"That sword isn't going to be much use in battle is it?"

"No, I guess not." Benn placed a protective hand over the hilt of the sword safely lodged in his belt.

"Well, I'd like to use it as a marker, to help find this place again after the catastrophe."

"Are you saying that the Horrific Catastrophe will destroy all traces of the paths and vegetation and other landmarks?" Benn looked worried.

Lyric nodded. "There's a reason why they call it horrific."

"OK then." Benn drew the sword and held it out toward Lyric.

Lyric focussed and the sword floated into the air and spun until the blade pointed downward. The blade seemed to glow momentarily, then the sword plunged into the earth until half of the blade was buried. "That should do it," Lyric announced, shifting her focus back to Benn.

"All good then?" Benn asked.

"All good."

Lyric took the reins, passed them over Nudge's head and launched herself, half floating, into the saddle. The morning light still glowed orange from the sunrise. They made good time with their preparations. Lyric turned Nudge toward the forest and urged her on. Benn mounted Polly quickly to keep up, and followed Lyric looking confused.

"Didn't we arrive from the desert side?" Benn asked.

"You have a good sense of direction." Lyric smiled, not altering her course. "I have spent years preparing the gorge for it to contain seed stock of all Vulcon's crop plants and fruit trees. They will be needed by the people later. Before we leave, I am going to try and protect it."

Benn nodded acknowledgement and followed behind.

They dismounted at the row of bushes that signalled the edge of the gorge. Benn secured the horses while Lyric made her way carefully between the bushes to the edge of the gorge. She sensed him arrive as she crouched near the edge of the cliff and placed both hands flat down onto the earth. She closed her eyes, and her hands began to glow where they touched the soil. The light seemed to focus on a point between her hands and it became intensely bright. Benn shielded his eyes with his arm.

Suddenly the light seemed to explode out over the top of the gorge and dissipated into a shimmering membrane that hung over the gorge forming a seal. The plants and animals below seemed totally undisturbed. Lyric opened her eyes, stood up and edged her way backward into the bushes. At that moment a hawk hovering above them dived toward a chick it spied in the gorge only to hit the membrane and bounce off. It flew away, shaken and confused.

"Well that seems to be working," Benn said, backing out of the bushes.

"It should hold for a few moons at least," Lyric looked satisfied with her workmanship.

They made their way back to the horses, mounted and set off toward the desert. Benn looked perplexed and Lyric noticed.

"What's the matter? You look troubled."

"You said back there that the protection should hold for—" He searched for words. "When exactly is the Horrific Catastrophe due?"

Lyric pulled up Nudge so she could face Benn directly, "In six cleads."

"Six cleads!" Benn was aghast, "Why didn't you tell me sooner? It is almost upon us. There is so little time to prepare."

"I wanted you to feel safe for as long as possible," Lyric explained, "I thought it would be more difficult to become accustomed to weirdness when you didn't feel safe." She urged her horse onward toward the light of the desert.

"Well I sure don't feel safe now!" Benn shouted behind her as he urged his horse on to follow, "I feel as though there is something I ought to be doing right now to prepare."

"There is," Lyric said, laughing. "You can help get us home safely."

Benn huffed and smiled. "Yes indeed, miss!"

They reached the edge of the forest and Lyric walked her horse out into the desert. Benn followed.

"Why are we going into the desert? Didn't we arrive under the cover of the forest edge?"

"We did. But I'm anticipating your next question."

Benn looked confused for a moment, then a look of curious realisation dawned, "What exactly is the Horrific Catastrophe?"

Lyric gestured toward the mountain, now in full view, with its peak shrouded in clouds, which still glowed in the morning light. "Have you noticed the tremors of the earth have become more frequent, longer and larger over recent months?"

Benn thought a moment, then nodded.

"There is a great fire building beneath the mountain, and that is what has been heating the wall of the cavern. In six cleads that fire will burst forth from the mountain, and rain down on the island of Vulcon."

Benn looked at the mountain in disbelief. "Surely not. The mountain has been the one constant in the history of Vulcon. Our legends tell how the Goddess formed Vulcon from the rock of the mountain itself. I cannot fathom that the mountain would pose a danger. Surely the Goddess would not unleash the mountain on her own people?"

As if to answer Benn's query, a tremor shook the earth beneath them. It took them a few moments to settle the startled horses.

"Are you OK?" Benn asked.

"Yes. I'm fine," Lyric replied. "Let's go home."

She turned Nudge back into the forest until she found the faint trail and they retraced their path back toward the Nye's farm.

CHAPTER EIGHT

Moth to a Flame

Lyric and Benn made good time, arriving at the final path near the farmhouse as the last light faded. As foretold, there was no sign of Protectors en route. Benn was worried the horses may not find the way in the dark, but Lyric reassured him her mother always hung a lantern to guide her home when she returned from Sanctuary. Sure enough, just as it became difficult to make out the path, a lantern light appeared and they followed it toward home.

The path through the farm was wide, so they could walk the horses two abreast. It was much easier to communicate this way than when riding single file, even when they could barely make out each other's faces.

"Lyric, before we get to the farm, I just want to thank you."

"What for?"

"For giving me a purpose."

Lyric was puzzled.

"You see, all of my life has been spent trying to meet other people's expectations. But that is a fairly hollow purpose. In retrospect, protecting and pandering to an overindulged Princess would have been the most purposeless and soul-destroying of all, and it would have lasted for the rest of my life. All six cleads of it," he said with a wink and grin. "I can think of no more satisfying purpose for a Protector than to try and protect the person who is trying to protect the people of Vulcon. Whether we succeed or fail, I am now a man of purpose and I have you to thank for that."

Lyric smiled. "I also need to thank you."

"How so?"

"Well, up until now, I always felt I alone was carrying the burden of being the Great Seer. I guess I'm still trying to meet my family's expectations too. Now though, I feel as though the burden is shared. I'm no longer facing it alone, and I have you to thank for that."

Benn nodded and they smiled at each other as they pulled in through the farmyard gate. At the sound of hooves on stone, Lyric's parents erupted from the kitchen to greet them. Lyric slid down from her saddle into a huge hug from her father. When she started to wriggle free, he held her at arm's length and asked, "Did he say yes?"

"He said yes." Lyric was then happily passed to her mother for another huge hug.

"Well done, Precious One," her mother whispered as she held her tight.

To Benn's great surprise, he received a solid man–hug from Lyric's father before being passed to Adria for a full, welcoming hug. It felt like a homecoming indeed. Benn looked awkward but happy. Lyric supposed Benn had never received a proper family welcome and she adored her family even more for treating him with such warmth and acceptance. The pair were ushered indoors with the promise of a hearty meal as Hann led the horses away and tended to them.

Lyric saw the room was even more sparse than when they left and baskets of treasured possessions stood by the door, ready to be transported to the City.

As they dined on roast chevon, vegetables and bread, washed down with pomegranate juice, Lyric and Benn were encouraged to relate the events of the last ten days. There was hearty laughter when Lyric recounted the expressions on Benn's face as the rock first hovered, and at the beginning of the first practice session. Benn blushed a little and laughed along, but he seemed too content in the moment to really mind. The main meal was followed by a deep–dish apple pie with goat curd. To Lyric and Benn, it felt like a feast. When they were thoroughly replete, Lyric and Adria rose to clear away the dishes. Benn sprang to his feet to assist, but Adria assured him the matter was well in hand and there were more important things to do. Benn sat down, looking quizzical, just as there was a loud knock at the door.

Hann opened the door to two men. One was surly, tall and muscular with a bulge in the middle. Benn recognised him as a potter from the City. The other a lean, weathered farmer. They greeted each other with easy and jovial familiarity, and Lyric's father led them to the table.

"Benn, I'd like you to meet Lyric's uncles, Uncle Renn and Uncle Lobb." Hann then resumed his seat.

Benn stood and greeted each man in turn, and when all were once again seated at the table, Uncle Lobb enquired, "Well?"

"Yes," Hann said with a satisfied smile.

"Excellent!" Uncle Renn was clearly pleased. "Let's get on with it then."

"Yes, yes, get the map," Uncle Lobb said.

Hann went to a nearby cupboard and carefully withdrew a large roll of leather parchment. He spread it out gently on the table.

By now, Adria and Lyric had the washing up well in hand and said nothing. They just smiled at each other and let the menfolk talk.

"You may have only just discovered the truth Benn," Hann said. "But we have been planning this for many years. We believe, however, there are significant deficiencies in our information, and your input would be much appreciated."

"I'll do what I can," Benn replied, looking relieved there had already been planning underway, and awkward because he assumed there hadn't.

"This is a map of the City," Hann said. "Here is the Port, the Palace and the city gates. This mark here indicates the city plaza, and toward the Palace end is the podium. The podium is close to the geographic centre of the City, so using it as a centre point, we estimate that Lyric will be able to protect the zone designated by this circle here." Hann was pointing authoritatively to each item in turn.

"So, half of the Port is included then?" Benn said.

"Yes," Lyric's father replied. "But only half. If we move to protect the whole Port, we lose protection of the city gates here, and the Temple here."

"Either way, the farms, including yours and my father's, are outside the protection zone," Benn said.

"It can't be helped," Uncle Lobb said, "Lyric can't protect the whole island, just the City."

At this point, with the clean–up complete, Adria motioned Lyric to follow her to the pantry room. They left the door ajar so they could hear the discussion as they began to load pots of preserved food into baskets, cushioning them with straw that was piled into the pantry for the purpose.

Uncle Lobb went on to explain. "We've sent children to tell all the farmers that the Horrific Catastrophe is imminent, advising them that when smoke appears at the top of the mountain, they should gather their families and livestock and enter the City for protection. They were warned that anyone outside the City would be unprotected."

"Wouldn't word of this have reached the Palace?" Benn asked.

"We expect so," Uncle Renn replied. "That's why we've asked children to convey the message. The Palace and the Royal Protectors have attributed it to a children's prank and reassured the farmers accordingly."

"When the smoke rises from the mountain, we need to be already in the City before the gates clog with farmers and livestock," Benn said.

"Yes," Hann replied. "We'll enter the night before, stay at Uncle Renn's home, and have the farmhands bring the livestock early in the morning. Hopefully our people reacting to the smoke will cause any farmers in doubt to follow suit."

"Well, that should make it easier to get Lyric to the Podium," Benn said.

"How so?" Uncle Lobb asked.

"Normally the Podium is well guarded. It is only for the use of the royal family, so Protectors are assigned in shifts to guard it from anyone else trying to use it. In total, there are usually two Protectors guarding the Podium and another two patrolling the plaza. However, with it being a market day, the number of Protectors will have been increased to four at the Podium and a further four patrolling the plaza. The large influx of farmers and livestock at the gates will cause some of the Protectors to be redeployed to the city gates to stop the influx and close the gates. Only a skeleton team of two Protectors will remain at the Podium."

"This is what we needed to know." Hann gave Benn a reaffirming pat on the back.

"Do you have a plan to keep the gates open?" Benn asked when he regained his breath. "After all, we don't want all the farmers and livestock trapped outside the City."

The men looked blankly at Benn.

"OK then," Benn said, thinking out loud. "Do we still have some helpful children available?"

The men looked at each other, then nodded in unison.

"Great," Benn said. "We need to issue them with pebbles. I can gather some of the right size. When the gates open at sunrise, the children need to sneak in and place pebbles in the bottom hinge of each gate. We used to do this as a prank when we were in school. The gates jam when the Protectors attempt to close them. It takes ages to reposition the gate and remove the pebbles, and that's after the time it takes for them to figure out the problem."

"That's brilliant!" Uncle Lobb was excited now. "You were right Hann, we do need the perspective of a young, capable Protector to make this work. If you explain to my eldest daughter what needs to be done, she can show the other children. Being a girl, her activity is likely to go unchallenged."

Benn seemed empowered by this vindication. "What is the plan to get Lyric onto the Podium?"

The men continued discussing the plans, detail by detail, late into the evening. Adria and Lyric, long finished packing baskets, crept upstairs to bed. Lyric was still lying awake when her father farewelled his brother and brother–in–law at the door and they made their way toward the City by lantern light. Uncle Renn was to overnight at Uncle Lobb's vineyard before entering the City in the morning. Over the years, the two uncles had grown to be close friends. A shared secret can do that.

This event was followed by cleads of preparation and the covert relocation of items and produce to the City. The Nye's farm was now almost devoid of possessions and food reserves. Some of their precious goats were sent to market, some were slaughtered and butchered on the farm. The meat was dried, preserved and relocated to house cellars in the City. The small flock of remaining goats was being yarded by the farm hands, ready to move to the City early the next morning. Benn and Hann loaded the last of the produce and possessions onto the wagon, covered them with canvas and secured the load with ropes. While the farmhands finished preparing the horses, each member of the family said their goodbyes to the farm and the house in their own way.

Lyric sat on her bed for a few moments trying to memorise the view from the window. She was recalling her life on the farm and the passing of so many seasons. It was a wonderful place to grow up, so full of love and laughter. Eventually she came downstairs to see Benn take the pillow from his bed in the kitchen and load it onto the wagon as a keepsake.

"Most comfortable pillow I've ever had," Benn said in response to Lyric's quizzical gaze.

Hann paced about all the rooms and buildings in silent homage. Adria stood in her kitchen one last time. She ran her hands over the benches, the table, the seats, the fireplace and the walls and began to cry. Slowly at first, but eventually in loud sobs. When Hann found her, he gently put his arm around her shoulders. She pressed close to him and sobbed into his chest, leaving a wet patch on his overshirt. Hann was discreetly wiping tears from his own eyes, while holding Adria close. When the sobs started to subside, Hann led Adria out into the farmyard and they all assembled at the wagon and donned cloaks. Hann stepped up to the driver's seat and Adria took the seat beside him. Lyric used the mounting stool to launch herself onto Nudge. In turn, Benn mounted Polly. As afternoon shadows became long on the ground, the procession moved out of the farmyard and onto the path toward the City.

The horses became suddenly agitated and as the family sought to soothe them, the earth gave a mighty shake. This quake was longer and stronger than those before. The farmhands and their families ran into the farmyard. It was safer on open ground. Large slabs of daub fell from the farmhouse walls into the once neatly tended gardens below. This time no one would make good the damage. This time, their final image of their beloved home was a house broken. The family wiped away tears, reassured each other with a touch and urged the horses onward.

The sun was low in the sky as the party approached the city gate.

"Prepare yourselves," Hann said.

Obediently they drew their cloaks tight around them. Lyric and Benn pulled their hoods low over their faces. To the Protectors at the gate, this seemed perfectly natural. The late summer evenings were cool. A chilly breeze came in from over the ocean and everyone was wrapping their clothes closer, so the family entered the City unchallenged. Vulcon was not at war with anyone, there was no civil disturbances and it was not the habit of the Protectors stationed at the gates to impede the flow of citizens to and from the City. The search for Benn had ceased as soon as the Queen received word he died in the haunted forest and her attention was quickly directed elsewhere. Still, as a precaution against being recognised by anyone who might inform the Queen they were still alive, Benn and Lyric kept their faces hidden as they moved through the streets. As was the custom, the city gates were drawn closed at dusk, not to be opened again until sunrise the next morning.

The Nye's made their way through the streets to Renn Aven's house. Uncle Renn had made a good life as a potter. The two storey, mud and daub home, was large by city standards, with an expansive, covered workshop and shop area at the front, and a mounting yard and stables at the rear. Uncle Renn was waiting in the mounting yard.

"They're here!" he shouted back through the open door into the kitchen.

The children tumbled out first. Tunn, a slight boy with clean-cut dark hair, a new grey tunic and shiny brown sandals ran forward. "Hello Uncle Hann!" he shouted, gleefully dancing around the wagon as it came to a stop. "Hello Aunt Adria," he said as he stretched up to peer at their load. Tunn was in his ninth year and soon to start his third year at school.

Little Keela raced out next, giggling and bouncing around the wagon and the horses. "Hello, hello, hello," she sang as she bounced about, her long dark locks wafting around her face in the breeze. Keela had just entered her sixth year and was due to start her first year of school in the fall. Like her mother, she had inherited the Sight, and Lyric knew the darling child would already be dead had she started school a year earlier. Poisoned.

By the time Benn and Lyric dismounted and drew back their hoods, Aunt Tyla finally emerged from the kitchen. She was a shorter, plumper version of Lyric's mother, with paler skin from spending much of her time indoors and in the shaded workshop. Her hair was neatly braided and pinned. "Welcome!" she called out, wiping her hands on her apron. She scurried over to hug her sister and Lyric as soon as the dismount from the wagon was complete.

"So good to see you Tyla." Adria squeezed her sister firmly.

"Any trouble on the way?" Uncle Renn asked as Hann dismounted.

"No," Hann replied. "All went smoothly, as foretold."

"Lyric," Keela said, hugging Lyric's legs.

Lyric smiled, untangled the little arms and bent down to give the child a proper hug. She then reached out to the approaching Tunn and gave him an affectionate hug too. During the embrace she winked toward Benn and placed a finger over her lips to signal that the children did not know she could converse. That would have been too great a risk. Children talking idly at school or at play could have compromised her camouflage.

"You're very clean today, Lyric," Keela said as she moved away from Lyric to investigate Benn.

"Who's this?" Tunn asked, gesturing toward Benn.

"I'm Benn." He moved forward with his hand outstretched. "Pleased to meet you."

Tunn seemed flattered at being greeted as an adult and vigorously shook Benn's hand. "I'm Tunn. Pleased to meet you too."

Benn felt a tugging sensation at the back of his tunic and looked down to see Keela smiling up at him. "Well hello," Benn said, crouching down on one knee. "And who may you be?"

"I'm Keela."

"Pleased to meet you Keela." Benn offered his hand to Keela, but she evaded it and launched herself at him to plant a big hug. Benn laughed as he struggled to regain his balance.

When Keela finally set him free, Benn was formally introduced to Aunt Tyla, who hugged him with great enthusiasm.

"Come in and eat," Aunt Tyla said, gesturing toward the kitchen which glowed with the light of a big fire in the hearth and enticed with the delightful aromas of cooking food.

"Yes, yes," Uncle Renn said. "Let's eat. My man will attend to the horses and we can unload the wagon after we have eaten."

The party happily made their way into the cosy kitchen.

They sat down to supper at a table that was just like the one on the Nye farm.

"Nice table," Benn said.

"Thank you," Uncle Renn replied. "Hann made it for us around the time he made the one at the farm. During his furniture–making phase."

Hann smiled and blushed a little.

"All in order?" Adria asked as they began to pass food around the table.

"All set," Uncle Renn replied, forking a large piece of chevon onto his plate. "Once the wagon is unloaded, I don't think we can squeeze another thing in. There's not even space left in that cellar for a rat, so they'll have to move elsewhere."

Benn said little as he was trying to gauge how much the little cousins knew.

"Thank you Tyla for this wonderful meal," Hann said, in between mouthfuls. "It's delicious."

"Well it should be. After all, you did supply all of the ingredients."

"Enjoy it," Uncle Renn interjected. "It may be some time before we are able to enjoy fresh, abundant produce like this again."

They all nodded, and the mood became suddenly sombre.

When every last morsel of the meal was consumed, Adria, Lyric and Aunt Tyla set about clearing the table and attending to the dishes. Hann, Uncle Renn and Benn unloaded the wagon and stowed the contents by lamplight. Once the children were safely in bed, upstairs, they gathered around the table and confirmed the arrangements for the next morning.

"The difficulty will be trying to get a good night's sleep," Adria said, stowing away the cleaned plates.

"Agreed," Aunt Tyla said. "Most important for you Lyric. You, more than any of us, will need to get a good night's sleep."

"I'll try," Lyric said.

"Yes indeed," Aunt Tyla continued. "That's why we've given you the guest bedroom upstairs. The room is packed with provisions, so it's a bit crowded, but you will not be disturbed. For the rest of you, we've set up bunks here by the hearth where it will be warm and cosy."

"Thank you Aunt Tyla," Lyric replied. "But I'm quite happy to sleep down here too."

"Nonsense, dear girl," Aunt Tyla said. "You need sleep more than any of us because you will be going the longest without it come the morrow."

All at the table indicated agreement and Lyric gave her aunt a conceding and thankful nod.

"Try using 'stilling of the mind' when you go to bed, Precious One," Adria said. "It will help settle your thoughts and prevent them from racing. This wonderful meal should help too. It's much easier to fall asleep on a full stomach."

"We're all so edgy, we will probably wake up much earlier than necessary," Uncle Renn said. "I, at least, will be keen to check if there is smoke from the mountain."

The men agreed.

Lyric, Adria and Tyla shared knowing smiles between them. They didn't feel the need to see the smoke. They already had.

After washing and changing, Lyric made her way up to bed and snuggled under the thick cashmere blankets. She was in no rush. Tonight, all those she loved were snug, dry and well fed. Tomorrow could take its time arriving.

Lyric awoke to cries of "There's smoke on the mountain Papa!" Tunn was leaning out of an upstairs window to see the spectacle. Lyric could hear the sound of people on the street. She had spent very little time in the City and did not know whether this was the normal level of noise for city streets at this hour, or whether the smoke had already caused a commotion. Today was the day, and it felt like a giant hand was squeezing her stomach. She dressed in her best clothes and made her way to the kitchen. A large breakfast was already laid out and everyone was gathered at the table and eating heartily.

"Thought we'd let you sleep as long as possible," Adria said.

"Thanks." Lyric took a seat at the table. Bowls of food and jugs of drink were passed in her direction. She scooped a pile of scrambled eggs onto her plate and poured a small cup of water.

"Is that all you're eating?" Uncle Renn said. "You'll need more than that to sustain you."

"Considering I won't be able to leave the Podium for the duration, it's probably best I don't eat or drink too much this morning,"

"Indeed," Uncle Renn said after a moment's consideration. He grabbed at some of the laden dishes. "More for the rest of us then!"

"Papa!" Tunn shouted. "Cousin Lyric just spoke!"

Lyric smiled. Outside her parents, her two aunts, her two uncles and Benn, no one had ever heard Lyric speak more than a word or two at time. Now that the day had come, there was no more need for camouflage, at least not within these walls.

"Of course, she did," Aunt Tyla said.

"But she has never spoken before, Mama," Tunn persisted.

Aunt Tyla and Uncle Renn looked uncomfortable. They looked unwilling to confess they were keeping a secret from their children all this time. At least not yet.

Lyric stepped up to the rescue. "I've always been able to speak little Tunn, I simply chose not to." She flashed a cheeky grin at her cousin.

"Well, you were very good at it. That's all I can say," Tunn said, trying to sound very adult. /p>

Everyone laughed at his earnest delivery. Tunn just blushed, smiled and fell silent.

"Grandma Aven will be arriving presently to care for the children for the next couple of days," Aunt Tyla said, "and your Aunt Avayne will arrive later with all of their children. They will all stay here while Uncle Lobb is helping us at the plaza."

Lyric could tell Aunt Tyla was choosing words carefully so as not to distress the children unnecessarily.

"We must all be very careful in the plaza today," Uncle Renn advised. "The Queen is still very powerful."

"Is she really?" Lyric asked, then gulped the last mouthful of water from her cup.

"Of course, she is," Uncle Renn replied. "She is still the most powerful person on Vulcon and we would do well to remember that, today of all days."

"Over the years Uncle Renn, I've had ample opportunity to observe the Queen in action, read the ancient parchments, practise power and study power. The question is, does she really have power Uncle Renn?" Lyric asked. "Or only the illusion of it?"

All the family were shaking their heads and looking confused. Only Benn smiled.

"Well, she has all the Royal Protectors on her payroll, and they do her bidding," Uncle Renn said.

"Is that really power or is it just influence by virtue of her wealth?" Lyric asked. "She can pay people to do her bidding or render them poverty-stricken if she feels aggrieved. What happens though if she loses her wealth?"

"Then they stop doing her bidding," Aunt Tyla replied while Uncle Renn was still pondering.

"So, is influence power, or just an illusion of power?" Lyric asked.

"Yes, yes," Uncle Renn said. "But some of the Protectors would do her bidding even if they weren't paid, simply because she is Queen. She still has the power to kill us at any time."

"Is that really power Uncle Renn? Or is it authority?" Lyric asked.

"Authority, I guess," Hann replied as he grabbed for more food.

Lyric continued. "Surely authority to govern can only exist with the consent of the governed. So, is it real power or another illusion of power? I mean, when the governed withdraw their consent—"

"Then she has no authority," Uncle Renn said.

"And if she were to be separated from her wealth," Hann said, "then she would also lose her influence."

"Exactly," Lyric said. "I eventually concluded that true, authentic power is what you can do, independent of wealth and authority. Kindness is a power, courage is a power, swordsmanship is a power, skill in your trade is a power."

"As is playing with rocks," Benn interjected with a teasing grin.

They all stared at Benn for an instant, then erupted in laughter. The children just looked confused.

"I know how to play with rocks," Tunn said.

"Me too!" Keela chirped.

They all laughed louder. Uncle Renn placed his arm around his children and managed to utter, "Yes you do my dears," in between heaves of mirth.

Lyric found the merriment a delightful distraction from the knot in her stomach and relished the moment.

"Well, there we have it." Uncle Renn said when he could finally speak. "All we have to do is rob the Queen of her wealth and the consent of the people, and she will be powerless. A daunting task indeed."

Lyric blushed and picked her way slowly through what was left of her meagre breakfast, under Adria and Aunt Tyla's approving smiles.

The kitchen door burst open and a determined, greying woman appeared. "Have you seen the streets? It's chaos out there! I had to cling to the walls just to make it here from the end of the street."

"Welcome Grandma Aven." Aunt Tyla leapt up and hugged her mother in law. "Would you like some breakfast?"

"Yes, Yes," the old woman said, eyeing the table for any bowls which still contained food.

By the time they finished breakfast, the street was even noisier. Hann peered out between the shutters of a downstairs window. Already the streets were filled with people, livestock and wagons. "It seems the farmers got the message."

"We'd better get underway," Benn said. "It will take a while to reach the plaza through all of these crowds."

Benn, Hann and Uncle Renn strapped on their studded leather breastplates, arm protectors and shin guards, all cleaned and polished for the occasion. Finally, they wrapped and fastened their sword belts, wiped and sheathed their swords and concealed their battle garb and weapons under thick woollen cloaks. Adria, Aunt Tyla and Lyric also donned cloaks. Lyric and Benn pulled their hoods over their heads and faces. It was best not to be recognised, at least until they were safely at the plaza.

Hann strapped a wooden chair to his back. He had carved it himself, to ensure it would be sturdy enough on the day.

Aunt Tyla and Uncle Renn hugged their children farewell and admonished them to behave well for their grandmother and to be good hosts to the visiting children.

"When will you be back Mama?" Keela asked. This farewell was different from those she was used to.

"We'll see you in a few days dear," Aunt Tyla said. "No need to worry. No matter what you see or hear. OK?"

"OK Mama," Keela said, holding her mother tighter.

"Be brave and look after your little sister," Uncle Renn said, gripping Tunn firmly by the shoulders.

"Yes, Father." Tunn's expression was now serious.

The parents disentangled themselves from their children, passing them to their grandmother.

"May the Goddess protect you," Grandmother Aven said, as the party made their way into to the mounting yard. She closed the kitchen door behind them.

Benn took Lyric's hand and entwined it firmly in his own. "I wouldn't want to lose you in this crowd," he said. "Don't worry Lyric, I won't let you go." He wrapped his other arm reassuringly around her and she melted against his chest, feeling the pressure of the metal studs against her.

Lyric felt a surge of heat rush through her. No matter what happened during the rest of the day, that one moment had already made the whole day worthwhile.

Hann and Uncle Renn took their cue from Benn, took their wives' hands and tried to give them a reassuring smile.

"All set?" Uncle Renn asked.

Hann looked around at the party. Their expressions apprehensive but determined, "All set."

Uncle Renn opened the gate onto the street. "May the Goddess be with you!"

"Thanks," Benn said, as the six of them spilled out onto into a river of bodies, carts and livestock, pouring and swirling relentlessly toward the plaza.

Lyric looked up behind and saw a single, mighty plume of black smoke rising from the top of the mountain, billowing and rolling high into the sky. A ring of cloud halfway up the mountain glowed white in the morning sunlight. Above it, the grey and brown of rocks and below it, the mountain's skirt of green forest. The sight was compelling, but Lyric looked away to concentrate on moving with the throng of people. Benn held her hand even more firmly and smiled reassuringly.

Hann and Adria were pushed away from them by the crowds, as were Uncle Renn and Aunt Tyla. Lyric lost sight of them in the sea of people, sheep, goats and cattle. Some people were trying to move wagons through the streets, filled with personal possessions and crates of chickens. The cacophony was intense.

"Father!" Lyric shouted toward where she last saw her parents.

"Don't worry," Benn said, "We expected this. We'll meet up again in the plaza. Besides, we're less likely to look suspicious if we all arrive separately."

Lyric nodded and kept tight hold of Benn's hand. They both pulled their hoods lower over their faces and flowed with the throng through the narrow streets to the plaza beyond.

Two Royal Protectors were forcibly and loudly making their way through the crowds in the direction of the plaza. Their bluster caused the crowd to part before them, so their progress was but little impeded. Benn sidled himself and Lyric behind them, giving them a rapid path to their destination. Lyric smiled at Benn, impressed. That was a clever move.

The crowds were even more dense in the plaza. As the two Protectors neared the podium, Benn moved Lyric to the side, and they were jostled and shoved as they skirted their way through the crowd to a position behind the Podium. Another team of Protectors was arriving with the Royal Litter.

"Were you expecting this?" Lyric asked, her voice loud over the noise of the crowd.

"No," Benn looked concerned. "It will be difficult to get you onto the Podium if it already occupied."

"Don't worry," Lyric said. "If it was going to be a problem, Mother would have said something."

Benn nodded and led Lyric to a position near the Plaza Sundial.

"We have until the eleventh morning hour, right?" Benn asked.

"Right." Lyric saw the tip of the shadow was halfway between the symbol for ten and that for eleven. Benn was searching the crowd for signs of Lyric's father as the Royal Litter stopped beside the Podium, was placed on the ground, and the Princess Brata alighted. The two Protectors who had unwittingly opened a path for Benn and Lyric approached the Princess as she took the last few steps toward the Podium.

"Your Highness," the tallest Protector of the two said as they both bowed low. "The farm folk and their livestock are flooding in through all of the city gates."

The Princess eyed them with impatience. "Well, have the gates closed then!"

The two Protectors bowed again as the Princess continued past them and began mounting the Podium steps.

"It would seem the Queen does not have the courage to face these crowds," Lyric whispered in Benn's ear. "She has sent the Princess to do the dirty work."

Benn whispered back, "She clearly has no idea, does she?"

Lyric shook her head and the pair watched the proceedings unfold, their faces still concealed beneath their hoods.

The Princess's Protector gestured for a number of the Protectors present to assist those who were sent to the gates. After all, there were more than two city gates. This left a skeleton team of only six Royal Protectors, and four would be required to carry the Royal Litter back to the Palace. This is what Benn expected would happen, but instead of being pleased, Benn's grip tightened on her hand.

"Ouch!" Lyric cried out.

"Oh, sorry." Benn loosened his grip a little, but he was distracted.

Lyric followed the line of his gaze to the Princess's Protector. As he turned, she could see his face clearly, it was Rikk. Benn looked like he was caught off-guard and was struggling to modify his plans to accommodate this development. The Princess took her place in the middle of the Podium and Rikk was standing vigilantly and respectfully at the side steps.

"People of Vulcon!" the Princess shouted in a commanding tone. "There is nothing to fear! The Queen and I foresee no danger, despite the plume of smoke from our beloved mountain. Go back to your homes and farms. All is well."

The crowd roared in anger and there were fists shaking in the Princess's direction. A single voice, louder than the others shouted back, "If you and the Queen didn't foresee this smoke and warn us, how can you be sure it is safe?"

The Princess suddenly looked vulnerable. An egg was thrown from the crowd and shattered on her dress. She cried out and raced toward the steps to Rikk who gathered her up and shielded her in the direction of the Litter.

Lyric saw a hand appear firmly on Benn's shoulder. She felt Benn immediately tense and swing around, only to relax when he saw Hann and Adria standing behind them. Adria was unstrapping the chair from Hann's back.

"Good to see you!" Benn was clearly relieved.

Lyric could see the two uncles working their way through the crowd to the front and far side of the podium. She looked at the sundial. The sliver of light between the shadow and the eleven symbol was shrinking rapidly. In the commotion, the Protectors who should be stationed at the four sets of steps to the podium had gone to assist the Princess's return to the Royal Litter and the podium was, at that moment, unguarded. Lyric sensed Benn would take advantage of the opportunity. Benn took the chair in his free hand and without releasing his grip on Lyric's hand, he quickly dragged her up the back steps onto the podium. He planted the chair in the centre of the podium and sat Lyric upon it.

"I will protect you as best I can, dear Lyric," Benn said as he took a step back. "The rest is up to you. May the Goddess be with you, with us all."

Lyric nodded and Benn strode toward the side steps, not far from the Royal Litter. She turned to see her father positioned at the rear steps. He pushed back his hood and cloak to reveal Protector garb, then drew his sword and held it upright in front of him in a position of vigilance.

Checking either side, Lyric saw her uncles were positioned at the far side and front steps. They too threw back their cloaks to display Protector garb and drew their swords into a position of vigilance. Once in position on the side steps, Benn similarly threw back his hood and cloak, and drew his sword, holding it upright in front of him.

The nearby crowd went silent, confused by the sudden turn of events.

"Get her off my Podium!" shrieked the Princess from the relative safety of the Litter. /p>

Rikk drew his sword and obediently made his way toward Benn, clearly stunned to see him.

"Hello old friend," Benn said as Rikk approached.

"Hello Benn." Rikk's face was a knot of confusion and consternation. He drew his sword. "Are you a ghost?" One of the other Protectors left the Royal Litter and was coming toward Rikk as backup. At the sight of drawn swords, the crowd moved away, creating a circle of space around the Podium.

"It would appear that rumours of my death were premature. And it would appear you have found yourself a bride." Benn nodded toward the enraged Princess.

"You know the rules Benn," Rikk said. "Get her off the Plaza Podium. Whoever she is."

"If she gets off the podium, Rikk, we all die today. Today is the day the Great Prophecy is fulfilled."

"The Princess said you went mad and ran off with the Wildling. Until now I didn't believe it. Now step aside!" Rikk lunged forward and Benn countered with his sword. The second Protector was soon upon them and Benn was valiantly warding off both swordsmen. Feats such as this had helped earn him the title of top graduate in his year at the Academy. The men stationed at the other steps knew this, so they maintained their posts, swords held upright.

Lyric tossed back her hood. The people seemed confused. At first, they did not recognise her without grimy skin and hair full of debris.

"Look at her eyes!" someone shouted from the crowd. "It's the Wildling!"

"The Wildling cannot save us, kill it!"

A crowd of twisted angry faces with waving clenched fists began to surge forward, stopping only when the defenders at the steps waved their swords in warning.

"Step back!" Uncle Renn shouted from his position at the front steps. "Step back or die today!"

The surge stopped, but not the anger of the people. They began to throw eggs and fruit. Lyric remembered that day when the children had tried to stone her all those years ago. They were angry and frightened. She had hoped their parents would be different. Kinder, wiser maybe, but they were not. They were just a mob of angry wild creatures determined to see her humiliated, or dead. In all her life, she never treated anyone this way. Why could they not see that she was not the animal? Today, the ones behaving like animals were they. Lyric's face fell as she just sat there, enduring the pelting, tears began to trickle down her cheeks. Her beautifully combed hair and the lovely dress her mother made were soon soiled with egg, and the debris of foul fruit.

Feeling safe in the Royal Litter, the Princess wore a smug grin as she watched the girl who took her Benn and humiliated her be humiliated in turn. She looked around for an item to throw, but it was not customary for the Royal Litter to contain eggs or fruit, and she certainly wasn't going to throw gold or jewellery.

The commotion from the crowd was so loud that few noticed the cattle begin to bellow. Benn did. As horses became restless and sheep bleated urgently. Benn, still fending off two swordsmen, bent his knees and braced his stance.

Sure enough, the ground shook. This was the biggest quake yet. Many were knocked to the ground, including the Protectors, and entire sections of crowd fell like dominoes. Lyric's chair toppled, throwing her forward onto the Podium. The stone was cold and hard and rough. It grazed some skin from her hand as she tried to break her fall. Benn flashed her a worried glance before turning back ready to deal with Rikk and the other Protector as they scrambled to regain their feet. She met his gaze, feeling wretched and desolate.

It was supposed to be her day of triumph, the day she fulfilled the hopes and expectations of her family, the day she fulfilled her destiny. She was not in triumph but on her hands and knees on the cold, hard, stone. The lovely, green dress her mother made for her, and the intricate braids her mother wove into her long brown hair were soiled with eggs and smashed fruit. The foul stench filled her nostrils. The crowd chanted,

"Eject the Wildling!" Lyric felt the sting of an egg smash on her cheek.

Ahead of her. Lyric could see Benn locked in sword combat against his best friend, fighting for his life, and hers. At the other edges of the podium, her father and her uncles were similarly in combat against Royal Protectors. She turned her head away from the sting, letting the slimy contents of the egg drip down her neck onto her dress. Lyric's eyes fixed on her mother, her face ashen in horror, her gaze soon diverted to the ground in disappointment. Today Lyric was disappointing her family and sealing their fate.

Just like the last time when the city folk used her for target practice, she felt powerless to deal with it. So many rules, so many constraints, so many expectations. Last time she huddled, waiting to be rescued. This time, no rescue would come.

Grandmother would have known what to do. Grandmother always knew what was to be done, what was best. Lyric missed her, needed her guidance, but she was not there. She felt humiliated and beaten. How had it come to this? Was there something she could have done to avert this? If she was more obedient from the beginning, perhaps that would have made a difference. No. It dawned on Lyric that had she always been obedient, she would never have befriended Benn and never had the chance to practise the skills necessary to help the people. She would have been even more powerless than she felt now.

Lyric knew she had the power to protect the people and she had the support of her family to do so. But here and now, with the Horrific Catastrophe imminent, she had no will to protect them. Why should she? All they ever did was shun her and seek to do her harm. Even if they thought her a mindless cretin, a Wildling, there was no excuse for such cruel behaviour. She had never done anyone any harm. Her only crime was to be wild and free and deficient in conversation. At that moment, she loathed the angry mob. She just wanted to lay there and let the mountain sweep them all away, sweep Vulcon clean of such despicable creatures.

As she was about to close her eyes and let nature take its terrible course, two little sets of fingers appeared at the edge of the Podium in front of her. A small head popped up in between them as a little girl half reached, half climbed the edge of the podium. Her hair beautifully braided, she was clearly loved. Her cherubic face frowning with concern.

"Hello dear sister," the child said, managing a weak smile. "I know you can save us. Please save us."

"What did you say?" Lyric's voice was feeble.

"Please save us."

"No, before that. What did you say before that?"

"Hello dear sister?"

"Yes, that was it. Why did you call me sister?"

"Mother says I should always treat young people as if they were my brothers and sisters, grown-ups as if they were my aunts and uncles, and old people as if they were my grandparents," the child said.

Lyric gave a slow nod. She was about to reply when a shrill voice broke through the commotion.

"Kyra! Kyra!" A well-dressed woman burst through the front line of the crowd. She gave Lyric a frightened, then despising glare, raced forward and grabbed the child by the arm, dragging her back toward the crowd. "Come away Kyra. What do think you are doing?"

"Talking to my sister," the child mumbled as she was dragged off. She managed one last forlorn glance at Lyric before she disappeared into the crowd.

Lyric could see that the White Fire seemed brighter around the child than around most people. The child's mother reminded her of her Aunt Tyla. When the woman took the child's arm, she saw the White Fire flow between them. Then Lyric started to look around. Really look around. She could see the faint flicker of the White Fire around each person in the crowd, as she always saw it around people. But now she looked more carefully, and she could see how shimmers of White Fire flowed between people. It was as if the White Fire was a great pool of radiant water and the people like jellyfish, full of water themselves, floating about within it.

Realisation suddenly flowed through Lyric, as if she was seeing clearly for the first time in her life. She suddenly knew that all people were connected, that one cannot diminish another without diminishing oneself, and one cannot exalt another without exalting oneself. She felt the White Fire stir within her. The stone no longer felt cold beneath her. At that moment Lyric knew she could save these people and beyond that, she could lead them. The actions of these people simply reflected the selfish and denigrating thoughts flowing down from the Queen. She was seeing the effects of the Queen's influence, but her influence could be different. She could help them become more than they were now.

The ground stopped shaking and Lyric pushed herself up from the stone and rose to her feet. Having regained her own footing, Adria climbed onto the podium and went to her aid.

Lyric raised her head and stood tall. "Stand back, Mother!"

In response to Lyric's stern, focussed expression, Adria stepped back, startled. Adria looked terrified that, after this humiliation, Lyric would slaughter the people herself.

Lyric stood tall and focussed.

"Look!" a woman shouted from the front of the crowd, pointing toward Lyric.

The debris began to fall away from Lyric's clothes and hair, as if repelled by some unseen force. When every last trace of debris was lying inert on the stone, Lyric shook her head and her long shiny hair swished and loosened, as if combed by an unseen hand. Then it fell, neat and tidy in to place.

"Sorcery!" a voice shouted. An egg flew through the air aimed directly at Lyric's chest, but it seemed to hit an invisible wall just beyond her clothes. It splattered and fell uselessly to the stone below.

Lyric could see that Benn did not look away from his adversaries who were lunging more feebly now as they tried to look past him to see what was happening on the podium. Nothing was happening that was new to him. She could count on him to remain attentive to his task.

The chair behind Lyric lifted into the air, hovered, righted itself and landed gently back into position. Lyric stepped back to it and took her seat. As the crowd watched in stunned silence, she untied her cloak and threw it back to cover the chair.

Although Lyric could see Benn was being challenged, she needed to focus. She wiggled herself into a comfortable position on the chair, sat upright, and placed her feet together on the stone of the Podium. She cupped her hands in her lap with her thumbs just touching, and partly closed her eyes.

The crowd gasped. "By the Goddess!" someone yelled. "Her eyes! Look at her eyes!"

Lyric started to glow bright and white, and under her eyelids her eyes glowed, intense white. The light around her became brighter and brighter. The second Protector dropped his sword and stepped back. Rikk and Benn had swords locked when Rikk saw what was happening and also stepped back, lowering his sword. Benn remained in a defensive position, so as not to be taken off-guard.

"What is happening?" Rikk asked, now needing to shield his eyes from the light with his hand.

Suddenly, the light around Lyric shot upward forming a column towering in the sky. When it reached a point well above the City, it stopped and formed a bright ball. Adria looked down at the Sundial. The shadow touched the centre of the eleven symbol and the top of the mountain exploded.

The crowd screamed as if in unison and dropped to the ground. A shower of rocks hurtled from the exploding mass toward the City. As the people saw them, they shrieked again and dropped back to the ground, grasping for anything they could use in a futile attempt to cover their heads, and holding their loved ones close.

The ball of light began to fan out in all directions as a barely discernible, flickering waterfall. The leading edge glowed dimly and was just visible to anyone looking closely. It steadily moved downward, creating a giant, shimmering dome over the City. Only, no one was looking closely enough to see it. They were cowering and terrified. As the airborne rocks loomed ever closer, it became clear these were not just rocks, they were huge boulders.

Lyric, still able to see through her partially closed eyes saw Benn, Hann, Adria and the two uncles hold their positions, though all the colour drained from their faces as the massive boulders, some as big as a house, plummeted toward them. Just as the first rock arrived, the leading edge of the shimmering shield touched ground in a massive circle around the City. One by one the rocks and boulders hit the shield. There was a bright flash where it hit, the bigger the boulder the brighter the flash. Then it would bounce off or roll down the surface of the dome. The sight was both terrifying and dazzling.

When the colour returned to her face, Adria, still on the Podium, took a deep breath and addressed the still cowering crowd. "People of Vulcon! Today is the day the Great Prophecy is fulfilled!" She gestured toward the mountain and the shower of boulders. "And this," she gestured toward Lyric, "is the Great Seer. Gift of the Goddess. Sent to save us all!" She paused a moment to increase the impact of her words. "Behold, Lyric of Vulcon!"

The terrified people in the plaza, many weeping and still crying out, slowly raised themselves to their knees and took in the terrifying sight of a glowing Lyric, a column of light and the flashing lights above them. Some cowered back down in fear and others bowed their heads in respect. Those near the edge of the plaza were passing the information back to those still in the streets and the message thus spread throughout the City.

Just as some of the people mustered enough courage to rise to their feet, there was a second mighty explosion on the mountain which sent everyone back to their knees. A chilling cry went up from a woman in the crowd. Everyone turned to see what frightened her so. A huge billowing black cloud flashing with red fire below and lightning above was racing down the mountainside toward the City like a great monster from the bowels of the earth. Again, there was shrieking and weeping and the terrified people repeatedly cried out, "Oh Great Seer save us!"

Within moments the shadow of the mighty cloud darkened the City, but Lyric did not flinch. She maintained focus and the light continued to stream from the earth, through her body and up into the shield. Now everyone, including Adria, stared ashen-faced and open-mouthed at the billowing black mass bearing down upon them. There was no time to react, it was too fast. There was barely time to take a breath before the looming cloud arrived at the City, surged over the dome and covered the whole surface in fiery hot ash. It completely obliterated the sunlight and plunged the City into an eerie near darkness.

With the white light of the column passing through Lyric and the faint glow from rocks and debris hitting the shield, the City was illuminated as if bathed in moonlight. It was sufficient for people to move about. Farmers were trying to calm the distressed livestock and herd them to open areas. Others were scurrying for lanterns and lighting them until the crowd looked like a sea of glowing faces punctuated by lamplight.

Many people in the plaza were still slowly rising to their feet, trembling and shaken. They were still in awe of Lyric, but they were frightened and angry. The outspoken among them had questions. Adria was still standing on the podium, ready. When she finally regained her composure, she called out to them. "Good people of Vulcon!" she shouted as loud as she could muster, "I am Adria, Seer, and mother of Lyric, the Great Seer. Do not be afraid. This has all been foreseen and our family has been making preparations for many years. The black cloud will plunge us into darkness for more than an entire day and the Great Seer will protect us until the land has been cleansed by rain."

"How is it the royal family did not foresee this?" A voice shouted out. The angry crowd rumbled in agreement.

"Good people of Vulcon!" Adria shouted out over the crowd, "The gift of Sight was lost from the royal family three generations ago." A murmur rose among the crowd, but Adria pressed on. "It seems they were unwilling to give up the privileges of royalty when the gift was lost."

The Princess, who was cowering in the Royal Litter, covered herself in a blanket, slipped out of the Royal Litter and melted into the crowd.

"The Prophecy spoke of murdered children," another voice from the crowd called out.

"There is no Fading Ill affecting our children," Adria replied. The crowd murmured with scepticism. "The royal family administered poison to any child who showed the gift of Sight at the commencement of their schooling. This is why the Greet Seer took on the guise of the Wildling, that she may live long enough to protect you and your families today."

The crowd was rumbling with outrage now and it intensified by the moment. Some were making their way toward the Royal Litter shouting, "Kill the murderers!" When they pushed aside the Royal Protector, they found the Royal Litter empty. The cry went up, "She is gone!"

Adria spoke up quickly to allay the worst, "The Great Seer wishes you not worry yourselves with the royal family now. Justice can wait. Now is a time for looking out for one another."

Rikk waved the Protector who was helping him battle Benn, to come closer. "Go to the Palace, arrest the former Queen and imprison her with the former Princess and former Protector Consort," he said. "Go quickly. They will no doubt attempt an escape."

"Yes sir!" The Protector saluted and smiled. "With pleasure sir." He jogged off toward the Palace and the crowd parted to make way for him.

"Just so you know," Rikk said as he turned toward Benn, "I found it difficult to believe you had gone crazy."

Benn smiled, but did not lower his sword. "Are we good then?"

Rikk smiled back. "Brata was seriously over-indulged and difficult to live with. I suppose you already knew that." He winked toward his old friend. "Thanks for breaking off the betrothal for me."

The two friends laughed together, renewing their bond. Rikk then took a position on the step below Benn. He turned to face the crowd and raised his sword into the vigilance position.

"You're still a great swordsman," Rikk said, turning his head to address Benn.

"Thanks, Rikk," Benn said. "And you haven't bested me yet."

"I'll keep practising then."

Adria nodded approval. Lyric now had one more Protector.

"Good people of Vulcon!" Adria shouted to gain the attention of the crowd. "Our family has been preparing for this day for many years. In her wisdom, the Great Seer has left instructions to ensure we all come through this as safely and equitably as possible." The murmuring of the crowd diminished as Adria continued. "Our first priority is to care for each other and care for what remains of Vulcon's precious livestock. That being so, all financial transactions are prohibited for a period of one clead."

The crowd restlessly murmured. A merchant shouted out, "What? You expect us to just give our wares away? We'll be ruined!"

Adria made a downward motion with her hands to try and lower the volume of noise from the crowd so she could be heard.

"For many months now, we have been secretly preserving the produce from our extensive farm and storing it safely here in the City, as have others in our family and some of our friends," she said. "We are prepared to share all of this with the people of Vulcon, for no monetary gain, to ensure no one goes hungry or thirsty in these trying times. We do not ask of you anything we are not prepared to do ourselves."

The crowd began to murmur again, but this time many heads were nodding. This was a good sign.

Adria continued, "This is a time for the people of Vulcon to come together and care for one another, just as the Great Seer is caring for us. Who is with us?"

There was a chilling moment of silence before the crowd began to applaud and cheer and wave their arms. Adria heaved a sigh of relief.

"Excellent! Let us begin," Adria said. "Tye of the family Marl, and Simm of the family Fenner, please raise your hands." Two hands dutifully appeared over the heads of the crowd. "These men will coordinate the building of fenced enclosures to contain the livestock in the school yard and on the lawns of the Palace. Timber and tools have been stowed in their cellars. Could any able–bodied man with skills in working timber please accompany these men to their homes so construction of enclosures can commence." A number of men hugged their womenfolk and children and made their way toward Tye and Simm.

"Thank you, thank you, noble sirs!" Adria shouted.

In a similar fashion, Adria delegated the distribution of food and water provisions, with items to be rationed such that the reserves would last out the clead. She explained that the water in the well would likely go foul or cease altogether and a number of cellars had been sealed and were collecting rainwater from house roofs for some months. "Remember, all drinking water must be boiled!" she shouted as the water delegates retreated from the plaza.

"Why?" called out a voice from the crowd.

"Because we have foreseen that if the water is not boiled, many people will become sick and die, especially the elderly and the children."

"That's a good reason!" the voice called back and a small group of people around him laughed and elbowed him in the ribs.

CHAPTER NINE

The Great Seer

Benn remained resolute at his post. Periodically he glanced toward Lyric. He was in awe. While practising in the desert, Lyric showed him how she could create a protective dome, but this was on a scale far greater than Benn imagined. This dome enclosed almost the entire City. He listened as Adria continued to make announcements and direct activities from the podium, pointing out that sitting about idly was not a good idea. She requested that, where possible, each family in the City should take a farming family into their homes. She called for menfolk to help with construction and distribution activities and the womenfolk were sent to prepare meals for their families plus some to share.

A young Protector returned from the Palace, jogging through the thinning crowd in the plaza.

"Protector Rikk sir," he said as he saluted, somewhat breathless, clenching his right fist and pressing it to his chest. "The royal family, I mean former royal family, are missing sir. They seem to have made good their escape before we arrived at the Palace."

"Thank you, Protector." Rikk returned the salute and looked toward Benn for direction.

"They can't have gone far. Anyone outside the dome will meet certain death and anyone inside the dome can be found later. Thank you, Protector."

The young man took the cue and saluted Benn, still panting and catching his breath.

As the people continued to disperse to their tasks, there was a commotion in the nearby streets. Those Protectors assigned to the city gates were returning to the plaza. Most of them stopped to take in the sight of Lyric and the column of light before rushing forward toward the podium. The first to arrive recognised Rikk and made for him.

"Returning from the East Gate, sir!" he said, puffing for breath, while saluting Rikk.

Rikk returned the salute. "At ease, Protector. I am no longer a senior Royal Protector." He gestured toward Benn. "This is now the Protector in charge."

The Protector turned to Benn and lapsed into despair. "I'm sorry sir, we couldn't save them," he said as he fell to his knees and tried to discreetly wipe tears from his eyes with his wrists. By now the others had arrived and they were assembled into a group, most of them were distressed and some were also wiping their eyes.

"What happened?" Benn stepped forward with genuine concern. His gut wrenched as he anticipated their tale.

"We were on duty at the East Gate this morning, and saw the smoke rise from the mountain," the Protector said. "We were expecting an influx of people and produce from the farms for market day, but there were so many, and they brought their livestock, and they just kept coming. It was almost like all the farms were evacuating into the City. Then Royal Protectors arrived and told us to close the gates. We tried to close them, but they were jammed."

The Protectors from the other gates voiced agreement, as similar events had unfolded at each of the city gates.

"Yes Protector, we instructed children to jam the hinges with pebbles," Benn said.

"Thank the Goddess for that," the Protector said. "Well, the gates wouldn't close, so the Royal Protectors tried to block more people from entering the City, but there were so many, with wagons and animals, and they just pushed the Protectors aside and kept coming in. Then a light appeared from the centre of the City and something came down from the light and blocked the road just outside the gate. The stragglers could not get through. They pushed up against the barrier screaming and crying out for us to let them in, but we could not. Then the rocks came down and many were hit. Finally, the dark cloud came, and all went silent and black." He looked at the ground, forlorn. "We should have saved more sir. If we hadn't tried to block the gates, we could have saved more people."

Benn looked down on this Protector and the group gathered behind him. They were trained since childhood to Protect the people. They were gutted by what they had seen.

"Do not hold yourselves to account, Protectors, you were not to know," Benn said. "You were not to know the royal family no longer had the gift of the Sight. You were not to know this was the day the Great Prophecy would be fulfilled. That this was the day the Great Seer would save Vulcon. You were trained to Protect the people of Vulcon and you dwell on those that were lost, this is a credit to you. Their loss is a great sadness, but dwell rather on how many have been saved." Benn waved his arm to indicate all the people currently safe in the City under Lyric's wondrous shield.

"The royal family were not Seers?" one of the Protectors asked.

"No," Benn replied. "The gift of Sight was lost from their family three generations ago."

"Then they have deceived us all!" The Protector was angry now.

"Yes, they have," Benn said, "and they will see justice, but first we must protect and aid the people."

The Protectors saluted. These were orders they could follow with conviction.

Benn could see that Adria had moved across the podium and listened to the exchange.

"Good Protectors of Vulcon." Adria addressed the gathered men. "In light of these events, the Palace must be prepared to receive a new Queen. Who of you is willing to serve the Great Seer and assist in this important task?"

All of the gathered Protectors raised their hands, keen to make amends for the loss of life at the city gates.

"Very well," Adria continued. "Take our Aunt Tyla to the Palace. She is an experienced Seer and she can help you discern who is loyal to the former Queen and who is willing to serve the Great Seer. As experienced Protectors, I'm sure you are more than capable of enacting the required change of staff."

"Yes, Seer!" the most senior Protector replied, with a brisk salute.

"We are at the service of the Great Seer!" another blurted out.

Aunt Tyla duly attached herself to the group of Protectors. Their muscular stature, fine uniforms and handsome faces were not lost on her. She gave Uncle Renn a sly grin and a wink before allowing the band of Protectors to escort her off to the Palace. Uncle Renn momentarily looked distressed, but a reassuring smile from Hann saw them both laughing loudly. As the greatest hazard passed, the Uncles, Hann and Benn lowered their swords into a more relaxed position with the tips resting on the earth and both hands resting on the hilt, ready to grasp and swing should the need arise.

"Nicely done," Rikk said, glancing at Benn and Adria in turn.

"Thank you." Benn felt pleased at Rikk's approval. Rikk's opinion had always mattered to him.

"If I may make a suggestion Benn," Rikk said. "You four Protectors are going to get pretty weary over the next day or so. Allow me to recruit some of the Royal Protectors to help. We can protect the Great Seer in shifts. Besides, after what some of the Protectors have witnessed today, having a job will keep them calm and focussed."

Benn looked to Adria and Hann who both nodded their assent. "Thanks, Rikk, that would be helpful."

Now appropriately authorised, Rikk set off on a mission to recruit assistance. He eventually returned with a group of eight Protectors. They moved people back, forming a defensive circle around the podium.

"This is the first shift," Rikk said to Benn. "As we have no sunlight, the sundial is useless, so we are setting up a water clock over there." Rikk pointed toward a small commotion behind the podium. "The shifts will change each time the clock is empty, around every five hours."

"I appreciate your support Rikk." Benn looked around at the rest of the family, each of whom nodded or smiled agreement. "We all do."

"Happy to protect the people who are protecting the person who is protecting us." Rikk gently elbowed Benn in the ribs. "It's going to be OK isn't it?"

"Yes Rikk. I think it's going to be OK."

The two of them chatted for a while. Benn summarised for Rikk the chain of events from the disrupted betrothal to their arrival at the plaza. Though he left out the details he thought Rikk didn't need to know. Rikk filled Benn in on what had happened at the Palace, the Queen's ire, the order to kill Benn and how he avoided being in the search party. He told Benn how the Princess quickly diverted her affections to himself. He felt flattered at the time, so much so he tolerated her bad behaviour. In retrospect he could see how the events indicated that neither the Queen nor the Princess had the gift of Sight, but at the time it had seemed unremarkable.

A little girl managed to edge her way through the crowd and between the Protectors. She stood for a while in front of Benn, just looking up at him, which was quite an effort on her part as she stood no higher than Ben's waist. Benn maintained his guard position and initially tried not to pay her any attention.

"Hello!" A small voice called out.

Benn looked down. "Hello."

"What's your name?" the girl asked.

"Benn. What's your name?"

"Tika."

"That's a nice name."

"So is Benn."

"Thank you."

"Are you a Protector?"

"Yes."

"When I grow bigger, will you be my Protector?"

Benn dropped to one knee to speak to Tika directly, "If I'm still available when you grow bigger, I'll give it serious consideration."

Rikk put his hand over his mouth to hide a chuckle.

"Where are your parents?" Benn asked, concerned.

"Over there." Tika pointed into the crowd.

Benn spied a woman handing out flatbread parcels to people in the crowd. When their eyes met, he looked down at Tika. The woman followed his gaze, caught sight of Tika and began rushing toward the podium to claim her wayward child.

Tika stepped over to Rikk. "Don't worry." She was trying to sound reassuring. "It will be OK."

Rikk looked surprised. "You know it's not polite to listen to other people's conversations, little girl."

"I know," she chirped, "that's why I don't do it."

Tika's mother arrived, grabbed her daughter by the arm and dragged her away while apologising profusely.

Rikk and Benn looked at each other and laughed.

"Seeing as you're now betrothed to a girl who can't be more than seven years old," Rikk jibed, "would you mind if I started courting Lyric?" Rikk tilted his head in Lyric's direction.

"Why would you want to start courting Lyric?" Benn looked surprised. "Wouldn't you rather date someone who didn't have the power to fry you to crisp?"

"Well, she is rather attractive, beautiful even," Rikk replied. "Good point about the crisp though. Now that I'm no longer betrothed to a Princess, I guess I'll just have to find someone else out there." Rikk swept his arm out gesturing toward the crowd.

"I'm sure there's someone out there for you," Benn said. He glanced back at Lyric, her face glowing in the light. Even with glowing white eyes, he could plainly see she was beautiful and he felt strangely pleased to have diverted Rikk from her.

During what was probably the night, women brought food to Adria and the Protectors and offered them a place to sleep in a house facing onto the plaza. Benn was weary, but reluctant to leave his post. Hann came over to him.

"You look tired Benn, and Adria too. Maybe you should take her to the house and get some sleep?" he suggested.

"I'm needed here," Benn protested.

"I'm needed here too," Adria chimed in.

"I can see that," Hann responded, "But you'll still be needed here tomorrow. Even more so. Remember the people are likely to become more restless when the Shield is due to come down. We'll need you both to be alert and able then. Besides, we can rest in shifts. The uncles and I will remain for this shift and you two can take over when you are refreshed and give us a break."

"He's right," Rikk said, "these Protectors and I can ably guard Lyric while you get some rest."

Reluctantly, Benn agreed and allowed the women to lead him and Adria to a room with comfortable beds where they could rest.

By what was thought to be midday the next day, they returned to their posts, refreshed. Then Hann and the uncles went off to rest, their posts being filled by diligent Royal Protectors. The cycle of shifts repeated, governed by the faithful water clock. Order was restored and all was running smoothly. Fences were completed and the livestock were relocated and provided with adequate water and feed. Some of the menfolk worked shifts around the livestock, removing manure and locating it to a large heap beside the Palace vegetable gardens. The strange situation was bringing out the best in the people of Vulcon. They were sharing food provisions, looking out for one another, and looking out for the children. Occasional disagreements and squabbles were either sorted by family and friends or brought to Adria for mediation.

After what seemed like much more than a day of darkness, people were starting to get concerned and irritable, and many who had dispersed were returning to the plaza. There were murmurings among the people. How long would this go on? How long would the food and water hold out? How long would the Great Seer be able to maintain the Shield? Would it be long enough to protect them? Suddenly a massive cracking sound rang out, so loud that people could feel the air vibrate.

"The Shield is failing!" a voice yelled from the crowd.

That's when the screaming started, and people started to flee for shelter. Rikk and the other Protectors looked to Benn for direction. Benn felt a pang of anxiety. He had not expected this. He turned his head to see Lyric, still unmoving, still glowing, and resolved that while she held true, he must also. Benn did not flinch from his position, and so, with trepidation, the Protectors held theirs.

Adria stood up from a second chair, which had been placed on the podium for her comfort when she returned from her first rest. She shouted at the top of her voice, "Good people of Vulcon! Fear not!"

Some of the people paused to listen.

"The Shield is holding firm!" Adria continued, "That was the sound of thunder. The rain is coming."

There were more mighty cracks and rumbles. People nervously spread the word among those who were fleeing. One by one they started to return to the plaza.

"Why is there no lightning then?" shouted a voice from the crowd, "Thunder follows lightning."

"We can't see the lightning!" another voice yelled back, "The dome is covered in ash."

Benn looked to Adria and she gave him a reassuring smile. She seemed pleased the people were figuring this out for themselves.

They heard the rain before they could see it. Gaps started to appear at the top of the dome and a dim light began to break through. As the gaps widened, and joined, dark grey storm clouds dusted with pink and pelting rain could be seen, although all in the City remained dry. The water was slowly but surely washing the ash from the dome. Hours later, when the rain finally stopped, the ash had washed down level with the top of the city walls. The clouds parted and beams of morning sunlight broke through, illuminating the plaza. The people began to cheer and dance. Accompanied by gasps, shouts and much pointing from the crowd, the shimmering veil lifted, and the column of light slowly contracted down until it disappeared under Lyric's feet.

There was still a massive plume of grey smoke rising from the mountain, but the wind had changed, and it was blowing over the farmlands to the east and out to sea. From the City, Benn could see the mountain had lost its green skirt. All was brown and grey and stark. A massive crater gaped at the northwest face of the mountaintop. The Vulcon they knew was gone. Changed.

Benn bounded up the podium steps to Lyric's side. She blinked a few times then opened her eyes. She looked from side to side upon the people, stood up, and promptly collapsed into Benn's arms.

"The Great Seer needs rest!" Adria shouted.

"Well, she certainly earned it!" a voice yelled from somewhere in the crowd. A cheer of agreement went up.

Benn swept Lyric up in his arms and proceeded to carry her from the podium. The crowd applauded as he descended the steps.

"Shall we use the Royal Litter?" Rikk asked as Benn reached the bottom step. "It still stands nearby."

"No. I'll take her to the Palace myself." Lyric was safe in his strong arms and he was not about to relinquish her to anyone. She moved in his arms, placed an arm around his neck and nestled against his chest. The scent of her filled his nostrils and something surged inside him. He was glad her tunic was draping beneath her as it would be embarrassing for a Protector to be seen as thus distracted. At that moment, Lyric felt light in his arms and carrying her to safety seemed like no effort at all.

The crowd parted, forming a clear path from the podium to the Palace. Benn carried Lyric all the way, through a multitude of 'thanks and cheers' from those lining the path. Adria, Hann, the uncles, Rikk and the Protectors formed a procession behind them.

Although Lyric was desperately weary, she nodded feebly to the well-wishers and tears started to trickle down her face. "Did I do it Benn?" she whispered. "Are the people safe?".

"Yes Lyric. You did it. The people are safe."

She nestled back against Benn's chest.

Benn carried her into the Palace, up the stairs, and into the royal bedchamber where he placed her gently on the bed. As he stepped back, Adria and two maids surged forward. They removed Lyric's sandals and her girdle and pulled a light cover over her. Benn stood quietly at a distance, watching his dear friend, the Lyric he had known, befriended and protected for so many years, drift away into sleep. When she awoke, she would be Queen. When she awoke, would she still want him around?

After all, he was just a humble Protector with no significant family connections, and she was the Great Seer. A chill ran down his spine at the thought and tears began to well in his eyes. Unaccustomed to such emotion, he stepped back and sat on a chaise against the wall to watch over her as she slept.

The room was unfamiliar, the shutters were closed, and the long, ornate curtains were drawn. Lyric was disoriented and she couldn't tell if it was day or night. A well-dressed girl who Lyric didn't recognise stood beside the bed whispering.

"Madam! madam! She's awake madam."

The girl stepped back in deference as Adria stood up from a chair beside the bed and leaned over Lyric.

"Mother," Lyric said, and started to look about the room. "Where's Benn? Are the people safe? Where am I? How long was I asleep?"

Adria smiled. "One thing at a time, Precious One." She stepped aside to reveal Benn, still in full Protector garb, sleeping on the chaise against the wall. "He's hardly left the room since he brought you in here."

Lyric remembered Benn carrying her to the Palace. She remembered the power of his arms and his scent. She loved the aroma of spices. Being in his arms felt good, safe, and warm. "I'm in the Palace?"

"Yes," Adria replied. "The Queen's chambers. You've been asleep all day and all night. Indeed, you've managed to sleep right through your eighteenth birthday. The people are safe but are getting restless. Are you up to rising for breakfast?"

Lyric pushed aside the covers and sat up. She felt weak and a little dizzy. She paused for a moment until her world stabilised before standing up with her mother holding her arm.

"She's awake!" Benn's voice came from behind Adria. He rushed over and took Lyric's arm from Adria, supporting Lyric as she took her first steps. "How are you feeling?"

Lyric paused and thought a moment, "Ravenously hungry."

"Good," said Benn, "Let's get you to the dining hall."

Lyric took a step forward, then stopped.

"What's wrong?" Benn asked, intensely concerned.

"Before I eat though."

"Yes?"

"I really need to go to the toilet!"

Benn blushed awkwardly, then turned Lyric and steered her toward the Queen's washroom. He seemed happy to let Adria and the maid take over when they arrived at the doorway.

When Lyric emerged, relieved, Benn was there. He took her arm and guided her from the royal chambers. Adria sent the maid ahead to ensure food was ready when they arrived. Hann, the two uncles and their wives were already seated at the table, and as Lyric entered the room, they rushed over and hugged and kissed her.

"Well done, Precious One," her father said as he stepped away. "You saved us all. I knew you would." He winked at Lyric.

Lyric sat down to a table lavish with ornate food, meats, vegetables, fruits, breads and cakes. Her eyes widened taking in the feast, then she turned to her mother.

"The people. Is there enough food for the people?" Lyric was concerned.

"The people have sufficient for now," Hann replied. "The maids and servants insisted they be allowed to prepare a meal to thank you for saving them."

Lyric looked about at the beaming faces of the servants positioned about the room. "Thank you all very much."

The servants, still smiling, bowed in unison.

"Eat, eat," Benn said.

Lyric sampled the foods, found all of them delicious and ate until she could eat no more. Her family and Benn joined her in the feast.

When replete, Lyric turned to the staff, "Please tell the cooks everything was delicious."

The servants smiled, bowed and a server disappeared to convey the message to the kitchen staff.

"Now to business, Precious One," Adria said. "The people are safe but restless. The former royal family are missing. The food is being managed and rationed according to plan. Now that there has been more rain, the height of the ash is about half the height of the city walls. As we foresaw, half of the Port is intact, but the entrance is blocked. There are massive rivers of rock, and fields of ash over what were the western farmlands. They extend far into the ocean to the west and the north, connecting to another large island which has risen from the sea. The new Vulcon is much bigger than the old Vulcon. Indeed, it would appear we are no longer a large island but almost a small continent."

Lyric listened intently to the details but felt a twinge of grief deep inside. The time of roaming the fields without a care were gone. It was now time for her to take on significant responsibility.

"The people are in need of leadership and reassurance," Hann interjected. "According to the traditions of Vulcon, as the Great Seer you are now the rightful Queen. I suggest we plan the coronation for this evening."

"So soon?" Adria queried.

"Yes," Benn spoke up, "I agree with Hann. In these difficult times, the people need to know there is strong, genuine, Seer leadership in the Palace."

Lyric observed that even her family were now treating her in a much more deferent and conciliatory manner. This would take some getting used to.

"Very well," Lyric said, "let preparations be made for a coronation this evening." She tried to sound regal.

"Excellent!" Aunt Tyla said, "I'll supervise."

The family agreed and Lyric's aunt left the room to organise the proceedings. Lyric knew her aunt took delight in organising large events which involved coordinating many people.

"Before the coronation, you will need to bathe and be dressed in coronation robes," Adria said. She was good at organisational details too. "I've sent for the Dean of the Protector Academy, the High Priestess and the Chief Magistrate so we can hold a rehearsal this morning. Are you feeling better now, Precious One?"

"Yes," Lyric replied. The sumptuous breakfast and the cheerful company of Benn and her family replenished her energy and she felt ready to take on the duties of the day. When she rose from her chair, Benn was instantly by her side to offer material support.

"It's OK Benn," she said. "I'm stronger now, after that magnificent breakfast. I think I can manage walking unaided." She flashed Benn a cheeky grin.

Benn took only a small step back and followed close by all day.

The shadows were lengthening on the ground when the procession left the Palace and made its way to the podium in the plaza. The crowds lining the way cheered and clapped as Lyric passed by in the Royal Litter, with the curtains tied open so she could see and be seen. Lyric gave cheerful and polite waves to the crowd as she passed by. Three solemn figures in ceremonial garb and an ornately carved wooden throne awaited on the podium.

"They've upgraded my chair," Lyric whispered to Benn who was walking beside the Royal Litter.

Benn flashed her an acknowledging and reassuring smile. "Indeed, they have."

Lyric lifted her skirts to avoid tripping on the dress her mother had spent many months sewing for the occasion. The fabric was the finest woven cashmere, dyed a dark green. It highlighted her green eyes beautifully. Over this was a long cloak dyed a rich scarlet. Although the dress was exquisitely light and comfortable, the cloak was heavy and cumbersome. Thankfully, after two good meals that day, Lyric felt strong now and up to the task. She mounted the steps as solemnly as she could manage, stood before the throne, gathered her dress and cloak evenly around her and seated herself slowly and deliberately. Benn took a position at the rear of the podium and her family took positions on the side steps. A circle of Royal Protectors kept the crowd at a respectful distance.

The three figures on the podium were the Dean of the Protector Academy, the High Priestess of the Temple of the Goddess and the Chief Magistrate. The Temple of the Goddess was located on a high point at the edge of the City toward the foot of the mountain. The High Priestess seemed much relieved that the protective shield had fallen just beyond the temple wall and the temple was spared.

The Dean nodded toward a row of final year Academy students positioned behind the podium. Three of them stepped forward and mounted the rear steps, each bearing a purple cushion. One of cushions bore the royal sceptre, another a crystal orb and the third a finely crafted, jewel encrusted, gold crown.

The Dean approached Lyric and addressed her in a loud voice, "Are you Lyric of the family Nye, Great Seer of Vulcon?"

"I am," Lyric replied, as loud as she could so the people could hear.

"Does any man or woman present dispute the identity of this woman?" The Dean continued.

There was silence and much head shaking in the gathered crowd. Deep inside, Lyric was half expecting someone to cry out she was just the Wildling, but it didn't happen. In the eyes of the people, the Wildling was no more.

In the absence of any objections, the Dean resumed. "Do you, Lyric of the family Nye, Great Seer of Vulcon, present yourself this day to the people, willing to serve as their Queen and guide?"

"I do," Lyric replied.

The Chief Magistrate then stepped forward. He took the sceptre from the cushion and held it before Lyric.

"Will you rule the people of Vulcon with wisdom and justice?" He cried out, his voice even louder than that of the Dean.

"I will."

The Chief Magistrate then proffered the sceptre to Lyric who took it and held it upright in her right hand.

Next the High Priestess stepped forward, took the crystal orb from its cushion and held it before Lyric.

"Will you use the gifts bestowed on you by the Goddess, in the service of your people?" The High Priestess was accustomed to projecting her rich voice over a crowd.

"I will." Lyric held out her left hand, and the High Priestess gently placed the orb into Lyric's cupped, slightly trembling, hand.

The Dean nodded approval, then slowly and gently took the crown from its cushion and placed it on Lyric's head. It fit securely. He stepped to one side, gestured toward Lyric and announced, "People of Vulcon! Behold your Queen!"

A mighty din of cheer and applause erupted from the crowd. Lyric stood slowly and the cheering became even louder. She was smiling wide but keeping her head very still, lest the crown be dislodged. It was heavier than it looked. She glanced to the side and saw her mother wiping away tears of joy. Even her father was wiping his eyes.

As the din died down, Lyric took a step forward to address the crowd.

"People of Vulcon, I vow to dedicate the rest of my life to your service."

The crowd cheered again. Lyric focussed and the orb and the jewel in the sceptre began to glow with a bright white light. There was a gasp of awe from the crowd, and as the light dimmed, the crowd cheered again. Lyric wanted to show them her ability was not just limited to the day of the Horrific Catastrophe, and she would use it in the ongoing service of the people. Her people.

"In light of recent events, it gladdens my heart to see so many people alive and well. However, like you, I mourn for those lost. Therefore, let us cause to be built a great memorial by the West Gate of the City to always remind us of the power of the mountain and of the lives that were lost."

This was met by general applause.

"The events of recent generations have taught us it is not in the best interests of the people of Vulcon for all governing power to be vested in one person. Therefore, I call on the Chief Magistrate of Vulcon, to sit down with the High Priestess, the Dean of the Academy, my mother who is an experienced Seer, and Protector Rikk who will represent our youth, to draw up a constitution founding an elected, governing Senate to make laws and preside over the day-to-day governance of Vulcon."

There was a murmuring in the crowd. This was unfamiliar and unexpected.

Despite the diminished response, Lyric persisted, "In accordance with the traditions of our people, only men of age may be elected to the Senate, but only women of age may vote."

The crowd paused a moment to consider this, then the women began to applaud. Soon the applause spread through the crowd and heads began to nod as the people began to realise the wisdom of this plan.

"We shall seek out the imposter royal family and see to it justice is done."

This triggered both applause and cheering.

"I ask for your patience. It will take time to restore Vulcon to its former prosperity. My family and I foresaw the difficulties we are yet to face and have prepared to ensure there is sufficient food, water and accommodation for all. I have faith in your strength, resilience, commitment and skills, and I can see that together we will rebuild Vulcon to be even better than we remember!"

Another loud cheer.

"Until livelihoods have been restored, the wings of the royal palace will continue to house members of our displaced farming community, the lawns of the Palace will continue to house the livestock so vital to the restoration of our farms, and the food reserves of the royal palace will continue to be shared with the people."

More applause and cheering.

"During the coming moons, I will be personally employing my gifts to aid in the necessary rebuilding work outside the city walls."

This generated modest applause as most of the people did not yet understand how Lyric would be able to help.

"Now that we all have something to celebrate, let the merriment begin!"

The crowd cheered and applauded. Musicians began to play near the edge of the plaza and people began to dance.

Lyric turned toward to the Chief Magistrate who smiled graciously and bowed. She repeated the gesture to the Dean and the High Priestess who bowed in turn. As she turned to leave the podium Benn and her family also bowed. This was more disconcerting than she expected. She wanted to rush to them and reassure them she was still just Lyric, but she held herself back. She was no longer just Lyric. She was now the Queen.

Benn stepped forward and Lyric accepted his arm for support as she descended the steps from the podium.

"Thank you," Lyric said, smiling at Benn.

Benn just nodded acknowledgement.

"I mean, thank you for protecting me while I protected the people," Lyric clarified, in case Benn thought she was merely thanking him for helping her down the steps. "Without you, I could never have done it, and I would not be Queen today. You were brave, capable and well... amazing."

"You are most welcome, my Queen." Benn led Lyric toward the waiting Royal Litter. "I'm glad you consider it a job well done, and I'm happy for you."

Lyric smiled, but she was perplexed. Benn's response had seemed cryptic and distant. She sensed something was not right, but she was too emotionally close to the problem to see what was happening. It took some fuss to eventually enter the Royal Litter with robes, crown, orb and sceptre in position, but eventually the procession made its way back to the Palace with citizens bowing and shouting out their congratulations as Lyric passed by. Although Vulcon's fields and forests were still a wasteland, for the people this would be a night of joy and merriment.

Once Lyric was suitably dressed and groomed, she left her chambers for the dining room. The wooden bench outside her door was empty. That was unusual, she expected Benn to be there. The sound of voices drew her to the parapet where she paused to breathe in the clear air of late summer and feel the warming rays of sunlight on her face. Her reverie was broken by the commotion below.

"What's going on?" Lyric asked, looking back toward her chambers. "Who are all these people and what are they doing here?"

Her maid, Tessa, a young woman of roughly Lyric's age, emerged and bowed. "They are suitors your Majesty."

"Suitors?" Lyric asked, confused.

"Well, your Majesty," Tessa explained. "As of last night, Vulcon has a new Queen who is neither bonded nor betrothed, so every family in the City with an unbonded son of age has come to seek interview with your parents."

"That's silly." Lyric was incredulous. "I have no need of suitors. I have Benn." She looked around, Benn was usually close by, but he was nowhere to be seen. "By the way, where is Benn?"

"He was seen leaving the Palace earlier this morning your Majesty," Tessa said, stepping back cautiously. Having seen Lyric's abilities, Tessa seemed worried that an emotional disturbance could potentially be fatal to those nearby.

"Leaving? Leaving to go where?"

"No one knows your Majesty. He left no word of his destination or his reason for leaving, nor any plans for his return."

Lyric felt sick, as though she was punched in the gut. She leaned against the parapet for support. Now his comment at the Royal Litter the previous evening made sense. She had thanked him for protecting her. The job he promised to do was done. He knew how much of a freak she really was and did not want to be bonded to someone like her. For a moment she wished Benn was mercenary enough to stay just to enjoy the privileges of Palace life, but Benn had integrity. That was one of the things she admired about him. The realisation he was honest, had integrity and chose to leave her felt like a second punch in her gut.

"Are you alright your Majesty?" Tessa asked looking intensely concerned. "Did I say something wrong?"

"No Tessa." Lyric composed herself. "You didn't say anything wrong. I appreciate your honesty and openness. I'm fine." That was a lie. She wasn't fine.

The dining hall was a grand room with high ceilings supported by mighty cedar beams. It was long enough to accommodate the grand cedar table and benches that stretched along the centre. Segments of the room and the table were illuminated by light coming in from large windows along one of the walls. Most of the table was empty, clean and shiny in the daylight. At one end there were plates of food and three place settings. Lyric arrived to find her parents just finishing their meal. They rose respectfully while she took her seat. It was strange to see her own parents treating her with such deference.

"Are you alright, Precious One?" Adria queried. Clearly Lyric looked as terrible as she felt.

"Benn's gone," Lyric said as she took her seat in a tall, ornately carved, wooden chair at the head of the table. There was still ample food, but Lyric had no appetite. She selected a few dried figs and pushed them absently around her plate before nibbling on one.

"Yes, Precious One," Hann said. "We heard." Hann looked pasty and uncomfortable in fine clothes sitting at a grand table. Lyric could see he would much rather be outdoors, overseeing farms and livestock.

"I don't understand," Adria said. "He promised to protect you, didn't he? Why would he go?"

"He promised to protect me while I was protecting the people from the Horrible Catastrophe, that's all. He kept his promise."

"Will you be OK?" Adria asked with deep concern.

Lyric just sat there a moment, brooding. She took a gulp of water from a silver goblet and gathered up a handful of the dried figs. "I'm sorry," she said as she rose to leave. "I need some time alone."

As etiquette demanded, her parents also stood, and they watched as she retreated from the dining hall. Lyric caught part of their conversation as she left.

"Does this mean I have to speak to all those suitors in the courtyard?" Hann asked.

"I think so," Adria replied. "But not just yet. Let's give it a little while."

Lyric dashed from the dining room and darted through the Palace rooms and corridors, scattering maids and servants in her path, then raced outside to a secluded and dark place she previously discovered. A place where she would be difficult to find. She sat on the cool earth in a shady nook between the bulging trunk of an ancient olive tree, a tall stone wall and a small sculptured hedge. She pulled her knees up, crossed her arms over them, lowered her head and wept. The sobs welled from deep within and she had no desire to try and stop them.

It was some time before she ran out of tears and finally looked up. Her body was stiff from sitting in the one attitude for so long. She leaned back against the tree trunk and stretched out her legs, her lovely robe gathering dust and debris from the earth. She remembered when dust and debris was her camouflage. She longed for the times when, as the Wildling, she roamed the countryside with Benn, when he didn't know how much of a freak she really was. But she realised that was a lie too. If their friendship couldn't survive the truth, perhaps it was never real at all, just a beautiful illusion. She wept some more at the thought of it. There were still a few tears left after all.

Eventually Lyric composed herself. She reconciled herself to her duty to the people. After all, it was her prophesied destiny to save the people and become Queen. The prophecy never said anything about her being destined to be happy.

There was still so much to be done, though it would feel empty without Benn by her side. She gathered herself up, dusted herself off, rounded up a handful of Royal Protectors and set out for the Port. It would need to be opened soon if Vulcon was to trade for the supplies needed to feed the people until crops could be established.

When Lyric arrived at the wharf, she could immediately see the problem. What looked like a flow of black water sat across the entrance to the Port. Only it wasn't water, it was solid rock and the entrance was thus sealed. In isolation, and exposed to the strange rock, the water in the harbour stagnated and festered. Dead fish floated on the surface and the stench was intense. Two of the Royal Protectors promptly donated their breakfast to the murky pool. Most of the others looked decidedly green.

Near the port entrance, Lyric selected the three Protectors who seemed the most able in the circumstances and showed them how to stand in formation around her. The same formation Benn had suggested was necessary. It stung the wound that he was not there to enact it, but Lyric was determined not to cry in front of these people. She must hold her composure and get the job done. A small crowd gathered to see how their new Queen would address the problem.

Lyric focussed on the stone. A pinpoint of intense blue–white light formed and disappeared into the rock, leaving small plumes of smoke. The plumes traced lines in the rock. Where the lines descended to the water's edge, hissing steam rose to mix with the smoke until the emissions became confluent and the rock was enveloped by a pale grey haze. Lyric broke focus and looked about, finally waving her hand to signal to the people standing nearby to move away. The remaining Protectors surged forward to push back the crowd. Lyric resumed focus and a mighty cube of rock began to lift up and away. The crowd hushed as the cube hovered a moment, then moved to the side and floated gently down to rest where people had stood only moments before. The crowd clapped and cheered, but even that could not soothe the ache within. She simply proceeded to move the next cube, and the next, and continued until the barrier was now just below the water level.

A stout man in a Phoenician tunic and sandals strode toward Lyric, and the surrounding Protectors raised their swords in warning. The man halted abruptly at a safe distance. "I must speak with the Queen."

Lyric finished the placement of another cube, broke concentration and turned toward the man. "Speak."

The man bowed low, fidgeting. "I am Kurn, captain of the trading vessel." He gestured back toward the ship. "Thank you for turning your wondrous abilities to the task of opening the Port. It is much appreciated. I am most keen to leave as soon as possible, your Majesty. Our supplies are running low and soon we will not have enough for the journey. Will the entrance be opened by nightfall?"

Lyric looked past him toward the ship. "Your ship sits low in the water for a vessel that is short on supplies Captain. What is your cargo?"

The Captain fidgeted even more and shuffled his feet. He looked truly uncomfortable. "Nothing of value to the people of Vulcon in these troubled times your majesty. We seek to lighten the burden on Vulcon's food supplies by conveying persons who no longer wish to remain on this island, back to lands in the east."

Lyric looked him in the eye. He seemed frightened and the colour drained from his face. "I should like to see your cargo for myself," she said and marched past him, Protectors in tow.

"That won't be necessary, your Majesty," the Captain said, now fairly dancing along at Lyric's side. "It's only a few passengers and our food supplies."

Lyric ignored his protests. She sensed he was hiding something. By the time she reached the vessel she could see it was crewed and set, ready for sail. There were ten crew above deck and she only had eight Protectors with her. Something didn't feel right. "Captain, please order your crew to disembark."

"But your Majesty, there is no need."

"Captain!" Lyric glared at him.

"Very well," the Captain said. "All crew leave the ship, immediately."

Lyric watched as the crew descended the plank to the wharf in an orderly fashion. "You four remain at this end of the plank," she said, pointing to four Protectors in sequence. "The rest of you with me."

The Protectors saluted and followed Lyric up the plank.

"Station yourselves here and here." Lyric pointed to the deck near the plank and a point near the steps down into the cargo hold."

Two Protectors positioned themselves at each station.

Lyric walked down the steps to the cargo hold and opened the door. She paused a moment while her eyes adjusted to the dim light before stepping forward. She expected to see a cluster of cowering citizens, but the hold was stacked with bags and crates. They lined the walls and formed mounds in the centre of the room. She stepped forward and untied one of the bags, gold spilled out. Lyric was hit with the realisation that the hold contained almost the entire contents of the Palace Treasury.

The celebrations in the streets and in the Palace went well into the night. Benn danced with Lyric until the musicians went home, too tired to play another note. It warmed Benn's heart to see Lyric so full of joy, and it stirred him deeper than he cared to admit as she danced in and out of his arms. He wanted to just hold her, close and safe, and show her just how much he had grown to care for her. Instead he eventually carried a weary Lyric, too tired to stand a moment longer, to her royal bedchamber where he placed her in the care of her maids. Benn gave orders that she be allowed to sleep for as long as she needed, then he slumped on the wooden bench outside her door, covered himself with his cloak and soon lapsed into a fitful sleep himself.

The commotion in the Palace courtyard started early in the morning. Benn woke to find his shoulder ached from sleeping on the hard, wooden surface. He swung his arm about to try and loosen the tight, painful muscles. He smoothed his tousled dark hair back with his hands and made his way to the parapet. Below him a queue of people began to assemble. Young men stood, agitated, alone or with their families. Rikk was in the line-up too looking painfully reluctant. His father appeared to be lecturing him, and his mother was wiping specks of grime off his wincing face with a kerchief. Benn knew what this was, and it cut him to the core to see it.

The new Queen was unbonded and every eligible young man was presenting to Lyric's parents to petition for permission to court their daughter. Every few minutes a new party would join the end of the line and each addition felt to Benn like his head was being slapped. Lyric was Queen now and she would be expected to bond for the advantage of her people. Perhaps the son of a wealthy merchant with good Phoenician trade connections, or the son of a major landowner to increase the royal estate, especially as so much land was lost under ash and stone. Benn had nothing to offer, no family, no wealth, no land, no connections; nothing but his devotion and his protection. That would not be enough. His contract was complete, he had protected her while she protected the people and seen it through to her coronation as Queen. He could think of no more acute torture than to remain at the Palace and watch Lyric bonded to another man. It was time to go, to give Lyric the space to form an advantageous bond. As he gathered his cloak about him and quietly left the Palace through a servant's entrance, he felt like a hot knife was cutting him open to his core. He couldn't even fathom where he would go. He wandered the streets aimlessly in the general direction of the temple.

Benn was too distracted, too tormented to watch where he was going. He was just taking one step at a time, not looking beyond the ground in front of his feet. He didn't see the woman step into his path until he crashed into her.

"Aunt Tyla," Benn said, as recognition set in. "I'm sorry. I wasn't watching where I was going."

"Clearly."

"Are you OK?"

"I'm fine, Benn," she said, straightening her tunic. "Where are you going?"

"I don't know. I'm considering throwing myself at the mercy of the temple."

"How about you start by throwing yourself at the mercy of my culinary skills? You look like you could use a good breakfast and a clean-up."

Benn's shoulders slumped, he wasn't sure if it was defeat or relief. "OK," was all he could manage, and he followed Aunt Tyla back to her home.

By the time Benn finished washing, Aunt Tyla had a hearty breakfast on the table and gestured for Benn to sit and eat. He didn't hesitate. He was famished. "Where is everyone?" Benn looked around, noticing the house was quiet.

"The children are with their grandmother for the day and Renn is in the workshop making more pots. The City always needs more pots."

Benn could only nod acknowledgement as his mouth was now full of food.

"So, why leave the Palace?" Aunt Tyla asked, munching on a dried fig, while watching Benn systematically consume every morsel of food on the table.

"Lyric is Queen now and it is time for her to be bonded for the advantage of Vulcon. I have nothing of value to offer."

"And you don't want to stand by and watch her bond to someone else?"

"Exactly," Benn said, and downed a pitcher of water.

"I see." Aunt Tyla began to clear away the empty bowls. "Would you mind coming with me Benn? There's something I think you should see."

"It's not like I have anything better to do." Benn wiped the water from his lips with the back of his hand. /p>

"Excellent." Aunt Tyla donned her cloak and the pair made their way back toward the Palace.

Benn felt more uncomfortable with every step. This was the very place he was trying to escape from and yet Aunt Tyla was leading him back. Back through the servant's entrance and back to the parapet overlooking the courtyard.

By now the queue of suitors was even longer, snaking out beyond the Palace and onto the street. Benn felt sick to his stomach at the sight.

"So, Benn, which of these young men below would you choose to protect and care for Lyric?"

The question was unexpected and perturbing. Benn began to study the young men assembled. He eliminated a few immediately on the grounds they were too well fed to be nimble enough to protect her. Then he eliminated a few more of his former classmates on the grounds of inferior swordsmanship, negotiating skills or mental aptitude. That left only a few real contenders, and he pointed them out to Aunt Tyla. Though it pained him, he conceded the contenders included Rikk. He was fairly certain Rikk's parents had insisted he be there, because they looked like they were guarding him lest he escape.

"A worthy group of contenders," Aunt Tyla said, leaning on the wall of parapet, unflinching. "Now Benn, could you please tell me which of these contenders is not secretly terrified of Lyric? Terrified of being incinerated without warning should she ever lose her temper. After all, how could someone be an effective protector and supportive companion to the Queen if he were secretly terrified of her?"

Benn obediently analysed the selection and soon realised that each of the remaining contenders seemed terrified of the prospect of being betrothed to the Queen, let alone being bonded to her. Even Rikk looked pallid and gaunt at the prospect, and he was the bravest young Protector there.

Aunt Tyla watched the expression on Benn's face change from gritted determination to stunned realisation. "So, Benn, who is the only young Protector on Vulcon qualified to protect our new Queen?"

"I am."

"I know that. Now you know that, and let me assure you, Lyric's parents know that."

"But Lyric only likes me as a friend. I doubt she ever considered me as a potential partner."

"Really Benn? If you're going to spend time around women, you're going to have to pay more attention. When you thought there was a power imbalance in your favour, when you were the star student and she was just the Wildling, did you make a move on her?"

"No."

"Why not?"

"Well, it wouldn't be decent for a Protector to abuse his power by taking advantage of someone who was vulnerable."

"Exactly. So, when the situation was reversed, and it was clear to both of you she was the Great Seer and the power imbalance was in her favour?"

The cogs were turning fast inside Benn's head now. "She did the same thing?"

"Precisely! Helpless victims of your own noble integrity, the pair of you." Aunt Tyla gave Benn a mock punch in the arm. "Tell me Benn, whenever Lyric had a choice, did she choose to be with you, or did she choose to be with someone else?"

Suddenly it felt like a myriad of puzzle pieces were assembling in Benn's head. Even as children, whenever there was an opportunity to spend a Fiveday together, Lyric showed up. When he went to the Academy, every clear full moon Lyric would be outside his window. When he was about to be betrothed to another, Lyric showed up. Was it possible? Had Lyric loved him all along? "I've been a fool."

"Understatement of the day, dear Benn."

Benn felt a twinge of desperation. "Am I too late? It's a very long queue."

"Follow me." Aunt Tyla led Benn down the servant's stairs into the bowels of Palace. They weaved through kitchens and workrooms and emerged through a small door discreetly located behind a curtain in the audience room.

Benn peered out to see Adria and Hann making themselves comfortable in two tall chairs on the podium at the end of the room and looking miserable about it. He felt a firm shove from behind and stumbled out into the middle of the room. The Protectors positioned around the podium surged forward.

"Wait!" Hann raised his hand. "Let him come forward."

The Protectors retreated to their posts. Adria's eyebrows were raised, and she looked like she was bursting to say something, but she deferred to her husband.

"Welcome Benn," Hann said. "You have something to say?"

Benn's mouth went dry and he struggled for words. "Yes sir. Yes madam." He glanced toward Adria, who was now smiling approvingly at him. "In accordance with the traditions of Vulcon, I humbly petition your leave to present myself to Lyric as a suitor."

The silent seconds seemed to drag out into an eternity.

Hann and Adria shared a glance, then just as Hann was about to make a considered response, Adria blurted out, "Well it's about time!"

Hann cast Adria a peeved glare. She had stolen his grand moment. He finally turned back to Benn. "You've been family all along Benn. You just didn't realise it." Then he turned back to Adria. "Does this mean we don't have to sit through all the other suitors?"

Adria smiled and nodded.

"That's a relief." Hann slumped back into the chair.

"You must go to Lyric," Adria said.

It was late morning now and Benn had left before the day's agenda was set. "Where is she?"

"She left with some Protectors to see about opening the Port, there is a Phoenician trading ship trapped there, keen to depart." Adria said.

Aunt Tyla, who was momentarily gazing into empty space suddenly looked ashen and leaned against the wall for support. "May the Goddess help us!"

"What is it?" Benn rushed to her aid. "What's wrong?"

"Lyric, at the Port. Phoenician ship. Cargo hold. Lyric is in great danger. Go now, go fast!"

Benn felt the sting of adrenaline in his skin. He had left Lyric unprotected. How could he have been so stupid, so selfish? And now she was in peril. He surged toward the great door of the hall and shoved it open. Racing along the assembled queue he pointed at each young Protector he could see. "You, you, you," he shouted in turn as he raced past. "Arm yourselves. You're with me. Now!"

Relieved to be spared the queue they gathered swords and fell in behind Benn as he raced out of the Palace toward the Port. Such was Benn's haste that only Rikk could keep up, and just barely.

"What is it Benn?" Rikk puffed between breaths.

"Lyric is in danger."

"May the Goddess be with us!"

Benn ran as never before. If Lyric was harmed, he would never forgive himself.

She caught a glimpse of movement in the shadows on her left, out of the corner of her eye. There was someone else in the room. By the time she saw the metal blade thrust from the shadows toward her chest, there was no time to react. She instantly realised the blade would find its mark, that she would die here, alone, without her beloved Benn. The turmoil of thoughts and feelings rendered her immobile, powerless to stop it.

A clink of metal on metal and the thrusting blade was pushed upward by another. Lyric felt the tip brush against her tunic. Her senses kicked in and she took a step back, away from the blades.

"Lyric, are you shielded?"

She knew that voice, that wonderful, warm voice, though harsh and stern now. She shook her head.

"Shield yourself. Do it now!"

"But then I can't protect you."

"I can look after myself if I know you are safe. Please Lyric, do it now."

The pleading in Benn's voice wrenched her gut. Lyric focussed and drew the White Fire into a shimmering shield around her. She was safe but the clang of blades told her Benn was locked in a fight for his life. Lyric stepped further back, against the wall, to give him more room to move in this confined space. The fight moved out of the shadows toward the light from the hold door and Lyric could just make out the snarling face of the former Protector Consort Dunn. She knew instantly that concealed among the cargo, there would be two other people.

Lyric turned toward Benn to warn him, just as Protector Dunn's blade scratched the skin of Benn's arm, drawing blood. Lyric gasped and Benn winced. Benn shot Lyric a steely glance that chilled her core before lunging forward and thrusting his blade home, through the chest of his opponent. Protector Dunn froze as if suspended from the blade in his chest, his face instantly white. Then he slumped to the floor. Benn withdrew his sword as the hulk of a man fell, blood pouring from his wound and puddling on the boards.

Before Benn could reach Lyric, a shrill cry rang out and a dagger blade propelled through the air toward Lyric's breast. It halted in mid-air, just before reaching its mark, and fell helplessly to the floor. The former Queen leapt up from behind some crates, another dagger in hand, and launched herself at Lyric, her face contorted in a snarl. "Usurper!" she shrieked in mid-air.

Instinctively, Lyric raised an arm to block the blow, so she didn't see Benn launch to her defence. All she saw was the tip of Benn's sword emerge from the left side of the Queen's chest. Lyric stepped to the side and the now inanimate body of the Queen thudded against the wall and slumped to the floor.

"Mother!" Brata suddenly appeared from behind a mound of bags. She slid over to where her father's body lay, retrieved his sword and launched herself toward Lyric, firmly holding and targeting the blade with both hands. Lyric ducked to the side, and the sword embedded in the wooden wall. With a sweep of her leg, Lyric knocked Brata off her feet and onto the floor. Brata barely hit the boards before Benn's blade ran her through.

Brata writhed there. "We could have been sisters," she whispered as the life drained from her.

"No Brata," Lyric said, stepping over the Queen's corpse toward Benn. "We have nothing in common."

Benn wiped the blade of his sword on Protector Dunn's cloak and inserted it back into his belt. "Sorry I was late," he said, nervously glancing at Lyric. "I ran as fast as I could."

Lyric looked about at the three corpses on the floor. "As I promised you, Jillen Felder, the murders are at an end." Lyric's expression suddenly changed to a frown. She strode toward Benn and slapped him hard on the cheek.

"Oww!" He rubbed the stinging skin. "I guess I deserve that for not being here to protect you when you needed me. I'm so sorry Lyric."

"That's not why I slapped you."

Benn looked confused. "Why then?"

"When you left the Palace without so much as a word, you were making a choice on my behalf. You were denying me a choice over my own life, leaving me with no options but to reign alone or be bonded to— to—"

"I'm so sorry, Lyric," Benn said, crestfallen. "I didn't realise."

"Don't do it again."

"I promise."

Lyric took a step closer, but Benn raised his hand to stop her.

"Wait," he said. "Speaking of choices. I've spoken with your parents and they have granted me leave to offer myself as your suitor." Benn dropped down on one knee in the congealed blood of Vulcon's former rulers.

Lyric knew the traditions of her people. All she had to do was ask the question and she would be betrothed to the man she had loved since childhood. She looked suddenly solemn, unable to fathom why a Protector of Benn's calibre would want to be bonded to a freak like her. "I wouldn't want you to do this just out of a sense of duty. I want you to be happy."

"Look, your Majesty," Benn said, blood soaking steadily into his tunic. "You've been my best friend since childhood, and I've been in love with you since the first time we swam at the beach. You do look rather fetching when you're not covered in grime, when your clothes are wet, and you're determined to thoroughly splash me with water. Anyway, I came back because Aunt Tyla led me to hope. I mean, is it possible? Could you possibly be in love with me?"

Lyric's head was spinning. The words she dreamed to hear were chiming in her ears. Could it be true? Her knees felt weak and tears were welling in her eyes. She struggled to maintain composure. Everything else in the room seemed to melt away. It was just her and Benn and this moment.

Benn's wide grin was distracting Lyric from the tears pooling in his eyes too. "So, your Majesty, if you still need me—"

"Every day," Lyric blurted out. "And are you sure you're not afraid of me?"

"No, your Majesty. I'm not afraid of you. You've been my best friend since we were children and you've had these abilities all this time. You could have fried me to a crisp a hundred times over, and with the way I treated you sometimes, I would have deserved it. Still, abilities or none, you're my best friend. Besides, I figure best friends are too rare to go carelessly frying them to crisps."

They both chuckled. When they looked into each other's eyes, the mirth stopped.

Lyric took a deep breath and tried to sound as solemn as she could. "Well then, in accordance with the traditions of the people of Vulcon; Benn, of the family Kreft, will you consent to become my bonded Protector?"

"It would be an honour and a privilege, your Majesty," Benn said with a solemn, gentle voice.

"Arise," Lyric commanded with a joyful smile.

Benn stood slowly and edged toward Lyric until they were almost touching. "Permission to kiss my betrothed, your Majesty."

Lyric liked the sound of 'my betrothed' coming from Benn's lips. He was so close now she could feel his breath on her face and the scent of him was intoxicating. "Granted," she whispered.

Lyric stood, in the midst of bags of gold, congealed blood, twitching corpses and the stench of death, somehow oblivious to it all and feeling more alive than she could remember. Benn placed one arm slowly around her waist and gently pressed her to him. He stroked away the tears on one cheek with his fingers. Lyric felt a great heat rising inside her and every touch tingled. She wasn't worried about accidentally incinerating Benn, but she wondered if she might explode. He cradled her head in his hand and gently drew her face closer to his, until their lips almost touched. She sensed he was giving her a choice and she was already decided. Lyric wrapped her arms around his neck and pressed her lips to his, gently at first, then ever more urgently and deeply. His strong embrace, his passionate kisses and the sheer warmth and scent of him washed away any doubts Lyric may have had about his feelings for her and hers for him. Even if she ceased to be Queen tomorrow and returned to a modest farming life, she would count herself the luckiest woman on Vulcon, as long as she could always be with Benn like this.

"Wow!" Lyric whispered when they finally paused for breath.

"Wow indeed!" Benn said. "I don't know about you, but I feel as if we have already been betrothed for a very long time. Would you mind if we kept the official betrothal as short as possible?"

"I think that is an excellent idea."

"We should probably go and speak to your parents, your Majesty."

"Yes," Lyric agreed. "Though I'd very much like a few more of those kisses before we leave."

Benn smiled. Lyric grabbed the front of his overshirt and pulled him closer to her. Instantly they were entwined, her fingers tracing the features of Benn's familiar face as their lips caressed in another long and passionate kiss.

Benn winced as he drew away.

"Your arm," Lyric said, gently examining the wound that was sending trickles of blood down toward Benn's elbow. She looked about for a suitable dressing and tore a piece of clean linen from Brata's tunic to bind the wound. After all, Brata would no longer be in need of it. "Oh, and thank you for saving my life," Lyric said as she finished tying the dressing in place.

"You're most welcome. I'm only glad I made it in time. Had I not, the torment would have been unbearable."

Lyric touched his face gently, moved by sentiment.

"There's something I don't understand Lyric," Benn said, gently placing his hand over hers. "This cargo hold pretty much screamed 'danger'. Why didn't you shield yourself? Why didn't you use your ability to deal with these... these traitors?"

"I'm sorry Benn. I didn't think to shield myself because I was distracted by my own thoughts and feelings. Also, I don't ever want to use my abilities to kill."

Benn shook his head, dismayed. "You really do need a Protector, don't you?"

Lyric looked deep into Benn's dark eyes. "Yes, Benn. I guess I do."

When the pair finally moved to leave the ship's hold, a familiar face seemed to suddenly disappear from the doorway. As Lyric's eyes adjusted to the bright sunlight, she noticed Rikk standing sentry by the entrance.

"You are a brave man, Benn Kreft," Rikk said with a grin as Benn emerged from the doorway.

"Protector Rikk," Lyric said, snapping Rikk back to attention.

"Yes, your Majesty." Rikk saluted his Queen.

"There are three corpses in there that are to be committed to the sea on the outgoing tide." Lyric pointed at the ocean spray crashing over what remained of the barrier. "Of the cargo, all but one bag of gold is to be returned to the Palace Treasury. Please see to it."

"Yes, your Majesty." Rikk saluted again and promptly began to organise Protectors to the tasks.

At the bottom of the plank, Lyric addressed the ship's Captain who was cowering nervously, even more so when he noted the Queen and her Protector were both heavily splattered with blood. "I will return tomorrow morning to finish opening the Port. You will take one bag of gold to trade for supplies for Vulcon. I will have a list of our requirements sent to you. When you return, we shall discuss trade further."

"Yes, your majesty." The Captain bowed very low and shuffled backward, out of the way.

Lyric and Benn set off for the Palace. "Now Benn," Lyric said as they left the wharf precinct.

"Yes, your Majesty."

"It doesn't feel right when you call me 'your Majesty'. Can we think of something else?"

"We can try, your Majesty," Benn said, with an impish grin.

Lyric gave him a playful shoulder nudge.

"Well, your parents have the monopoly on 'Precious One' so what about 'My Queen'?"

"No." Lyric giggled. "Still too formal, and it reminds me of someone I didn't like much."

"Well, I can't just call you Lyric," Benn said. "That's not respectful enough for the Royal Court. How about 'Your Highness'?"

"No."

"Your Radiance?"

"No."

"Your Magnificence?"

"No."

"Your Beneficence?"

"No."

"Your Freakiness?"

"Absolutely not!"

Still locked in debate, the pair made for the Palace, their bloodied state attracting stares and murmurs from the city folk.

It was two days before the bonding ceremony and Benn was annoyed. He had hoped to spend the day with Lyric, in preparation for the coming ceremony. He had plans for Lyric's safety on the day and he needed time to brief the Royal Protectors. However, in the face of the pressing needs of the people, Lyric agreed to hold a public audience in the morning. Assembled in the Audience Room, Lyric sat on a throne at the centre of the podium. Benn stood at her right side in full ceremonial Protector regalia. His sword was drawn and the tip was touching the floor, in vigilance position. Seated on smaller chairs on either side were Lyric's parents.

The ornate pattern on the mosaic floor incorporated a large arc, centred at the podium. The space inside the arc remained clear for petitioners and outside the arc the room was filled with citizens, standing tightly packed.

"Being Queen is more intimidating than I expected," Lyric said. "But when you are here, I feel more confident I can do a decent job of it."

Benn took her hand and gave it a reassuring squeeze.

The Palace Paige, in white tunic and black overshirt, announced each citizen as they stepped forward from the crowd.

"Citizen Temm, of the family Drolt, your Majesty!"

A man in his late twenties stepped forward. Benn recognised the bound boots and brown tunic of a farmer. Brush marks were apparent where he had tried to remove traces of ash from his garb.

"Your Majesty." He bowed low.

Lyric nodded acknowledgement. "Your petition, Temm Drolt?"

"Thank you for your indulgence, your Majesty." He looked at Lyric's shoes as he spoke, not daring to look the Queen in the eye. "I am a humble farmer. Our lands lie on the eastern edge of the ash field. I thank you for the assistance you have sent. Together with the workers, we have excavated, and all but repaired, our home and farm buildings. The fields have been spread with manure from the livestock in the City and are being ploughed to mix the ash and manure into the soil. We would like to re-plant the orchard and try to get some crops of vegetables sown and grown before the winter fully sets in, but with all the trees and crops destroyed by ash, there is nothing to plant." Temm raised his eyes hopefully to Lyric's face. "Can you help us?"

Lyric turned to Benn. "It is time."

"Yes, my Light." Benn knew what this meant. The last touchstone of his time with Lyric before the Horrific Catastrophe, was about to be handed to others and irrevocably changed. From here, the only path would be onward.

"Citizen Drolt," Lyric said, "thank you for your petition. This situation was foreseen. During the last ten years I established a Sanctuary, in a deep gorge, in what was the Haunted Forest."

The crowd murmured and Temm just looked at Lyric in amazement.

"In the Sanctuary, I collected samples of Vulcon's most productive fruit and crop plants, to act as a source of seed and propagation material for this day. Before the Horrific Catastrophe, I placed a shield over the gorge to protect its contents from the ash."

Temm, the other farmers in the room, and their wives, looked as if a great weight was being lifted from their shoulders.

"On the day after the Bonding ceremony, let a small team of farmers, including yourself," she gestured toward Temm, "led by my father — one of the few who knows the location of Sanctuary — be sent forth to collect the required plant material for the re-establishment of crops and orchards. These farmers may also have access to the palace orchards and gardens as they will contain plant material of use. Is this sufficient, citizen Drolt?"

Temm bowed low. "Amply sufficient your Majesty. I thank you for your care and foresight."

"Take care, farmer Drolt," Lyric said as Temm stood straight and turned to go. "Use the resources of my Sanctuary sparingly and tend it well. It serves us well now and may one day be needed to serve the people of Vulcon again."

Temm turned back and bowed again, "I shall take special care, your Majesty."

As Benn watched Temm disappear back into the crowd, he mused on how neither Temm, nor any of those gathered, could really understand how significant Sanctuary was to them. He saw Lyric hold her face solemn, as such attachments could be construed as a weakness in a leader, but he felt her reach toward him and squeeze his hand.

The Paige stepped forward again, accompanied by a raggedly dressed, ungroomed man of middle age, his face partly concealed by a hood.

"Citizen Donn of the family Kreft, your Majesty."

The man stepped forward and bowed low.

Lyric nodded acknowledgement and glanced toward Benn.

Benn was stunned and he could feel the blood draining from his face. He hoped it didn't show. Having to maintain composure in front of the gathering was going to take some effort.

"Your petition, Donn Kreft?" Lyric proceeded as if it was just another citizen.

The man stood upright and pushed back his hood. Benn regained composure and was biting his lower lip, his face etched with resolve.

"Your Majesty." The words seemed to grate as he spoke them. "I am also a humble farmer. As my lands were nearer the City on the west side, my home, fields and livelihood have been utterly destroyed. As father of your betrothed, I humbly request a place be found for me at Court."

The gathered murmured. Benn looked to Lyric, to see what she would do. Lyric glared back at Donn and waited until the commotion subsided.

"It would appear this is a family matter, rather than a matter of State," Lyric said. "However, as it has been raised in this forum, let it be dealt with in this forum." She turned to Benn and loudly announced, "Whatever course of action you choose, shall be done."

Benn was taken by surprise. He rubbed his lower lip with his forefinger in contemplation, feeling a surge of anger rising.

Now Donn looked apprehensive.

It was some time before Benn stepped forward. "As I recall, the last time we spoke, you were outraged I was not to be betrothed to the then Princess Brata and that I dared protect Lyric. You declared I was no longer your son and sent me from the house with nothing but the clothes on my back." Benn turned to Lyric. "As you were present at the time, my Light, does this concur with your recollection of events?"

Lyric frowned. "Indeed, it does Protector. Please continue."

"I further note, it is law in Vulcon that only women of age can possess land. My mother died when I was an infant, and in the absence of aunts or sisters, you continued to farm the land that was rightly forfeit to the Crown. The lands you claim as your own, rightfully belong to Queen Lyric, and you cannot lose land you never owned. The Crown owes you nothing."

The crowd was murmuring throughout the whole speech. Donn looked crumpled, but Benn was not done yet. "Nevertheless, you did house, feed, clothe and raise me. So, even though you were very clear I am no longer your son, some livelihood would seem in order."

Donn lifted his head a little, looking hopeful.

"I am satisfied you have demonstrated your skills are in farming," Benn said at his leisure. "Therefore, I suggest you be assigned as a paid farm labourer to the farms that are being reclaimed on the eastern edge of the ash fields. I am to understand they will soon be in need of additional labour to plant and tend crops."

Donn looked crushed again. All his hopes of a high life at Court were dashed. The crowd murmured. This was a harsh judgement. Benn returned to his position at Lyric's side, his anger was satisfied. When Lyric looked at him, her expression was unexpected. This was the expression she wore when she was remembering, thinking, feeling and deciding at the same time. It was beyond him how she managed to do that, and it made him nervous.

Donn accepted the judgement, a broken man. He bowed low and turned to go.

"Wait, citizen Kreft," Lyric said.

Donn turned back toward the throne and bowed low again. He looked like he was expecting further pain to be inflicted.

"I require you be honest and open with your Queen," Lyric said. "Can you do that?"

Donn nodded.

"Please, tell me about your daughter."

Benn felt slapped again. What was Lyric doing? He had no sister. It was just him, and his father, and his mother was dead. The look on his father's face surprised him, his expression torn and wan.

"Please no, your Majesty. There is too much pain there."

Benn was confused. His father had not denied it. Suddenly he wanted answers. He looked to Lyric and she cast him a concerned glance before turning to stare down Donn, forcing a reply.

"Aria was the joy of my life," Donn finally said with a sigh. "She was happy, bright and playful. I could not refuse her anything. When she wanted a puppy, I hunted one out. She called it Quo and they played together, grew together. She adored her baby brother and delighted in any small task she could do to help care for him. I would have done anything for her, but I could not save her. When she came down with the Fading Ill, there was nothing I could do. It broke my heart to watch my beautiful child fade and die. Quo remained by her side until the burial, then she cleaved to the child's mother."

Benn knew what this meant. The big sister he never knew he had, was a Seer, murdered by the Queen for her gift. He fought back shock, outrage and great sorrow to try and hold his composure. He would not have succeeded but for Lyric placing her hand over his in a gentle gesture of reassurance. He looked to her and Lyric gave him a nod, signalling him to take over from there.

"Tell me about my mother," Benn said with a slight break in his voice. "When and how did she die?"

Donn crumpled to his knees. "I've told you the story before."

"Tell me again. Omit nothing."

"Myra, your mother, was the love of my life. The land was indeed hers and it gave me much joy to work it beside her. It brought a good living and with the birth of Aria and yourself, our happiness was complete. When Aria died, it broke both our hearts. She began to weep over you whenever she tended you. You had barely completed your first year. At the time I didn't realise, she was saying goodbye. Three cleads after our dear Aria passed, Myra gave me this." Donn removed from around his neck a small roll of chamois parchment tightly bound with leather thong. He held it out and Benn stepped down to take it. "She told me to look after you and to ensure you grew to be bonded to a Seer. She made me promise. The following day I took the produce to market. When I returned home, you were crying in the house and she and Quo were floating lifeless in the creek. Drowned."

Benn could feel tears welling in his eyes. He fumbled to untie the thong and unfurl the parchment. This little piece of leather was suddenly the most tangible connection Benn had to his mother. The ink was faded but legible.

Know that you are the love of my life

Know that Benn is the joy of my life

He is our hope for the future

Keep him safe

Care for him

Do this for me, my love

Keep your promise to me lest all Vulcon be lost

All my love always

Myra

Benn could not believe what he was reading, so he read it thrice before handing the parchment to Lyric. She read it and met his eye, the tears welling in her eyes mirrored his own. His mother was a Seer. Somehow, she had concealed it from infancy. When Aria died, Myra knew her fate. His mother then set in motion a chain of events that would lead him to Lyric. Keeping the promise kept his father going. He valiantly strived to see Benn married to what he believed was the only remaining Seer on Vulcon. Now he understood his father. Now he even understood why his father would not tolerate having a dog on the farm.

Benn strode toward his father, raised him to his feet and embraced him. "Father".

"My son."

Benn held his father at a distance and looked him in the eye. "I have avenged the death of my sister and my mother." Then he embraced his father again. This time when he pulled away, he turned to present his father to Lyric. "I would like to petition that a place be found for my father at Court."

"Granted," Lyric said. "But it will not be a life of ease, Donn. There is still much to be done and your farming expertise is needed. You shall accompany my father on his expedition to my Sanctuary."

Benn smiled. His family was whole again. Donn bowed low.

"But first, I fear you are in dire need of a meal and a bath," Lyric said with a cheeky smirk. She gestured to one of the servants present who stepped forward, took custody of Donn and led him from the room.

Benn walked over to Hann and whispered, "Please watch out for him. See that he is well cared for."

Hann gave a solemn nod and Benn returned to his place beside Lyric.

"How long have you known?" Benn whispered to Lyric.

"Since just now," Lyric whispered back. "I recalled my grandmother once saying that your mother's death was a double tragedy, so I took a chance."

"Thank you, my Light."

Lyric gave Benn a caring smile before turning in readiness to address the next petitioner.

"There is still much to be done to help the City and the land recover," Benn said.

Lyric called one of the servants to summon the City Engineer. It was time to plan how they would reopen the gateways and the Port so work could begin on the land and trade could resume.

When Lyric raised her plans at lunch her family didn't question that she should help. Much to her surprise the points of dispute were what she would wear and how she would get to the gates. Her mother insisted she should wear full dress robes befitting her new role as Queen, but Lyric insisted she was going to work, not to conduct a ceremony, therefore more practical attire was required. Adria also insisted she be transported in the Royal Litter, but Lyric wanted to walk to the gate and engage with the people.

The following morning, Tessa dressed Lyric in a white tunic with a gold chain girdle and a calf-length, cashmere, hooded cloak in a rich royal blue, fastened by a gold brooch festooned with gems. Her hair was neatly braided and coiled upon her head, fastened with gold pins and a discreet gold tiara. Not the garb her mother hoped for but practical enough for the task ahead. She emerged into the sunlit Palace courtyard, still cool from the chilly night and was delighted to see three horses in fine, royal tack.

Lyric half-danced over to the first horse, which looked resplendent in a finely embossed, soft leather saddle and a similarly embossed leather bridle. "Poppy, you look wonderful," Lyric said as she stroked the horse's neck. Poppy was brushed until shiny and her mane decoratively braided. Pausing only a moment, Lyric moved on to the next horse. She wrapped her arms around the shimmering grey neck and hugged tight, taking in the familiar scent and warmth. "So good to see you, Nudge," she whispered. "I've missed you." As soon as Lyric released her grip, Nudge gave her a solid shove which threw her off balance.

"Sorry, your Majesty," the old and experienced stable hand holding Nudge's reins said. "Shall I find you a better-behaved mount for today?"

"Not at all," Lyric said with a smile. "Nudge and I are old friends. I wouldn't have her any other way."

The old man looked confused but obediently led Nudge to the mounting steps. Practical as her garb may be, it was still some effort to manage the attire and step into the saddle. Lyric arranged her cloak evenly over Nudge's back, then cheerfully took the reins. Benn duly mounted Poppy and Rikk mounted a beautiful bay mare made ready for the day. Hann had suggested Lyric should have two Royal Protectors on that day. Benn agreed and assured Hann he would select someone suitable.

The trio made their way from the Palace through the streets of Vulcon toward the East Gate. The people smiled and waved and bowed. Nudge arched his neck and stepped proudly through the streets as if all the adulation was meant for him. Lyric compared this to the Royal Litter and the band of Royal Protectors the old Queen always used when out in public and concluded that the happier the people were, the less protection a Queen requires.

They arrived at the East Gate to find Marc, the City Engineer, waiting. A small crowd was gathered. Benn and Rikk dismounted promptly and Benn aided Lyric to dismount with a semblance of elegance, although standing so close to Benn tended to take her breath away. She took a moment to smile at

Benn and regain her composure before allowing him to escort her to Marc, who was unrolling a scroll of parchment.

"Please stand back everyone!" Benn ordered, waving people away from the gate. "We need space to safely open the gate."

The crowd obediently drew back. Benn, Rikk and one of Marc's men stepped forward, lifted the large wooden beam which functioned as a mighty gate bolt, and put it to the side. Then they pulled on the great metal rings and the massive structure slowly creaked open. The crowd cried out and mothers rushed to cover their children's eyes with their cloaks and usher them away. Marc lowered his parchment and stared. Benn glanced to see if Rikk was OK. He was looking rather pallid. Lyric stepped forward.

There was a gap, about the length of a horse between the gate and the wall of rock and compressed ash that rose to the height of a man. This was the side which was least affected. The West and South Gates would be worse. At the bottom of the rock–face was a charred skull grotesquely embedded as if pressed against the edge. This is the limit that her shield had reached on the east side of the City. The remains of those who had not made it in time were embedded, down against what was once the path into the City. Lyric took a deep breath and strode to the exposed skull. She reached out her hand and touched it gently.

"I'm sorry," she said to the skull. "I wish I was able to save you too." Lyric turned and walked back to Marc. "As we discussed, the lower layers of rock at each gate contain the remains of our esteemed citizens. They are to be set aside and used to construct the great memorial. They will help us to be mindful of the power of the mountain, and they will ensure we never forget them." She then strode toward Benn. "Time to create a perimeter," she whispered.

"Yes, my Light." Benn moved to address the crowd. "Good people of Vulcon!" Benn called out. "Please step back and give the Queen some space. We wouldn't want anyone to be accidentally hurt."

Benn and Rikk shepherded the crowd back until they formed a large semicircle centred around the gateway. Lyric escorted

Marc to a position closer to the crowd before returning to stand just inside the gate. The two Protectors took positions on either side of her with their swords drawn and the tip placed on the ground, ready to be swung at a moment's notice.

"Remember what I said, Rikk," Benn called over to his friend. "No matter what you see, your job is to remain composed and protect the Queen."

Rikk nodded, but he looked nervous, nonetheless. Still, what could be more remarkable than Lyric's shield? He grew accustomed to that after a while.

Benn turned to Lyric as a signal they were ready. Lyric took a deep breath and focussed. A bright bead of light formed at the centre of the rock-face, about a cubit below the top. It stretched out to form a thin glowing line and disappeared into the rock leaving a smoking trail. The crowd murmured and watched mesmerised. Presently the entire slab of rock above the line began to lift up into the air. Loose, pumice pebbles from the top tumbled into the gap below. The crowd gasped and took a step back. Rikk moved to take a step back too but glancing over he saw Benn confidently hold his ground and smile approvingly at Lyric, so he resumed his stance.

Wafts of smoke appeared from multiple points on the slab and the entire structure broke up into cubit-size blocks with shiny, smooth edges. The blocks wafted to one side and were deposited on the top of the surrounding ash field. With this the crowd was in awe, and prayers to the Goddess could be heard in the murmurings that followed.

Rikk stared wildly at Lyric, then at Benn.

"I told you," Benn said with a grin. "Her Majesty likes to play with rocks."

Rikk took a moment to comprehend, then laughed with his friend as they took positions for the next round of excavation.

After every two tiers, Lyric would pause for a brief rest and to consult with Marc to ensure the path being created met with his specifications. They originally planned to return to the Palace for lunch but the people, having adjusted to this new form of earthworks arrived at noon with an array of food and some tables and chairs. Word spread and many came to see the spectacle, so even the High Priestess of the temple was there to join them for lunch.

Tier by tier Lyric cleared a path from the East Gate to the fields beyond. She carefully set aside the blocks from the lower levels of the path into the gap between the old city wall and the rock–face, so they would not be desecrated before they could be used for the memorial. By the time the sun was low in the sky, the work was done, and the weary party returned to the Palace.

The following days saw Lyric, accompanied by Benn and Rikk, use the White Fire to carve out access from the West and South Gates. After the passing of a moon, the gates and Port were once again open. Thanks to Lyric's ability to carve and move the compacted ash rock, great corridors were constructed from the gates to the western ash and rock fields beyond.

In what seemed to Lyric no time at all, it was the day of the Bonding ceremony, but there was business to be attended to before the afternoon's festivities. It was too soon for Lyric to allow herself to be nervous and excited just yet, she needed to focus on the task at hand. After thanking Tessa for dressing her well and complimenting both the dress and the ornate braided hairstyle interwoven with pearls, Lyric made her way to the meeting room. Benn greeted her at the door, bowed, kissed her hand and escorted her inside. Lyric took her seat in the high back chair near the centre of the room. There was a wooden table at elbow height to her left. Benn stood vigilantly by her right side.

A loud rap on the door echoed through the room.

"Enter!" Benn shouted.

The doors opened and the Palace Paige stepped forth, "Jonn of the family Forje. President of the Vulcon Senate, your Majesty."

"Enter," Lyric said.

A well-groomed middle-aged man in dress-tunic and overshirt moved forward and bowed low, fidgeting. "Your Majesty."

"Please be seated Mr President," Lyric said as she gestured to a comfortable chair nearby.

Jonn nervously proceeded to the chair and sat down.

"Congratulations on your election as Senate President, you are a worthy choice," Lyric said. "I understand congratulations are also due on your daughter's school entry results."

"Th—thank you, your Majesty," Jonn replied.

"I understand Tika was one of three girls in this year's intake found to be a Seer."

"Yes, your Majesty. It was a great surprise for us. In light of recent events, we are glad she started school after your coronation. She is an only child and much loved."

"And now highly treasured by our community, Mr President," Lyric said. "In light of the testing results, my aunt, my mother and I have given the education of Seers much thought. We have decided they will attend school with the other children for three days each week, however on the Fourday, the Seer school will be reopened, and they will be tutored by myself and the Seers of my family. Will this be acceptable to you and your family, Mr President?"

Jonn could not conceal his astonishment. "Speaking on behalf of my family, and no doubt the families of the other two girls, we are exceedingly grateful for your attention to their education. Your proposed arrangements are most acceptable."

"Excellent," Lyric said with a smile. "Now, to other business. I have proposed that the President of the Senate attend a meeting with me on each Oneday. An opportunity for you to provide a briefing on the working of the Senate and to petition for ratification of laws and motions passed by the Senate. You have indicated this arrangement is acceptable to you, therefore welcome to our first briefing session. I trust we can build a positive working relationship for the benefit of the people."

"Thank you, your Majesty," Jonn said while removing a sheaf of parchments from the belt of his tunic and unrolling them. "As the first act of the new Senate, a motion was passed to thank your Majesty, on behalf of all Vulcon, for saving the people from the Horrific Catastrophe. I petition for ratification of this motion."

Lyric caught Jonn's wry smile and met it with one of her own. She took the parchment, placed it on the table beside her and, as she applied the Royal Seal, announced, "Motion ratified."

Jonn proceeded to the next item, "The second motion passed by the Senate was to acknowledge the wisdom of the Queen in the establishment of the Senate and to undertake to strive to be worthy of the faith placed in the Senate by the Queen and by the people."

Jonn passed the parchment to Lyric who received it with another smile and proceeded to affix the Royal Seal. "I'm pleased to hear it. Motion ratified."

Jonn lifted another sheet of parchment from the sheaf, this time looking rather more nervous. "In light of recent events, the Senate wanted to take action to assist the people to put the darkness of the past behind them and move forward with confidence. It was agreed that the power of the mountain and the protection of the Goddess be acknowledged. To this end, the Senate has passed an Act stating that the name of the island of Vulcon be changed to 'Atlantis', in honour of our beloved Goddess, Atlanta. The name of this City shall be 'Atlantis City'. Finally, the name of the mountain shall henceforth be 'Mount Vulcano'."

Jonn looked nervously at Lyric, trying to gauge her reaction. Lyric concentrated to keep her face expressionless, then she looked up at Benn, "What do you think Benn, can you live with Queen Lyric of Atlantis?"

"I have known you by many titles, my Light," Benn replied. "Some not so pleasant. Queen Lyric of Atlantis sounds noble enough."

"Indeed." Lyric smiled knowingly at Benn, turned back to Jonn and reached out her hand to take the parchment. After affixing the seal, she extended it back to Jonn. "The first Act passed by the Senate is hereby ratified."

"Thank you, your Majesty." Jonn carefully stowed the parchment back in the sheaf. "I believe that concludes our business for this meeting." He made to rise from his chair.

"Not quite," Lyric interjected. Jonn, surprised, sat back down.

"I have a few items of my own to discuss,"

"Yes, your Majesty." Jonn was looking nervous again.

Lyric removed two sheets of parchment from her robes and placed them on her lap.

"I have looked into the future of our land, Mr President," Lyric said with a hint of sadness, "and I have decided a new prophecy is in order. As the title 'Great Prophecy' has been previously used and has unpleasant connotations, Benn has suggested this prophecy be titled the 'Lyric Prophecy'."

Lyric handed the parchment to Jonn and smiled up at Benn who returned the gesture and placed a reassuring hand on Lyric's shoulder.

As Jonn read the prophecy, a range of emotions passed over his face. "It would appear the workings of the Senate were not a surprise to you?"

"When one is a Seer, Mr President, life contains fewer surprises," Lyric said. "Please indulge us and read it aloud. I would like to hear if it reads as intended."

"Certainly, your Majesty." Jonn held the parchment out before him and proceeded to read:

"Atlantis shall be blessed with peace and prosperity for many

years hence

Then, in the twentieth generation of the family of Nye

Mount Vulcano will awaken once again

The earth shall shake, and the seas shall rise up and swallow

Atlantis

Little trace of our fair lands shall remain above the waves

So in the nineteenth generation of the family of Nye

Let the people and ways of Atlantis be dispersed among all the

peoples of the world"

There was silence for a short while as all present absorbed what was read.

"That reads well, my Light," Benn said, breaking the silence.

"Yes," Lyric said. "You are troubled, Mr President?"

"Will there be no Great Seer to save Atlantis from this catastrophe?"

"No Mr President, not this time." There was sadness in Lyric's voice. "But there is hope, Mr President. Because the event is foreseen, we can take steps to save as many of the people of Atlantis as possible when the time comes."

"How so?" Jonn was intrigued.

"This brings me to my next item," Lyric handed the second sheet of parchment to Jonn. It contained a diagram and some written annotations. "I propose a memorial be built in memory of those who lost their lives in the Horrific Catastrophe, and to function as a signal to the people of Atlantis to prepare for what is to come. Let the memorial be built on the north side of the road outside the West Gate as a great pyramid with nineteen tiers. Let the first tier be built now, engraved on the east and west sides with the names of those who lost their lives, and on the south side facing the road, with the Lyric Prophecy. Let 'Generation One' be engraved below the Lyric prophecy. When our first child is born, let the next tier be built with the Lyric prophecy engraved on the south side and 'Generation Two' engraved on the other three sides. Let the pyramid tiers continue to be built in this manner until the nineteenth tier, which is to be engraved on all four sides with 'Beloved of Atlantis. Leave now.' for all to see."

Jonn carefully added the parchment to his sheaf, "There is much wisdom and foresight in this plan. I shall take this to the Senate for debate. I'm sure the necessary Acts will be passed with minimal discord."

Lyric smiled and rose to leave. Jonn rose accordingly. Clearly the session was ending. Jonn bowed low to the Queen and began to walk to the door. He paused about half–way and turned.

"Your Majesty," Jonn said.

"Yes?" Lyric acknowledged him.

"There is a rumour among the people that on the day of the Horrific Catastrophe, you saw the Goddess herself and this enabled you to save us. Could this be so, your Majesty?"

Lyric paused a moment, recalling her vision on the day. "Suffice to say, Mr President, I saw what I needed to see to save the people."

Jonn bowed, accepting that no further detail would be forthcoming. "Your Majesty, were you not Queen, you would make a capable politician." He smiled graciously.

"I think that went well, Benn," Lyric said, watching Jonn leave.

"Very well, my Light," Benn said, taking Lyric by the hand and leading her from the room. "We have a ceremony to prepare for." Benn gently kissed her hand.

"Indeed, we do." Lyric smiled and blushed.

The moment they left the room, Adria, Aunt Tyla and a flurry of maids descended upon them. Their mission was to have her fed, dressed and decorated on time and they were passionate about it. During the planning process, Lyric realised the bonding ceremony was not so much for the benefit of the bonding couple (that part only took minutes) but rather for the benefit of the families, or in this case, the entire nation of Atlantis. As soon as Lyric acquainted a reluctant Benn with that realisation, they were content to take a step back from the process and watch all the participants enjoy the planning and preparations. Lyric did step up on a few occasions to curb suggestions that were getting out of hand. After all, the dress would have to be sufficiently functional that she would be able to walk, sit, enter and alight from the Royal Litter, and hopefully even dance.

Lyric glimpsed Benn sidle out a side door. He was to prepare for the ceremony at the Protector Academy. The Seers predicted blustery, chilly winds for the entire week, precluding a dignified outdoor ceremony, and the Grand Hall at the Academy was by far the largest hall in the land, so was chosen as the venue.

When Queen Lyric finally stepped out of the Royal Litter onto the steps of the Grand Hall, a great roar went up from the assembled crowds. Huge as the Grand Hall may be, it would still not contain everyone. Many would remain outside to be informed of the proceedings by word of mouth. The skirt of Lyric's dress began billowing and Lyric could feel the icy wind on her skin. The palace maids formed a barrier to protect her from the chill and help usher her into the building.

Adria and Aunt Tyla, dressed in their finest, fussed about her, righting any ornamentation which had drifted during the course of the journey. The elaborate construction of her hair was further topped with the colourful, bejewelled, royal tiara, from which a banner of the finest cloth flowed behind. Lyric's dress of soft, cream fabric was gathered and wrapped about her to enhance her fine figure. It was embroidered with pearls and gold thread and wafted around her ankles as she moved. She wore a pair of white slippers of soft kid leather also adorned with pearls and gold embroidery. In her hands she carried the white ceremonial scarf, tied in a large decorative bow. Everything back in place, Adria and Aunt Tyla stepped back to survey their handiwork.

"Beautiful," Aunt Tyla said, clutching a kerchief as a talisman against imminent tears of joy.

"You look radiant, Precious One," Adria said, a tear already running down her cheek. She brushed it aside and turned to the Royal Protector. "Are all assembled?"

He walked to the entrance doors raised the peep flap and surveyed the situation. Satisfied he turned back to Adria, "All assembled and ready madam."

"Well, we're ready then," Adria said.

"Not quite!" Lyric interjected. "An important member of the party seems to be running late."

"Of course," Adria said. She was so swept up in the proceedings she had forgotten.

Adria turned toward the side door of the vestibule, "Protector, please check if the remaining member of our party is in sight."

The Protector proceeded to the side door and as he opened it, a finely dressed woman and young girl tumbled through. They both bowed deeply to Lyric who smiled acknowledgement.

"So sorry we are late your Majesty," the mother gushed, breathless. "The gardener at the Palace was tending roses especially for the occasion. Given the auspicious nature of the event he was most tender and ceremonial about parting with them, so the process took longer than expected."

The women laughed together, Knutt the head gardener at the Palace was highly skilled. Only he could have guaranteed rose petals at this time of year. But he was very particular about his botanical charges and he functioned on 'garden time', a time all his own which he declared was dictated by the garden itself.

"It's a wonder he parted with them at all," Lyric said, trying to make her flower girl feel much more relaxed. "May I see them?" Lyric bent down slowly as the girl approached, carefully carrying the large basket festooned with ribbons. Lyric took a handful of the petals and held them to her nose. "They smell lovely!" She held the handful out toward the flower girl who took a deep sniff.

"Mmmm, wonderful!" the child said, looking much brighter. She leaned in toward Lyric and whispered, "I'm a bit scared."

Lyric smiled and took her little hand in hers, "You are a Seer, my dear Tika. This doesn't mean we are born brave. We become brave by practising courage. Shall we practise some courage today?"

Tika smiled meekly and nodded. Her mother beamed with pride.

"Well then," Lyric said, releasing Tika's hand to rise and stand tall, "are we ready?"

They glanced at each other, and Lyric nodded to the Protectors at the inner door. The doors were swung open, musicians began to play, the assembled turned and gasped, and the procession made its way down the aisle of the Grand Hall.

Tika led the way, dutifully strewing rose petals ahead of Lyric who walked gracefully, calmly and evenly, despite Tika dancing about in excitement. As Lyric walked through the shafts of sunlight streaming in from the great windows, her dress and jewels caught the light and glowed. Adria completed the rear of the procession with Hann, in full ceremonial Protector garb stepping forward as they left the vestibule to take Adria's arm and escort her down the aisle. A prouder family was rarely seen.

As they approached the front rows, the President of the Senate turned to view the procession and looked astonished and delighted to see Tika leading the way. Tika gave a little squeal of delight to have surprised him so.

Waiting in front of the podium was Benn, standing proudly in ceremonial garb, decorated with the sashes and medals of a Royal Protector who was acknowledged by the Academy as having provided service to the people above and beyond the call of duty. He was scrubbed clean, freshly shaven and his dark hair oiled and slicked back to fully display his chiselled features and penetrating dark brown eyes. For a fleeting moment, even Lyric barely recognised him. He looked more handsome than even she could recall.

The look of awe on Benn's face soon gave way to a welcoming smile as his eyes met Lyric's. Rikk, proudly filling the role of brother, placed a reassuring hand on Benn's shoulder.

Presiding over the ceremony was the High Priestess of the Temple. Ever so grateful the temple was spared from the calamity, the matronly and wise woman had insisted on conducting this most auspicious ceremony. She wore the azure ceremonial robes of the High Priestess, embroidered with the symbol of the Goddess; three white flames in deep teal circle. On her forehead, the triangle symbol of the mountain was painted in black, making her look even more solemn and impressive than usual.

As the procession arrived at the podium, Tika ceased strewing flowers and walked along the front row to her proud mother who had a seat waiting. Rikk took his seat in the front row beside Donn. Lyric stood beside Benn and passed the scarf to the High Priestess, who untied it and draped it around her own neck.

"Silence!" roared the High Priestess, her voice easily projecting through the entire building. The Grand Hall fell silent. The ceremony began.

The High Priestess turned to the Nye family, "Do you, family of Nye, accept this man, Benn, into your family as a full member and Protector, to serve your family according to the traditions of our people?"

Hann stood and proudly announced, "On behalf of the family of Nye, I accept Benn into our family according to the traditions of our people."

The High Priestess turned to Donn and Rikk, "Do you, Benn's family, relinquish Benn henceforth to serve the family of Nye, according to the traditions of our people?"

Donn stood up. "On behalf of Benn's family, I relinquish Benn to the family of Nye, according to the traditions of our people."

"So be it." The High Priestess beckoned Lyric and Benn to follow her onto the podium.

The service continued with the High Priestess adhering to the traditional rituals, encouraging the couple to honour the Goddess by their service and honour their family with children. She included a comment that children would also honour all of Atlantis as the land was in need of more Seers. Lyric observed that despite her solemnity, the High Priestess was capable of a subtle, wry smile when she deviated from the traditional ritual.

The High Priestess took Benn's wrist, "Will you, Benn, take Lyric as your bonded partner for life, to love, to honour and to protect? Will you protect and provide for her and her family, all the days of your life?"

"I will," Benn said loudly, while smiling warmly at Lyric.

The High Priestess took Lyric's wrist in her other hand, "Will you, Lyric, take Benn as your bonded partner for life, to love, to honour and to protect? Will you nurture and care for him and your family, while serving the people of Atlantis, all the days of your life?" There was that wry smile again. Lyric liked this woman, she reminded her of Grandmother.

"I will," Lyric replied, as loud as she could manage, while shooting a smile at Benn.

The High Priestess placed Lyric's hand in Benn's, took the scarf from around her neck and tied it around their joined hands. Then she took Benn by the arm and turned the pair to face the audience. "Behold! Lyric and Benn of Nye, and of Atlantis!" Another wry smile.

The audience rose to their feet, applauding and cheering loudly. Lyric and Benn raised their bound hands high, eliciting another wave of applause and cheering. Lyric could see her mother, Aunt Tyla, and even her father, wiping away tears.

Tika tore herself away from her mother, raced toward the aisle and began strewing more rose petals in the path they would walk. She danced and skipped her way back down the aisle.

The newly bonded pair walked slowly down the aisle, graciously acknowledging the guests. When they entered the vestibule they paused, apprehensive, while the great outer doors were slowly swung open and they stepped out to a cheering, waving, mass of people. They raised their tied hands in the air and the crowd roared. Celebrations in the plaza would continue long into the night.

The Royal Litter waited at the base of the steps. In accordance with tradition, once all saw the bond, Lyric and Benn untied the scarf together and Lyric draped it around Benn's neck, planting a gentle kiss as she did so. The gesture elicited another rousing cheer from the crowd. Lyric alighted the Royal Litter and Benn walked beside holding her hand.

As the Royal Litter made its way through the plaza toward the Palace, Lyric could see in the distance the top of the tree beside the schoolyard. She recalled the day she first met Benn, when he rescued her from the stones. So much had happened, so much had changed. Benn accepted her for who she really was, and they would be together always. Now it was Lyric's turn to wipe away tears of joy.

The End